MW01094961

FRIENDS HELPING FRIENDS

Also by Patrick Hoffman

The White Van

Every Man a Menace

Clean Hands

FRIENDS HELPING FRIENDS

A NOVEL

PATRICK HOFFMAN

Atlantic Monthly Press
New York

FIRST EDITION

Published simultaneously in Canada
Printed in the United States of America

The interior of this book was designed by Norman E. Tuttle of Alpha Design & Composition.
This book was set in 12-pt. Abobe Garamond Pro by Alpha Design & Composition of Pittsfield, NH.

First Grove Atlantic hardcover edition: March 2025

Library of Congress Cataloging-in-Publication data is available for this title.

ISBN 978-0-8021-6412-4
eISBN 978-0-8021-6481-0

Atlantic Monthly Press
an imprint of Grove Atlantic
154 West 14th Street
New York, NY 10011

Distributed by Publishers Group West

groveatlantic.com

25 26 27 28 10 9 8 7 6 5 4 3 2 1

For Charlotte Sheedy

FRIENDS HELPING FRIENDS

Bunny Simpson picked a shirt off the floor and stuffed it into his bag. His boss at the cigarette store had just warned him that a pair of Denver police detectives had been looking for him. They had his DMV photo printed out and everything. "Plainclothes," she said like the lack of uniform meant even more trouble. She told him to take the day off and get his affairs in order. For Bunny, that meant going home, packing a bag, and catching a bus up to Grand Junction. He'd hide out with his mother, let the dust settle. That was the plan. Denver was done.

"Jesus, Bunny, what the hell am I gonna do without you?" asked Uncle Rayton from the couch.

"Don't go all *what am I gonna do without you*," said Bunny. "I got enough problems as it is."

"I'm not saying for survival, I'm saying for company," said Rayton. "It's gonna be lonely here. Who am I gonna eat my burritos with? Who am I gonna share a beer?"

Bunny heard the question, but he didn't answer. He was too busy searching for any last items that needed grabbing. He was only twenty-four; he didn't own many things. Still, he felt like he was forgetting something crucial.

Bunny called Rayton his uncle, but they weren't related by blood; he was more of a family friend. Rayton was in his sixties; he had sad eyes and a weather-beaten face. Fifteen years ago, the man had been in a car accident, and now both of his legs, right at the knees, ended in stumps.

Bunny had been living with him for three and a half years. He helped keep the place tidy, he helped get Rayton into his wheelchair, and he helped push him to his destinations, too. For that, he got a sofa to sleep on and a shower to wash in. He kept his things in the corner of the room. It wasn't a fancy place; it was a mobile home in a trailer park in Elyria-Swansea. But it was safe.

Bunny looked around, spotted a book, and held it up: *Modern Card Counting*, by Rod Roland. "I'm gonna borrow this, if that's cool?"

"Keep it."

"I got your belt on, too," said Bunny. The belt was too long—it pointed out at the side like a wind vane.

"Trouble like this doesn't just go away," Rayton said. "It's better to clear it up. Take your hit. You don't want to have nothing hanging over you. It's gonna turn you into someone you're not. I've seen it before." Rayton took his cap off, brushed his hair back with his hands, and pulled the cap back on. "I know you, Bunny, you can make something of yourself."

"I appreciate that," said the younger man.

"You got a handsome face," said Rayton. "You could end up being a CEO with a face like that."

"I got these scars, though, too," said Bunny, touching his jaw.

"They add to the whole thing. Real talk, Bunny, you could go a long way with that face."

Bunny zipped the duffel bag closed. "I gotta just figure it out," he said, looking around the trailer. He realized he might not see this place again and he shook his head. *Things sure could change fast*, thought Bunny. *You could wake up fine in the morning, find yourself running with a bag in the night.*

"It's the way you handle yourself," said Rayton.

Bunny looked at the man and saw tears in his eyes. He walked over to him, bent down, and gave his big shoulders a hug. Rayton smelled like maple syrup and cigarettes. "I'll be back," Bunny whispered.

That was Bunny's last moment of peace. When he stepped outside, he was met by a semicircle of six cops in green tactical uniforms. They had shotguns pointed at him and they barked that they were the police and they told him to "*get the fuck down on the ground!*"

Next thing Bunny knew, he was flat on his stomach, dirt in his mouth, looking at black boots. They yanked his arms behind his back and cuffed him. Bunny's neighbors were gathering. One of them had his phone out and was taking video. Bunny turned his head the other way and looked toward Rayton's trailer. The cops had gone in there, too, and Bunny could hear a commotion. "Hey!" yelled Bunny. "He's handicap!"

He felt a knee on his head and the side of his face pressed into the dirt. He braced himself to hear gunshots from inside the trailer, but thankfully there were none.

More of his neighbors gathered. There was all sorts of hollering going on now. Bunny hated to be the center of attention like this, and he closed his eyes and prayed to Jesus for help. *Help me, and help Rayton, too, please God, just help with this one.*

Eventually, with his hands behind his back, they lifted Bunny to his feet. He looked for Rayton but didn't see him anywhere. They marched Bunny through the trailer park, turning him sideways at one point to fit through a narrow passageway. Bunny felt a mixture of shame and notoriety; cuffed up like that, he couldn't help feeling like a bit of a bad boy.

On the other end of the lot, a dude named Herman asked Bunny if he was alright. "No," said Bunny. "I'm not alright." He wanted to say, *What the hell does it look like?* But he held his tongue.

They walked him all the way out to Adams Street, where four Denver police cars sat parked and waiting. To Bunny, everything looked more vivid than normal. The adrenaline in his body made the clouds and fences and street and cars and everything else pop out crystal clear.

The cops put him in the back of a squad car, and buckled him in. He sat there with his wrists hurting from the cuffs. The seats were made of hard plastic. The car floor was dirty. Some spit had dried on the nearest window. Bunny took a deep breath and cursed all the choices he'd ever made. Getting cuffed up and marched past his neighbors? That seemed like the worst possible ending to his story. *Shit,* he thought, sitting there, shaking his head. Truth was, Bunny didn't have the perspective to understand what was happening. Getting cuffed up and marched out like that wasn't the end of his story. It was just the beginning.

Six days earlier, he'd been selling a pack of Pall Mall Super Slims to a heavy-bosomed older lady in a bubblegum-pink T-shirt. The receipt was printing out of the machine when he saw his friend, Jerry LeClair, pull into the lot. Jerry's Blazer kicked up a little cloud of dust when it stopped. Bunny ripped the receipt from the machine and gave it to the lady. She thanked him, smiled, and turned to leave. Bunny watched her walk to the door, and then he watched Jerry come in.

"Hey man," Jerry said, sniffling a little. Jerry, at twenty-six, was older than Bunny. He was a little chubby and had long eyelashes. Bunny, on the other hand, was slim, wiry; and while Jerry's skin was smooth, Bunny had little scars on his hands and face. Jerry wore a white T-shirt, with a gold chain underneath. He was Bunny's best friend. They'd met four years ago at a punk rock show in a warehouse in Golden.

"I said I'd pay you on Saturday," said Bunny, knocking his knuckles on the counter. He owed Jerry sixty dollars, but he didn't want to be hassled for it, especially not at his place of employment.

"Come on, man," said Jerry. "I'm not here for that." He stepped to the counter, leaned on it like he was at a bar. Then he whispered, "I got this thing, though, if you wanna maybe make five hun—"

"I can't hear you," said Bunny. "Why you talking so quiet?"

"I said, I got this thing if y'all wanna make five hundred."

"What kind of thing?"

"Remember that MILF I was telling you about? The one I sold the Var to?" Jerry, among other hustles, sold steroids to gym-goers. Var was short for Anavar.

Bunny nodded. "Yeah."

"She wants someone to get rough with her ex-husband."

"Rough sex?"

"Not sex, man—to fight him," whispered Jerry.

Bunny knew he didn't want to see his friend that morning. This was the exact kind of shit he didn't want to get involved in. Still, five hundred, though. That was a lot of money. "Five hundred to split?" he asked.

"Five for you."

"How much is she giving you?"

"Don't worry about that, player, I'm contracting you out. You can set the price when you contract me out."

"Five hundred, though?"

Jerry laid it out for him. The husband went jogging every day. He ran through Washington Park. His route took him off the main path and into a less populated area. They'd run into him there, exchange words, and get in a little scuffle. That was it. It wasn't their kind of work, that was for sure, but it seemed easy enough.

"Why's she wanna do it?"

"I don't know, man, either she's tripping, or the dude's tripping. I didn't give her a questionnaire and make her fill it out."

Bunny imagined the so-called *less populated* area. Then his thoughts shifted to a church he used to attend. Pastor Dan with his hands rubbing all over Bunny's body, rubbing down between his legs. *Jesus is love and love is play.*

"I'm sorry, man, I can't do it," said Bunny, feeling agitated. "I'm trying to stay on the straight and narrow."

"I need help on this," whispered Jerry. "Look at me. I'm not built for that kind of work. I'm not a roughneck."

"I'm not, either."

"You like to fight, though."

"I hate fighting."

"You're good at it."

"I'm sorry, dude."

"Alright," said Jerry. He took a deep breath and sighed. "Give me a pack of those Winstons, then."

Bunny put the pack on the counter.

"Interest on the sixty," said Jerry, picking up the cigarettes and giving them a little shake.

Alone again, Bunny scanned a pack of Winstons. Then he pulled out his wallet. He had one ten-dollar bill in there, and he used it to pay for the cigarettes. His boss kept a tight track on the inventory. Muttering to himself, he took three dollars from the register and put it into his wallet, then he took a quarter and stuffed it loose into his pocket. The rest of the day, nobody came in except for some shift workers from the refinery and a tweaker or two. Bunny felt uneasy the whole time. Nervous and anxious.

When he got home that evening, he found Rayton sitting on the couch, surfing his computer.

"Did you eat any of those oranges?" Bunny asked. He could already see the bag sitting unopened on the counter.

"Oh man," said Rayton. "I was sitting here, yapping my gums on the phone to Marky and them and I forgot all about those oranges."

"You gotta eat the oranges," said Bunny. "Fruits and veggies, man. You need your vitamin C. Social worker said that."

"I know," said Rayton. "Grab one and let's have some." Bunny ripped open the mesh bag and flopped down next to Rayton on the couch. Without talking, they both peeled their oranges and piled their peels next to them like little plates.

"Thank you, Bunny."

"For what?"

"For being such a good boy."

"Shit," said Bunny.

At dinnertime, Bunny lifted Rayton from behind, kicked open the front door of the trailer, carried him out to his wheelchair, and set him down as best he could. Even without his lower legs, the man was still heavy. Bunny had to pull him backward through the dirt until they got to the sidewalk; then he could push him normally.

For dinner, Rayton treated them to frozen burritos at the convenience store. The clerk heated them up in the microwave. While they waited, Rayton told him that the landlord had been hassling him for rent. They owed $780.

"Damn," said Bunny.

"Yep," said Rayton.

"Hold on," said Bunny. He felt a little sick with anxiety, but he stepped back outside and called Jerry. "I'll do it," said Bunny when his friend picked up the phone.

"I knew you would," said Jerry. "I had a feeling. Don't worry, we'll make it easy."

⁂

The woman who'd asked Jerry to beat up her ex-husband was a thirty-seven-year-old lawyer named Helen McCalla. She'd met Jerry buying steroids. If she hadn't decided to get anabolically enhanced, none of this would've happened. That was an undeniable fact.

Until a couple months ago, she'd never considered using steroids. She'd never even thought about it. She liked lifting weights, and since her divorce a few years ago, she'd become sort of obsessed with working out. But steroids? To her, that had seemed like something for professional athletes and freaks who wanted to look noticeably larger. People like Sam Kaminsky, for instance.

Sam was a guy at her gym. He was a smooth talker with huge, hairy shoulders. One day, they were standing near the kettlebells, and he asked her out. He did it in a casual way. *Flirty,* thought Helen. She agreed to get a drink.

Two nights later, they met at a bar in Union Station. She told him about herself, told him she was a lawyer, told him she'd grown up in the Bay Area. He said he was in real estate. There was something mannered about the way he acted, but it wasn't a bad date. Helen enjoyed herself; they shared some laughs. And while she was standing outside waiting for her Uber, he mentioned that he used steroids. He just said it, like it was nothing to hide. Like he was proud of it.

"What?" said Helen, aghast.

"Testosterone, Winstrol, Equipoise. We all do it."

The rest of that night was a blur. They didn't hook up or make any plans. And when she lay down in her bed, she didn't think about him. Instead, one word played through her mind: *steroids.* It was the idea of it that thrilled her. There were pills that could make her stronger. It didn't have to be freakish. Why hadn't she thought of this? Everything clicked into place.

Two weeks later, at the gym, near the squat racks, she brought the subject back up. Smiling, trying to make it sound like she was joking, Helen asked, "Do girls ever use it?"

She knew the answer; she'd gone on the internet as soon as she sat in the Uber that night. Still, the conversation had to start somewhere.

Sam nodded toward a woman whose name Helen didn't know, but whose body—her backside in particular—she'd noticed and admired.

"Ah," said Helen.

"Pushing the envelope," said Sam, licking his lips and raising an eyebrow.

Two days later, Sam's steroid dealer, Jerry LeClair, picked Helen up in his Blazer. Neither of them, of course, had any idea how drastically this meeting would alter the course of their lives, but if their destinies had been written on individual decks of cards, those decks, right then, were being shuffled, cut, and mixed together.

Helen was surprised by the steroid dealer's appearance. She'd expected someone like Sam. This guy didn't appear to even work out. His car smelled like marijuana. Still, they introduced themselves and shook hands. He pulled back out onto Logan Avenue. "Sam's cool," he said. "He's got that Hollywood vibe."

"Yeah," said Helen. *So Hollywood,* she thought. She wiped her sweaty palms on her lap.

"He's so Hollywood," she said, smiling.

"He said you wanna start with the Var?"

"Anavar?"

"It's four hundred dollars for two hundred forty pills," said Jerry. "Ten milligrams a pill, but Sam said you're gonna wanna double up on that, take two pills a pop, three times a day." He took a breath. "Dip your toes in," he said. "I'm not a doctor, though, so I can't offer medical advice."

Helen started taking the Anavar the next day. She didn't feel anything for a week, no mood swings, no digestive problems, no menstrual issues, no appetite changes. She felt the same. Then, on the ninth day, when she started her normal twenty-pound dumbbell bench press, it felt like she was using ten-pound weights. It was too easy. She had to stop and look at the weights in her hand. She grabbed the twenty-five-pound ones. Same thing. Her workout that day was intense, it was grueling, but when she finished, she wanted more.

The changes to her body came fast after that. Within a month, her waist had shrunk and her muscles, *all of them*, had grown. That first cycle ran for eight weeks. At the end of it, she felt people looking at her differently. Not some people, *all of them*. At work, her female colleagues—lawyers, paralegals, secretaries—looked at her with barely hidden contempt. Her male colleagues responded by either forcing themselves to ignore her—the effort was unmistakable—or cranking up the sexy vibes, staring into her eyes too long, turning and watching her walk, looking her up and down. Did she mind all that? No, she did not.

Her workouts kept getting more intense. She wore tighter clothes. She grunted like the men. She dropped heavy weights onto the ground. She strutted through the gym, her arms held out from her sides like a cowboy, and stared without shyness at herself in the mirrors. She loved it. She loved everything about it.

It wasn't just the drugs; her diet changed, too. She started making batches of boiled chicken and cabbage that she'd blend with water and salt and drink like a smoothie. Twenty ounces, three times a day—this in addition to the three protein shakes she'd make. Protein, protein: *fucking protein.*

Her girlfriends didn't express any concern. If anything, they made her feel better about the choice. "You look fantastic," said Lynn. "Is it that Sam guy?" she asked. "Are you dating him?"

They were eating sushi. Helen pulled the plate of fish closer to her. "No, it's this diet. This chicken, cabbage thing."

Lynn squinted at her, took a sip of her sake. "Well, whatever it is, yeah, I'm jealous."

Another friend, as Helen walked up to the table at a different dinner, looked her up and down and said, "Jesus, Helen, are you on steroids? You're looking so built."

"Yeah," said Helen, pretending to inject a needle into her buttock. "I'm trying out for *American Gladiators*."

At a restaurant one night, she asked Sam what other supplements she should use. He leaned his head a little, looked at her neck, looked down her body. "When you finish this cycle, you could take some ephedrine, to slim down a bit. Boost your workouts."

She did. And it worked. The pills made her feel even more in control. She felt, just as Sam had predicted, *boosted*. All her co-workers, her tired co-workers, her slovenly co-workers, the tired masses: they just didn't get it.

She didn't notice any change in her mental state. She didn't notice a shift in her mood. She didn't think she was acting erratically. She didn't, as they phrased it in law school, think that she was suffering from a *defect in reasoning*. The brain is a delicate thing, though; it's hard to stay objective about one's own mental state.

About a month after her first steroid cycle ended, Helen found herself parked down the block from the home of her ex-husband, the Honorable Tad P. Mangan. Tad was a civil judge in Denver's district court. They'd met right after Helen moved to Colorado. He was from the area, he had a lot of friends, and when she first arrived, she was lonely. So she married him. Four years after the wedding (three years ago), he told her he'd fallen in love with his clerk, a twenty-five-year-old recent law school graduate named Vanessa.

Helen hadn't planned on going to Tad's house that night. She'd been headed to a mall to pick up a new set of exercise clothes. But the store was closed. The idea came to her unbidden in the parking lot: *Tad's house.* Just to see it.

She'd never been there before; she'd only looked it up on Zillow, looked it up on Redfin, examined it on Google Maps (street view and satellite), and studied the pictures his new wife posted on Instagram and Facebook, zooming in on every little pathetic detail: the botanic wallpaper, the globe lights, the brass fixtures, all of it so trendy.

Now, parked down the block, hands on the steering wheel, she leaned and looked at the house. The kitchen lights were on. The grass was mowed. Tad's SUV sat in the driveway. Helen imagined the scene in the kitchen. Vanessa would be cooking their dinner. She'd be hovering over a pan of stir fry, a recipe no doubt gleaned from some mommy website. Tad, in her mind, had just walked in and wrapped his hands around Vanessa's pregnancy-distended belly. He was probably telling her how much he loved her: *I love you. I love you.*

There was a time when he would say that to Helen. In fact, he used to say it all the time. He'd say it in the morning when they woke, and in the afternoon when they spoke on the phone. He had a deep voice, too. He would say "I love you" almost every single day. They were words, though. Empty words. The final time he'd said it had been the literal day before he'd announced to her that he was in love with another woman. He was dropping Helen off at the office. She stretched her neck for a kiss on the lips. It was a cold, snowless, brown winter morning. "I love you," he'd said. There were dark clouds in the sky.

The next night, after work, when she came home, he seemed to be in an odd mood. Distant. They had roasted chicken. Roasted potatoes. Salad greens tossed in oil and vinegar, freshly ground pepper and Malden salt on top. Wine opened for the occasion, decanted and breathing. She was living *that kind* of life. And after dinner, he'd taken a deep breath, like he was steadying himself. Then he said, "Helen, I have to tell you something." She knew right then.

Eyes red, he told her he'd fallen in love with his law clerk. "The girl with the makeup?" Helen asked.

"Yes," said Tad.

Rather than fighting about it, Helen had dropped into business mode. She went straight to their bedroom and started packing suitcases. He followed her and tried to convince her to stay until they sorted everything out. She didn't cry in front of him. She waited until she was in her hotel room for that.

Sitting there in her car now, staring at the house, she shook her head. It wasn't that Tad had done some unthinkable thing. Helen herself had slept with two men while she was married to him—one a colleague at the law firm (a mistake), the other a much younger man she met in a bar on a business trip. No, it wasn't the infidelity, it was the *not being chosen* part that bothered her. Unselected, left behind.

Right then, an old, gray-haired woman walking a little terrier approached Helen's car. The woman dipped her head at Helen as though preparing to speak. She probably wanted to say something friendly. Helen turned the car on and drove away. She did not look at Tad's house as she drove by. He might've been gazing out the window.

Stopped at a red light, she realized her pulse was racing like she'd done something wrong. Then, in her head, she heard the words: *You will not be okay until you make him pay*. Clear as day. It was as though God had spoken to her. God or an angel of some kind.

Helen's eyes stayed on the red light. Her hand went up to her hair, and she brushed it off her forehead. The ephedrine was making her head tingle. She looked in the mirror, stretched her face taut, turned it side to side, and looked at its best and worst angles.

That night, she tossed and turned in bed. The Xanax couldn't cut through the ephedrine and sleep would not come. She wasn't a bad person. But she wanted to do bad things. She wanted to hurt Tad the way he had hurt her. She wanted to even the score. Was that so wrong?

Two weeks later, Helen hit the gym to get some cardio in before work. She ran on the treadmill, alternating between a sprint and a slow jog. Her monitor was tuned to Court TV, and she watched footage of defendants attacking their lawyers and family members attacking defendants.

In the shower, her thoughts, as they often did, went back to Tad. Specifically, to when he proposed to her. They'd been skiing in Crested Butte. It had been toward the end of the day.

They were right at the top of the Paradise Bowl. She skied over to him, and they looked out at the view. Tad pressed his pole into his heel lever and freed one boot, then the other. Helen remembered thinking, *What are you doing?* He was smiling at her in a weird way; he took his gloves off and dug in his pocket. Helen thought he was going to force her to take yet another selfie with him. Instead, he pulled out a ring box and dropped to a knee.

All you have to do is make him pay. The shower sprayed down on her. *Stop*, she told herself. She turned the water off. *You're not thinking right.* She grabbed her towel and dried her chest and underarms, dried between her legs. Then she got dressed and went to the mirror. She touched up her lipstick with her finger. A younger woman walked behind her and said, "Good morning."

"Good morning," said Helen, smiling.

In her car, she pulled out her cellphone and texted her steroid dealer: *I need to talk to you about something.* She hit send and felt a brief wave of panic. She waited for a reply, but nothing came.

Helen was an attorney at Sigworth, McKenzie & Harper. She handled corporate contracts and compliance. It was a very mid-tier job, she wasn't passionate about it, but she was on track to make partner. That was the goal. Make partner this year, and professionally, everything would be settled. Now, during her weekly meeting with Donnie, her supervisor, her mood continued its descent. His mediocrity represented everything wrong with her life. Right then, he sat listening to her status report with an eyebrow raised, like he distrusted her. "And the Emerson case?" he asked.

Helen's phone buzzed in her hand. She looked down at it and felt Donnie's eyes go from her face to her breasts. A text had come in from Jerry: *Wassup?* She set the phone face down on her leg and continued filling Donnie in on the status of the Emerson case.

"Bill those hours," Donnie said, shifting his gaze to his monitor and using his mouse to click open an email. The meeting was over.

Walking back to her desk, Helen texted Jerry: *I need to see you tonight.* She added a smiley emoji and hit send.

At 7:07 p.m., Jerry picked her up outside her apartment. She had already told him it wasn't to purchase anything, she just wanted to talk. This appeared to make him nervous. He was quiet when he picked her up.

Helen pulled the visor mirror down and fixed her hair. Then she got straight to the point. "I need a couple guys to beat someone up." She turned and looked at him. "Do you know anyone that could help me with that?"

He chuckled and turned to her, and his face transformed into what Helen would describe as a kind of pantomimed hip-hop shock. "Oh, you're not fucking around?" he said. He licked his lips and changed lanes.

"I'm willing to pay twenty-five hundred dollars," said Helen.

"What kind of dude is this? It's not Sam and them?"

"No, this is my ex-husband. He's a—" She considered saying *judge* but thought better of it. "He's a lawyer."

"Where the hell you gonna fight a lawyer?" asked Jerry.

"You ever hang out in Washington Park?"

"Yeah."

"Well, he goes running there every morning." She had confirmed this after her first visit to his house, with two additional morning visits.

"Is the dude big like Sam and them?"

"He's a skinny, middle-aged man. I don't think he's ever been in a physical altercation in his life."

They stopped at a light. Jerry sat there thinking. "Twenty-five hundred?"

"Yeah," she said.

"I'll get my little homie to do it with me. He's a bad boy."

Helen took a moment and thought about it. Tad had ruined the past few years of her life. She hadn't been happy since he told her he had cheated on her. She might never be happy again. She may have suffered a permanent, nonhealing wound. This would be a way to right that wrong, to restore order in the universe. After that, a fresh start. Spring and flowers. New beginnings. After that, she would dedicate herself to becoming a better person. A kind person. A generous, sharing, open, kind person. She just needed a clean slate.

"Can you do it next Tuesday?" she asked.

"Mm-hmm," said Jerry, nodding his head. "I think so."

❧

The day after that car ride, Jerry went to the cigarette store and tried to recruit Bunny for the job. Bunny said no. Jerry, feeling anxious about the whole thing, left with his pack of Winstons. He didn't know what he was going to do. He certainly wasn't going to do this alone. Now he was in a parking lot in Northglenn, waiting to sell some acid to a kid who worked at the Best Buy. The kid was late, though, and Jerry was getting a little ticked off.

"Sorry," said Johnny when he got in the car. He still had his blue work shirt on. "My boss was yammering on the God talk."

"There's thirty cut on that sheet, right there," said Jerry. He nodded at the center console and the kid opened it up and took the sheet of acid wrapped up in a Ziploc bag. He looked at it on his lap, like he was examining jewelry.

"Those wolves were more popular."

"I just sell it," said Jerry. "I don't design it."

"Well, you could tell them," said Johnny. He leaned forward so he could get into his back pocket. "If you wanna be successful in business, you can't just take things the way they are. That's business rule number one-oh-one, man." He changed voices for a second. "Smash the Like button," he said. "You want me to pay you in Ethereum?"

"Come on, dude," said Jerry.

"You gonna come around one of these days," said Johnny, digging into his pocket. He handed two fifties and a twenty. "Here you go, my G."

Jerry folded the bills and put them in his pocket.

"I'll give you another twenty if you take me downtown," said Johnny.

Jerry held his hand out and Johnny pressed another twenty into it. They had a deal.

As soon as they were out of the lot, the kid opened his bag and pulled out a Denver Nuggets jersey, the old one with the rainbow mountains. When he was done putting it on, he opened the bag of acid and ripped one of the tabs off and placed it on his tongue. "Yes, sir," he said. "Time to make some money."

"You gonna sell it on the street?"

"A party tonight," said Johnny.

"And who'd you get it from when you get busted?"

"A frat boy in Boulder," said Johnny.

"That's right," said Jerry.

Jerry's phone rang, and when he looked at it, he saw it was Bunny calling. "Wassup, Bun?"

Bunny told him he'd do the job on the husband.

"I knew you would," said Jerry. "I had a feeling. Don't worry, we'll make it easy, man."

He ended the call and looked at Johnny. "All we do is grind," he said. He held his fist out and Johnny bumped it. "Grind-and-scrape, scrape-and-grind."

❧

Four days later, the day before they were supposed to do the job, Bunny was in Five Points helping a friend move a sofa to his second-floor apartment. His friend, Carlo, was a black dude in his fifties. He promised Bunny forty dollars to move the couch.

The couch, sitting on the sidewalk, was wrapped in blue moving blankets held in place with ribbons of beige packing tape. Carlo had a cigarette in his mouth, and he looked down at the couch, then turned and looked up at his apartment, then scanned the block for a moment like he was looking for another set of hands to help.

"Well," said Carlo, flicking the cigarette away. "Let me pop that door real quick." Bunny watched him unlock the front door to the building and disappear into it. He came back out a moment later and arranged a piece of junk mail near the latch to hold the door open.

The couch itself, when they moved it, was heavier than Bunny had imagined, and he strained under the weight of it, shuffling his feet and puffing air.

"It's a sleeper," said Carlo.

At the front entrance, Carlo held the couch with one hand, pulled the door open, and kicked the mail out of the way. "Set it at that first turn," he said, nodding toward the stairs.

They struggled up to the first turn and set it standing tall on its side. Carlo continued up the stairs to unlock his apartment. Bunny stood there, both hands on the couch, staring down at the front door. His back ached, and he told himself he was too young for that to be happening.

The scent of beef stew came to Bunny's nose from a first-floor apartment, and he noticed how hungry he was. All he'd eaten that day was one big bowl of cereal. He was going to use these forty dollars to buy some more frozen burritos.

He listened for Carlo but didn't hear anything, so he fantasized about working a job where he made enough money to buy whatever he wanted. He'd buy hamburger meat and buns and ketchup and frozen French fries and Coca-Cola and make himself and Uncle Rayton a nice home-cooked meal.

"Sorry, had to piss," said Carlo, coming back down the stairs. They got the sofa into the apartment without too much fuss, and then

Bunny, brushing his pants with his hands, looked around. The place was dusty with cat fur and smelled like kitty litter. There were books stacked everywhere.

"You got a lot of books," said Bunny.

"Yeah," said Carlo. "The pornos are over there." He pointed toward the window and cleared his throat. "Make yourself at home." Then he went to the kitchen, and Bunny heard him opening and closing drawers like he was looking for something.

Carlo came back to the living room and held two twenty-dollar bills out for Bunny. "Here you are, my kind sir," he said.

Bunny took the money. "My back aches," he said.

"You want a massage?" asked Carlo. "I'm certified," he added. "Certified massage therapist."

"Nah, I'm cool," said Bunny.

"You wanna smoke some crank?" asked Carlo.

It had been about six months since Bunny had smoked any crystal meth. Not because he had quit, more because he hadn't been running with that crowd. He thought about it for a second. There was a nagging, anxious feeling in his gut; it'd been there all day long and he suspected that it might go away if he got high. Also, Jerry was gonna pick him up around five in the morning. Maybe it made more sense to stay up all night. "Alright," said Bunny. "But I'm gonna keep the forty dollars if that's cool? I'm kind of broke right now."

Carlo cut the packing tape with some scissors, and they pulled the blankets off the sofa. It was blue and printed with flowers. They pushed the thing into its place. Bunny stared at it for a minute and wondered if he was making a mistake.

Carlo put some international music on the stereo, then he brought out a glass bubble pipe and they smoked a modest amount of crystal meth and passed the pipe back and forth and drank some red wine from a big bottle.

For a while, it was all going well. Bunny was enjoying himself. He was feeling empowered, and his anxiety had all but disappeared. Carlo, between hits on the pipe, smoked cigarettes and kept the wine flowing. He told Bunny about some kind of fantasy book he was writing. He outlined the plot for him, talked about mountains and wizards and trolls and warriors having sex with girls. Bunny said it sounded like a movie.

Then, after a bit, Carlo's mood started to change. He was high but he got a little edge to him, too, like he was high and sullen at the same time. He got back onto the massage topic and kept trying to convince Bunny to take his shirt off, until finally it was too much and Bunny told him that he had to get going.

Bunny barely realized how high he was until he stepped back outside. It was dark now, the streetlights were on, and he decided that rather than waiting on the bus, he'd walk home.

He walked all the way from Five Points, listening to hip hop straight from his phone and talking to every person he passed. "Nice night!" he'd say to one person. "I like that shirt!" he'd say to the next. He was high and happy to not try and hide it. He felt totally unrestricted. He felt capable of doing anything.

Rayton was asleep when he got home, so Bunny lay down on the couch and listened to music on his phone and jerked off and skimmed the internet, until it was time to get up and meet Jerry.

Earlier that same Monday night, a few minutes after ten p.m., Jerry picked Helen up in front of her apartment. She wore spandex pants and a hooded sweatshirt. "Damn," Jerry said to himself when he saw her. *Maybe I should start using that shit*, he thought, referring to the Anavar. She looked like a professional athlete, or a reality TV star. She looked good.

He smelled perfume when she got in the car, and underneath that, alcohol. It occurred to him that she might not be totally sane, and he felt the area above his eyes tense up. His music was playing too loud; he leaned forward and turned it off.

"So, in terms of what you're going to do—" she said, jumping right into business mode, "—what I'm envisioning is just like, well, let's go over there, I wanna show you where I think it should happen."

Jerry drove her to Washington Park, and she told him to do a U-turn and pull over next to the park, near the basketball courts. "He loops around that, and then he cuts back directly through that field toward that playground. See that over there? Always the same thing, he's a creature of habit."

Jerry leaned forward in his seat to see where she was pointing. He was feeling, suddenly, very nervous about this whole thing. It was a stupid idea. He could feel it in his gut.

Helen showed him her phone. "This is him," she said.

Jerry studied the picture. He saw a middle-aged, corporate-looking guy. He was skinny and, at first, didn't seem scary at all. Then Jerry looked at the eyes and thought he could see a little anger in there. His nervousness increased. "Yeah," Jerry said. "Hmm."

"I was thinking," Helen continued, "you guys should sit over there, near the playground, and like, you could be drinking beers. So, it would look kind of . . ."

"Random?" suggested Jerry.

"Yeah, like it just happened."

Jerry's palms were sweaty, and he wiped them on his shirt, one at a time. Then he blew through his lips, like he was cooling some soup. "Man," whispered Jerry.

"I'm gonna give you six hundred tonight. That's a deposit."

"Alright," said Jerry.

She talked for a while about how she envisioned the confrontation. Jerry zoned out, stopped following her words, and instead watched the way she used her hand to emphasize her points. He couldn't help thinking how hot she was. They were parked in a car, and it was night, after all. *That's how these things happen*, he told himself. He looked directly into the woman's eyes to see if the feeling was mutual.

"I don't want any permanent damage. I don't want any broken jaws or, you know, knocked unconscious, nothing like that."

"Yeah, okay," said Jerry. He used his thumb and finger and brushed at his little mustache, making sure there wasn't any food there. *You're either going to do this or not*, he told himself. Then he leaned over and kissed her.

She pulled her head back a little, but she didn't turn away. She also didn't kiss him back, so Jerry wasn't sure what to do. But he kept kissing her on the mouth, which was awkward. He put his hand on her breast, and he started squeezing it through her tight bra. Whatever was happening, it was something, there was no denying that.

"Not a good idea," she whispered, finally, turning her head away.

Jerry wiped his mouth. "I hear you," he said, leaning back. Then he added, "I'm sorry." He looked out at the soccer field. "It's just . . ." He wanted to say, *You're so pretty*, but he couldn't get the words out. He looked at the trees without their leaves. A childhood memory of running laps on a similar soccer field passed through his head. A friend of his had told him not to look at his feet while he ran. *Look forward*, the kid had said. *Easier that way.*

"He has to learn a lesson," Helen said, like the kiss had never happened. "He's gotta know this world isn't his personal playground and there are bad things that can happen to him. He thinks he's untouchable."

After that, Jerry, feeling a little depressed, drove her home. Before getting out, she put a hand on his knee, which revived him. She looked him in the eye and said she was going to text him a message that he should ignore. "I'm going to say I don't want to speak to you anymore. Just on the off chance that law enforcement ever looks at my phone." Jerry didn't like the sound of that, but he didn't say anything, because she was already pulling out an envelope from her sweatshirt pocket.

Before leaving the car, Helen reminded him of their plan to meet the following Friday evening. Then she kissed him on the cheek. Her lips were a little wet. She handed him the envelope with six hundred dollars in it. He felt fully alive.

Fifteen minutes later, as Jerry turned onto his block, his phone buzzed. He looked at the text Helen had sent: *You need to leave me the fuck alone. Leave my friends alone. Don't ever call me again.* For a second, he was confused, then he remembered she had told him to ignore it. Still, it created a bad vibe, and later, after everything had played out, he looked back on this moment and regarded it as a tiny spark that started a much larger fire.

Every morning, at 4:10 a.m., Tad Mangan woke up without the assistance of an alarm. He prided himself on that fact and told whoever he could whenever the opportunity presented itself. Vanessa, his pregnant wife, lay quietly snoring, with her back to him. They'd left the heat too high; Tad was hot.

He thought about a dream he'd just had. He'd been hosting some kind of political event. There were tables of guests, and he had to get up and make a statement. He was wearing skinny jeans and they were extremely tight. He found himself standing there for a moment, all eyes on him, struggling with the jeans, trying to pull them up. That's all he could remember. What the hell was that about? He didn't wear skinny jeans. Never had, never would.

He got up, put on his bathrobe and slippers, and brushed his teeth in the bathroom, turning his face side to side, appraising it. *It's odd to age*, his father used to say. *One day you're young, the next you're not.*

Routines were important to Tad. He had a firm belief that if you followed the right ones, if you stuck to them, you would optimize yourself and be able to achieve all your goals, whether they were professional, romantic, athletic, or otherwise. Thus, every morning, during the time it took to brew his coffee, he allowed himself to check the weather and read the sports headlines. While he *drank* his coffee, he moved on to the markets and news. He didn't linger when he finished. He emptied the dishwasher and put his mug into it. Every weekday morning, always the same routine.

Before going to bed, he'd left his running clothes hanging on a chair in the office. Now he pulled them on. In the living room, he stretched his quads, calves, hamstrings. He gripped his hands behind his back and bent over, stretching his shoulders and opening his chest. He spent a moment visualizing his form, and even moved his hands a little to remind himself not to cross too far over his center plane. He rolled his head in circles, first left, then right. He wiggled his fingers and told himself not to grip his fists. Energy efficiency.

He didn't listen to anything while he ran, no music, no podcasts, no audiobooks. Society, in his opinion—and he was an actual judge, mind you—had become too distracted with this need for never-ending entertainment. Nobody could do anything without being amused anymore.

Vanessa would listen to her self-help podcasts every chance she got. She was addicted. Not him. He wanted to hear his own breath.

Loosen your shoulders, Tad told himself, starting out, and he felt their grip soften. Above, in the dark sky, a star blinked, and Tad wondered whether it was a satellite. He made a right, veered into the street, and headed toward the park. His feet felt light, but his right hip was a little sensitive. *Inflammation*, he thought. *Need to cut the wheat.*

On the next block, he thought about his pregnant wife. Warm and sentimental thoughts. She was a miracle. Such a pure heart, so kind. He pictured her, saw her smiling, saw her face and hair. A dog barked from behind a fence, and Tad thought about a different woman, an attorney named Monica. He pictured her near her desk. He saw the white skin on the back of her hand, saw the veins underneath the skin. She wore lipstick, shades of red, that looked expensive and seemed out of place in the courthouse. He pictured her lips around his dick.

A streetlight had stopped working, and this, momentarily, distracted him from those lustful thoughts. He cursed the city government. *What the hell was wrong with these people? It's called routine maintenance.* The woman, Monica, popped back into mind, and then vanished just as fast.

He entered the park. This was the part of the run he most enjoyed. There was something liberating about running underneath the big sky. These dark, early hours gave him an almost religious feeling. *Man, loose, running, field*, he said in his head. He repeated it: *Man, loose, running, field.*

It was cold out, and the turf under his feet felt stiff. He had to pay attention; the last thing he needed was a twisted ankle. He could sense a few cars driving on the streets around him, their lights making yellow impressions in the periphery, their engines humming quietly.

Loosen your shoulders, he told himself again, starting off toward the farthest soccer goal. Somewhere, across the city, an ambulance was rushing to an emergency. The sound of the siren brought on a wave of bad feelings related to his ailing mother, who was, at that moment, sleeping in a nursing home in Fort Collins, dreaming about God knows what. Tad ignored the anxiety and focused on his breath: *Unlabored*, he instructed himself. *Make it unlabored.*

From the field, he headed toward the playground. He felt his lungs working efficiently now.

His stride felt lighter, too. *This*, he told himself, *this is why I run.*

Across the field, about a hundred yards in front of him, he noticed two men watching him. *You want to stare at a judge?* Tad felt his eyes narrow a little, felt his mouth curl up, not exactly in a smile, more like the face a dog makes right before it bites.

Bunny was trying to act cool, but his anxiety was rising by the minute. As a child, he'd gotten in trouble because he kept wetting his bed. His mother had taken him into the bathroom, thrown him into the bath, and forced his face down in the water, not like she was drowning him, but in a humiliating way. Sitting in the park now, Bunny remembered the water, saw his mother's face, saw the tub itself, discolored, not white like a clean tub should be.

"Yo," said Jerry, breaking his trance.

Bunny looked up and saw a man jogging toward them. *Fuck.* He had hoped the dude might be a no-show. The guy was tall, and Bunny felt an overwhelming feeling of fear. He stood up from his seat and then lay down on the picnic table and stared up at the sky. *Help*, he thought. A full-fledged panic attack was moving in.

"What are you doing?" asked Jerry.

Bunny wanted to say, *Nothing, just sitting here*, but he couldn't get the words out, so he squinted at Jerry and shook his head. Jerry dipped his own head and watched the jogger, then he turned in a circle, taking one last look for witnesses. Then he turned back to Bunny.

"Get the fuck up," he said.

Bunny forced himself to sit on the table. The man was about forty feet away and headed straight toward them.

"Look at this dude," said Jerry. "His ass is coming to fight *us*."

The man slowed his jogging but kept on track toward them with his head jutted out a little like he was trying to make their faces out through bad night vision. He was about twenty feet away. Bunny glanced back toward the street and saw a car drive by.

"Fuck you looking at?" said Jerry.

"What?" said the man, confused.

Bunny, biting his own lip, watched him. He wasn't scary, but he had a mean face. Jerry stepped toward the guy. Bunny tried to grab his friend's arm and pull him back, but Jerry shrugged him off.

"Wassup?" said Jerry, walking toward the man. He sounded angry. They were close now, touching distance.

"Excuse me?" said the man.

"Don't! " said Bunny.

It was too late. Jerry sent a jab at the guy's face. It caught him square between the lips and nose. The man staggered back, then righted himself and raised his hand like he was about to sneeze. Blood gushed out between his fingers and a low moaning sound came from his chest.

Jerry was moving toward him again, but Bunny caught his friend's arm and pulled him back. "No, no, no. It's chill, it's chill."

"You mother—" roared the man.

Before Bunny knew what was happening, the man grabbed hold of Jerry and they clenched up and thrashed around in a circle. Bunny heard panting, and growling, and feet scuffing the grass.

"Hey!" called Jerry, like he was asking for help.

Bunny grabbed the jogger by the shoulders and was pulled into the circle. Without thinking about it, he headbutted the man right above his ear. It was a solid blow, and the man staggered a few steps and then, in the same motion, turned and ran away.

"Fuck," said Jerry to himself. Then he yelled out, "Fuck you!"

Bunny, suddenly scared that he'd dropped his phone, patted his pockets and searched the ground. He found his phone in his pocket. "Jesus," he said. His forehead felt warm, and his stomach queasy.

"What the fuck, dude?" said Jerry, his face looking like he might cry. "You were supposed to fuck him up."

"I did," said Bunny. "I headbutted him. I got him pretty good."

"Dude."

"He was bleeding," said Bunny. "You saw him. What do you want me to do, kill the guy?" They walked as fast as they could to the car. Bunny stuffed his hands into his pants pockets.

He never liked violence; he hated it. The headbutt resonated in his head, and he knew in his bones that this whole thing had taken a bad turn and it was going to lead to serious and consequential trouble. He had a good sense for that kind of thing.

Before entering his house, Tad examined himself in the reflection of his SUV's window. His nose didn't appear to be broken, but the smear of blood on his face alarmed him. His chief concern at that moment was making sure Vanessa didn't see him like this. The last thing she needed was unnecessary stress. *You're a good man, for that*, he told himself. *A frigging good man.*

In the kitchen, he pulled a long sheet of paper towels from the roll, bunched it up and wet it in the sink. Before he cleaned his face, though, he placed the soppy towels back on the counter, went to his office, grabbed his phone, and took pictures of himself. It felt ridiculous to pose like this, but he wanted evidence of what those punks had done to him. The first few pictures made him look old, and he had to adjust the angle and retake them. He looked like his father. *Same eye-bags, same sagging face.*

Once he was clean, he took his phone and walked back to the park. He certainly wasn't going to have the cops respond to his house. That would be worse than the assault itself.

His nose wasn't broken, it was just a small cut on the nasal septum. Still, that didn't diminish what this was. This was an attack. He'd been ambushed. He thought about his recent decisions; there hadn't been any controversial cases. He handled civil claims, and all his recent cases had been depressingly boring.

The police arrived six minutes after he placed the call. He'd requested that they not respond with their sirens on as he didn't want to make a disturbance, and, in fact, they honored that request. He also told the dispatcher that he was a judge in Denver's District Court. The dispatcher hadn't seemed particularly moved by that information and simply repeated it back to him.

The officers, when they arrived, seemed very young. They looked like college students. "Mr. Mangan?" the first cop, a stubble-faced white kid, asked.

"Judge Mangan," said Tad.

"I'm sorry?"

"It's Judge Mangan," repeated Tad. "I'm a District Court judge, Bannock Street."

The two cops exchanged a look. "Was that—" began the first cop, "—was that part of the incident, sir?"

Tad took a step back, turned, and looked at the east side of the park. The sky was brightening with daylight. "Yes, it was part of it," he said. There wasn't evidence of that, but he couldn't help himself. He wanted this thing to be taken seriously.

The first cop turned to his partner. "We better call the sarge," he said. The partner nodded.

The sergeant showed up eight minutes after she was summoned. A uniform-wearing woman in her fifties, heavyset in the legs, she walked from her car to them with what appeared to be a stiff back.

Tad described to the three cops what had happened. When he finished, the sergeant looked at the officers, then scanned the park like she was searching for unnoticed witnesses. She asked if the assailants had said anything.

"Just a bunch of *F you*'s," said Tad. "*F this, F that.*"

"Were they waiting for you?"

"They appeared to be waiting for me," said Tad, his voice becoming a little high-pitched with emotion. His cellphone vibrated in his hand. He glanced down and, upon seeing his pregnant wife's name, sent the call to voicemail.

"I'm gonna be honest with you, Judge," said the sergeant. "This thing can either be a big deal,"—she snorted, raised her eyebrows, held her hands out like she was measuring a fish—"Feds, all of it. Or we treat it as a random incident, two punks, an assault in a park. That doesn't mean we don't investigate. Just . . . you know. Your call."

Tad felt like he wanted to cry. His nose hurt; his head hurt. This was humiliating. It was all so humiliating. The last thing he wanted was to be sat down and questioned by FBI agents. He looked at his phone. "Random act," he said. "I think it was just a random act. But—" He looked at the sergeant, growled. "I want you to arrest these men."

"Oh, we will," she said. "We're going to do everything we can to find your assailants." She turned to her young officers. "Call it a Code Nine, let's go."

More cops responded. The sergeant stayed and helped supervise the whole process. Tad sat in a squad car and made a statement. He sent the pictures of his injuries to the sergeant. He watched other people jogging by.

Before leaving, he thanked the sergeant. She scratched behind her ear and gazed at the ground. "I hope the rest of your day goes better than this," she said.

At home, he found Vanessa waiting for him. He'd already called her and explained—in the most relaxed way he could—what had happened. "An altercation," he'd called it.

"Taddy," she said. "Oh, my Lord, what have they done to you?" She'd already put her makeup on.

"Nothing," he said.

She was wearing her bathrobe, the belt tied around her belly. She raised a mug of coffee to her lips, blew on it, sipped.

"Were they . . . ?" she asked.

"What?"

"Well, who was it?"

"Just two drunk bums."

"Homeless men?" she asked, her face incredulous.

"Not— I don't know, just two—"

"Were they . . . ?"

"What?"

"Black?"

"What?"

"I saw a vagrant in the park yesterday," she said, collapsing her eyes and tightening her lips as though warning him not to suggest what he seemed to be suggesting.

Vanessa was only twenty-five, but in that moment, Tad could see her in her midfifties, her sixties, her seventies. *What have I done?* he thought. *What have I done? How did I end up here?* Helen wouldn't have freaked out like this. She wouldn't have jumped to any racist conclusions. She wouldn't have tied her bathrobe around her belly like that, either. Makeup first thing in the morning? *Oh God*, he thought, *who have I married?*

Vanessa touched his arm. She put her head on his shoulder. "Do you want me to make you breakfast?" she asked. He didn't answer. "Do you want me to *mmmmmm*?" she made a kind of whiny noise, her code for sex.

"I can't right now," said Tad. He kissed the top of her head and walked toward the stairs—he needed to take a shower and get to work.

❧

"I'm sorry I was short with you back there about the money," said Bunny. They were in the car, driving back from the fight in the park. Bunny was fussing with his seatbelt; Jerry, both hands on the wheel, drove.

"Nah, dude, I get it," said Jerry. "I'll give you two hundred when I drop you off."

"I appreciate that," said Bunny.

"And I'll get you the rest when this chick pays me."

"That's wassup," said Bunny.

They rode in silence for a second. They were on Twentieth Street now. Bunny looked at a billboard advertising Powerball. His thoughts jumped from Powerball to rich people to fancy cars to skiers and then finally settled on the man in the park. "Who was that dude, though?"

"Just some dude," said Jerry. "Some dude with the wrong ex. This girl, though," he squinted at the road ahead of them. "She's fine as hell. She's lightweight vibing me, too."

"She's rich," said Bunny. "Paying for all this."

"Yeah, man. She's a business lady. Corporate. Older, but I'm like, shit, we're cool. I'm cool with all that," said Jerry. "I need a rich girl. That's the kind of lifestyle I want."

"Tell her to get a friend, and we could do something," said Bunny.

"That's wassup, player," said Jerry. "Take them out to dinner, dancing, and a movie. Me, you, her, and her. You gotta dress up, though."

"Yeah," said Bunny.

"Get in your nicest clothes and hold all the doors open."

"We could go for a walk. Take them on a nice walk in the mountains."

"Yeah, I don't know if that's what kind of ladies these are."

They rode in silence for a few blocks, then Jerry turned to Bunny and asked him what he was thinking about.

"I was thinking about this teacher I once had," said Bunny. "Ms. Sanchez, a nice teacher, a nice lady. She used to hug me when I was feeling down, grab me by the shoulders, look me in the eye, and say, 'You could be anything you want to be in this world, Bunny.'"

"Ms. Sanchez," said Jerry, like he was talking to himself.

"Yeah," said Bunny. He thought about how Ms. Sanchez's perfume smelled like roses. How her clothes were always clean and pressed. He'd like to call her up. *What the hell should I do with my life?* he'd ask her. *Like just tell me, what the hell should I do with myself?* She'd probably say he needed to go back to school, get his GED. Then she'd say he had to go to college. Go to college and study business. *You could be a businessman, Bunny.*

They continued bumping along the road. Bunny looked at a homeless man who was riding a bike next to them and then he closed his eyes again and he felt space all around them in a distinct way, like he could really tell that they were on a planet floating through space. *We're on a big, giant planet, and we're floating in space.*

⁂

The following morning—twenty-eight hours and thirty-four minutes after the incident in the park—Jerry, lying in bed in the basement, awake and ruminating, heard his doorbell ring. He listened as his mother crossed from the kitchen to the front of the house.

The sound of the door opening was followed by the low notes of a man's voice. Friendly, but not a neighbor. The words weren't clear, but Jerry had the distinct impression that the visitor was a police officer.

Jerry got out of bed, stepped into some shorts, pulled on a sweatshirt, and crept to the front side of the basement. On his tippy toes, he peeked out the egress window. He could see two sets of men's legs. On the street, he saw an unmarked Ford Fusion.

Jerry raced back to his room, pulled his shoes on, and went straight to a rarely used back room. As quietly as possible, he unlocked and opened the door and stepped into a dank-smelling storage room. On the far side of the room was a door that opened to a stairway up to the backyard. As Jerry fumbled with the lock, he heard his mother's voice call down, "Jerry."

Outside, he shut the door and stood there at the bottom of the stairs, listening. He could go for the back fence, but that would leave him exposed from the living room window. Instead, he took the stairs two at a time, then hunched close to his building and moved for the neighbor's yard directly next to them.

The fence between their yards was tall and wooden. Jerry grabbed the top, pulled himself up, whipped his legs over, and landed on the other side with a thump that knocked the wind from his lungs. The fence had stabbed into both of his palms, and he checked them for blood but there was none. He looked toward the neighbor's house and didn't see any sign of life. He peeked back toward his house and didn't see any movement over there, either. He moved for the neighbor's back fence.

When he landed in the next yard, Jerry found two kids, probably five years old, playing near their back door. They both stood when they saw him. Jerry put his finger near his lips and motioned for them to be calm. They watched him with their mouths hanging open as he made his way to the gate at the front of their yard. "Sorry," he said to the two boys as he passed. "Sorry," he repeated.

The gate to the street was unlocked. As he made his way out, he heard one of the boys say "Mommy." Jerry picked up his pace. When he got to the sidewalk, he looked back and saw the two boys had followed him out of their backyard and were staring after him. Their faces looked mad, like they wanted to fight.

Jerry broke into a light jog and moved south toward the larger street that fed these little cul-de-sacs. He realized he hadn't grabbed his wallet or his phone, and he cursed himself up and down as he went.

An older man—skinny, bald, and red-faced—stepped out of his house and stared at Jerry as he jogged past. Jerry, squinting against the sun, forced himself to smile and kept going. *Just going for a jog*, he chanted in his head. *Just going for a jog.* When he reached the larger road that ran perpendicular to his own, he headed south. The streets were quiet. Nobody else seemed to be out.

He had the vague idea of getting to Wadsworth Boulevard and borrowing someone's phone. *I'll leave town,* he thought. *Go to San Diego.* Maybe this was the kickstart his life needed. What had he been waiting for, really? There was never going to be a better time than now. He'd lay low for a minute, get his money together, then just go. California.

He looked up and saw a young woman walking toward him on the sidewalk. She didn't belong in Arvada, she looked like she was from downtown Denver or something. She wore a halter top and had bright-red lipstick on, and her hair was dyed black. Jerry, conscious of his running form, tried to move more gracefully. For a second, he forgot his problems.

He was about to say hi when he saw her face change. She looked scared. Jerry realized she wasn't looking at him, though; she was looking beyond his shoulder. He followed her gaze and saw a black-and-white Arvada Police SUV speeding toward him.

Jerry stopped and turned and faced it and the lights popped on. The car screeched to a stop. The doors flung open, and two cops jumped out. They didn't have their guns drawn, but they both had their hands on them, and they looked like they were itching for a reason.

"Down on the ground!" said the first one.

"Get down on the ground!" said the second.

Jerry put his hands up; he got on one knee, then the other, and then he lowered himself down to the sidewalk. His face was away from the cops, away from the girl, and toward the grass lawn of a nearby house; the sod looked like a rug with little white roots.

He felt a knee on his back, and both of his arms were yanked, and he felt himself being cuffed. He heard the cops cursing him and telling him not to resist and to stay still. He could feel his cheeks puffing out with each exhale. His forehead was sweaty, and his back, too. The sidewalk was warm from the sun.

"Fuck," he said. "Damn! My arm, dude."

One of the cops was calling something in on the radio. *There goes California*, thought Jerry. *Kiss all that goodbye.*

By the time they lifted Jerry back up, arms cuffed behind him, the girl he'd seen had disappeared. In her place was the Ford Fusion. The two plainclothes cops got out. He recognized their jeans and sneakers.

One of them looked Middle Eastern. He stepped to Jerry, looked at his face. "LeClair, that you?" The cop looked over at his partner, a white dude wearing jeans and a sweatshirt. "That's him, right?"

The white one squinted down at Jerry. "Yeah, that looks like him to me." He looked at the uniformed Arvada cops. "No ID?"

"Nothing on him."

"You gonna make us print you? Or you gonna tell us you're Jerry LeClair?" said the white one.

"I'm Jerry."

The Middle Eastern cop looked at him like he'd never seen someone so dumb. "You know running makes a consciousness of guilt, right?"

"I'm just jogging," said Jerry. "Last time I checked, that's not a crime."

They brought Jerry downtown, to Colfax Avenue, and booked him on a felony arrest warrant for assault, battery, and attempted robbery. The last charge shocked him the most: *We didn't try to rob nobody!*

At the jail, after being processed and printed, the deputies searched his anus, under his balls, and inside his mouth, even poking around between his gumline and cheek. When they were done, they handed him a stiff yellow jail suit that smelled like vomit. He pulled it on, and they walked him straight to an interview room.

Jerry had to wait in there, alone, for a few hours. The room was clean, but it had glass walls on each side, which made him feel watched and made it hard for him to relax. Finally, those same two detectives from his house stepped into the room. Jerry blinked up at them from his seat.

They looked tense and grumpy. The white one—he had a big forehead and thin hair—set a manila file on the table and put a lined notepad on top of that and then organized their corners flush. Then he straightened back up and stood there staring.

"Jerry LeClair," he said, looking right into Jerry's eyes. He pulled out a business card and read from it: "You have the right to remain silent, anything you say can and will be used against you in a court of law."

"Excuse me," said Jerry.

"Hold on," said the cop. "You have the right to an attorney. If you cannot afford an attorney, one will be appointed to you. Do you understand these rights?"

"We just gonna get right into it?" asked Jerry.

"Oh, you're in it," said the white one.

"You attacked a judge on video," said the other one.

"A judge? What the fuck y'all talking about?"

"The Honorable Tad P. Mangan."

"Do you know what *laying in wait* is?" asked the white one, taking a seat right across from Jerry.

Jerry knew he shouldn't be talking to these guys. *Ask for a lawyer. Ask for a lawyer. Ask for a lawyer.* But he forgot. In the heat of the moment, he simply forgot. "Laying in wait?" he said. "I wasn't laying in wait. For real, I don't know what the hell you're talking about."

"Oh yeah, we got a regular psychopath here." The other cop had a coffee in his hand, and he sipped from it.

"I don't know what the hell you're talking about," repeated the white cop, jotting Jerry's words down in the notepad.

Jerry told himself to just shut up for a second; let them talk. *First person who speaks loses*—a negotiating lesson he'd learned online. *Control yourself.* He sealed his lips tight, pulled a long breath in through his nose.

"Jerry," said the white one. "Look at me. I'm detective Baron,"—he then pointed at his partner—"this is Detective Mousa. We're not park police, my dude. This is not a scuffle. We're Major Crimes." He nodded. "Yes, sir. You attacked a judge, Jerry. Damn near put him in a coma."

Detective Mousa tossed his coffee cup into a little plastic trashcan. "You parked on South Franklin."

"All those houses have cameras," said Detective Baron. "All of them."

Jerry stared down at the table. He crossed his arms in front of himself. The detective facing him opened his file and pulled out a printed photo and looked at it. Then he slid it across the table, face down.

Jerry lifted it up and saw a still image of his Blazer. Beyond the car, he saw the park. Helen had instructed him to park blocks away. *Multiple blocks*, she'd said, *and then walk*. She told him three times. His ears started ringing. A molar in the top right of his mouth began to ache. His brain hadn't been working right to make him forget that. *Slow down*, he told himself.

"A Blazer?" said Detective Mousa. He sat down next to his partner. "Come on, man."

"So what?" said Jerry.

"There's a reason you're already in the jail and not on Cherokee Street," said Detective Baron. "Shit,"—he held his hand out like he was offering a handshake—"look at you, you're already dressed in yellow. You gonna walk one way down that hallway. Yep. We don't need anything else on you. We could go to trial tomorrow, get a conviction before the lunch break."

"Jury will barely deliberate," said his partner. "Open and shut."

"What do you think the DA will make of this?" said Detective Baron. He turned and looked at his partner.

"Judge got attacked," said Detective Mousa. "My guess is they're gonna want to prove a point."

"Don't want to upset a judge. You upset one judge, they're all gonna get pissed off," his partner added.

"They're a cabal," his partner added.

"And they're gonna all be watching this one. You fucked up. You fucked up so good, my friend."

They sat in silence. Outside the interview room, voices in the jail could be heard hollering. Down the hall, a jail door slammed shut. Jerry felt, suddenly, freezing cold, like it was winter, and he was lost in the woods. He rubbed his hands together trying to warm up.

"We're going to need a name," said Detective Baron.

Helen forgot to mention this dude was a fucking *judge*. That seemed like a relevant piece of information. He considered giving her name up but realized that would put him in deeper. That would elevate this from a stupid incident all the way up to premeditation. Jerry knew enough to understand all that. He bit his lip and stared at the table.

The white cop said, "Look here." He opened his file, pulled out another piece of paper, slid it to Jerry. Jerry turned it over and saw a picture of himself in Circle K buying cigarettes. Clear as day. High definition. He'd bought cigarettes right after the fight.

"This is your last chance, genius," said Detective Baron, dropping his voice down to a barely audible whisper. "This is your one last chance to get in the good graces of the prosecutor who's gonna be looking at your file in about thirty-five minutes. We can tell her you're a good kid. You're helping us. Or we can tell her you're a punk, a scumbag who ambushes judges at night. But we need to know the name of your friend."

They sat in silence.

"You didn't drive to pick this dude up?" Detective Mousa whispered. "And then you dropped him off?" He dropped his voice, too. "Location will be right there."

"We'll find him," said the other one. "The question is if it's today, or tomorrow. But your hesitation, your failure to assist us, is pissing me off, and it's going to piss everyone else off, too."

"Give us his name."

When Jerry first met Bunny at that warehouse party in Golden about five years earlier, Bunny had still been a kid. He carried peanut butter and jelly sandwiches in a Ziploc bag. Over the years, they'd become best friends. Fucking Bunny, man. He hated to do this, but they would find him. They'd find him right there on the phone. Jerry had texted him, *On my way.* They had Bunny dead in their sights. And if they looked at his phone, they might have Helen, too.

"You gonna vouch for me?" Jerry asked.

"Hell yeah, we will," said Detective Baron. "I give you my word on that."

"His name is Bunny Simpson."

"Bunny? Is that his real name?"

"I don't know. But I'm gonna tell you the truth, now. He didn't have anything to do with this. It was me that got in the fight with the dude. And that dude started the fight, word to God, I don't care if he's a judge or not. Bunny tried to break it up. He's a good kid. And there was no robbery involved. That's bullshit, too. That's my statement, write all of that down in your notes right there."

Jerry closed his eyes for a second. He saw himself lost in the woods again, snow on the ground, a black creek running by. A sad, peaceful feeling came over him. When he opened his eyes, the white cop was looking at him with a little smile in his eyes, but it didn't look friendly. It looked mean and satisfied.

That same morning, Bunny took the 49 bus to the cigarette store for work. He'd treated his uncle to pizza the night before, bought a whole large pie, and they drank a few beers, and Bunny had slept well and woke up feeling refreshed and good. His only worry was that he hadn't heard back from Jerry. He'd texted him a few times and called twice. Nothing. It was almost like his friend had just up and disappeared. The guy still owed him $240, too.

The RTD bus, headed for Commerce City, was about half full. Most of the riders were Latinos on their way to work. There were three passengers that looked homeless; two of them dozed with their necks bent at odd angles. The driver, a woman, had a little pocket radio, and she was listening to some ragtime being played on a piano. Bunny worried she might get in trouble for that.

While he rode, Bunny daydreamed about his future. He'd start working construction. Then, once he'd obtained financial stability, he'd start an organization that helped other young men and women find work in construction, help train them. Yep, then maybe he'd get into politics. Find a wife, get married, have kids, a house, all of it.

The bus bumped along and turned onto Holly Street. This was a nice, quiet neighborhood with trees and fences around the homes. Yeah, he'd get a home just like one of these. Get a truck. Someone behind him rang the bell and the driver pulled up to the stop. Air hissed from the suspension as the bus jerked down like an old horse. A lady got off.

Bunny checked his cellphone. Still nothing. He thought about an incident he'd witnessed as a kid. He must've been about six or seven. His father hadn't jumped ship yet, and they all lived together as a family. Their house, at that time, was still in Grand Junction. It must've been a weekend day because Bunny's father was home and not working. Bunny had been on the side of the house with his little sister, Reecey, digging a hole in the ground and pretending to look for water.

Two pickup trucks pulled into the lot. That was enough of an unusual event to make Bunny and his sister—who must've still been wearing diapers at the time—stop digging. They crept over to the side of the house and watched, the way kids do when strangers show up.

The trucks, in Bunny's memory, were big, dark-colored, old, rusted, and dented. Some number of men stepped out, and Bunny's father, who'd been working on his own car, placed a tool down on the ground and set about cleaning his hands with an old rag. He held his shoulders up as the men walked toward him, like he was expecting them to say something. Bunny could tell his father was scared. He'd never seen him look like that before. Right then, he noticed his uncle Willard, his mother's brother, was one of the men. The man was large, he had a dark goatee, and a mean face. Bunny had never liked him.

"Carol, go back in the house," said his father. Bunny looked for his mother but didn't see her anywhere. Soon, Bunny's father and uncle started arguing. Bunny didn't understand what they were talking about, but he remembered his uncle telling his father that he was gonna take him by the hair and drag him down the damn street.

Nothing happened that day. There was no violence. Just talk. But Bunny still remembered how frightened his father had looked. He'd never seen him like that. That image stayed in his mind.

Later, when Bunny was a teenager and he became more curious about his family's history, he learned that his uncle—sometime after that incident in the front yard—got sent to prison at the Limon Correctional Facility. He served twelve years on a manslaughter charge. Apparently, he beat a man to death. Bunny's mom told him that.

Bunny watched an older lady get on the bus and sit down in the front. His mind went back to his father, who had left the family shortly after that incident in the yard. "Your father's gone," his mom had said. Sometime shortly after that, his mother got caught up in a burglary case. Bunny and his sister had to go to a foster home for a few months. The foster home hadn't been that bad, though. The parents were Christian, they had four kids of their own, and they lived in a nice, light, clean house; they had plenty of food to eat. Bunny had been able to stay together with his sister, Reecey; that made everything easier, at least. After a few months they were allowed to return to their mom. These days, Reecey was living in Green River, Utah. She already had two kids, so now her life was pretty much taken over with all that mothering nonsense. Bunny only talked to her once every few months or so. She seemed old now. They were so different.

Bunny wanted kids, though. He wanted a bunch of them, but he needed to have a better career than selling cigarettes in Commerce City. He was gonna need a girlfriend, too. He looked around the bus, made sure he hadn't missed any potential romantic partners. He didn't see any possibilities and he sat there biting his thumbnail. His eyes went back to the houses passing by, and he thought about his father again. He didn't even know where the man was. He was probably in a prison somewhere. Locked up in a cage for some bullshit.

Either that or dead.

Bunny finally got off the bus at East Sixty-Ninth Avenue and Monaco Street. He had to walk a few blocks over to the cigarette store, and he put his hands in his pockets and headed that way. On the walk, he gave himself a little motivational talking-to. He said that everyone he was going to meet that day was going to provide him with an opportunity to learn something. All he had to do was look for it and keep himself open. *You gotta stay open*, he said to himself, looking down at the ground and kicking a little pinecone.

When he got to the AAA cigarette store, he saw that his boss, T-Ma, was still there. She drove a Ford F-150, with the black windows, and Bunny wasn't quite sure how she afforded that. The thing was clean, like it had just been washed, and Bunny took a nice, long look at it. There was another car in the lot, a little Toyota.

When he got inside the store, he saw T-Ma behind the counter helping the driver of the Toyota fix his e-cigarette.

"Wassup, T-Ma?" said Bunny.

"Bunny boy," she said, shaking her head and giving him a nasty look.

Bunny pulled his phone out and confirmed he wasn't late. He grabbed a broom from behind the counter and said he was going to sweep up out front. The doorbell chimed when he left.

Outside, he set about sweeping the dust off the concrete floor. Why, he wondered, was his boss so upset? When the customer came out, Bunny went back in and again asked T-Ma what was up.

She was in her midforties; she was kind of a mother figure for Bunny. She'd lived a hard life, which you could see on her face, but she'd been sober for years and was on a roll of good luck. Right then, she looked at the door where the customer had just left, then turned back to Bunny. "Two cops came in here this morning looking for you."

"What?" said Bunny. "What do you mean, two cops?"

"Just what I said," said T-Ma. "Two *plainclothes* detectives came in here with your DMV photo all printed out." The anger in her face grew deeper. "I told them you were *not* working today." She raised an eyebrow, dropped her voice. "Let you get your shit in order."

"It's just a little thing," said Bunny. "A little altercation."

"I don't want to hear about it," said T-Ma, "but listen to me for a second, Bunny." She took a big hit off her vape and blew out a cloud of smoke. "Nobody's ever been serviced by talking to the cops. They gonna sit you down, and they gonna wanna have a statement from you. It never helped anyone. You hear me? In the whole history of crime, nobody ever talked their way out of trouble."

Bunny was familiar with the philosophy, always had been. He nodded solemnly.

T-Ma glanced toward the lot, like she was making sure the cops hadn't returned. "So, what you gonna say is, 'Respectfully, sir, I don't know what this is about, but I think I should try and talk to a lawyer before I speak with you.' Get yourself a public defender. Cops gonna try and press you and make it sound like talking is the only way you could get yourself out, but don't believe anything they say. They're not helping you. They're trying to lock you up for as long as they can. Repeat: 'I wanna talk to a lawyer.'"

"I'll get it straightened out," said Bunny.

"Yeah, hopefully you will," said T-Ma, shaking her head and looking at the counter in front of her. Bunny wanted to hug the woman, but he hesitated, and the moment passed. Then, after saying goodbye, Bunny went back out to Monaco Street and headed toward the bus stop. She was a good friend, and he was never going to see her again.

From there, Bunny went home, packed his bag, said goodbye to Rayton, and got arrested. They swooped right in on him. Made their whole big to-do about it. Perp walked him through the trailer park and everything.

They didn't take Bunny straight to jail. First, they brought him to the station for an interview. They processed him, took his phone away, took pictures of him, printed him, moved him from one holding cell to another, and then finally they brought him to a cramped and brightly lit interview room. He was still dressed in his street clothes.

Bunny half expected to see Jerry waiting for him there. He was escorted into the room by a black woman in a uniform. She pointed at the seat near the far wall and told him to sit down. Then she stepped back into the hallway and locked Bunny inside. Her perfume lingered in the air.

Bunny looked around for a camera and spotted one in the corner of the ceiling above him. He looked at the little markings that other people had scratched into the wall. He saw one that read SCREEMO, and below that he saw two Nazi SS symbols.

Bunny's wrists were cuffed in front of his body. He looked at the keyhole and, for something to do, imagined picking the lock. Then he thought about that priest who used to fondle him. It started when he was ten and continued until he was fourteen. The guy was called Pastor Dan. He probably wasn't much older than Bunny was now.

Bunny started fighting around that same time. The more fights he got in, the more people seemed to want to fight him. He ended up with the reputation of a fighter, which was probably the reason Jerry asked him to do this stupid thing in the first place. He looked at his knuckles and told himself, *You gotta do better than this. You gotta grow up.*

His thoughts shifted to one of his past fights. It happened at a high school football game, Grand Junction against Fruita Monument. He'd gone to the game with his buddy Carlos. They were only in the seventh grade, but they were both drunk from sipping on some cooking wine that Carlos had stolen from his mother's kitchen. They were leaving the game in the middle of the fourth quarter when Major Montero, a kid a year older than Bunny, walked right up to him and bumped him hard, on purpose. They fought right there, outside the stadium. The sky was lit up with lights. Hundreds of people stood watching, but nobody intervened. Bunny, in the interview room, thought about that. Something snapped in Bunny during that fight. He went berserk. The kid Major must've had something snap inside him, too, though. He didn't back down at all, and they fought like wild cats, swinging and scratching.

Bunny opened his eyes and looked at the table in front of him. He thought about Pastor Dan again. He saw the Pastor's face looking up at him from between his own legs. He saw his dick in Pastor Dan's mouth.

His thoughts were jolted by the door opening. Two plainclothes detectives stepped into the small room. They were dressed casually, jeans and button-up shirts. One was white, and one looked Middle Eastern or Indian.

"Bunny Simpson?" said the white one. "I like that. That's a cool name. You gotta be a country star with a name like that." He brushed at his pants. "You need anything? You want a Coca-Cola?" They were trying to butter him up.

Bunny stayed silent.

"We need to talk to you about that issue in the park," said the other one. Bunny didn't speak.

"Right now, we think you might just be a witness, that's it. But we still gotta read you your rights."

"Keep everything on the up-and-up."

They read him his rights, and when they were done, the white cop looked Bunny up and down. "So?" he said, a friendly look in his eyes. "What did you see? Tell us what you saw happening there in Washington Park?"

"I want a lawyer," said Bunny. He felt good saying it, too. He saw the anger in the cops' faces and that added to his good feeling.

"We want to do this the friendly way."

"I want to talk to a lawyer, please," said Bunny.

"Okay then."

The two cops stood. "You know he was a judge, right?" asked the white one. "Lawyer," said Bunny, looking into his eyes and making his voice sound a little more authoritative.

The cops left after that, and Bunny thought about things. What the hell were they talking about? A judge? Bunny was so hungry his stomach hurt; he felt a little lightheaded. He daydreamed about cooking a big pot of beef stew. He'd be living in a house with Uncle Rayton. Chopping up the onions and carrots. Browning the beef. Pour some beer into it. Bread and butter. He would love to eat some white bread with butter on it. That would do him just fine. Bread and butter, he'd take that alone, right then. That would be enough for him.

Jerry, meanwhile, was being held on the fourth floor of the Denver Downtown Detention Center. The room he was in looked more like a place for meetings than a jail. It was a low-ceilinged, open room with three rows of bunkbeds running front to back. He counted twenty-eight other inmates. They were over capacity, so Jerry had to join three other newcomers on the floor in the back of the room.

He didn't know anyone when he first arrived. Didn't recognize any faces. It was a mixed crowd, whites, Blacks, Latinos. They all kept pretty much to themselves.

On the ground, in the back with him, were two white guys. One looked homeless—he was malnourished and had a wild red beard and matted brown hair. Scabby sores around his mouth. He seemed mentally disturbed and sat with his back to the wall, muttering to himself.

The other white guy was friendly enough. He was a little soft in the gut, and he had long, thin black hair and wire-rimmed glasses. He had an intellectual air to him, and Jerry could imagine him teaching at a college or something. Jerry kept his distance, though; the guy had a pedophile vibe, and Jerry didn't want to associate with that.

The third dude on the floor was Latino—Mexican or Salvadorian or something. He said his name was Ivan. He had a casual air, like he was used to being in jail and wasn't that bothered by it. He was a strong dude, looked like he worked with his hands, and Jerry aligned himself and took his cues mainly from him.

The room was lit by large fluorescent lights. It was windowless and smelled like dirty laundry and cafeteria food. The black guys in the front of the room did most of the hollering, but the white guys near them carried on, too, all of them chattering about this and that all day long.

Things started badly that first day. There were two guards watching the room, and one of them walked back to Jerry and took him out of the pod and down a hallway to get his sleeping mat and blanket. This guard was a big white guy. He had a sunburnt face and a huge neck. His knuckles looked swollen and rough, like he'd been punching a wall to toughen them up. His shoulders were nearly twice as wide as Jerry's, and his shoes stretched out at their sides, like overpacked duffel bags.

On their walk down the hall, the guard kept repeating Jerry's last name, muttering "LeClair" to himself like he was trying to make sense of it. "Is that French or something?"

"French-Canadian," said Jerry.

The guard turned to him and chuckled, but not in a friendly way. "LeClair," he said again, shaking his head, like he couldn't believe what kind of guys they were sending in these days. Jerry's eyes stayed on the linoleum floor.

When they reached the closet with the bed stuff, the guard took a long time going through his key ring. He snorted when he found it, looked at Jerry, looked all around like he was making sure they were alone, then unlocked the door and pulled it open. Jerry saw a large walk-in closet.

The guard had a distant look on his face, like his mind had gone somewhere else. "Go on," he said. "Grab a blanket and a mat." Jerry had to brush past the man to enter the closet. After he did, the guy turned and followed him in and blocked the doorway with his body. All of Jerry's stress signals switched on at the same time.

"LeClair . . ."

"Yeah, that's me," said Jerry, picking out a folded blanket and a plastic-covered mat, the kind made for a kid who wet the bed. He turned and faced the guard, holding the mat between them.

"You'll get on alright in here. We look out for each other." The guard's gaze went from Jerry's eyes to his shoulder, then down his flank to his hip.

"I appreciate that," said Jerry.

"Yup," said the guard, cleaning his teeth with his tongue and bending his head a little, like he was appraising Jerry. "Yeah, everybody gonna act right, we try to help each other." He nodded. "We call this the mellow wing. Ain't no need for problems." He was speaking almost in a whisper.

"Shit," said Jerry, smiling and shaking his head.

"I'm serious."

Jerry watched the guard scratch himself around the crotch and then give his dick a little squeeze. When Jerry looked at the man's face, he saw him staring back with an expression like *You wanna fuck with me?*

Down the hall, Jerry heard a man's voice saying "Hempstead" or "Hampstead" or something. The guard sighed and stepped out of the doorway and looked in the direction of the voice. Then he called out, "Sarge," and stepped back further still.

Jerry followed him and saw another guard escorting a few inmates toward them. The inmates walked in a line holding their hands behind their backs. One of them wore a Covid mask. A different one, a black dude, looked at the guard and Jerry and the open closet and said, "Shit, y'all need a camera on this wing. Y'all ain't supposed to be alone with us."

"Move along," said the guard who was walking them.

The big guard held his hand up at Jerry, telling him to follow the inmates.

When they got back to their dorm, Jerry saw one of the white inmates near the front of the room watching him with interest. The inmate looked at Jerry, then looked at the guard, like he was asking, *Did you?*

"Go on back, LeClair," said the guard. "No fussing, no fighting. Recreation at fifteen hundred."

"You stay on Colfax?' asked an inmate when Jerry walked past. The guy was laying on his bunk. He had tattoos inked out on his neck, like he'd had them covered up.

"Nope," said Jerry.

"You don't ride with Ritchie and them?"

"No," said Jerry. "Sorry, I don't."

When he got to the back of the room, the three other guys there set about moving their mats to make room for him. He had to set his mat closest to the toilet, which wasn't a good place to be. Jerry considered arguing, considered trying to make the long-haired guy stay there, but decided to hold his tongue.

It was a horrible place to sleep. Men kept shuffling to the commode all night long. There was a stomach virus going around the jail. It seemed like every inmate had diarrhea. There were no walls around the toilet, so the men sat there facing Jerry, groaning and exploding. The lights were on, and the floor was cold.

He thought about Helen. He should have known better. Should have known right when she started talking about beating someone up. What kind of woman uses steroids anyway? How'd he get involved in all this?

In the morning, he called his mother collect from a payphone. She was pissed. "Jerry, they said you attacked someone."

"Who said that?" asked Jerry, holding the phone away from his ear and speaking right into the mouthpiece.

"The police! They said you jumped a man in the park."

"Mom, it's a mix-up," he told her. "Listen, though, I'm gonna need help bailing out."

"Sweetheart, I can't help you with this one. We told you to stop all this nonsense. Did we not say you had to stop? Brian and I both said you had to stop all this foolishness."

Jerry pictured the guard grabbing his dick and staring at him. He thought about telling his mother that he was going to get raped in here, but he held off. If she didn't want to bail him out, he wasn't going to beg her. He'd call Helen instead. He just had to get her number somehow. Problem was, he didn't even know her last name.

Shortly after Bunny got moved into his jail dorm, he befriended an orderly named William. The orderly was a an older black dude with chapped lips and a gold-capped front tooth. The man claimed to have access to information, and Bunny asked him if Jerry LeClair was in the building. The orderly came back later that afternoon and told Bunny that Jerry was in the house. He pointed at his feet. "One floor down. I could get him a note," said the orderly.

Bunny had never been in jail in Denver. He'd served six months in Grand Junction on a drug case, but that was eventually dismissed. Then he got picked up another time, on a receiving stolen property charge. Back then, he'd been told that he shouldn't accept help from anyone, that they'd expect payback later. But he liked William, and he always wanted to give people the benefit of the doubt.

"See that guy back there," said William, nodding toward a black dude in the back of the room. The guy looked like he was in his mid-forties, a big guy; he was talking to two other inmates. "He's called Car Shop. He'll give you paper and a pen. Write up a little note, I'll get it to your boy."

"Alright, thank you, sir," said Bunny. "I'll think about that. I appreciate it."

"No problem, little man. We all gotta help each other in here. Tell him William sent you." He winked at Bunny and pushed his mop and bucket away.

Later that day, Bunny ended up near Car Shop. He introduced himself and told the bigger man that William, the orderly, had said he might be able to lend him a pen and paper.

Car Shop's hair was shaved so close it looked like he used a razor. He had a scar under his eye. He looked over Bunny's shoulder, like he was trying to see if William was still there. "Yeah, G, I got you," he said. Then he led Bunny over to his bunk, opened a plastic file. "How much paper you need?"

"Just one piece, if you got it," said Bunny. "And a pen, too, if you got that."

"You could borrow this one, but you gotta give it back. It's the only one on the wing."

Bunny went back to his bunk, ripped a little piece from the larger one, and wrote a message as small as he could: *Jerry! WTF man? Hell you get me into?* He thought about it for a second, then added, *No hard feel tho, bro. I hope you cool. Let see if r lawyers can set up a meeting with us. Alright G. Stay cool.* He signed it, and then drew a little hand making a peace sign. He took the note, rolled it up like a cigarette, and hid it under his mattress.

The dudes in Bunny's immediate bunk zone were all white. There was a guy above him who had a shaved head and seemed dope sick.

Bunny wanted to offer to switch bunks with him, but he hadn't had an opportunity yet.

In the bunk next to them, was a slim dude who seemed tense. He had his hair combed straight back, and he sat there with his arms crossed in front of him. Above him was a more heavyset guy. He was ruddy-faced and had a little beard coming in.

"Careful who you talk to," said the tense one, nodding toward Car Shop's bunk.

Just like that, Bunny was activated. He wanted to fight. Wanted it bad right then. That feeling could pop right up in Bunny, sometimes. He was trying to work on it, but that's how it was.

"You got me twisted, man. I talk to whoever the fuck I want."

The tense guy stood from his bunk. "Alright kid, calm down," he said.

Bunny started to take his slippers off. If he was going to fight this guy, he didn't want to be slipping around like he was on ice. But the dude walked away, went right over to the guards' station, and started talking to them. Bunny thought, *Boy, you better not be trying to snitch.* But the dude didn't seem to be saying anything about Bunny, because the guards didn't turn and look his way.

After talking to the guards, the guy walked a wide circle through the whole dorm before heading back. When Bunny saw him coming, he pulled his socks off and stuffed them into his slippers, then pushed the slippers under his bed with his bare foot.

The guy walked back up to Bunny and held his hand out for a handshake. "I'm sorry, man. No disrespect."

Bunny reached out and shook the man's hand. It was clammy, and for a moment, Bunny tried to pull his hand back, but the guy gripped it tight. Then he let it go. Bunny wiped his hand off on his pants and looked at the guy. He had a little cut right below his Adam's apple. Dark eyes. A little bit of stubble. He said, "We gotta stay up in here," which Bunny took to mean, *the whites gotta stay with the whites.*

"I'm cool," said Bunny.

"Put your shoes back on," said the guy.

"You're gonna learn to stop telling me what to do."

The guy turned away from Bunny, a pained look on his face. He got back into his bunk, picked up some paperwork, and busied himself reading it, his jaw muscle twitching the whole time. The guy above him, the bigger guy with the stubble, looked at Bunny and shook his head a little, like he was telling him to knock it off.

Bunny pulled his slippers back out from under the bed. He sat down on his own bunk and pulled his socks on, made them nice and straight, and then put his feet back in the slippers. Then he stood up and paced around, waiting for his food to come.

The jail was on some kind of lockdown right then, so the food was brought to them instead of vice versa. An inmate wheeled the food in on a cart and stacked the boxes up on the guards' desk, and then the guards called each bunk quad over, one by one, to collect their food.

When Bunny finally got his little dinner box and brought it back to his bunk, he opened it, and saw a bologna sandwich wrapped in Saran wrap. It had mayonnaise on it, and that was it. Next to the sandwich were three slices of apple that had already turned brown from the air. There was a smaller box next to the apple. Bunny opened it up and found some frozen broccoli that had been microwaved and had cooled back down. Next to that was a brownie, which actually tasted pretty good. He forced all of it down but didn't feel satisfied when he was done. He felt hungry and grumpy.

That night he lay in his bunk and tried to sleep, but the dope-sick guy above him tossed and turned all night long, moaning and whining. The place never got quiet. The lights stayed almost all the way on. Bunny thought about his uncle Rayton. He said a little prayer for the man. Then he thought about all the girls he'd ever known.

When he finally fell asleep, Bunny dreamed about an old friend of his, Faheed. The guy had committed suicide about six years earlier. In the dream, Faheed and Bunny were playing on a grass slope. They were roughhousing. Rolling in the grass like they used to do when they were kids. Then Bunny was inside a house. He was peeing in the bathroom, and there was a mirror behind the toilet, and he looked at his reflection, but he couldn't see any arms on his body. He had no arms.

He woke up before morning and thought about Faheed. Bunny always liked dreaming about dead people, he liked to see them again and couldn't help feeling spiritual about it. It felt like a little visitation from the other side. He didn't like the stuff about the arms, though. That made him feel ill at ease.

Bunny and five other inmates—feet shackled, hands cuffed behind their backs—were marched through an underground corridor that connected the jail to the courthouse. After passing through a series of checkpoints, they were forced to wait in a windowless holding cell. All this just to get arraigned.

None of the men had any paperwork yet, and there was no television. They sat with their heads hanging. One guy talked more than anyone else, going on and on about some kind of constitutional issue, until the man next to him told him to shut his mouth, and the one doing the talking complied.

Eventually, the men, as a group, were called into a courtroom. One of the deputies told them to sit in the jury box. A judge was on the bench. The men were then called up one at a time for arraignment.

Two civilians, watching the proceedings, sat in the gallery. A couple of public defenders and a few private attorneys came and went. Bunny kept waiting for Jerry to be brought into the room, but he didn't see any sign of his friend.

Eventually, before Bunny was called up, one of the attorneys walked over to the jury box and asked, "Which one of you is Bunny Simpson?"

The lawyer's name was Adam Rendelman. He looked like he was in his sixties. His suit was loose and wrinkled. He had baby skin and a mustache. He wore glasses, and his hairline was receding. Despite his appearance, the man moved around the courtroom confidently.

There was something theatrical about him. He had a presence, and Bunny, when he had time to reflect on it all, thought that must count for something.

When Bunny raised his hand, Rendelman told him to step over to the side of the box. "I'm your lawyer," he said. He nodded toward the judge, who was busy discussing something with a couple of other attorneys. "He appointed me. I'm private counsel, but your co-d already got a public defender, so you're with me."

"Nice to meet you, sir," said Bunny.

Rendelman smiled at Bunny with his eyes, as though to say, *Don't bullshit me, kid.* He looked at the other inmates, then looked at the judge and—lifting his hand to the other side of the courtroom—called out, "Your Honor, may we?"

"Go ahead," said the judge.

Rendelman led Bunny across the courtroom. When they got to the other side, safe from prying ears, the lawyer looked at Bunny for a moment, then whispered, "I've never seen a situation quite like this."

Bunny had no idea what the man was talking about.

Rendelman lifted the file in his hand. "I read the police report. This shouldn't be a felony. If you decide you want to fight this, we can fight it."

"Thank you," said Bunny.

"But—and there is a big *but* here, Mr. Simpson—the district attorney has informed me that they intend on *going hard* at you. She said—her words—'He is going to spend a *long time* in prison.'"

Bunny's heart sank like a bag filled with rocks in a lake. He was hoping to be released that day. He'd actually believed that was what was going to happen. His eyes searched the room for the district attorney. *This was not a real thing*, he wanted to say.

"She said,"—Rendelman cleared his throat—"'it has to be double digits.'"

Bunny's mouth went dry. The lights in the courtroom suddenly seemed evil, like he was already in hell, and he was just opening his eyes to it. He looked at the men on the other side of the courtroom, the inmates. Two of them were watching him with blank expressions. "It was a little fight," said Bunny, blinking back tears.

"Bunny— Do they call you Bunny?"

Bunny nodded.

"You're being arraigned today on felony charges of assault, battery, and attempted robbery. We're going to plead *not guilty*— Okay, if—"

"It was just a little thing," said Bunny, interrupting. "A squabble. There wasn't no robbery." He thought about mentioning the woman but held his tongue. He thought about his mother for a moment, too. Saw her in her old kitchen. It occurred to him that if he went to prison now, that might be the only way he would see her—in his memories. And those memories would fade. He pictured her face, clear in his mind, looking sad at his predicament, at the world, at everything. *Lord, help me*, thought Bunny.

"We could go to trial, and you could win. We could walk you right out that door," said Rendelman. "Depends on the jury." The lawyer looked over at the judge, squinted for a moment. "You're a young man, you wanna live your life."

"That's right," said Bunny.

Rendelman changed tracks. "When I stand in front of a jury," he said, turning toward the jury box, "when I look at them . . . Do you understand what I'm trying to get at?"

"No," said Bunny. "I don't."

"I try and connect with them. I try and get a sense of how they relate to the man or woman I'm standing next to. In this case, that would be you, Mr. Simpson. It would be *you* standing there with me." He licked his lips. "A trial, a criminal trial, will be won or lost in that jury selection." His face grew angry, like Bunny was arguing with him. "It doesn't matter what evidence they put up against you. It's the jury. They're going to decide on whether they *like* you or not."

"I'll testify," said Bunny.

"No, no. No, sir. Not on my watch."

"Shit," said Bunny. "They got my back to the wall, then."

"Well, that's what I'm trying to tell you," said Rendelman. He looked around the room again, then turned back to Bunny. "The district attorney's name is Pamela Bunbury. She's not a nice woman. She's unhappy. But"—he wiggled his eyebrows at Bunny—"she's not a boat-rocker, if you understand my meaning?"

Bunny nodded, then folded his arms in front of his chest.

"All that is moot," said the lawyer. "It's a moot point. I'm saying—forgive me, Mr. Simpson, I'm circling back to the original point, if you'll bear with me—what I'm saying is that this case presents an extremely unusual set of circumstances."

"We didn't know he was a judge," said Bunny.

"Oh." Rendelman said, smiling, "the judge, yes, His Honor. That's not even what I'm talking about. That's a bad piece of this puzzle, but that's not what I'm talking about."

"So, what are you talking about?" Bunny was starting to lose patience with the man.

"What I'm talking about is Ms. Bunbury has informed me that she is willing to make a deal on this case. You'll plead guilty to all the charges—"

"I'm not—"

"Hold on," said Rendelman. "You'll plead guilty to all the charges and receive a suspended sentence. All of this will be sealed, of course. The public won't see it. Your case will disappear. In exchange,"—his eyes circled the courtroom again—"in exchange for your cooperation."

Bunny turned away from his fellow inmates, covered his mouth with his hand. "They want me to snitch on Jerry?" he whispered.

"Not Jerry."

Bunny saw sadness in the man's eyes. "They want you to cooperate in an ongoing federal investigation."

"Federal investigation?" said Bunny. "On what?"

"Well, this is why I'm saying it's unusual. They won't tell me. They want you to sit with some ATF agents. They won't tell me what it's about. They need you to sit. I'll be there with you, but they won't tell me anything about it beforehand." He shrugged. The sadness in his eyes was gone. In its place was amusement.

"Jesus," said Bunny.

"They're going to make you an offer." The lawyer shrugged. "My advice is we hear them out."

Ninety minutes later, two deputies led Bunny out of the courtroom. They walked him straight down the public hallway. Civilians stood here and there, and Bunny, in his yellow jail suit, felt like an apprehended maniac. The deputies steered him to a conference room at the end of the hall. Rendelman followed behind.

Inside the room, Bunny saw two men seated on the far side of a table. They were white guys in their thirties or forties. One of them was a redhead. He wore a blue windbreaker without any insignia. He had large freckles on his face. The other looked Italian. He had short brown hair and beady eyes, and he wore a white button-up shirt, tucked in, no tie. Both were in decent shape and both had a grumpy vibe, like they wished they were anywhere else. In the middle of the table was some audio equipment that looked like it was for conference calls. Standing to the side was a middle-aged white woman wearing a pantsuit. Her skin was dull and unhealthy; Bunny thought she needed sun. She was on her phone, texting, but she stopped as soon as Bunny entered the room.

"Good afternoon, Mr. Simpson. I'm going to record this meeting for our records, but this is all unofficial," said the man in the windbreaker. "It's an informational meeting. Take a seat." He turned on a small digital recorder.

Bunny sat.

"My name is Agent Howley,"—he gestured to his partner—"this is Agent Daniel Gana, we're with the Bureau of Alcohol, Tobacco, and Firearms." He looked up at the woman standing next to him. "This is—"

"Pamela Bunbury, district attorney's office."

"Pamela. And with you is your own counsel." He looked at Rendelman. "Sir?"

"Adam Rendelman, R-E-N-D-E-L-M-A-N."

"Mr. Simpson, as we informed counsel, this is not an interrogation. This is not a proffer session. We're not asking you for any information. I'm still going to read you your rights, even with your lawyer here. And just so we're clear, you are being detained, but *not* by us. You can end this meeting anytime you want. Walk down that hall and they'll take you back to your cell. All you have to do is tell Mr. Readyman—"

"Rendelman."

"—Rendelman that you're done, and we'll end it."

"Okay," said Bunny.

The ATF agent read him his rights again.

"I understand," said Bunny afterward.

Because they were ATF agents, Bunny had grown fearful that they were going to ask him about his work at the cigarette store. On occasion, his boss had been known to buy black-market cigarettes. She got them from a Native American dude who brought them up from the Ute Reservation near the New Mexico border. Bunny had already decided he wasn't going to say anything against T-Ma. It didn't matter what they threw at him. Lock him up. Throw away the keys. His lips were sealed on that front.

"We're going to make you an offer," said the redheaded agent. "The offer will stay on the table as long as this meeting lasts. You won't be able to think about it. It expires when you walk out that door."

The brown-haired agent, Gana, cleared his throat. "You have to tell us yes or no, today," he said.

"Guys, please, come on," said Rendelman.

"Excuse me, sir," said Agent Howley. "We can end this right now. If that's what you want."

"We're willing to hear you out, but if my client says he wants to think about it, that will be his choice."

Agent Howley smiled, but not in a friendly way. "Bunny, we are investigating an organization in Denver. Our operation is being coordinated with the FBI and the Denver Police Department. The group we're investigating is a *Christian* organization." He stopped talking for a moment and stared at Bunny to see if that stirred anything in him.

Bunny shook his head, turned and looked at Rendelman. The lawyer nodded once, like keep listening. Bunny glanced at the district attorney, who was still standing. She crossed her arms in front of her chest and stood there blinking.

"We need a volunteer to join the group," said Agent Gana.

The redheaded agent started back in: "You're looking at—what did we say he's topping out at?"

"Twelve years," said the DA.

"Twelve years. You're facing twelve years in prison, Mr. Simpson. Hard time in the state pen. If you agree to join the group, and if you give us information that we deem helpful, you can walk out of here today."

"Join the group?" said Bunny. "How the hell am I supposed to join a group? What'd you say they were?"

"Bunny," said the redheaded one. "You have to understand something: We didn't pull you in here randomly. We didn't just pick the first guy we saw. As soon as your fingerprints hit IAFIS, we received an alert."

"I don't know what that is," said Bunny.

"Your name was on a list. We put it there. We were waiting for someone on that list to get arrested. And you did it, Bunny. You hit the jackpot. You got arrested for a serious felony."

"What list?" Bunny asked.

The redheaded agent opened a paper file on the table. He took out a sheet of paper but left it face down. "Your uncle is the leader of this group, Bunny."

"What?" asked Bunny, incredulous. "Uncle Rayton? He's not leading any groups, that man is—"

"Not Rayton." The agent pushed the piece of paper across the desk. Bunny picked it up and looked at a color copy of a photo. It showed a man, an older white man, a big guy, looking like he was speaking to a group. Bunny stared at the picture. It was his uncle Willard, his mother's brother. He hadn't seen him in years, but there was no forgetting that face.

His eyes stayed on the picture, but his mind went somewhere else. He saw a glass break in his mother's kitchen. It wasn't thrown, it was an accident. It fell off the counter. Then, still in his mind, he looked out his mother's kitchen window, toward the yard. He saw a truck, some dust in the air, and then he came back into the room he was in.

Bunny felt too weak to speak. He sat there rubbing the side of his forehead. Then he rubbed his eyes like he was waking up. Then he looked up at the prosecutor woman.

"Would you like a tissue?" she asked.

"Yes, please."

Bunny watched the woman step to the side of the room and bend down to her purse. He couldn't help thinking about having sex with her. She grabbed a tissue, brought it to him, and he blew his nose.

"I don't really know him," said Bunny. "I don't know any group."

"I think what my client is wondering," said Rendelman, "is what type of case are you making against this group?"

"Conspiracy, racketeering," said Howley. "It's a VICAR case, 924Cs, B1As, it's big."

"What's that mean?" asked Bunny.

"It means," said Rendelman, "it's a criminal enterprise with guns and drugs, Bunny." Rendelman looked at the agents. "Are there bodies?"

"We can't comment on that," said Howley.

"I don't know anything about this," said Bunny.

"We understand," said Agent Howley. "We're going to be guiding you."

"We're gonna coach you," said Agent Gana. "We'll mentor you."

"I don't think that man has any kind of positive feelings toward me," said Bunny. "I haven't seen him since,"—Bunny saw a flash of Uncle Willard's face, growling like a mad dog—"well, since I was in, what, since his son died, and that was . . ."

"Family, Bunny," said Agent Gana, touching the table with his palm, shaking his head. "End of the day, strained or not, there is no tie as strong as blood. We believe in you."

"I believe in me, too," said Bunny. "Problem is, I don't think he does. He doesn't really like our side of the family." Bunny took a deep breath. "My mom. He's not, like, a close family member, is what you could say."

"All you gotta do," said Agent Gana, "is just be yourself. We'll put you together, we'll arrange that. You show him you're interested in volunteering. He's gonna look kindly on that, whether he's happy with your mother or not. You cannot discount family bonds."

"You can't," said the other agent.

"How much would you need me to do?" asked Bunny.

"Bunny, we have CIs working all over the place. Not just this case, all over the place. They give us info. That's what we want from you. We're not asking you to lead this group. We're not asking you to commit crimes with them. We're asking you to meet up with them, get to know them."

"Be our eyes and ears," said Gana.

"Tell us what you're seeing," said Howley.

"Then testify against him?" asked Bunny.

"No," said the cop, raising his eyebrows, shaking his head. "We might use your information, but you're going to remain masked. Your name will never be used. We're not going to ask you to appear in court."

"Can we get that in writing?" asked Rendelman.

Gana smiled. "I'm afraid we can't put anything in writing on this one, sir. This is a *deal* that we're making with her," he gestured to the prosecutor.

Rendelman sat up straighter. "And just for my understanding, what is the criterion for your so-called happiness? In other words, how do we know your demands are going to be reasonable?"

"As we said, this isn't the first time we've done this," said Gana. "If Mr. Simpson gives good, consistent info, we're going to be happy. That's it."

"We're pretty easygoing," said Howley. Both agents smiled and looked down at the table.

Bunny looked at his lawyer. The man was shaking his head. "And what is the time frame on the suspended sentence?" asked Rendelman. "In other words, how long is my client going to have to do this? Surely, this arrangement can't be expected to carry on indefinitely."

The agents looked at the district attorney.

"We said eighteen months," she said. "This is an eighteen-month deal. If they stay happy for eighteen months, your client has satisfied the terms of this agreement. His guilty plea will be withdrawn and his case dismissed."

"Remuneration?" asked Rendelman. "Can you pay my client for the days of work he'll inevitably miss?"

Howley looked at Gana, who nodded. "We're authorized to give one hundred dollars a day," said Howley.

"When he's in the field," said Gana.

Bunny liked the sound of that. He let his eyes close, and he pictured clean laundry. He saw himself folding clean clothes, setting them on a bed somewhere. Nice clean clothes on a clean bed in a clean room. He thought about his uncle Rayton. He saw the man pushing himself around on the ground. Bunny opened his eyes. "I'll do it," he said. He knocked on the wooden table with his knuckles for good luck. "I'll do it."

At that exact moment, Helen, driving south on Corona Street, toward Tad's house, had her hands on the wheel and her eyes on the road, but her thoughts were playing over an incident from her middle school days. It involved a group project for Spanish class.

There were three other girls in the group. Helen's mother had driven her to Laird's house. After being dropped off, Helen had walked up to the door. A beautiful, flowering bougainvillea framed the doorway. She remembered a feeling of pride. These were A-list, top-notch girls.

She rang the bell. Laird opened the door for her. Helen was just stepping in when the other girl told her, "You don't have to come in. I thought Jodie told you. We'll do it for you."

Helen said she wanted to help.

"It's fine, you don't need to," said Laird, smiling, and inching the door closed. That was the worst part. That smile, almost twenty-five years later, still haunted her.

Right then, a motorcycle drifted into Helen's lane and snapped her out of her memory. She hit the brakes, put her hand to the horn, but didn't honk. "Fucking asshole," she said. Her eyes went down to the documents on the seat next to her. She still co-owned an investment property with Tad. He had asked her to sign some insurance documents and mail them to him, and Helen, partly because she didn't have stamps, but also just to mess with him, had decided to hand-deliver the documents to Tad's house.

She continued driving, and her mind drifted to a different girl from the same class. Eloise made frequent appearances in Helen's dramatic memories. The girl had been accidentally burned with kerosene during a camping trip. She'd missed two months of school, and when she finally returned it looked like her face had melted and dried back hard. Her hairline was disfigured.

Eloise, thought Helen as she drove. *I should have done better by you.* Bougainvillea bushes and Eloise's face played in Helen's head; she breathed in and breathed out.

At the next stoplight, she studied her own face in the mirror. "Oh, Eloise," she said quietly, turning in the reflection. She vowed that she was going to get on Facebook that night and see if Eloise was out there.

She'd friend her, it wasn't too late. She could help. "I'll friend you," Helen whispered. She tapped the steering wheel. "I'll friend you."

When she got to Tad's house, she was shocked to see Tad's SUV in the driveway. It was a weekday, after all. Helen parked right next to his car. She killed the engine and gathered the documents on the seat.

At the door, she didn't hesitate. She reached out and pressed the doorbell, and listened to the gongs ring out in a descending scale. She felt a mixture of feelings. On one hand, she felt mischievous, like she was pulling some kind of prank. Mixed with the mischief was the anger she always felt toward Tad. He was an asshole. Finally, on top of everything, she felt a weird horniness. While she waited, she grabbed the top button of her shirt and pulled it a little lower. She hadn't really been thinking about sex with Tad, that hadn't been her plan. Not that it wouldn't be amusing to sleep with him in his new house. In the bed of his pregnant wife. She pursed her lips. That would seem like fair play. Her tongue probed around her front teeth, making sure they were free of the salad that she'd had for lunch.

The door opened and Helen found herself standing face to face with Vanessa.

"Hey," Helen said, forcing a smile onto her face. For some reason, she hadn't considered that the woman would be here.

"Oh, my goodness," said Vanessa. She seemed visibly alarmed. They hadn't interacted since before the divorce. "Hi," she said, through weirdly squinted eyes.

"I have the papers Tad wanted me to drop off," said Helen, holding them up.

"Goodness, come in! Come in!" said Vanessa, looking utterly flustered.

Helen had never been inside their new home. She stepped in and sniffed the air. The place smelled a little musty. The furniture in the living room seemed too small for the square footage. Helen's gaze went to a cluster of framed pictures on the wall. She stepped that way. One of the photos showed the happy couple skiing. A selfie that Tad had taken. Helen forced her jaw not to drop. *No, no, he hadn't proposed to her like this!* Her forehead began to sweat.

"Yeah," said the young woman, sweeping a hand to indicate the room. "Still needs some . . ." She changed tack. "You look great," she said. "Can I offer you water?"

Helen accepted the water. She wanted to torture the girl. It was the first time they'd ever been alone together. She wasn't just going to walk away from that. They went into the kitchen, and Helen watched the woman fill up a glass of water without speaking.

"Are you feeling okay?" asked Helen, making a face and looking down at her belly.

"Oh," said Vanessa, rubbing the top of it. She handed Helen the glass of water. "You know, it's— I get a little sick in the mornings. But Taddy's been so good to me."

Helen considered throwing the glass of water in her face. She considered assaulting her. Ripping her pajamas off. Chopping her hair off with a knife. Throttling her. Strangling her. Banging her head into the floor. Destroying the house. Burning it down.

"Is he?" she raised her eyebrows suggestively.

"Oh, he's so excited. You should see him. He's blossoming. I mean, as a man. You know, as a father. I'm . . . It's . . . I'm so glad you came over. You are such a doll." She took a small step toward the door.

Helen smiled. She sipped from the glass and then set it down on the counter. There were dishes in the sink, and Helen made sure to spend a moment letting her eyes linger on them. She looked down at the documents in her hand, held them out to Vanessa. "Will you give these to him?"

"Of course. You must promise to come back. Can you come back and drink a glass of wine with us? I think we all could . . . You know?"

Helen was about to leave, but an overwhelming urge came over her. She felt like she had to say something about the fight. She knew she shouldn't, but she couldn't stop herself. "Tad mentioned the umm . . ." For the sake of deniability, she let the sentence hang there.

"Oh," said Vanessa, appearing to somehow intuit what she was saying. Her eyes became wet with tears. "It's horrible. The world is getting really . . . You know?"

"Yucky?" said Helen.

"Exactly," said Vanessa, moving toward the door.

Helen, following her, spoke a silent curse: *I hope you rot in hell, you fucking bitch.* Vanessa, for her part, seemed to be thinking something similar.

Bunny, right after that meeting with the agents, pled guilty. They cleared the courtroom for him, and he stood there at the dais with Rendelman and answered all kinds of questions from the judge about understanding this and understanding that. The DA, Ms. Bunbury, stood next to them and responded each time the judge spoke to her. When they finished, she gave Bunny a tight smile, and walked away fast enough to stir up a little breeze.

"Well, that's it, kid," said Rendelman.

It took hours to get processed out. Finally, when he was dressed in his street clothes, in his shoes, given his phone, his money, his wallet, his change, his keys, his lighter, he found the same two ATF agents waiting for him on the civilian side of the sally port. They hadn't said anything about waiting for him, and Bunny, when he saw them, felt his face get hot.

They didn't speak. The redheaded one, Howley, just nodded, like *Follow us.* Bunny jammed his hands into his pockets, put his head down, and followed them out. People stood here and there in the lobby, and Bunny felt discouraged by the sloppiness of it all. This wasn't how it was supposed to be done. They were about to get him labeled a snitch.

They led him right out of the building and into the night.

"We're gonna give you a ride home," said the brown-haired one, Gana.

Bunny followed them across the street to a fenced-in parking lot. On the way, Gana saw a plainclothes cop he knew, and they exchanged a silent fist bump. The cop looked Bunny up and down while he passed, like he was trying to memorize his appearance. Bunny frowned, shook his head, and kept his eyes down.

"Hop in," said Howley, opening the passenger door of a beat-up old SUV.

Bunny got into the backseat and pulled his seatbelt on. He could smell Mexican food lingering in the air, and not in a good way. Rendelman's voice was looping in his head, just saying a bunch of words and legal phrases. Bunny wished he felt more happiness at getting released. But he only felt dread.

Gana sat in the driver's seat. "Take you to your uncle's place over on— Tell me again, where is that?" asked Gana.

"East Fifty-Second and Adams," said Bunny.

"That's right," said Gana. "Y'all some east-siders."

Bunny felt himself squint. He felt like the cops were messing with him somehow. Like they had ill intentions.

"Bunny, listen," said Howley, turning in his seat and looking at him. "It's gonna be important that you don't speak about any of this. You can't tell your uncle Rayton. You can't tell anyone."

"I won't," said Bunny, but he knew that was a lie, he was going to tell Rayton as soon as he got back.

"For your own safety," said Gana. He put the car in reverse and backed up. "For his safety. People talk."

"We're easygoing," said Howley. "You'll see. We're gonna keep it on the real, though. You help us, we help you." The cop turned and reached his fist out, and Bunny cleared his throat, leaned forward, and bumped fists with the man.

Gana was headed for the boom gate at the exit. They pulled out onto West Colfax and Bunny looked around at the scenery and after a little bit he saw the Capitol building. He'd only been locked up for two nights, but it felt a lot longer than that. It felt like the seasons had changed and he'd aged a few years.

Out of the blue, Jerry popped into his mind and asked him what the hell he was doing. A feeling of panic gripped Bunny. How had he taken a deal and not even thought to try and arrange one for his friend? He leaned forward, put his hand on Howley's headrest. "You think we could offer my friend the same deal?" he asked.

"LeClair?"

"Yeah."

"Nah," said Howley. "He doesn't have what you have, Bunny. He's not family."

"You're lucky," said Gana, looking in his rearview. "Not a lot of people gonna get this kind of deal, man."

"What am I gonna tell him, though?" asked Bunny.

"Tell him your lawyer talked the DA into believing you didn't have no part in it. Tell him you got a good fucking lawyer. Tell him you got Ren-Dog on the case."

"He's gonna be fucked up, though," said Bunny, referring to Jerry.

"He's gonna be fucked up until his lawyer tells him that you didn't snitch. That's all he's gonna be worried about. People's cases get dropped, man, it's not rocket science. Tell him to hire Rendelman next time. Not some public pretender."

They drove past a homeless encampment: ramshackle tents, shopping carts, and tarps. A man, shirtless and muscled, stood outside and watched them pass and then bent down to fuss with something on the ground. Bunny thought about the last thing his lawyer had told him. "It's a good deal," he'd said. "Let's just hope they honor their end of it and remain reasonable." *Honor their end? Remain reasonable?* What the hell does that even mean? Bunny sat there biting his thumbnail.

Howley turned in his seat again. "We'll pick you up tomorrow. I'll text you when. We gonna have a little meeting. Just the three of us."

"Start coaching you up," said Gana, looking in the rearview.

"I get paid a hundred?" asked Bunny.

"Not tomorrow," said Gana, smiling with his eyes. "You gotta be hunting to get paid. Active duty if we gonna write that up."

"Shit," said Bunny. "Work is work."

"Don't worry, big boy," said Howley. "You'll get your money."

"Just got his ass out and already worried about getting paid?"

"I'm trying to figure it out," said Bunny.

"This boy's a fucking whip, man."

"Shrewd," said Gana.

"Tell you what," said Howley. "We'll buy you lunch. How's that sound?"

Gana hit the brakes for a yellow light, and they all leaned forward in unison.

"You gotta live for something bigger than money," said Howley. "You gotta find meaning in the world. Can't just be living scam to scam. Chasing the next hustle. You need a plan, man. Set goals. Accomplish them. Shit, we'll start right here. I'm telling you, this could be a good thing, linking up with us. A good partnership."

"Good friendship," said Gana.

"Yes, sir," said Bunny. He cleared his throat and thought about the $240 that Jerry still owed him. Was he gonna get that? He looked at the road and his mind shifted to Uncle Willard. He had a clear vision of the man sitting in a barber's chair, getting his hair cut. He wondered, for a second, if he'd seen that in real life, or if he was manufacturing it out of thin air.

The light changed, and they started moving again. The cops continued lecturing him all the way until they got close to Rayton's house. Bunny asked to be let out a couple blocks away.

"Yeah, we got you," said Gana, pulling over. "Okay, matter of fact, this spot right here,"—he pointed at a bench in the park—"see the bench. That'll be our little pickup spot."

"Alright," said Bunny.

"We don't wanna hear nothing about 'my phone's not working,'" said Gana. "You wanna go back to jail? Try that on us. Tell us your phone's not working. You'll be headed for state time. Don't fucking try me, dude."

"Okay," said Bunny.

"Take a shower," said Howley. "You don't wanna bring them bed bugs into the home."

"True story," said Gana.

Bunny got out and closed the door. He had to work not to slam it. He didn't like these two. He didn't like the way they thought they were so much better than him. Shit, they weren't better than him just because they were cops. These dudes needed a reality check. He shook his head. *Thinking you're the best of the best because you're a cop.*

Bunny walked straight across the park, looking around to see if anyone was out. Nobody was. The moon was about three-quarters full. There were little clouds framing it like a drawing. It was a nice, cool night. *Yep,* thought Bunny. *It is better to be on the outside, though. That is for sure.*

The next afternoon, Jerry ran into the orderly who had passed him the note from Bunny. Jerry had written his own response in the margins of a tiny piece of paper ripped from a paperback. His message said, *Yo bro! I'm sorry man. I didn't want u to get pinched for this. Keep it locked. No talking. No phones. Lets def get up with the lawyers. Peace bro. Ain't no thing. I'll get you thru.*

The orderly was mopping on the other side of the room. Jerry already had the note rolled up in his sock and he went straight over to the man. A mounted television played above the area.

Jerry pretended to watch it.

"Hey, pop," said Jerry to the man.

The guy stopped mopping and frowned. He didn't seem to recognize Jerry. "You gave me that note from the kid upstairs."

"Oh, yeah," said the man. He leaned on the mop and stood there looking like he was trying to remember something.

"Can you bring him one from me?"

"The boy's not there no more," said the man, shaking his head.

"What do you mean?"

"I was just up there," the man said. "You want me to find out where he is?"

"If you could," said Jerry, "I would appreciate it."

"I got you." He turned and pushed his mop bucket toward the guard booth.

Jerry stayed where he was. On the television, an infomercial was selling a bow-flex rowing machine. Jerry was reminded of Helen. She should've bailed his ass out already. Thinking about her was painful. He pictured their kiss in the car. That had been a lifetime ago. *You were free, you could kiss whoever you wanted. Out there a free man. Young, capable—*

Right then, a ruckus on the other side of the dorm kicked up. One inmate, a white dude, was hollering at another white dude, "No, you will not!" His voice resonated through the dorm.

The other guy turned on him and they grabbed each other by their jail shirts. Jerry instinctively moved closer to the wall. The two men pushed against each other, trying to get an edge. It seemed like everyone was hollering then, and right when they started swinging, the guards got to them and pulled them apart.

There were only two guards in the dorm, but one of them was the big guy, the one who'd been sweating Jerry, and he pulled the first man to the ground. He got the guy on his belly and put a knee on his back. By that time other guards were running into the dorm, their key chains and belts rattling.

The big guard, his knee on the man's back, locked eyes with Jerry. He was in the middle of a struggle to get the man's arm out from under him. Jerry looked away for a second, but when he looked back the guard was still staring right at him. His mouth was tensed up like he was lifting weights. It felt, to Jerry, like a kind of show. It felt sexualized somehow. He didn't like it, and it made him feel sick. Finally, the guard got the man's arm behind his back, and he looked away from Jerry and down at the man.

The man under the guard yelled in pain, and some of the other inmates started yelling, too. By then, the other guards had joined the fray, and Jerry couldn't really see what was happening anymore.

"Bunk down!" the guards yelled after the fight was over. "Bunk down! Bunk down! Every man, get in your fucking bunk!"

Ever since Helen had stopped by the house, Vanessa, Tad's wife, had been upset. In fact, she'd been weaving in and out of variations of the same argument for a few days. "I just don't understand why she couldn't text first," said Vanessa.

They were standing in the kitchen, Tad scrolling on his phone, Vanessa on the other side of the island. She couldn't stand when he did that, and right now, under these circumstances, this phone scrolling, it was enough to get her blood boiling.

"I mean, she was just standing there, looking like she was about to be picked up for a date!" said Vanessa. "Like she was in a movie! With her body all—that's *enhanced*, she paid money for that—just standing there."

Tad sighed.

"She was surprised when I opened the door. Do you understand? Like she thought *you* were going to open the door. Like she expected it."

"I had no idea she was coming," said Tad. "I told you that."

Vanessa continued chopping her cauliflower. "It's disruptive," she said. "I'm carrying a child." She touched her belly, raised her eyebrows. "Dr. Peña says stress is not good for the baby."

"She also said don't stress about stress." Tad put his phone in his pocket.

Vanessa went back to chopping the cauliflower. Her mind stayed on Helen. "I'm just confused why you're still talking to her," she said.

Tad shook his head. "I'm not talking to her. She's a flipping psychopath. I needed her to sign those documents, that's all. There's no grand conspiracy here."

"Well, if you're not talking to her, I'm confused why she is asking about that *thing* that happened." Vanessa pointed her knife toward the street. "Like, really? You have to talk to her about everything."

"I never told her anything about that," said Tad. "Why would I tell her that?" He scratched his head and appeared to be racking his brain to make sure he hadn't told her that.

"Did you feel like you couldn't come talk to me?" She looked at her hand on the chopping board and thought about slicing her ring finger off. *Take your ring. Take your freaking paleo casserole and shove it up your dang a-hole.* She took a deep breath. "Honey," she said. "I'm sorry, it's just, I don't know, I thought we—"

"We do, munchkin." Tad walked around the island, wrapped his arms around her from behind. He rubbed her belly. Kissed the back of her neck. Then he stopped. "She said she heard I got attacked?"

"Are you freaking texting her?" asked Vanessa, taking his hand off her belly.

"I'm not texting her."

"That woman just gives me the willies. She's so, I don't know. She's scary. She's weird."

"She's a hurt girl who likes to hurt people," said Tad. He shrugged, like that explained everything and there wasn't any more to be said.

They ate their dinner. Later, they watched a true crime show on TV. Vanessa let all her bad feelings evaporate. She let Tad give her a foot massage. She called her mother. She cleaned the kitchen.

She had to wait a while, but Tad finally fell asleep. Then, quietly, she crept over to his bedside table, unplugged his cellphone, and stood over him to make sure he wasn't stirring.

She crept into their bathroom and closed the door. If she glanced at his text messages, just one little look, she could finally stop with all this nonsense. Grunting, she lowered her baby-carrying body down onto the toilet and swiped the phone open. The passcode requirement was on, and she entered his pin, 2289. It didn't work. Her eyebrows furrowed. She entered it again; it still didn't work.

He changed his passcode. Why in the world would he do that?

She took a deep breath and peed. She was so uncomfortable. Being pregnant was a holy blessing, there was no denying that. But it was awfully uncomfortable. She closed her eyes. *Lord help me*, she prayed. *Lord, just help me. Please. Help my baby. Help my husband stay on the path. Help my mother and father stay healthy.*

⁂

Bunny, lying on the couch, fussing on his phone, received a text from Agent Howley: *Bench 10:30 am.*

A second text followed immediately after the first: *Got this?*

Bunny responded, *Yes.*

The car, when it pulled up, was a different SUV. This one was newer, cleaner. Its windows were blacked out just like the first one's. The agents were playing country music at a high volume, but they turned it down when they pulled up.

Clearing his throat and dusting his pants, Bunny made his way to the vehicle.

"Damn, Bunny, we didn't say wear battle fatigues," said Gana, referring to the camouflage pants that Bunny had on.

"I know, I'm just wearing them," said Bunny, feeling stupid.

They started driving, and Bunny looked all around for any kind of snooping eyes. Then he looked down at his pants and rubbed at a little stain with his thumb.

"Your uncle was happy to see you?" asked Howley.

"Yes, sir."

"You tell him he has us to thank for that?"

"Nah, just said I got sprung."

"Good boy."

They drove Bunny all the way over toward Ruby Hills and parked on South Jason Street just off West Mississippi Ave. It was kind of an industrial spot, beige-walled warehouses standing here and there.

There was a used car lot in the middle of the block, and Gana turned the engine off and pointed at it. "Alright, Bunny, you gonna start grinding tomorrow," he said. "You're gonna apply for a job over there. Wear a button-up shirt."

"Tucked in," said Howley.

"Tucked in," said Gana. He turned in his seat and looked at Bunny. "Shave your face, trim those little whiskers off."

"I don't really know cars like that," said Bunny, leaning forward and looking at the dealership.

"It's not a mechanic job. You are starting at the bottom, and that's what you gonna tell them. Say you willing to clean up, sweep, clean the toilets, take the trash out, but—you gotta stress this—*only* if they agree that they will train you up." He looked at Bunny. "Say it."

"Clean, sweep, toilets, trash, but I want to be trained," said Bunny.

"To sell cars," said Gana. "You gotta say it like you mean it."

"And that's the only way you'll do it," said Howley.

"And that's the only way I'll do it. Train me to sell a car."

"Alright," said Gana. He looked at the auto lot for a second, turned back to Bunny. "Owner of the shop is a dude named Monte Ventola. He's a veteran, a Marine."

"He's a bad boy," said Howley. "I don't know if you know this, Bunny, but a Marine vet is not about to put up with no bullshit."

"That's why I put these pants on," said Bunny.

Howley smiled. A big truck drove past, and all three men tracked it with their eyes.

"You don't need to play a character," said Howley, turning serious again. "Just be yourself. If you try and act the part, they're gonna sniff you right out."

"Do a good job, stay positive, keep your head down, your mouth shut, do your work," said Gana.

"That's it?" asked Bunny.

"That's it," said Howley. "Get in the good graces of this man."

"And then if you do all that, if you do it right, Ventola will introduce you to your uncle Willard," said Gana.

"Reintroduce you," said Howley.

A depressed feeling came over Bunny. While Howley droned on about Willard being happy to find him, reconnection, family ties or something, Bunny thought about his mother and about Willard's mother—his grandmother, Minnie. She was a grumpy old trout. Mean to everyone except Bunny. She had rough hands, hardened from working on the farms, picking plums, apricots, cherries. Bunny remembered being patted on the head by those hands. He liked it. He liked her attention. Liked her rough hands. He loved her.

Minnie died when Bunny was eight. She was run over walking home from a bar. Hit and run. Bunny hadn't thought about any of this in years, and a heavy sadness settled in his gut.

"You understand what we're saying?" asked Howley.

"Yeah, I got you," said Bunny. He took a deep breath, looked at the auto lot. "How d'you know they're trying to hire someone, though?"

"Posted an ad on Craigslist," said Gana.

Bunny nodded for a second. He took a breath and then asked, "I get to keep the money I make?"

"Yes, sir," said Gana.

"And you're gonna pay me a hundred a day while I'm there?"

"Can't do that," said Gana. "Sorry."

"That's not gonna qualify as field work," said Howley. "Unfortunately, they're kind of ballbusters about that. You gotta be undercover. All the way."

Bunny blew air through his teeth.

Howley busied himself texting someone on his phone.

Gana started the car. "Take you back."

"I thought we were going to get lunch," said Bunny. He had every intention of squeezing these cops for every penny they had.

"Shit, that's right," said Howley, looking up from his phone. "Go by that Carl's Jr. on Colorado Boulevard," said Howley. "You like CJ?"

"Yeah, I do," said Bunny, drying his palms on his pants. "I love it."

For a moment, while they drove away, he thought about his grandmother again. Gramma Minnie. Walking home from a bar, stars above her head, like that. *Damn, man,* thought Bunny. *Hope she wasn't feeling no pain. Dying alone on a road in Grand Junction.*

⁂

Helen, standing near a bar on Blake Street, waiting for her date to show up, was talking to Tad on the phone. He had called her, and against her better judgment she had picked up. They'd gotten through their greetings and now were edging their way out onto a quiet battlefield. It was sunset, the sky was pink.

"Thanks for bringing those documents by," Tad said. He had a little tone to his voice, which made her feel scared of being exposed and angry at being accused. Like, *How dare you?*

"Mm-hmm," she said.

Right then, she saw her date—Sam from the gym, the same guy who introduced her to Jerry—approaching. She'd been sleeping with him on and off for a couple months. She put a finger to her ear and quarter-turned away from him. Life was coming at her from all directions.

"Vanessa said you asked about the park?" said Tad.

"I have no idea what you're talking about," said Helen. "What park?"

Right then, a homeless woman approached Helen; she held her hands in the shape of a bowl. Helen nodded to her left, toward Sam, and the woman walked that way. Helen watched Sam pat his pockets and tell the woman he didn't have any money.

On the phone, Tad was still talking about the park, but he was only saying that nothing happened.

"I honestly have lost the thread," said Helen. "What are you saying?"

"Do me a favor, Helen. Just text me before you come to the house," said Tad. He then claimed he had to go and ended the call. Helen turned her attention to Sam and batted her eyes at him. The homeless woman had continued down the sidewalk.

They entered the bar and ordered skinny margaritas. Sam, while they waited for their drinks, talked endlessly about some deal he'd closed that week. Helen listened, but only partly. Mainly, she was playing over what had just happened. She wanted to feel more happiness. This was the moment she'd been waiting for: an admission from Tad that he'd been hurt. That's all she wanted. She didn't feel happy, though. Truth was, she didn't feel anything.

The night before, after still not having heard from Jerry, she did some online snooping. First, she did a deep dive on his Instagram. But there was nothing there. She looked at news stories but came up empty there, too. Then, on a hunch, she logged onto the Denver Inmate Locator website and punched his name into it. Her worst suspicions were confirmed. He was there, alright. He'd been locked up. He'd been sitting in jail this whole time. Helen, in her living room, broke into a sweat. The first move she made was to review the text messages she'd sent him.

There they were. *Leave me the fuck alone.* Those should hold up, she thought, mentally patting herself on the back. Still, it wasn't an ideal situation.

Back in the restaurant, meanwhile, Sam was going on and on about meditation. "I meditate every day," he said, tapping his chest. "Every morning. Twenty minutes. Every night, twenty minutes." He shrugged and looked over Helen's shoulder at two women who had just walked into the bar. His eyes shifted back to Helen. "Changed my life."

"I need something," Helen said. She took a deep breath and stared at the bar for a moment. *I need something*, she thought. "Let's get another drink," she said.

They drank their second drink and then had a third. Sam talked about some new super set routine he was doing at the gym. Then he did some mansplaining about muscles. They both drank two pints of water and then, after he paid, they went out to the street.

He told her he'd give her a ride home. At a red light, he casually put his hand on her leg. She put her hand over his and held it there. This felt awkward, but she kept it there for a few blocks.

Outside her apartment, he asked if he should come up.

"Nah," she said. "I don't think so."

Sam pretended not to hear her. He leaned over and kissed her. With his left hand, he started pushing on her breasts. Helen thought of Jerry, and she pulled her head back and leaned away from Sam. She unbuckled her seatbelt. "I should go," she said.

"Alright," said Sam, shrugging. A dark mood came over his face.

As she made her way to the door, she continued to think about Jerry. She imagined him locked up and sick. He probably had some kind of disease. Hepatitis or something. HIV. He was stuck in jail. It was her fault. She needed to nurse him back to health. *Fuck*, she thought.

By the time she entered her apartment lobby, her worry had grown into a feeling of genuine anxiety. There was a mirror in the elevator, and as she went up, she turned and studied herself in it. Her body looked good; she was happy about that. She looked strong. A mare. She cupped her breasts in her hands and squeezed them, the same way Sam had just squeezed them. Then she raised her right hand up near her face, turned her eyes to the hand, and whispered, "I love you." Then she began kissing the back of her hand. She used her tongue and kissed it until the elevator chimed and the doors began to open. She was on her floor.

Bunny, with his hands in his pockets, walked across Ventola's lot and looked at the cars. He read the dates on the stickers. Most of them appeared to be about ten to fifteen years old. The cars were clean, but they didn't look shiny; one even had some dents on the hood and roof like it had been left out in a hailstorm. Bunny saw some 2010s, a few 2012s. The newest one he saw was a 2017 Chevy Cruze, red and cheap looking. It was early, and Bunny didn't see a single person outside. He wondered if the place might be closed.

The sales building looked like it had been built in a hurry. Like it had been raised during some kind of natural disaster. The walls looked like they'd been made with cheap particle board. The exterior of the building was painted greenish brown. There weren't many windows, and the ones there were had bars on the outside and plastic blinds on the inside. A sign above the door read, VENTOLA AUTO, CARS TRUCK & SUV. On the door itself was a poster that read, SHOW ME THE CAR FAX.

Bunny opened the door, and an electric chime sounded. A woman at a desk looked up. She was a white woman, in her sixties. Her face looked like she'd been smoking cigarettes for the better part of her life. She looked worried. "Help you?" she said, leaning forward, like she was shocked to see that someone had appeared out of thin air.

"Hi," said Bunny. "I wanted to drop off a resume for the job."

The lady seemed disappointed by this news; she frowned and shook her head. "Bring it here, honey," she said. As Bunny walked over, he smelled burnt coffee in the air. There was a room behind the woman. It had windows, but its blinds were drawn. Bunny could hear a couple of men inside having a discussion.

The woman's desk was covered in disorganized paperwork and garbage. Bunny's eyes passed over the remnants of a fast-food breakfast—grease-stained wrappings, ketchup, crumbs. Some empty soda cups.

"Ma'am," he said, holding out a resume that the agents had typed up for him. "I saw the job on Craigslist."

The woman narrowed her eyes at him, looked at the resume for a second, half turned to the room behind her, and then turned back to

Bunny. She wiped her nose with her finger, sniffled, looked back down at the paper in her hand, and frowned. "Bunny Simpson?" she said.

"That's me."

"What kind of name is that?"

"It's the name my mother gave me."

"My mother named me Blanche. I never liked that, either." She looked back down at the resume. Bunny watched her lips move over the words *Commerce City.* "Hold on for a second. If they finish, you can talk to Monte."

"Yes, ma'am. Thank you." Bunny checked his shirt, made sure it was still tucked in, front and back. He smoothed his pants at his sides. Turned and looked around the room. There were three other desks, none of them occupied. A calendar on the wall showed some sexy women gathered around a muscle car. A few Avalanche posters hung here and there.

The woman, Blanche, kept clearing her throat in the cadence of a military snare drum player, *mmm-mmm-mmm-mm, mmm-mmm-mmm-mm.* Bunny looked to her to see if she was trying to tell him something, but she had her eyes on her computer monitor.

Eventually, the office door opened, and two men walked out. The first was a skinny white dude. He wore a tucked-in shirt and had thin brown hair that looked like it had been combed with Vaseline. He had a nervous energy coming off him, and he looked at Bunny with suspicion.

The second man was bigger and taller. He appeared to be in his midfifties. His barrel chest stretched his shirt, a blue button-up. He wore a tie loose around his neck. He was clean-shaven, but his face gave Bunny the impression of a walrus. He looked mad, and his eyes went from Bunny to the door, to the woman. "Blanche," he said, like she'd done something wrong.

"He wants to apply for the job," Blanche fired back.

The man—Bunny figured he must be Monte Ventola—looked at Bunny full on then. "This is a maintenance job," he said, like he was arguing a point.

"Yes, sir," said Bunny.

"Cleaning up," said Monte. "Breaking down boxes. What the hell you want to do that for? That's Mexican work." He raised his chin a little, scowled down on Bunny.

"Well, sir,"—Bunny took a little step forward—"I'm happy to do it. But I wanted to talk to you first." Bunny felt clumsy reciting his script and he had to take a moment to get settled. "I wanted to see if I did this job, if I did it properly, if there might be a path to me selling cars here one day. I don't care how long it takes. I'll do the work, but I want to sell cars."

"You hear this?" said Ventola.

"Oh yeah," said the smaller man.

"He wants to sell cars," said Ventola.

"He's a whippersnapper," said Blanche.

"Yes, ma'am," said Bunny.

The big man leaned over Blanche's desk, looked at the resume. Bunny could hear him breathing through his nose. "Bunny," he said. "You gonna come in here and sell cars?"

"Yes, sir, I'm gonna sell cars, here, or somewhere else, but I'm gonna be selling a whole lot of cars."

"Monte Ventola," said the big man, holding his hand out and then crushing Bunny's hand when they shook. "This here is Jimmy Dean," he said, indicating the smaller man. "He's our head salesman." He turned to Jimmy Dean. "What do you think, Jimmy? You think he's a car salesman?"

"I think he could break down boxes," said Jimmy humorlessly.

Ventola's eyes went back to the resume. He squinted. "AAA Cigarettes on Monaco? Yeah, I know that spot. That's the ah,"—his hands described a square—"it's the little building out there on Monaco?"

"Yes, sir," said Bunny. "I been working there a few years."

"Cheap cigarettes," said Ventola, speaking to the other man. "Cheapest in town."

"That's the place," said Bunny.

"Okay," said Ventola, giving Bunny a final looking-over. "We'll give you a call."

Bunny thanked the three of them and then walked out the door. He felt, as he crossed the lot, high, like he'd pulled off some great scam. *I should've been selling cars this whole time,* he thought. By the time he made it to the street, his feeling of optimism had already started to fade. Sure, he'd succeeded at the task he'd been given. The agents, waiting in their car, a couple blocks away, were going to be pleased. And that was the point. The problem was, this meeting got him one step closer to being reunited with Uncle Willard. And that was something he was not looking forward to.

"Why'd they let Bunny out, though?" asked Jerry, tapping the table with the flat of his hand. He was in a tiny interview room with his public defender, April Costa-Tenge.

April appeared to be in her late thirties. She dressed casually that day, sweater and jeans. She was pretty, but didn't give off any of those vibes, so Jerry didn't think about her in that way. She had a large stack of files with her. This was the second time they'd met. He had the impression she didn't like him.

"I don't know why he was released," she said, shrugging. "I'll ask the DA. There's nothing in here"—she touched the top file—"that suggests he is cooperating. But Mr. LeClair, listen to me for a minute, you need to stop thinking you're the victim. And you definitely don't need to make—What's his name?"

"Bunny."

"You definitely don't need to make Bunny mad. I'll have our investigator talk to him. He might be the only witness in this case. There's nobody else who saw what happened. We need him. Do you understand what I'm saying?"

"Yeah."

"Okay, so, you were telling me why you were in that park."

"Before we get into that," said Jerry, "let me ask you something. What if, hypothetically—" He was about to ask her if Helen having paid him to beat this guy could help him at all, but he had second thoughts. He didn't fully trust that this lawyer would keep his secrets. "Never mind," he said. He put his hands together in front of his face like he was praying, then he dropped them back down to the table. "We were in the park because we were bumming around. We didn't have anywhere to go. We were driving around, and we came across the park and we were hanging there, and then that dude came by, and he starts talking shit to us—"

"Hold on," said the public defender. She had him go back over the early part of the night. Jerry had made that part up. He'd been at home compulsively masturbating, there hadn't been any earlier part. But he made up a whole story about having been with a couple of girls, smoking weed in the car.

The lawyer asked for the girls' names, and Jerry said, "Oh no, they don't want to get involved in something like this, trust me."

Later, Ms. Costa-Tenge wanted to know what the man in the park had said. Jerry made something up about this, too. He did it on the fly. He said the guy had seen them sitting there, and he'd said something about "getting a job," or how they had to "get the hell out of there, or something." The lawyer squinted at him. "Some Karen shit," said Jerry. "'You need to get out of here!' Something like that."

Jerry felt self-conscious at the way his lips were smacking together. He was antsy and he looked around the room and rubbed his shoulder with his hands. He felt ugly. His skin was dry. Stinking jail clothes. His fat body on its small frame—he was a fat little garden snake.

The lawyer began questioning him about his past arrest. The one for selling cocaine. Jerry outlined the case for her, told her about his punishment, pointed out that it was a bullshit case. He thought about his mother and his eyes filled with tears.

Finally, at the end of the interview, Jerry managed to steer the conversation to the guard who'd been harassing him. "He's named Janko," said Jerry. "Big guy. He's been harassing me."

The lawyer, for the first time, seemed to become interested. "What do you mean?"

"He's been, like, following me around, and he gets, like, a— I'm not trying to be crude."

"Go on."

Jerry lowered his voice. "He gets an erection, and he just follows me everywhere and moans and kind of threatens me." There had been another incident in the hallway, where the guard, Janko, had appeared to get an erection.

"Jesus," said the lawyer. Her eyes shined empathetically. She reached across the table and squeezed Jerry's hand. "I'm going to help you file a complaint and I'm going to ask that you be released on your own recognizance. Barring that, we'll get you transferred to the county jail. You should've been sent there already. I don't know why they're holding you here, some kind of administrative bullshit going on."

Jerry sat up straighter. "Thank you," he said. He wanted to say, *I really do appreciate you*, but he worried she might think he was flirting, so he held his tongue. Instead, after a moment, he said, "One other thing. If I had someone who could help pay the bail, do you think you could call her?"

"I told you that."

"Okay, it's a little complicated, though."

The lawyer narrowed her eyes, cocked her head.

"I don't have her number, but her name is Helen McConnell, or McDonald, or something. Helen McSomething."

"Okay," said the lawyer. She jotted down the info on her notepad. "Anything else? Work? Does your mom know her?"

"Well, she's a lawyer."

"Okay, that'll be easy, then."

Jerry watched her write down the word *lawyer* and circle it.

"It's complicated, though," said Jerry.

"Why?"

"We're a little . . ."

"You're what? Involved?"

"If you just called her and told her you're my lawyer and said that you thought she might be willing to help me out with the bail."

"I'll try," said the public defender. "Judge set it at fifty thousand dollars, though—which is fucking insane—but she would have to pay"—she calculated in her head—"five thousand dollars to get you out." The lawyer's face became skeptical. "Would she pay five thousand?"

"I think if you tell her that it would be *best for everyone* if I was out, she might be willing to help. Put it like that."

The lawyer's eyes narrowed further. "Okay," she said. She gathered her files, went to the door, called out to the guard, and told him she was done. Then she left Jerry in the room and went on to her next interview. A guard came to the door, told Jerry to wait for transport, and locked him in.

Jerry sat there. "Best for everyone," he said, again, quietly. He thought about his mother. He couldn't believe that she wasn't going to bail him out on this one. That was going to be hard to get over. He'd have to move out. There was no question about that. *I get it, Mom,* he said in his head. *I do have to straighten up, but this is no place to be.* He looked at the cinder block walls, reached out and ran his finger in the smooth place between the bricks.

He had a bad feeling about mentioning Helen. His hairline started to sweat, and then his underarms. Most of his anxiety centered in his belly, though. He stood and walked to the door, looked out the little window, but couldn't see anything. He gave his dick a little squeeze.

"Damn, get me the fuck out of this bitch," he whispered to himself.

Two days later, Helen, while she was at the gym, missed a call. Her phone had been tucked into the pocket in the back of her pants. She listened to the message between sets of military presses: "Hi, Helen, my name is April Costa-Tenge, I'm a public defender. I'm representing Jerry LeClair in a criminal matter he has here in the Denver court. Umm, Mr. LeClair thought it might be good to reach out to you. Can you please give me a call when you have a chance. Call me on my cell at (720) 499-6691. Thank you."

Helen, after listening, went straight back to her military presses. Then she did her seated cable rows, standing rows, and seated lat pulldowns. All of it was done in a haze, though; like her body was only half there. On the way to the locker room, she had to work to not bump into anyone.

In the shower, she soaped herself up. Two women were chatting nearby. One of them was saying, "I don't know, if he doesn't call back, that doesn't necessarily mean he doesn't want to date." *Yes, it does,* thought Helen. *Yes, it most certainly does.* Then, in a bad humor, she shut the water off, clenched her jaw, dried herself off, and got dressed.

Walking to her car, Helen eyed the mountains to the west, the snowy peaks up top. Earlier that day, a co-worker, Brenda, had asked Helen if she wanted to get lunch with some of the girls. Helen had demurred. Now she went over the phrasing she'd used: *I wish I could. I have too much work.* She didn't have too much work, and she wasn't sure exactly why she'd said that. Instead, she had lunch alone, at her desk, surfing online sales. *Next time I'll say yes,* she told herself. *Next time I'll say yes.*

Helen unlocked her car and got in. She sat there for a moment, the frown back on her face. Then she did a half turn in her seat and looked around the parking lot. She pulled out her phone and called the lawyer back.

"This is April Costa-Tenge."

"Hi, it's Helen McCalla, I'm returning your call?" She tried to make it sound like a question as a way of implying that she had no idea what the woman was calling about.

"Hey! Yes, hi," said the public defender.

Helen stayed silent.

"Umm, Jerry LeClair suggested I call you. Do you know Jerry?"

Helen focused her mind. "A little bit."

"May I ask where you know him from?"

"From the gym." She sniffled.

"Well, look, I don't know if you know anything about this, but Jerry is in a significant amount of trouble. He thought . . . you might be able to help pay for his bail? It's been set at fifty thousand dollars, so out of pocket, you'd have to pay five K. Is that something you might be able to help him with? I think we'd have a much better chance to fight his case if he was out of custody, and he does, as I mentioned, have significant exposure on this case."

"I can't do that," said Helen. The words came out sounding flat and emotionless, and she thought about saying it again in a different way but froze.

The public defender cleared her throat. "Ms. McCalla, I had to google you to find out who you were. Jerry couldn't remember your last name. But one of the top entries was a wedding announcement for you and Judge Mangan."

"Okay."

"Judge Mangan is the victim in Jerry's case."

Helen stayed silent.

"They got in a fight in a park. Sorry, excuse me. I should've said that this conversation is protected, and I absolutely won't disclose anything you tell me. But, I mean, do you know anything about this?"

"No, I don't," said Helen. Her gaze went back up to the mountains. She ran through different responses she could make and decided that perplexity would probably suit the moment best. "I don't understand," she said. "I knew Jerry was in jail, but I didn't know what for. You're telling me that Tad was the victim of some fight? What the hell happened?"

"They had an altercation in the park. It was early in the morning. Judge Mangan was allegedly attacked while jogging."

"Oh, Jesus. He's always jogging."

"There was another guy with Jerry, a Bunny Simpson. Do you know him?"

"Never heard of him." Helen felt like she was regaining her footing. "This is insane. Can you email me the police report?"

"I'm afraid not," said the public defender.

"Where did this happen?" asked Helen.

"Washington Park."

"Yep, that's where Tad lives. But what the hell? This is so— You know what I mean?"

"It's a strange case."

"I like Jerry. Underneath the facade, he's a good kid." Switching into a confiding tone, she said, "But I probably should stay away from bailing him out, given—you know—my relationship to your victim."

"Is the judge a violent person? Does him fighting make any sense to you?"

"I mean, does the man have an anger problem? Yes. Does he have a short fuse? Yes. Can I imagine him fighting someone—fighting Jerry in a park? No. Between me and you, that doesn't sound like him." Helen forced her mouth into a smile. "I'm so sorry, I should go. But tell Jerry I'm really sorry to hear from you. Does that make sense?"

The public defender tried again, but Helen held fast and ended the call.

She sat there fuming. Had Jerry lost his mind? What was he thinking bringing her name into this? It occurred to her that he was trying to threaten her. Having his lawyer call was his way of saying that he was going to try to get released by offering evidence against her.

Helen looked down at her phone, swiped it open, and did a quick whirl through her instagram: *Friends, kids, babies, ads, sunsets, more kids, bullshit, more ads, babies, garden, gym, cat.* She swiped it closed and redialed the public defender.

"Yes?"

"Hi. I'm thinking about it. I want to try and think about it and see if there is a way to help."

"Okay."

"I'm sorry, I'm not trying to brush you off, it was just a little shocking to hear about this. I'm really confused. If you could tell Jerry that I'm trying to think about it. Also, maybe tell him that it feels really dangerous to get my name involved."

"I'm sorry?" said the public defender. "Dangerous?"

"I'm saying, if someone started turning over rocks, and they found out that Jerry was stalking me, or something."

"Was he stalking you?"

"If someone started pushing in the wrong direction, I'd hate if they found that out. That's all." She tried to make her voice more friendly sounding, but she was losing control of herself. "Maybe tell him he should be careful."

"Ms. McCalla, is there something you want to tell me? Did he stalk you?"

"God, I don't know," said Helen. She paused for a moment, then added, "But it seems like it would probably be best for your client to keep my name out of it. I really have to go now."

She ended the call. Then, with her fingernails, she sat there tapping her skull through the part in her hair. Her chest and heart felt panic-stricken. Above the mountains, dark clouds showed a storm coming from the west. This wasn't good.

❧

It was 9:42 p.m. when the agents came for Bunny. He gave a fist bump to the kid he was sitting with, got up from the bench, jogged over, and hopped into the vehicle. The agents were quiet. "Who was that?" Howley finally asked.

"That's Dante," said Bunny.

"You told him who we are?" asked Howley.

"Hell no."

"So what'd you say?"

"I said, 'That's my ride,' I gave him a fist bump, and I left."

"Low profile," said Gana, whispering it like he was mad. He put the car in drive and started moving.

"He sat with me. What you want me to do, tell him he can't sit there? That's gonna make a bigger fuss than what I did."

"You're on your way to the pen, man," said Gana, driving.

"Nothing I can say, then," said Bunny. "What do you want?"

"Okay, come on," said Howley, keeping the peace. "Now, Bunny." He turned in his seat to face Bunny. "Ventola?" he said.

"I got the job. I start tomorrow."

"Alright," said Howley, speaking to Gana. "See?" He turned back to Bunny. "You did well," he said. "But you gotta understand, we're trying to help you. Okay? You gotta work like your life depends on it. Show up on time. Just do whatever they tell you to do. Pay attention. Do things right."

"I'm a good worker, man, you don't need to worry about that," said Bunny.

"They say, clean the toilet, you clean the toilet," said Gana. "Spotless. Military style."

"You standing there, you see that old lady carrying a bag, you gotta hop up and offer to carry it for her," said Howley.

"I'd do that anyways," said Bunny.

They watched a man on an electric bike pass by in the opposite direction.

"I'm gonna stress it, and then we can drop it," said Howley. "*Ingratiate*. Make them like you."

"They already like me," said Bunny.

They drove through some brick warehouses on East Forty-Ninth Street, headed out toward Montbello. Bunny looked at the buildings and imagined himself rich enough to have a place like that. He could park some motorcycles in there. Open a motorcycle shop, sell some custom choppers. Build a whole community. Chopper City.

They stopped at a light. The agents kept prattling on about mindset and operational integrity, but Bunny wasn't paying attention to that. He was thinking about his old boss, T-Ma. She used to say things like *Life is boring, boring, boring, until it's not.* Then, Uncle Rayton appeared in his mind. Last night, the man had proclaimed he'd be happy eating those frozen burritos for breakfast and dinner every single day. He'd be fine with that, *happy as a clam in the sea*, he'd said.

Howley, still talking, mentioned Willard, and Bunny thought about something that had happened when he was about four or five years old. He'd been on his uncle's lap, looking up at him. Willard said he had a magic trick. He shifted Bunny from one knee to another, then took a cigarette butt and put it on a white napkin. *Now look here, Bunny, see this.* He poured some water onto it, closed the napkin, and rubbed it with his hand for a long time. *Ready? One, two, abracadabra, three.* He opened the napkin and revealed some disgusting brown-and-yellow slime. It looked like coughed up phlegm. Willard laughed uproariously. That was the trick. That was the whole thing. Bunny had hated him ever since.

The light turned green, and Bunny scratched his ear. He'd like to drive up to Grand Junction, put on a nice button-up shirt, and tell his mother what was happening. *I'm working for the Feds now, ma. They got me trying to investigate Uncle Willard.* His mother would be pissed. She'd say, *Those agents don't give a God damn about you. You stay out of this shit, Bunny.*

Bunny cleared his throat. "You gonna give me my hundred if they take me to meet him?"

"Yeah, man, shit," said Howley. "You in the field then. Yes, sir, we'll write that up. Hell yes. And it will be approved."

They drove through a new development on Central Boulevard. On one side, wild grass—brown and shaggy. On the other, cheap new apartments. Gana wheeled the car around and started heading back toward Bunny's neighborhood.

"In the field," said Bunny, out loud to himself. He pictured his mom chopping some chicken thighs for tacos. His sister showed up, arguing with his mother. Bunny suddenly realized he had no idea what these agents wanted him to do. "What am I supposed to do when I meet him?"

"The same thing you're doing with Ventola," said Howley. "Just be a good boy. Mr. Nice Guy. Let him recruit you. That's the key. He's gotta pull you in. Shit, you could even resist a little. Tell him you're busy. Play hard to get. He pulls you in, then you gonna be our eyes. That's it. It's not complicated."

"Shit's gonna happen fast. You'll see," said Gana.

Bunny's palms sweated. He did not want to be part of this. He'd almost rather be back in jail.

Only thing he liked was the idea of those hundred dollars a day. Put that on top of whatever he was making at Ventola's. That was pretty good money.

He could become a car salesman. Matter of fact, maybe that's why these agents had come into his life. In the deeper sense. Something guided them to him. He was open to that. Bunny had a spiritual side. *Shit, we all got a path, man.* He scratched his neck, looked out the window, rubbed his chin. *Maybe these guys are helping me*, he thought. *Gotta stay open to that possibility, too. Can't close yourself off to that.*

Later, after they dropped him off, Bunny drank some beers with Rayton. He told the man the Feds wanted him to be their eyes and ears on Willard.

Rayton shook his head mournfully. "I don't like this, Bunny. I don't like this at all."

"I know," said Bunny. "I don't either."

❧

Bunny started working at Ventola's. He spent his first day cleaning trash from behind a back fence. It was an awkward space and he had to squeeze himself between a building and the fence and take each piece of trash, straighten himself back up, and throw it over the top of the fence. It was a hot day, too.

Ventola came out and looked at his progress. "I haven't seen it that clean. Not once."

"Thank you," said Bunny.

"If you could do that on the whole thing," Ventola said. He gestured at the lot and then turned a half circle and glared out at the street like he was watching for surveillance. Bunny, when he felt Ventola's eyes come back on him, dropped his own gaze to the ground. There was a cigarette butt there; he bent down and picked it up.

"There you go," said Ventola.

Bunny hit the entire lot, picking up trash from every nook and cranny. He had to get under all kinds of cars and pick up plastic bags, newspapers, candy wrappers—he even found an old used condom. He worked into the afternoon, and when he finished, Ventola came back out. This time he was accompanied by Jimmy Dean, the head salesman. "Look at this," said Ventola.

Jimmy Dean walked out and looked around, blinking at the sun like a man waking from a nap. He looked at Bunny and nodded. Bunny pointed at the four large black trash bags he'd filled. "Yes, sir," said Jimmy Dean. "That does look nice. Good job, young man."

"Thank you," said Bunny.

Right then, a Buick sedan—gray, 2010—pulled into the lot. Bunny saw three white guys inside.

"Go on," said Ventola. "Ask Blanche if she wants you to do anything in there."

"Yes, sir," said Bunny. "Unless you want me to sell these guys on a car."

"They're not buying," said Ventola. "Go on."

It was a Colorado plate: HWY 3735. Bunny repeated it in his head. The men didn't get out, and instead Ventola and Jimmy Dean approached the driver's side window and spoke into it.

When he stepped inside the main building, Bunny found Blanche standing at her desk, bent over, looking into a drawer. "I can't find my charger," she said.

Bunny walked over and looked all around the desk for it. Then he got down on the ground and found it underneath the desk. "Here it is."

"You sugar plum!" she said, before coughing into her fist. Bunny asked if she wanted him to do anything else.

"Monte needs to lay the hell off you," she said. "He's working you to the bone. Look over there on that desk." She pointed at one of the sales desks. "Donut alert," she said. "Have one."

Bunny walked over, opened a waxed box of donuts, and grabbed a classic glazed. His stomach growled.

"Take a break," said Blanche.

"Thank you," said Bunny. "I'm gonna wash my hands." He set the donut down on a napkin.

"Right in there," said Blanche.

Bunny went to the back bathroom. It was filthy inside, and it occurred to him that he was going to have to clean that, too. He took out his phone, opened his notes, and typed *HWY 3735*.

Then he lifted the toilet seat and peed. Then he washed his hands with soap and dried them with a paper towel. He inspected himself in the mirror.

Bunny grabbed his donut and walked over to one of the windows and looked out through the slotted blinds at the men. Two of them had gotten out, so now there were four men standing outside. The driver, talking on his phone, stayed in the car. The two guys appeared to be in their forties. One wore a baseball cap with the brim bent hard. The other was hatless and had a full head of brown hair. They dressed normal but had a scuzzy vibe. Bunny watched as one of them opened the trunk and all four men gathered around to look inside. They stood there for a minute, looking in. One of the visitors was pointing things out and explaining something. Ventola nodded.

Bunny took a big bite of donut and kept watching. Right then, Ventola turned and looked directly at him, like he'd heard Bunny say something. Bunny stepped back from the window.

"I spilled my coffee," said Blanche.

Bunny grabbed some napkins from next to the donuts and went to her desk and started blotting the coffee up.

"Crap," said Blanche.

He felt her right next to him, smelled her perfume. She was dabbing at spots here and there. Bunny, getting more napkins, looked around the office. There was a security camera mounted on the far wall. It was unclear if it was operating, but Bunny noted it, and thought to himself that he better not steal anything from these people.

Right then, the front door opened, and the bell chimed. Bunny and Blanche both looked up. Ventola and one of the visitors entered the room. Bunny looked at the man. He was ugly.

"What the hell'd you do?" asked Ventola.

"I spilled my coffee!" said Blanche, nearly growling at him.

Bunny opened some more napkins and gave the desk a final wipe.

Ventola led the man back to his office, and as they passed Bunny and Blanche, the man and Bunny looked into each other's eyes. Ventola closed the door behind them. Bunny glanced at Blanche. She shook her head at him once, which Bunny thought could mean either *leave it alone* or *damn this coffee*.

Bunny pulled Blanche's trash bag out of the little bin, spun it, and tied it closed. "I'll take this out," he said.

"Thank you, honey," said Blanche.

Back outside, Bunny put the trash bag into one of his larger black bags. The Buick had moved to the far side of the lot, and Jimmy Dean had popped the hood on an orange Chevrolet Aveo and appeared to be showing the other two men the engine.

Ventola and the man came back outside and walked toward the others. Bunny noticed the man was carrying a little duffel bag now, the kind you might bring to a gym. His hands had been empty when he'd gone in. Bunny was certain of that.

Bunny walked back into the office, grabbed his half donut, went to one of the chairs, and sat down. He ate the donut slowly. Those men were either buying or selling drugs. That was Bunny's theory. He'd been around long enough to recognize that. They were probably looking in the car for a place to stash it.

Bunny, chewing his donut, thought about trying to steal the stuff, but then realized that wouldn't work. He'd like to, though. He looked over at Blanche. She was scrolling on her computer, probably looking at Facebook or something. Bunny finished his donut and licked the sugar glaze off his fingers.

When he went back out to the lot, Bunny saw that the Chevy Aveo was gone. The Buick, the men who rode in it, and Ventola himself were gone, too. Jimmy Dean, meanwhile, right near the entrance, was showing a Latino family a truck. Bunny moved closer so he could hear the man's selling routine.

"That's a fifteen hundred LT LT1," said Jimmy Dean. "Eight cylinder, five-point-three liter, it's got some get-up-and-go. Forty-nine thousand miles on it—under fifty, mind you. Trailer hitch, it's a beaut. *Muy bonita. ¿Me entiendes?*"

"It's a nice truck," said the man.

Bunny went back to his cleaning. *I'll get some wax,* he thought. *I could wax the cars and make them shine. Make them sparkle out here.*

A few days after speaking to his lawyer, Jerry was transferred to the county jail out on Smith Road. Things didn't get any better, though. In fact, they got worse.

After waiting around, he was reprocessed, reprinted, rephotographed, searched—anal cavity and all. Then they made him change into a different uniform; this one was forest green and smelled strongly of another man's armpits.

Eventually, a deputy—short, white, with big ears—escorted Jerry to his new dorm. While they waited to get buzzed in, the deputy said, "Oh, LeClair, yeah." Jerry looked at him. "You the one who made a complaint on Janko." The door buzzed. The deputy pulled the door open, dropped his voice to a whisper, and said, "You gonna get on fine in here."

Jerry stepped in and looked at two levels of cells running on the north and west sides of the room. The guards were stationed in the far corner. A little kitchenette with a sink and a water cooler sat in the center of the space. Around the kitchen a handful of round tables sat bolted to the ground, their tops marked like chess boards. The floors were made of shiny concrete. The place was clean, but to Jerry it smelled like a mixture of fast food and hospitals. There were no windows.

"Hanson," called the deputy who'd escorted him. "He's here. Show him around."

Hanson was another white guard. Jerry thought he looked like a military man, a Marine or something. He stood near the kitchenette, and when Jerry stepped into the room, he walked out to meet him.

"LeClair," said Hanson, "walk over to those stairs and head up to your cell, it's 2-H, up on top." He pointed to the second floor of cells.

Jerry noticed a group of black inmates down in the common area stand up from their table. He looked around for the white inmates and saw some sitting at another table, watching him.

"Go on, that way," said Hanson, pointing toward the stairs to Jerry's right.

Jerry set off toward the stairs, his paperwork getting clammy in his hands. He could feel the whole room's attention on him. Like everyone was waiting for something. *Hit first,* thought Jerry, pumping himself up but also feeling scared and depressed and lonely.

Right before he reached the stairs, Hanson yelled out, "Hey!"

Jerry turned toward the guard. Hanson pointed to the second story and said, "Go on up, 2-H."

Jerry turned back to the stairs and was hit in the face with some liquid. It came from the nearest cell, a holding cell under the stairs. His first thought was that someone had spit water on him; it was warm. He tried to peer into the cell but the door, besides a little slot, was solid. He touched at the liquid on his face and pulled his hand back and saw that it was brown. His next thought was that it was coffee. It took him a second to realize it was shit. Someone had thrown their liquid human shit on him.

Frantically, he wiped his face with his hands and then with his shirt. He could hear all kinds of hollering behind him. All the inmates stood now, and they were all yelling different things. Jerry pulled his shirt off, wiped himself with it again, and whipped it to the ground.

"What happened?" said the guard, Hanson, walking to him. He had a little smile in his eyes, though, like he knew exactly what had happened. Like he'd arranged it himself. Another deputy behind him was smiling, too.

"Nothing," said Jerry. "I need a new shirt. This one's dirty."

Hanson walked over to the cell where the shit had come from. "Crosby," he said into the slot. "Prone down. Prone down on the ground." He turned to Jerry. "Go on up. It's safe now, LeClair. You're good."

Jerry considered fighting the guard. He wanted to. He thought about swinging for his face. It wouldn't end well, though. Instead, shirtless and humiliated, he headed up the stairs.

On the second floor, he made his way down the row of cells, trying not to look in any as he went, but also keeping an eye out, too. There was a skinny black dude in a do-rag standing on the gangway, and when Jerry passed him, the guy whispered, "Fuck on, man."

Hanson was trailing Jerry from the ground floor. "Bunk down, LeClair, before your ass gets written up."

Jerry found cell 2-H and he stepped into it. There were two beds, one above the other, built right out from the wall. Next to the beds was about eighteen inches of walkway. In the back of the tiny cell, there was an open metal toilet and a sink above that.

Jerry washed his hands as best he could with the little trickle of water that came out of the sink. He rinsed his face, then turned and started to check his pants.

"Take the top bunk, I'm on the bottom," said a voice at the door. Jerry looked and saw a big inmate, white, 250 pounds, a bushy beard and short brown hair, looking into the cell. The guy had a jail shirt in his hands, and he threw it to Jerry. "I'm Hopper," he said. "Come out here. Make sure you don't have any feces on you."

Jerry stepped out of the cell and performed a turn for the man. Hopper looked him over. "You're alright," he said. "Fucking guards, man. Don't let 'em get in your head." He looked down at the main floor. "See 'em." Jerry stepped to the rail and saw the guard, Hanson, escorting an inmate to the door.

"Brought him in just for you, now they gon' take him out: a hitman."

"I don't have words for it," said Jerry. "I really don't."

"They said you filed a complaint on a deputy downtown."

"My lawyer did."

"Don't let him do that no more."

"Yeah, no shit," said Jerry.

"Don't be filing no complaints. Your lawyer fucked you up. Throw some shit on him next time."

"It's a her."

"So, shit on her, then."

"I will."

Hopper looked him up and down for a second. "Let me see your paperwork," he said. "Them boys down there gonna need some reassurances."

Jerry considered denying the request, but he knew he shouldn't. Also, he didn't mind having the men down there know he wasn't a pedophile or a rapist. He grabbed his paperwork and handed it over.

Hopper leafed through the pages. "Mm-hmm," he said, handing it back. "Okay, I'll tell 'em. Let's go."

Hopper led Jerry back downstairs and brought him to the table where the white guys were. Everyone was still watching, but not with as much interest.

"This is Jerry LeClair," said Hopper, pointing his thumb at Jerry. "That's Floyd right there." He indicated one of the seated men. Floyd looked about forty. He had a goatee, short-cropped hair. He was wiry, but strong. Jerry sensed he was probably the leader of the group. He had that kind of gravitas.

Hopper pointed to the man next to Floyd, a guy with long brown hair, and said, "That's Mickey Boo-Ride." There was a handful of other white guys behind them, but they weren't introduced.

"Consider this your orientation," said Floyd.

"Okay," said Jerry.

"No laying in your cell, except for bed-down. We make our bed every day. No fighting." He nodded toward the black guys. "We're cool in here. It's a mellow pod. Stay in line, don't start no shit. Unless we tell you to. Then your ass better be moving fast and mean."

Jerry nodded. "I got you," he said.

⁂

Helen, in the dressing room of a clothing boutique in Cherry Creek, pulled her shirt off, faced the mirror, and scrutinized her body. She raised her left arm and, with her other hand, ran her finger along the line of her deltoid muscle. She turned and looked at her back. Her muscles were unmistakable. Still, she couldn't help feeling anxious about aging. It was an ever-present fear. Mostly it stayed in the background, but it never really stopped humming.

She pulled the shirt—a white poplin blouse with ruffled shoulders—over her head. Then she pushed the curtain aside and stepped back out onto the sales floor.

"I love it," said the salesman.

Helen looked in a larger mirror. She moved her head and shoulders side to side. "I don't know," she said. "I don't know about this neckline." The shirt had a square neckline; it looked odd on her.

"It's modern," said the salesman, shrugging. "I think it's hot."

Helen's phone rang. She stepped over to her purse, which was sitting on a chair, and fished her phone out of it. She had saved the public defender's number in her phone as "Jerry.lawyer," and that's what she saw now.

Helen believed in facing these things head on. She made a little face to the salesman, moved toward the windows, and answered the call.

"Hello?"

"Ms. McCalla? April Costa-Tenge, Jerry's public defender."

"Yes?"

"I spoke to Jerry. I told him you weren't interested in bailing him out. That you were concerned the police might perceive some type of stalking element. Jerry wanted to call you himself. I said he *cannot* do that. Those calls are recorded. If he calls you, I'd prefer you not even accept it."

The lawyer continued talking, but Helen got caught up on the idea that the calls were being recorded. She looked out the window of the store and saw a white van parked on East Third Avenue. Helen, nervous, frowned and rubbed her forehead. *Was this call being recorded?*

"I'm sorry," she said, interrupting Jerry's lawyer. "I'm in a store right now."

"I'll get to the point," said April Costa-Tenge. "I agreed to call you on his behalf *if* he promised not to call you himself. That was the deal."

"Okay."

"Jerry thinks that maybe if you don't want to get involved, if you don't want your name in any of this—which is understandable, I get it—he suggested that maybe you could *loan* the money to someone named Sam? Is that a mutual friend of yours?"

"How much did you say it was, again?"

"The bail has been set at fifty thousand dollars. You could put collateral down for the fifty—say, a house—or you could pay around five thousand, depending on some factors, to a bail bondsman."

Helen stayed silent for a moment. She probed a back molar with her tongue and watched an unleashed dog walk by on the street. Its owner, his hands in his pockets, followed behind.

"I'm not going to keep bothering you with this," said the public defender. "I literally agreed to call you just to keep *him* from calling. But I thought I would float it. I mean, I do think it would be better for him to be out. He's having a pretty rough go of it. We could fight this case much more effectively with him out."

Helen turned from the window to another mirror. She looked at herself in the blouse, pulled at the hem. It occurred to her that if she didn't do anything, Jerry could very well pull her into this. Yes, she could say he was stalking her, but it would all be so complicated. She had to bail him out. If she could do it and keep her name out of it, all the better. "Okay," she said. "Let me talk to Sam and see if he'll do it."

"Wow," said the public defender. "Fantastic. That is not how I expected this call to go. I'm very pleased. Thank you. This is my cell, call me as soon as you hear from him."

Helen walked over to the salesman. "I'll take it," she said, referring to the blouse. "Can I wear it out?"

"Of course!"

Helen, wearing her new blouse, walked to her car. The sky was bright blue. The man with the unleashed dog stood on the corner, watching her. Was her new neckline ridiculous? She glanced down and thought, *No, it's not.* Then she fished her fob out of her bag and beeped her car unlocked with it.

Once she was in the car, she grabbed her phone and took a selfie. She thought about posting it on Instagram, but her face, her eyes in particular, looked too sad. Instead, she sent it to Sam with the text *Drink tonight?*

Bunny was in the middle of waxing a car when he saw a souped-up Ford F-150 pull into the lot. It parked right next to the main building; Bunny kept his eyes on it because he thought they might be looking to sell the truck. He liked it. It was black and lifted. He'd like a truck like that.

The door popped open, and Bunny saw his uncle Willard step out. There was no mistaking the man. An immediate feeling of fear pumped through Bunny's body. It felt like a switch had been hit. He turned off his polisher and set it down on the ground. Then he wiped his hands on his pants and stood there watching as Willard Haggerty made his way into Ventola's building.

Bunny looked around the lot and then out at the street. Ventola had a mechanic named Juan Carlos, who was working on a car near the garage. He didn't seem to have noticed Willard's arrival, or Bunny's reaction. His focus was on the engine.

Bunny, ready to call the agents, pulled out his cellphone. But he didn't call them. Instead, he walked toward the street. When he got there, wanting to distract himself, he scrolled through his feed on Facebook. He saw stupid shit, memes. Then he saw a girl from Arvada who he thought was hot, and he liked her photo.

"Fuck," he said out loud, jamming his phone back into his pocket. He walked over to the far fence and did fifteen push-ups, trying to burn off some of the adrenaline. Then he went back to the car he was waxing, picked up his electric polisher, and—moving to the passenger side so he could keep his eyes on the door—continued waxing the car.

The monologue in Bunny's head sounded like: *Okay, okay, okay, calm. Calm. Calm. Calm.*

Running alongside the words were images: he saw his mother, their yard, trucks, and snakes. "Fuck," he muttered to himself. He didn't want anything to do with any of this.

Bunny switched the polisher off, set it down, and began rubbing the car with a hand cloth. The panic he'd been feeling began to subside;

now he embarked on a pep talk: *Okay, you got this. You got this. Let's go. Let's fucking go. Ninja style. Fucking ninja style. Come on, dude.*

The office door popped open and Ventola walked out, Uncle Willard trailing right behind. Bunny had already planned his approach, and he started walking that way like he was going to fetch a bucket. This led him straight toward the two men.

"Bunny, get over here," said Ventola.

Bunny headed that way. Willard was in his sixties now. He was a large man, over six feet tall and two hundred and something pounds. He had a dark mustache, and Bunny couldn't help wondering if he dyed it. He had lines in his face and the same mean, dark eyes that Bunny remembered. They were locked on Bunny right then and their expression did not look friendly.

"Bunny, pull those pallets from the truck," said Ventola, pointing to a stack of about eight wooden pallets in the back of Willard's truck.

"Bunny?" said Willard, squinting. "That's not Bunny Simpson?"

"Hey, Willard," said Bunny.

"Oh Lord," said Willard. "Jesus help me." He turned to Ventola. "That's my nephew."

"What?" said Ventola.

"That's me," said Bunny, rubbing his hands on his pants.

"That's my sister's boy," said Willard. He licked his lips and grabbed Bunny by the shoulders. Bunny noticed the prison tattoos under the man's sleeve. He'd forgotten about those. "Oh my. This is a shock," said Willard. "How's your mother?"

"She's okay," said Bunny, looking at the ground and feeling suddenly sad. "She's alright. She's still up there in Grand Junction." Bunny breathed in, gathered himself.

"And your sister?"

"She's good. She's in Green River. She's got a couple kids, now."

"Damn, almighty," said Willard. "I'm gonna have to borrow this kid," he said, looking at Ventola. "You know that, right?"

Ventola frowned, looked down at the ground.

"Come on," said Willard.

Bunny waited for Ventola to give him a signal.

"Go ahead," said the car salesman. "Take those pallets out first."

Bunny unloaded the pallets. His adrenaline made him feel like he was floating. He had to work to make himself look calm and not bothered or nervous.

When he finished, he got into the truck. It smelled like cigarettes. There were some large canvas folders, filled up with paper. They looked like construction blueprints. "Push those over," said Willard. Bunny pushed them to the middle of the bench seat. "I haven't seen you since Frazier passed," said Willard.

Frazier was Willard's only child. He was a couple years older than Bunny. He died six years ago. Overdosed up in Grand Junction. *Grand Junky*, as Bunny and his friends liked to call it. He died in a truck with a needle in his arm. Bunny and his mother went to the funeral. His mom and Willard weren't talking at the time, but Bunny—in a suit that was borrowed and too large—had gone over to his uncle, shaken his hand, and offered his condolences. "Well," Willard had said at the funeral, "I told him not to mess with the hard stuff."

Willard's glove box popped open and interrupted Bunny's memory. Willard said, "That thing," and reached over and slammed it shut. "I'm remarried now," said Willard, out of the blue. "I have a new wife." Bunny thought about his old wife, a woman named Lucille, Frazier's mother, a sad lady that Bunny never knew very well. She was probably dead, too.

Willard sat there staring at Bunny; his left eyelid twitched a little with his pulse. "Tell you what," he said. "Let's go get us a cup of coffee from Star-bucky. You gonna tell me about yourself. I take these meetings as a gift. The Lord gonna put you where he wants you. Yes, sir. You can count on that."

"Okay," said Bunny. He pulled down the visor mirror and checked his face, made sure there wasn't any oil or wax on it.

Willard started the truck and backed up. Bunny, when they pulled away, noticed Ventola near the door watching them. The man had his arms crossed and didn't look happy.

They pulled out onto West Mississippi Avenue and headed east, away from the mountains. Bunny, as they rode, thought about a fight his mother and Willard had gotten into once. Bunny couldn't remember exactly how old he was at the time, but he was very young. They were staying in the apartment of a friend of Bunny's mother, a lady named Joyce, who lived out on Flat Top Lane. Willard was there; there was all kinds of arguing. There were broken dishes. His mom was crying. Some men from another apartment got involved. It turned into a whole thing. Bunny and his sister hid in Joyce's room with the television. *The Price Is Right* was on. They pretended not to hear any of the arguing going on outside, and Bunny gave his sister a hug. Told her he loved her.

Willard slowed down for some traffic, and Bunny thought about Agent Howley. *Make him like you*, the agent had said. "It's good to see you," Bunny said. He felt a pit in his stomach. He didn't like to lie. "Been a long time."

"Thank the Lord for bringing us together."

"Yes, sir," said Bunny. "Amen to that."

"You go to church?"

"No, sir," said Bunny, remembering how Agent Gana had instructed him to lie only when he absolutely had to.

Uncle Willard, while they drove, filled Bunny in on the whereabouts of some of their relatives. Bunny knew the names but didn't really have a sense of who they were. His own family unit had been isolated from the larger family, partly because of Willard and his mother's rift.

They pulled into the parking lot of a Starbucks on Santa Fe Avenue. "Yes, sir," said Willard, parking the car. He turned and looked at Bunny. "You're a good-looking kid. You look like your mother. Just like clean creek water." He killed the engine. "I don't like to use the drive-thru," he said. "I prefer to go in."

They stepped into the Starbucks. Cool air greeted them. A few techie-looking customers glanced up. The two of them must've looked like father and son, standing there.

"I like the cold brew, with the whipped cream and the caramel," said Willard.

"That sounds good to me, too," said Bunny, looking at the workers and brushing some dust off his shirt. "That sounds nice."

They brought their drinks to a table by the windows and sat down. "I been thinking about your mother," said Willard.

"Yes, sir, me too," said Bunny.

"She's had a hell of a time."

"Mm-hmm," said Bunny. He took the lid off his drink and ate the cream off the top. Caramel and salt, it tasted good, and Bunny became lost in it for a second.

Willard sipped from his own drink and got a little spot of whipped cream on his mustache. He looked at Bunny with shining eyes, and then, very quietly, almost whispering, he said, "Bunny, I always was very fond of you. Me and your mother have had our differences, but I always was very fond of you."

"Thank you," said Bunny, shifting in his seat.

"How the hell did you end up with Ventola?" Willard asked.

The older man was staring at Bunny with such intensity that for a moment Bunny forgot what his answer was supposed to be. His heart thumped inside his chest. He looked down at his drink, sniffled, looked back up into his uncle's eyes. "Craigslist," he said, finally. "I saw an ad on Craigslist."

"You hit the ball out the park," said Agent Gana, later that same night.

Bunny sat in the back of the agents' SUV. They were driving in Riverside Cemetery, right near Bunny and Rayton's place. Bunny had just finished telling them that he'd made contact with his uncle and been invited to work at the ranch in Castle Rock. Ventola had signed off on it and everything.

"I knew this kid was a gamer," said Howley.

"Natural-born killer," said Gana.

"Thank you," said Bunny. "Said I could start this week."

"What kind of work does he have in mind, Bunny?"

"Building something. Construction."

"Damn, Bunny," said Gana, "you about to get yourself an award."

They rode in silence for a second.

"You think I could get that hundred, though?" asked Bunny.

"Hell yeah," said Gana. "But we gotta put in the request. You'll get it. It's not coming from our pockets. It takes a little time."

"Okay," said Bunny.

"Keep track of those days in the field," said Howley. "Write them down somewhere. Don't write what you're doing, just jot down the dates."

"Yep," said Gana. "We'll turn that in."

"You gonna be triple billing," said Howley. "Ventola owes you a check. Your uncle Willard gonna pay you. Treasury gonna pay you. What the hell you gonna do with all that money?"

"Maybe get a car."

"That would be nice," said Gana. "A man needs a car in this town."

"Hold up," said Howley, digging into his pocket. "I'm gonna give you a hundred, right now. Fuck it, man." He pulled out a roll of cash and peeled off five twenties. "Show you we're for real," he said, holding the money out. "Act of good faith."

"Thank you," said Bunny.

"There's gonna be a lot more where that came from."

Bunny looked out at the cemetery. All those tombstones. He thought about his mother and worried that he was going to have to bury her one of these days. Then, just like that, he realized that these agents were going to make him betray his uncle Willard. He'd already known that, but suddenly he *really* knew it. Sweat from one of his armpits rolled down his side. Bunny, for about the hundredth time, wondered what the hell he'd gotten himself into.

❧

"You want to bail out Jerry?" Sam's face looked confused. "The kid who sells steroids? I don't understand."

"He's in jail. I don't know," said Helen. She hadn't really planned her argument. They were in a Cuban restaurant on Larimer Street. She looked around impatiently. They hadn't ordered drinks yet.

"What'd he get arrested for?"

"His lawyer said it was some kind of assault in a park."

"We should start a GoFundMe," said Sam. "Half the guys at the gym would throw in for that! It would be no problem!"

"Sam, we don't need to raise the money. I said I'm happy to pay for it, but I need you to be the one who puts your name on it."

Sam scrutinized her. His gaze went from her eyes to her cheek, then dropped to her lips, then ticked back up to her eyes. "Wait, you're not fucking this kid?"

Helen felt herself begin to blush.

"You're blushing!"

"Sam, come on. He's like, what, twenty-two?"

The waiter came and Sam ordered vodka sodas for both of them. "No more sugar," he said, speaking to Helen. "No more margaritas. We're done with that."

"Extra limes on the side, please," said Helen to the waiter. She looked back at Sam, made her lips pouty for him. "What do you think? Can I write you a check?"

"Is he going to pay you back?" asked Sam.

"Of course."

She knew Sam had already made his decision. He wasn't very good at masking his intentions. Still, he'd have to be drawn out. She leaned back in her seat and with both hands reached up to her hair, untied it from its ponytail, pulled it up, and let it drop: Kalahari melon shampoo. She loved the smell of it.

"Will you do it?" she asked.

"Sign my name?"

"Yeah."

"Alright," he said with a shrug.

They drank four vodka sodas each and after dinner they ended up in the parking lot. Sam, drunk, had become sulky. He leaned against her door and wouldn't let her open it.

"Let's go to the Snowplow and have one more."

Helen protested that she had to hit the gym in the morning. He put his big arm around her and pulled her to him. "I need to fuck you," he whispered in her ear. "I'm sorry, I just do."

Helen, at that moment, didn't feel attracted to him. It had been a few weeks since they'd had sex, and she thought they were done with all that. Still, she let him guide her to his SUV. She let him open the back door and pull her in. From there, something shifted in her mindset, and she became the aggressor. She got on top of him and started rocking back and forth. She was aware that she didn't feel tenderness—she felt a kind of hostility. It felt more like a tussle than a romantic interlude. Her pants were tight, and she had to work to get them off.

"Do you have a condom?" she whispered.

"I got snipped," he said.

Helen wondered why he'd used a condom the other times she'd had sex with him, but she didn't ask. They started kissing again. Helen pictured a high school teacher of hers. She used to masturbate and think about him. He was an older guy, Mr. Roberts, but there was something sexual about him. He had a big dick and walked around with it bulging in his pants. He taught history.

Helen, still kissing, opened her eyes and looked out the back window. There was a couple getting into a car nearby. She'd noticed them in the restaurant. They were in their thirties, white, sober-seeming. They both were skinny, had perfect posture, and looked like they worked as art gallerists or architects or something. Helen had hated them in the restaurant, and she hated them outside of it. Sam, under her, shifted around and pulled his pants and underwear down. She grabbed his dick and with some effort got him inside of her. He came almost immediately, grunting like a beast.

Afterward, while she pulled her pants back on, he said, "Sometimes, I just can't resist you."

It struck Helen the wrong way and she became annoyed.

Sam must've sensed something. "What's up?" he asked.

"I'm just sick of you," she said. "And everyone like you."

"What the fuck?"

She wanted to say, *Because I don't want you to* sometimes *not be able to resist me. I want you to always want me. I want you to want to live with me. To share a bedroom. To cook together. Go on trips. Fly places. Watch TV. I want to be like that couple in there, the architects. I don't want this with you, but I want it with someone, and the fact that you don't want it with me fucking hurts my feelings.* Instead, she said, "Because you're an asshole."

His face became grim. He pulled his pants up. "Fuck you, Helen."

"You just did—for almost a full second."

"What happened to you as a child?"

"Nothing," said Helen. She closed her eyes. "I'm sorry," she said. "I'm feeling a little weird."

"Dude," said Sam. "It's not nice."

She needed his help, so she gave him a little push on the shoulder. "You're my guy," she said, smiling. "You're my big guy."

That seemed to cheer him up. They sat there in the backseat for a bit. She kissed him in different spots on his face. Then she got out of his car and drove home alone, drunk and lonely.

Bunny was in Castle Rock. He'd taken the bus from Denver and now stood waiting in front of a generic motel, the kind you might find on a highway. He was the only person standing there, and he felt nervous and kept adjusting his pants and sweatshirt.

The agents' instruction had been minimal. *Just go. Get the lay of the land. We're not even gonna mic you up. Play it natural.* Bunny scratched himself, squinted against the bright sun, and looked at a couple of empty landscaping trucks that were parked on the side of the road. *Wish I was working that job*, Bunny thought, *instead of this one.*

Right then, his uncle pulled up. Bunny, stepping from the shadow of the portico, nodded to him. Willard looked around like he was searching for a lost dog. Bunny raised his hand and waved, the old man stepped on the brake, and the truck lurched to a stop.

When Bunny got in, he noticed a sad expression on his uncle's face. For a moment, Bunny worried the man knew everything. But then Willard said, "You look just like Frazier," referring to his dead son. "You move like him." Bunny remembered the way Frazier moved. He saw him throwing a beer bottle at a store on North Avenue. He saw his sneering face. Truth was, he'd never been a big fan of Frazier Haggerty. Still, Bunny managed to whisper, "I miss him."

"Me too," said his uncle. "That's why I called you out here." He looked at Bunny. "Family gotta stick together. That's one thing I've learned with everything we went through."

"Yes, sir," said Bunny.

Willard put the truck in drive, and they started rolling out. "The ride was okay?" Willard asked, like he wanted to change the subject.

"Yeah, it was alright," said Bunny. He buckled his seatbelt and watched a man hurrying into one of the other motels. Bunny's face was tense, and as they drove along, he tried to relax the muscles around his eyes. He tried to relax his shoulders, too. *Come on, man*, he told himself. *Be cool.*

They drove to the edge of town; then they got onto a smaller road and followed along the side of some old train tracks. There were fewer and fewer houses out here. Willard did most of the talking, and Bunny tried to stay engaged, but he felt a little foggy and had to work to follow the flow of conversation. Most of it involved Willard saying how happy he was to have Bunny working out there instead of with Ventola. "You don't wanna mix with all that," said Willard. Bunny suspected he was referring to the drugs, and he made a little grunting noise to signal he understood and agreed.

At one point, they passed by an abandoned house. Willard slowed down and looked to his right. There was a truck parked next to the building. Two men with shaved heads sat in it. The driver flashed his brights once, and Willard sniffed and then sped on again. Bunny, feeling like the men were keeping watch over something, turned in his seat and looked back after them.

"Friends," said Willard. "Friends of the family."

Eventually, they arrived at the property. From the road, it looked like a big ranch. The only difference was it had a barbwire fence that followed the road as far as Bunny could see. Willard hopped out of the truck and unlocked a swing gate. Bunny, while he waited, counted three signs warning against trespassing. The signs themselves had bullet holes in them. When his uncle got back in, Bunny said, "Y'all got a ranch out here?"

"Fourteen hundred acres. Yes, sir. Sixty head of steer, but we wanna get more. I wanna have two hundred. That's my goal. Self-sufficiency. Get us off the grid."

Bunny felt the old man looking at him like he wanted to make sure Bunny understood what he was saying. Bunny nodded: *Yes, I do.* Then Willard pulled the truck forward, through the gate, and hopped out again. *He moves pretty good for an older dude*, thought Bunny, watching him in the side view mirror. Willard jumped back in and said, "You could open and close it next time. That could be your job."

"I will," said Bunny.

They bumped along a dirt road. There were still some hills out here, but they were the last ones before the plains started and everything became flat. If they kept driving in a straight line, they'd eventually hit Kansas. There were some bristlecone pine trees and some dry, scrubby bushes; the mountains were behind them. It was spring, but the winter grass was still yellowish brown. At one point, they passed a burnt-out old truck, rusted and destroyed. There was something spooky about it; it felt like a crime scene. Willard exhaled through his nose, like *Yep*, and they continued bumping along.

A moment later, they wheeled around a bend, and the road became fenced in; ten-foot-high corrugated metal walls stood on either side for about forty feet. There were lights on top of the fence, but they were shut off. The walls made Bunny feel claustrophobic. The place felt menacing.

"It's quiet out here," Bunny said.

"That's how we like it."

They exited the fenced part, rounded another bend, and then approached a kind of compound. Bunny saw two newer-looking cinder block buildings, but besides those, the place seemed chaotic and not planned out. Bunny was a little taken aback by the mess of it all. To the left of the buildings, a row of smashed cars sat piled on top of each other, like the beginnings of some kind of fortification. Next to the cars was a structure that looked like an old garage. Its frame was made of mismatched wood—some of it looked rotted—and its walls had been covered with plastic sheets. A few other ramshackle buildings sat spread around the place. Some mobile homes sat here and there, too.

Bunny saw collections of scrap metal, wire, and tires. There were heaps of disorganized lumber, like a whole house had been scrapped and piled for parts. Bunny counted a half dozen beat-up trucks parked at different spots, along with two other regular cars. A few tractors and a couple four-wheelers. The ground in front of the buildings was dirt, and loose trash lay spread out on it, like a garbage bag had been ripped open and the wind had moved the stuff around.

Bunny's eyes went to a group of shirtless men standing outside the bigger building. They didn't look friendly, and they stopped what they were doing and watched the truck approach. A few other men were shoveling loose sand from the back of a truck, and they stopped their work and watched, too. All said, there appeared to be a little over a dozen men and a few women outside. Everyone there was white.

"Y'all got a whole thing out here," said Bunny.

"It's a camp," said Willard. "Yes, sir. A place where boys become men, and men become soldiers." He pulled to a stop and killed the engine, then scratched his chest for a moment. They both got out of the truck, and Bunny stood next to him.

"There's my wife, right there," said Willard, pointing at a group. He cupped his hands around his mouth and yelled out, "Bess, come over here. Meet my sister's son." He turned to Bunny. "She gonna have dirt on her hands," he whispered. Bunny didn't know what he meant by that.

Before coming over, Willard's wife turned and said something to another woman. The other woman walked away. And Bess, wearing what looked like some kind of frontier woman's dress, walked over to them.

Willard introduced her to Bunny.

"I've heard so much about you," said Bess. She seemed younger than Willard, maybe in her forties. Her face looked like she spent a lot of time in the sun, though, like she'd lived her whole life in it. Her hair was brown, with a little gray on the sides. She was a large lady, with a large bosom, and she came right up to Bunny, put a hand on his shoulder, looked into his eyes.

"Praise Jesus," she said. Bunny could see her front teeth were brown. "I always wanted a boy named Bunny."

"Let's go," said Willard. He grabbed Bunny by the arm and pulled him toward one of the cinder block buildings. Bess, scowling at the ground and muttering to herself, trailed behind.

A pit bull came out from the far side of the lot and trotted toward them. Willard yelled, "Go on!" and the dog turned around and reversed course. "We got two dozen of them out here," said Willard. It was only then that Bunny became aware of a distant chorus of barking. "Gonna set the cages so you could let them all loose at once. Twenty-five hungry dogs," he said, turning and looking at Bessie with a crazed smile on his face. "Imagine that!"

They got to one of the cinder block buildings and Willard told Bunny to wait outside for a second, and then he disappeared into the building.

"Need good men like you out here," said Bess. "Not that sort." She nodded toward the other men.

Bunny didn't understand what she meant, but he said, "Happy to do it."

"You have any kids?" asked Bess.

"Not yet," said Bunny.

"Shit," said Bess, seeing something she didn't like across the way from them. "I'll be back," she said.

"Okay," said Bunny.

He watched her walk for a second, and then he watched a fly buzzing near the ground. Then the door of the building swung open, and Willard and another man came out. The new man had a shaved head. He appeared to be in his forties; he wore jeans, work boots, and an orange T-shirt. He had a holster on his belt, with a black Glock on one side and some extra clips on the other. His face looked a little tense.

"Flesh and blood," said Willard, speaking to the man.

The guy stepped forward and extended a hand. "Nelson," he said. Bunny gripped his rough hand, shook it, and told him his own name.

"You came in from Denver?" Nelson asked. He seemed to be watching Bunny closely, like he was trying to detect any lies.

"Yeah, just now," said Bunny.

"Trying to work out here?" asked Nelson.

"Yes, sir," said Bunny.

"You good with a hammer and shovel?"

"Yeah," said Bunny. He looked down at the ground and scratched his chin.

Uncle Willard cleared his throat and spoke. "Bunny, go on with Nelson to his office. He wants to do a bit of an intake interview."

Bunny followed the man into the building. The place had an institutional feel: a school or a jail, but not quite finished. All the lights were off, which made the hallway unusually dark. It was cool inside, too, and they walked in silence.

"Come on in here for a second," said Nelson, pointing to a room at the end of the hall. He then held the door open for Bunny.

The room was small. Nelson flipped the light on and then sat himself behind a wooden desk.

He pointed at a metal chair and Bunny took a seat. Behind Nelson were a few stacks of legal boxes filled up with paper. A window to Bunny's right looked out toward the plains. Hanging in the center of the window was a fly strip, dotted with dead flies.

"It's your uncle's place, but I manage it," said Nelson.

Bunny nodded like he understood.

Nelson turned and pointed at an engraved sign hanging on the wall. Bunny read it: WE MUST SECURE THE EXISTENCE OF OUR PEOPLE AND A FUTURE FOR WHITE CHILDREN.

"You got a problem with those fourteen words?"

"No, sir," said Bunny. His forehead became a little warm. He didn't like that racist shit, but he had a role to play.

"I'm gonna need a copy of your ID."

"Shoot, he didn't tell me that."

"Next time."

"Yes, sir," said Bunny.

"Tell me your date of birth and your address. Matter of fact, tell me all the addresses you've lived at."

"As an adult? Or a kid?" asked Bunny.

"Both," said Nelson. "Tell me it all."

Bunny told him as best as he could remember, and the man jotted it down onto a yellow legal pad.

"What's your real name?"

"Bunny Simpson."

"You use any other names?"

"No."

"You been arrested before?" asked Nelson.

Bunny nodded.

"When was the last time?"

Bunny's heart rate sped up. The agents had told him his recent arrest wouldn't show up. Still, it made him nervous to lie. He looked at the ceiling like he was calculating time. "A couple years ago," he said. "In Grand Junction."

"For what?"

"That was a little mix-up with some stolen tools." They sat in silence. Bunny sniffled. "And some drugs."

"You still using?"

Bunny shook his head.

"Show me your arms."

Bunny turned his arms up and looked down at his own veins. A cop had made him do that downtown, just about a year ago.

"You got any tattoos?"

"No, sir."

"Good, we don't advertise anymore. You understand what I'm saying?"

"Yeah," said Bunny.

Bunny realized he was tapping his foot, and he stopped. Nelson kept his eyes glued on him. Finally, Nelson said, "Alright." He raised his eyebrows. "It was nice to meet you. We always looking for new men out here to join our little crew of do-gooders. If everything goes well, and it feels right, we may want to make it a little more formal down the road. You understand?"

"Yes, sir," said Bunny.

After that, Nelson introduced Bunny to the men shoveling sand. There were three of them. They all had their shirts off. One of them was extremely hairy: wiry fur covered his chest, shoulders, and back. One of them had his head shaved bald; he had spiderwebs tattooed on his face and Nazi symbols on his chest and arms; apparently, he hadn't gotten the memo about not advertising. The third guy seemed grumpy and had short brown hair and eyes that were set close together. The skinhead and the guy with the close-set eyes appeared to be in their thirties. The hairy man looked like he was in his late forties. Bunny was used to characters, but these men seemed particularly rough.

A few minutes later, Bunny set to work and started shoveling sand into bags. By the end of the day, he was exhausted and sunburnt, and his hands were calloused.

After introducing Bunny to the men, Nelson returned to his office, and looked at the notes he'd jotted down. The kid, for reasons he couldn't pinpoint, had left him feeling uneasy. He pulled out his cellphone and dialed an associate, Byron Santner, a deputy at the Jefferson County Sheriff's Department.

"Wassup, Hoss?" said Byron. He sounded like he'd just woken up.

"Need you to run someone for me," said Nelson. He paid Byron $150 a pop to run people on the sheriff's NCIC system. Byron, if he found anything, would print the records and mail them in an unmarked envelope. Every month or so they'd meet up, and Nelson would pay the man in cash. After Nelson gave him Bunny's info, they chitchatted for a minute and then ended the call.

Nelson, frowning, tapped his knuckles on the desk. Then he headed back outside. He watched Bunny shoveling sand. The boy seemed to work hard; that was good. Then, out of nowhere, the word *homosexual* popped into Nelson's mind. *Ah*, thought Nelson, *he might be gay.* The thought left him feeling queasy. He'd have to keep an eye on Bunny.

Right then, Willard stepped out from the door behind him. "You know what Rhonda and them are doing?" asked the old man in an ill temper.

"No," said Nelson.

"Using that frozen beef to make chili."

"That's not a problem," said Nelson. "I can get more tomorrow."

Nelson had only known Willard for about three years. The man still made him nervous. They'd been introduced through Nelson's benefactor, an older man named Buford Heinz. Mr. Heinz was heir to a meatpacking fortune. He'd been funding White Power movements for almost forty years. He was a creepy old dude, but he had deep pockets and plenty of friends.

Nelson, for his part, had been involved in the movement since he was a teenager. As a young man in Denver, he'd been a skinhead. When he was twenty, he got arrested for a brawl in which a kid had his jaw broken. The judge gave Nelson a choice: prison or the army. He chose the latter.

The military, of course, set him further along his path. He met plenty of people there who were friendly to the cause. After six years, when he got out, Nelson dedicated himself full-time to the White Power movement. He started getting involved with some of the fascist organizations: he linked up with groups like the National Socialist Coalition and Patriot Arm, and started attending meetings with European Identity Front. It was through that last group that he met Buford Heinz.

Mr. Heinz was something of a kingmaker. The old man liked to pretend he was a cowboy, but it was clear he'd never worked a day in his life. His hands were too soft. He liked Nelson, though. Two months after they first met, Mr. Heinz extended a coveted invitation up to his ranch, outside of Vail. That was an important step. A man with ambitions, like Nelson, needed funding. He became a regular visitor up there. His military background served him well. Mr. Heinz would trot him around the ranch, holding his arm like a little trophy, introducing him to other clammy-handed rich men.

During one of those meetings, Mr. Heinz told Nelson he had an idea. They were standing in his library, looking at one of his antique guns. "Our group," said Mr. Heinz, pointing down at the little pistol, "lacks muscle. We're not tough enough. I'm tired of seeing these antifa bastards holding their own against us. It's embarrassing."

"I hear that," said Nelson.

"I know someone who can help us with that."

Nelson turned and looked at him. "Who?"

"A man by the name of Willard Haggerty," said Mr. Heinz. "Yep, ol' Willard is a doozy, you'll see that as soon as you meet him. You two would get on, though. He's a rancher, a real one"—Mr. Heinz motioned toward the window—"not like these other ones. No, Mr. Haggerty . . . How should I say it. He's got a unique background. He's got some money. Little bit, but he's got some. Served time in prison. He's got connections to *that* world. He's a good man, though.

"We've had some good heart-to-hearts. He's a Christian man. Now look, some of the things he's involved with would be frowned upon by our friends. Thing is, he *understands* that we're in a war. The war has already started. Not everyone realizes that yet. There will be some unsavory things that happen, we might have to make alliances with people we never imagined we'd be doing business with. Criminal types. The way I see it, though, his group might be a little rough. They're not refined. But our group is a little soft. We're not ready for war." Mr. Heinz licked his lips, intertwined his fingers. "I wanna merge the two groups."

A meeting was arranged. Nelson drove to a bar in Pueblo, Colorado. The bar was a musty-smelling place with elk heads hanging on the walls. It was closed, but a biker-looking guy let Nelson in, offered him a beer, and had him sit at a table. Ten minutes later, Willard Haggerty walked in. The bartender, after exchanging a few words with the man, disappeared into the back, leaving them alone in the room.

Nelson had already researched the man. Byron, his sheriff friend, had called an associate, a CDOC intelligence officer, who confirmed that Willard had been a yard captain for the Western United Aryan Brotherhood. Western United was a Colorado State Prison spin-off of the larger gang. "Still in good standing," the intel officer told Byron, referring to Willard's status.

Nelson liked him right away. Mr. Heinz had been right about that. Willard was an impressive figure. He had a seriousness to him. Nelson remembered thinking, *Yes, I would go to war with this man. He is a leader.*

Nelson didn't want to beat around the bush. He didn't want to pretend to not know Willard's background, so eventually, after some small talk, he said, "You served time at Limon?"

Willard squinted. "That's right."

Besides that, the two men never mentioned prison, or the gang, again. In fact, Willard only said two things that even hinted at it. The first, in reference to a discussion on discipline, was "Well, we do follow our bylaws." The second, referring to the fact that they were even having this sit-down, was that it had been "Council-approved." The Council, Nelson learned later, was made up of five prisoners, all serving life sentences, all of them in solitary, two of them at Limon, and three of them at CSP in Cañon City. They were the leaders of Willard's group. Their communications mainly ran through the guards. People like Byron and the CDOC intel officer.

After they'd gotten through their preliminaries, Nelson got down to business. "I want to relay an offer to you. It comes direct from Mr. Heinz himself."

Willard tilted his head, then nodded like *Proceed.*

"Mr. Heinz told me about your ranch. The one out there in Castle Rock. He wants to rent it from you. He wants to help you develop it. Turn it into a place where our friends can find refuge. Where we can train. Learn discipline. Learn to work the land. Learn to build. I'm gonna be honest with you," said Nelson.

"Please," said Willard.

"Reason he wants to rent it from you is, well, he wants to help underwrite *your* endeavors."

"And why would he want to do that?" asked Willard.

"He thinks some comingling between your group and ours is gonna be good for both sides."

Willard made a face like he didn't like it. "I'm gonna be honest with you, now," he said. "I know Mr. Heinz. I've met him. I can't really see myself taking orders from him."

"He's not gonna be involved like that. Nothing hands-on at all. He's just the money man."

"How much does he want to rent the place for?"

"He thinks twenty-six thousand two hundred fifty dollars a month is a fair price. And he's gonna pay for the materials and labor to help build it up. Let you increase the value of your property."

"Hmm," said Willard. His eyes got a far-off look to them. "Let me think about that. Talk to my people." He reached his big hand out, and the two men shook.

Two weeks later, Willard got back to him. The deal had been approved. They were in.

All that had taken place three years ago. Now, Nelson stood there watching Willard's nephew shoveling sand. His mind shifted from that first meeting in the bar to a fantasy where he was a military leader. He pictured himself walking along a row of soldiers, shaking hands like General Patton. He saw all the soldiers, in their uniforms, dirty from war, gathering around him. *Men,* he said in his mind, *it gives me great pleasure to—*

"Do me a favor," said Willard, interrupting his daydreams. "Go check on that food."

The kitchen was on the ground floor of the other cinder block building, which they called South House. When Nelson got there, he found Rhonda and one of her women looking down into a huge pot of chili. Nelson had built the kitchen. He learned how to do that in the army. He was proud of it, too. The stove had enough cooking power to feed a few hundred men. Two large industrial refrigerators stood on one wall. Next to them were two additional freezers. On the stove, nestled inside a cooking cradle, was a fifteen-gallon pot. Right next to the burners was an extra-large gridle. Nelson looked at it now.

The splash guard was leaning, and he gave it a little wiggle. Under the gridle was a grease trap. He pulled it out and checked that, too.

"If you wanna cook, then come in and cook," said Rhonda. She was a heavyset lady in her fifties. She'd served time for drugs. She was a good cook, but a nasty woman. The other one helping her was named Joyful. She was much younger, in her twenties. She had a scar on her neck like her throat had been cut at some point. Her face was a little distorted, too, like her mother had been drinking while she carried her. Nelson sometimes fantasized about raping the girl. He'd do it right there in the kitchen. He could tell she wanted it.

"Don't leave all those dishes piled up," said Nelson, pointing at the sink.

"We're not," said Rhonda.

Nelson walked back outside and jumped on his four-wheeler. He rode it down the small dirt road, over to what they called the Dig Site. The Dig Site was where they were going to make their new dorm, a low-slung building that eventually was going to sleep forty men.

Nelson expected to find a bunch of guys down there working. He was shocked to find only one, Tall John, who was just sitting on a tractor doing nothing at all.

"Where the hell is everyone?" asked Nelson.

"They went to go get more cement."

"Why?"

"We need it."

"Why'd they all go?"

"It's just J. D. and Relly."

"There's only three of you?" asked Nelson. "Where's everyone else?"

"Mr. Haggerty sent Thomas and them to fix the roof on the cow shed."

Nelson turned and looked toward the cow shed, but he couldn't see it from where he was. "Y'all are crossing too many signals," said Nelson.

"I agree," said Tall John. "I tried to tell them that."

Nelson shook his head and rode the quad back toward the main compound. He thought about going to the cow shed and bitching the men out, but he'd had enough arguing for the moment. Instead, he decided to go to the kennel to check on the dogs. The kennel had been set up in an old barn made of dark wood. It was about a quarter mile from the main compound. They'd put cages into the stalls, cement floors, built them out and everything. The dogs were kept in there.

Bill Sorrentino was out there tending to them. At sixty, Bill was older than everyone else in the camp except for Willard. He had a similar vibe to Rhonda's, grumpy all the time. His face looked sour, and his muscles and skin hung from his bones. The dogs barked loudly when they heard Nelson riding up but quieted down when he got off the four-wheeler.

"How are they?" asked Nelson.

"Everyone's good," said Bill, nodding toward the cages. "Tricky bit Martha, though. Got her on the neck."

"God damn it," said Nelson. He looked down at the ground and saw an old, sun-bleached candy wrapper. He felt anger overtaking him. A little switch flipped. He walked toward the cages and grabbed the poke stick that lay near the front. The poke stick was a broom handle that had been whittled down to a point. All the dogs started barking again.

Nelson walked down the row of cages. The place smelled noxious, like shit and piss. He stopped at Martha's cage. She got up when he arrived. She was a brown girl with a white belly and snout. She put her nose near the cage; Nelson put his hand down there and she sniffed him. He bent down, pushed her head to the side, and looked at her through the bars. Her neck was cut. It looked like Bill had treated it with Neosporin.

They kept Tricky at the end of the line. He was a mixed Staffordshire Bull Terrier, gray and wide-bodied. He gave more trouble than any of the other dogs. Nelson, hot with anger, walked to his cage, bent down, and looked into it. Tricky was already up and staring at him, a defiant look in his eyes. He was rocking back and forth like he wanted to play.

Nelson took the stick and stuck the dog hard in the shoulder. Tricky yelped and bashed himself against the far side of the cage.

"You gonna bite her?" yelled Nelson. He jabbed at the dog again. He knew he shouldn't be doing this, knew it wasn't right, but he couldn't help himself. He jabbed at Tricky again and again. The dogs nearby rioted in their cages. "You gonna bite her?" Nelson yelled, spit flying from his mouth. "You gonna bite Martha?" He poked the dog a few more times, saw some blood, and then realized that Bill Sorrentino was standing behind him saying "Alright, alright" like he wanted him to stop.

Jerry woke in his cell convinced he was in his mother's basement. Even with his eyes open, it took a second to understand where he was. Then he heard his cellmate snoring and the sound of a lightbulb buzzing. He tried to force himself back to sleep but couldn't do it.

After breakfast, down on the main floor of the pod, he was allowed to make a phone call and he dialed his lawyer's desk number. He was surprised when she answered and even more surprised when she told him the good news: Sam and Helen would be bailing him out. He should be released in the next few days. If he wasn't, he should call back. Then she ended the call.

Jerry looked around the pod. He felt like he was high on speed. On the way back to the center tables, he passed a guy called Tall Clarence, who was vocally born-again. "Praise the Lord," said Jerry.

"Praise Jesus. Yes, sir," said Tall Clarence, bumping elbows with him.

Suddenly, all the men in the pod didn't look as mean as they had. In fact, Jerry had a moment in which he anticipated missing these men.

"Getting bailed out," he said to his cellmate, sitting down next to him at one of the tables.

Hopper turned his head and appraised him. "Is that right?" The big man's face didn't look happy, though; it looked skeptical.

"My girl's gonna put it up," said Jerry.

"Okay," said Hopper. "Congratulations."

Jerry stared at the chess markings on the table and fantasized about attending college. He'd be in San Diego, studying programming. Fuck all this.

There was an older man in the pod with them, a skinny white guy who held himself with straight posture and stayed aloof from everyone else. Jerry, in his mind, called him the Professor. It was unclear what he'd been charged with, but nobody messed with him, and he seemed to garner a level of respect. He approached Jerry after lunch. They were at the foot of the same stairway where Jerry had been hit with the feces. The man motioned with his finger for Jerry to come to him. "I knew a kid just like you in Wyoming," said the Professor. "I worked oil rigs back then."

Jerry, feeling confused, leaned back. But the Professor stepped closer. "Converse County," he said. "You ever been there?"

Jerry shook his head and looked around the room to see if anybody was watching him. Nobody appeared to be.

"Carried himself like you. Same face, too. You believe in reincarnation?"

Jerry felt himself becoming uneasy. He didn't know what this man was rambling about, and he didn't want any trouble, but the man had cornered him. From up close, his eyes looked wild, like the eyes of a person desperate for water.

"He got pushed off the back of a truck," said the Professor. "On the highway. Hit his head on the concrete." The man tapped the back of his head, then turned so his gaze was directed right at Jerry. "Life is strange," said the Professor. "You never know which way . . ."

Jerry waited for him to finish, but he didn't. He just shook his head and then walked to his cell, which was on the ground floor.

Jerry walked straight to the guard area. "Any court calls?" he asked.

"Not today," said the guard at the booth. "Not for you."

Behind him, two inmates were arguing. One of them was yelling "You ain't a Crip" at the other.

"Stand back from me," said the one being yelled at. "Go on!"

Jerry looked back toward where the Professor had gone, and he saw him standing outside his cell looking at something on the ground. His lips were moving, like he was still talking.

First night back, the agents texted Bunny and told him to wait for them in the park. Sunburnt and exhausted, he hurried outside. A half hour passed and they still hadn't picked him up. It was almost midnight. The area was deserted of people. The houses looked cold and lonely. Dry wind blew through the park.

Finally, a car pulled up. It was different from the SUVs he'd previously been in. This one was a gray sedan; its headlights were yellow. The windows were darkened. Bunny, with his shoulders stooped, walked to it like a scared cowboy.

The front door popped open, and Bunny leaned his head in. He became a little wary when he found Gana in there alone. It didn't feel right to meet one-on-one.

"There he is," said Gana.

Bunny smelled alcohol on the agent's breath. The smell made Bunny think of his mother. He pictured her fussing around while he pulled his seatbelt on.

"You did it," said the cop. "You made it out. Congratulations."

"Where's your other guy?"

"Look at you," said Gana. "You're a little detective, aren't you?"

"I'm working on it," said Bunny. "If you'll teach me."

Gana put the car in drive, and they started to move. "It's gonna be me and you," said the cop.

They drove past an old man wearing dirty clothes. He stood almost in traffic, talking to himself, and pointing at something on the ground that didn't appear to be there, perhaps a snowman, or a dog. Bunny bit his lip, crossed his arms, and watched the man.

"Tell me everything," said Gana. "Go on. Tell it in the order it happened."

Bunny told him the story. He described Willard picking him up, talked about the wife. He told him about Nelson and the intake interview.

Gana nodded at the part about Nelson in a way that made Bunny think he must've been familiar with the man. Like he was already a target.

They looped around to Harrison Street next to Vazquez Boulevard, and when Bunny told him about the three men he worked with, the agent pulled over next to a dark storage lot, killed the engine, took out a notepad, and wrote down Bunny's descriptions.

Then Gana pulled some printed satellite images from a file and made Bunny point out the building where Nelson talked to him. Gana used his phone to light the paper. It took Bunny a moment to sort it out, but then he pointed at the biggest building and said, "It's right there, I think. That one." He tapped the paper. "They call that the Big House."

While Gana jotted down some other notes, Bunny thought about Willard. His uncle had given him a strange look when they'd said their goodbyes. Bunny, at the bus stop, was just about to hop out of the truck. Willard said something like "It's a pleasure to have you here." And Bunny, trying to joke, said, "Next time, you could shovel with us." A look came into Willard's eyes. It looked like he wanted to cut Bunny's throat. It looked like he was ready to do it right then.

An older memory followed right behind that one: Bunny had been at a party in high school, at a place way out in the desert, at a trailhead near Redlands. Dirt and stars. Someone had brought Bunny to Frazier. His cousin appeared to be passed out drunk on the ground. Bunny bent down to look in the boy's face. Frazier's eyes were open, and he was both there and not there at the same time. And now he was dead.

"Wake up, Bunny," said Gana.

"I am awake," said Bunny.

"You look all goo-goo gah-gah," said Gana.

"I'm tired."

"Next order of business. We need you to try and map out the place, a little more detailed. Mainly on where your uncle keeps his office, where he keeps his records. You know what I'm saying?"

"Yeah," said Bunny.

"Take some pictures with your phone."

"You think that's a good idea?"

"That's gonna be top of the mark for you."

"Mm-hmm."

"Don't say *mm-hmm*. Say, *Yes, sir.*"

"Yes, sir."

The lights from the cars on Vazquez Boulevard passed over Gana's face. It made him look ghoulish. Bunny looked away and stared down at his own knees.

"Bunny," said Gana. They sat in silence for a long moment.

"I understand," said Bunny.

"I don't know if you do," said Gana. "I'm gonna say this because we're alone right now. This ain't gonna work if we don't trust each other." He dropped his voice. "My partner's gonna want to end this arrangement at your first screwup. He told me that. He said, *I hope he does give us an excuse.*" Gana put his pen on his lap and scratched his scalp with both hands. "He thinks you're a drug addict. Thinks you're not gonna be straight with us. That your loyalties are gonna lie with your family. I told him, *Nah, Bunny's gonna do what's right.*" Gana reached out, put a hand on Bunny's shoulder.

"I don't know what to say to that," said Bunny.

"Say *thank you*," said Gana, giving Bunny's shoulder a squeeze.

Bunny took a moment and stared at the passing cars. The anger he felt in his belly spread out through his body. "I've been doing everything you wanted," Bunny said. "You ask me to do something, I do it. So tell your partner if he wants to send me back, quit talking about it and just do it."

"Damn, Bunny. That's the spirit. That's what I'm talking about right there." Gana turned the key in the ignition, revved the engine, and looked at Bunny with a little smile that seemed more antagonizing than friendly. "You're a fucking G, man." Then they pulled out of the parking lot, and they rode in silence back toward Bunny's house.

"I'd buy you a beer, but I got a girl waiting for me at the bar," said Gana.

"Next time," said Bunny.

When Bunny got back to the trailer, he took out the little notebook he'd bought at the drugstore and made his first entry. He wrote the date, and that he was digging sand with the three dudes. Next to that, he wrote: *Gana*.

Uncle Rayton was already in bed, sleeping and snoring. Bunny lay down on the couch, put his hands behind his head, and stared up at the ceiling. First day in the field.

When they finally called Jerry to court, he found a different public defender standing in for his own. This one was older, a little frumpy in her clothes, but she had a no-nonsense attitude that Jerry found reassuring. April Costa-Tenge, he was told, was in the middle of a trial. The new lawyer talked to the judge, and the judge said Jerry had been bonded out. After answering a series of questions, Jerry was told when his next court date was. Then the judge moved on to the next case.

From the courtroom, the guards brought Jerry back to the first jail he'd been at. He half expected to find Janko waiting for him. Instead, they escorted him directly to processing, where he had to sign some documents. A deputy handed him a trash bag filled with the clothes he'd been wearing: a sweatshirt, some underwear, a pair of shorts, and some running shoes. He'd been in such a rush, there weren't even any socks. There was some confusion over his phone, but in the end, it was determined that no phone had been processed. Jerry changed his clothes behind a temporary, folding screen. He was instructed to throw his dirty jail suit into a large hamper.

They led him through a series of locked doors and released him onto the civilian side. Outside, when he finally looked at the blue sky and mountains, he felt a little happy and a little angry, all of it mixed up. "Shit," he said to himself. "Fresh air."

With no money to call his mother, he started walking down Colfax, headed toward a friend's house. He'd ask for a ride, go home, shower, get sorted out. Eat some food. Relax, get his life back on track. It was time to be better. While he walked, he fantasized about Helen, saw himself with her in her office clothes.

Near the end of the block, a homeless man stepped in front of him and interrupted his romantic daydreaming. "Got a dollar?" the man asked. His hair was matted, and his teeth were stained dark brown.

Jerry pointed back toward the jail and said, "I just got out."

"Got a nickel?"

"Come on, man, gimme a break," said Jerry, walking past him.

The friend whose house he was walking to was named Angel. He was one of Jerry's customers. He bought a lot of acid on a regular basis. He lived in a brick apartment building on Humboldt Street, just off East Colfax. He lived closer to the jail than anyone else Jerry could think of.

At the building, Jerry realized he didn't know which apartment the man lived in. He always just picked him up on the street. He stood there for a second, not knowing what to do. Then a woman walked out the front door. Jerry asked her if she knew where Angel lived, and without even questioning him, she said he lived right above her in apartment 312. She even held the door open for Jerry and smiled at him.

He took the stairs two at a time to the third floor. It felt suddenly like everything was getting sorted out. Like he'd been stuck in an astrological rough patch and was only coming out the other side just then. Like his stars were finally aligning. Things were looking up.

He walked down the hall searching for 312. He felt a little nervous; it seemed strange to stop by unannounced. He could hear noise coming from the apartment, so he put his ear to the door and recognized the sound of a television playing; then he heard a kind of muffled laugh. Jerry knocked on the door.

The room inside went totally silent, TV and everything. Jerry stepped back and brushed his hair with his hand. There was a peephole on the door, and it went dark, so Jerry waved a little hello.

The door opened and Jerry found himself facing a tall, skinny, pale, blond-haired dude with eyeliner on. He wore some tighty-whities and nothing else. A chemical smell came wafting out of the apartment.

"Is Angel here?" asked Jerry.

"Babe! Someone's here for you!" said the man, speaking over his shoulder.

A second later, Angel appeared, also wearing his underwear, but with the addition of a T-shirt. He looked panic-stricken, and it took him a second to recognize Jerry; when he did his face shifted into a smile. "Oh my God! It's Jer-Bear LeClair! Come in!"

He held the door open, and Jerry stepped in and saw another shirtless man in his underwear sitting on the couch. This guy had brown hair on his head and acne on his chest, and both of his ears were pierced.

Angel introduced him to the two men. The man who'd opened the door was called Rascal, and the one on the couch was Curtis.

Jerry—with his hand on his head like he had a headache—explained his situation. He said he just got out of jail, and he needed a ride home to Arvada. He shook his head. "Don't have my phone, or wallet."

"Yeah, okay," said Angel. "First sit down, take your shoes off, and smoke some of this coke." He pointed at the coffee table.

Jerry slipped his shoes off, put them on the mat. He looked at the table and saw a little pile of yellowish-brown crack rocks. He immediately started sweating and rubbed his face. This was not in his plans. But he needed a ride, and it did feel like an appropriate way to say *fuck you* to the police and the jail and everyone else on this planet. He sat down on the couch.

Rascal loaded the glass pipe with a fresh rock and passed it over. Jerry told himself, *Nah, you're not doing this*, but he held the pipe to his lips and Rascal used a butane lighter and lit it for him. Jerry heard the crack sizzle, and he sucked the smoke in.

He took a few hits from the pipe and then felt suddenly and entirely focused. Like he'd had his head underwater and now it was out. After passing the pipe back to Rascal, he told the three men, speaking in a monotone, about how he'd ended up in jail.

"Is your buddy still in?" asked Angel.

"Nah, he got out," said Jerry.

"He's snitching," said Rascal, shaking his head. "Nobody gets out. Trust me, I'm a paralegal. Also, I served time in Utah. Nobody gets out. People snitch, and *then* they get out. That's how it works."

Jerry looked at the television, which was muted. On the screen, a home video of a man jumping off his roof onto a trampoline played. Jerry turned his eyes away before the inevitable injury.

"He'll testify against you," said Rascal.

Jerry looked at Angel, who pointed at Rascal and mouthed, *He knows.*

"You have to understand, these things are matrices of opposing forces," said Rascal. "They want to convince him to snitch. It's your job to convince him not to." He raised his eyebrows and tilted his head like: *You understand?*

They spent the next forty-five minutes smoking crack, and then Angel became all business and got his two friends to put their clothes back on and said they were going to drive Jerry home.

Staggering outside into the bright sunlight, they piled into Angel's car. Jerry sat in the back with Curtis. There was a Bible on the floor, and Jerry picked it up. Angel saw him looking at it and said, "We all go to church. You should come with us sometime. It's chill."

"Okay," said Jerry. He handed the Bible to Curtis, who began flipping through it like he needed to find a specific passage.

Angel started the car and the stereo played house music. A woman sang: "Let yourself be free." Angel checked his reflection in the mirror, rubbed at the corners of his mouth, and then pulled out of his spot and turned left onto East Colfax. Jerry, meanwhile, stared out the window and prayed his mother wouldn't be home when he got there.

"Here we go," said Curtis, reading from the Bible. "First Corinthians, fifteen thirty-three: *Be not deceived: evil communications corrupt good manners.* See?" He leaned forward and stared at Jerry with a maniacal look in his eyes. "No snitching."

They drove Jerry to Arvada; Angel and his friends talked over each other the entire time.

When they arrived, they all got out of the car, and for a second Jerry was scared they were going to try to come inside. Instead, they gathered around him like they were consoling a friend who'd just received horrible news. Then they hugged him and got back in their car and left.

Jerry turned toward his mother's house and gazed at it. Anxiety and guilt pushed down on him, and the grandiosity and power that came from the crack pushed up on him. There were no cars in the driveway. He was still high, but he felt a little sick to his stomach. He walked to the side of the house and found the fake rock that held a spare key. Then he went inside.

❧

The dude with the spiderweb tattoos was supposed to give Bunny a ride back to the ranch. His name, appropriately enough, was Spider. He lived in Five Points, on Champa Street, so Bunny had to take an early bus to meet him. His house was a one-story brick bungalow, but Bunny didn't go inside because Spider was already sitting in his car with the engine running.

"You're early," said Spider, talking through his open window.

"I know," said Bunny, shrugging and shaking his head.

Spider nodded him in, and Bunny got into the front seat.

"Bunny and Spider," said Spider.

"I was thinking the same thing on the way here," said Bunny.

"We could be in a movie," said Spider. He turned and looked at Bunny. "You need coffee or anything?"

Bunny told him he was good, and they set out toward Castle Rock. They rode in silence for a minute, then Bunny asked Spider how he'd hooked up with Willard.

"I met Nelson online," said Spider. "On Facebook. He introduced me to Mr. Haggerty."

Bunny nodded.

"How'd you meet him?" asked Spider.

"He's my uncle," said Bunny.

"Mr. Haggerty?"

"Yeah."

"No shit?"

"Family," said Bunny. "My mother's brother, yep."

"Damn," said Spider.

Bunny noticed the man sit up a little straighter; he put both hands on the steering wheel like he realized he had a VIP in the car. "Yeah," said Bunny. He couldn't help himself. "Uncle Willard."

"Is your mother involved?" asked Spider.

Bunny didn't know exactly what he meant by that. "No, not really. She's just up there in Grand Junction."

"She must be proud of you, though."

Bunny shrugged. When he was eight years old, Bunny had walked into his mom's room looking for some dinner and found her passed out on pills. She wouldn't wake up. That was shortly after his father had disappeared from their lives. Bunny ran and got a neighbor lady, who slapped his mother hard in the face, shook her violently, and then dragged her to the bathroom, rolled her into the tub, and turned the cold shower on. It was a horrible memory. He wished he didn't have those kinds of thoughts. He had to stare out at the road and force himself to think about other things.

When they finally got to the ranch, they texted Willard and waited for him to unlock the gate. Bunny and Spider both got out of the car and shielded their eyes from the sun with their hands. "We should've texted him about ten minutes ago," said Spider.

Bunny nodded and then found a little piece of broken concrete on the ground; he threw it at a fence post but missed. A few minutes later, Willard pulled up in his truck. He hopped out and walked to the gate. He wore a wool sweater, and his face, to Bunny, looked preoccupied.

"Give me a key next time, I'll open it," said Bunny.

"I will," said Willard. "We'll get you a copy."

Bunny jumped into Willard's truck and Spider followed them in his own car and they drove down to the compound. When they were rolling, Willard turned to Bunny and, with his gravelly voice, said, "We used to hunt elk out at White River."

"Yeah, I remember that," said Bunny.

"Bowhunting," said Willard. "You ever come with us on any of those?"

Bunny shook his head.

"You should've."

"I wish I had," said Bunny.

At the compound, after parking, Willard walked Bunny around to the back of the Big House. There were a few scattered groups of men working on projects here and there. At a truck, two men stood unloading tools. Willard brought Bunny to them. One of them was the man with the hairy back from last time. His name was Arnold D.

The other man had short brown hair; he wore jeans and a dirty, threadbare T-shirt. He wasn't tall, or big, but he had a mean face and looked like an ex-con. This was the first time Bunny saw him. "That's Hostetler," said Willard, pointing at the man. "This is Bunny Simpson."

Hostetler nodded at Bunny, then turned and looked out toward the plains like someone out there had called his name. Bunny watched the man. He seemed a little off in the head.

They worked through the morning, digging a trench for a septic system that had to go in behind one of the smaller buildings. Willard set them up, gave them instructions on where to dig, and then he disappeared back into the main building.

The work was difficult, it was hot in the sun, and the ground they dug was rocky and dry.

Bunny wished he'd worn shorts instead of jeans. He cursed the cops for getting him involved in this. He cursed Willard, too. Cursed his mother, while he was at it, for bringing him into this family, into this world.

At lunch, Willard's wife served them each two tuna fish sandwiches wrapped in paper towels. That seemed to be part of the deal in working out there: lunch was free. She gave each man a cold can of Coca-Cola, touched Bunny's fingers when she did that, and gave him a little smile. Nothing else noteworthy happened all the way through lunch. And then all hell broke loose.

It started as an issue between Spider and Hostetler. Hostetler had been picking on the man all morning, saying he was a pussy, this and that. Spider, for the most part, took it, and didn't say anything back.

After lunch, Spider was sitting in the shade of a truck. Hostetler tried to tell him to get up. Spider ignored him, and Hostetler spoke down at him: "Get the fuck up."

Spider told him to fuck off and Hostetler lifted his boot and stomped down on Spider's bald head, catching him hard on the side of his skull. It made a hollow *thunk* noise. It was a vicious attack, and shocked Bunny right to wide awake.

Bunny reacted without thinking. He grabbed Hostetler from behind and lifted him and flung him away; the man lost his footing and fell on his backside. There was a long moment where Hostetler sat still like he hadn't decided what he was going to do yet. Then he started to get up.

Bunny heard hollering coming from the main building. His eyes stayed on Hostetler, who was up now and moving toward him, his head going side to side like a snake's. Bunny gestured with his left hand, like *Chill.* But the dude didn't want to chill; he raised his fists up near his chin.

Time slowed down: Hostetler sent a fist toward Bunny's face and Bunny slipped to the left and the fist went sailing by. Right after that, Bunny got caught between the lip and nose and he felt his head snap back and he saw black for a second and he tripped backward but he kept his feet under him. Hostetler came thrashing toward him again and Bunny's fist smashed into the man's face. Hatred boiled up in Bunny's body, in his chest and face and back and arms, and he felt himself growling and his hands started flying and he was stepping and punching, and the blows were landing. Finally, Hostetler crumpled down on his butt and then lay down on his side, covering his head with his arms. Bunny whipped around, looking to see if anyone else wanted to test him. Spider was on his knees by then, rubbing his head where he'd been kicked. The hairy guy, Arnold D, looked at Bunny with a scared expression on his face and began cleaning up the lunch stuff.

Bunny turned toward the main building and saw Nelson and Willard walking fast toward them. Willard's wife stood on the stairs. A handful of other men were looking on, too. Bunny looked back at Hostetler, and saw that he'd turned himself forward, so he was on his hands and knees. Bunny looked down at his own hands and saw a little blood on his right knuckle. It scared him and he felt the world squeeze in on him and he wiped the blood on his pants.

"What happened?" yelled Nelson.

"He kicked him in the head, and I didn't like it," said Bunny, speaking down toward the ground.

Hostetler, by then, had repositioned himself again and now sat on his butt, holding his knees with his hands. His nose and mouth and chin were covered in dark red blood. He dabbed at it with his hand and looked at his fingers. Tasted it on his lips.

Bunny watched as Nelson went to Hostetler. "We don't fight!" he yelled. "Get up!" Hostetler, a little wobbly, pushed himself up. Nelson took the bottom of Hostetler's shirt and wiped his face with it. "This ain't a fucking prison farm. You're not a bunch of coons." He turned and looked at Bunny. His face looked enraged. "You understand?"

Bunny nodded.

Willard walked to Hostetler. "Come with us," he said.

Willard and Nelson led Hostetler toward the main building. Bunny, Spider, and Arnold D all watched them go; then they returned to work. They started digging again. Bunny felt sick from the violence. He felt weak digging the dirt. He wanted to leave. He didn't want to be around this place anymore.

About fifteen minutes after they went back to work, they heard a gunshot. All three of the men turned and looked toward the sound. They couldn't see anything, but a moment later they heard a second shot. "Jesus," said Bunny. "What the fuck is that?"

They never saw Hostetler again, and at the end of the day, Willard, looking stone-faced, told the men, "We need discipline above all else. This is not a place for unorganized men. This is a place for Christians. Do we understand each other?"

After that, another two weeks passed without incident. There was a lot of digging, a lot of waiting, a lot of cleaning of the property, but nothing else noteworthy. Then, one morning, Bunny ran into his uncle near the garage where most of the tools were kept.

"We gonna have some campers here today," said Willard. He was wearing a Stetson and he took it off and wiped his hairline with the back of his hand.

"Kids?" asked Bunny, confused.

Willard turned toward him, smiled. "Some of them are young."

"You gonna bring out your horses?" asked Bunny.

"That would be nice," said Willard. "Horse camp. No, Bunny, these men are training self-defense."

"Shit, okay," said Bunny.

"Patriotic, God-fearing young men," said Willard.

"That's wassup," said Bunny.

"Willing to protect our country."

"America," said Bunny.

"You willing to fight for it?"

"Like join the army?"

"Join *our* army?"

"Long as I don't gotta hurt nobody," said Bunny.

Willard chuckled like Bunny had told a funny joke. Then he said, "Good boy."

Bunny, feeling uneasy, walked back to meet the other men.

They worked all morning. In the afternoon, Bunny heard what he thought was a truck pulling up, and he excused himself to take a piss. The truck was actually a van—clean, new, and white. Bunny, peeing, watched it park in front of one of the smaller buildings across the way from him.

Finished, he walked over to see what was going on. By then, some men had gotten out.

Bunny counted seven of them. Nelson and Willard were standing there, too, but they had their backs to Bunny. Willard's wife stood off to the side; she had a camera in her hand, but she wasn't taking any pictures.

Bunny was confused by what he saw. The men who'd gotten out of the van all looked weird. That was the only way he could describe them. They looked young, too. All of them looked like they hadn't seen the sun for months. One of them returned Bunny's gaze, but the rest just stared down at the ground. The one that was looking at Bunny had thin blond hair in a swoop, combed over to one side. He was tall and thin.

"Bunny's welcome here," said Willard, apparently responding to something Nelson had said. Willard pointed to one of the men from the van. He was stouter than the others, older too. "This is General Dearing," he said. "General, this is my nephew, Bunny Simpson."

"Son," said Dearing, stepping forward and looking at Bunny.

The man was ugly. He had a huge head, a soft chin, and beady little eyes. The skin around his nose was red. His clothes—he wore tan pants and a blue button-up shirt—were clean and pressed. General Dearing lifted his hand and Bunny, tongue-tied, shook it.

Bunny's eyes went to the boys behind Dearing. They were all watching Bunny now, frowning and staring at him. For a second, Bunny wondered whether they were foreign. They seemed different like that. They didn't appear to be hardened, like the other men that Bunny had met at the ranch. They seemed like they might live with their mothers or something.

About an hour later, things took another ominous turn. Bunny had returned to his digging, but the other men were taking a break. They were standing around, drinking water and wiping their hands on their pants. Suddenly, a loud *boom* sounded. It was followed by a series of *booms*. It was clearly the sound of a large gun being fired.

Bunny looked at Arnold D. The man had a creepy smile on his face. "That's an AR," he said.

"Who's shooting?" asked Bunny.

"Them boys that came," said Arnold D. He looked back toward the big building, then looked at Bunny. "Making sure their tactical is up to snuff."

In the background: *Boom-boom-boom-boom-boom.*

Bunny, feeling nervous, didn't say anything.

"What'd you think we were gonna be doing out here?" Arnold D asked.

"I don't know," said Bunny. He felt a few of the men staring at him. "I know I'd rather be shooting guns than digging ditches, though."

"You wanna join them boys," said Arnold D, squinting over toward the gunshots, "all you gotta do is volunteer."

They were all silent for a moment, listening to the sound of the guns. Then they went back to their digging. The shooting, with breaks here and there, continued all day. Sometimes more than one gun. Sometimes more than two.

The tall, thin kid with the blond hair who'd been staring at Bunny was named George Milbier. He was nineteen years old. He'd grown up in Lakewood, just outside of Denver. His parents were both alive and still lived together. His father worked as a mechanical design engineer; he'd been at the same firm his entire career. His mother was a homemaker. George had two older sisters. Both lived in California; the younger one was in still in college, the older one had graduated.

George never fit in with his classmates. His childhood and teen years could best be defined by a sense of otherness. He wasn't athletic, artistic, or academic. He wasn't a bad kid, either; at least, not in the traditional sense. He just struggled to make friends. He was a lonely kid.

Once, during gym class in seventh grade, he tried to talk to a female classmate. He'd practiced what he was going to say. They were playing volleyball. George was in the front row, near the net. He turned and, feeling like he was levitating, spoke to a girl behind him. "You know," he said, reciting his lines, "volleyball was invented in Massachusetts." The girl's face looked confused, like she didn't understand why he was speaking to her. He continued, "They used to call it Mintonette—" But right as that word left his mouth, he felt his pants and underwear get yanked down to his ankles. A boy from the other team had ducked under the net. George, horrified, pulled his pants up and ran to the locker room. He hid in a toilet stall and cried.

That same week, he started sneaking into his parents' room and masturbating onto his mother's pillow. He didn't know why he was compelled to do that, and he became overcome with shame after each incident. But he didn't stop. His feeling of isolation continued to grow. He started peeping in windows when he was fourteen. He'd wait until dusk and then he'd go walk around near Kendrick Lake. There were a few houses in the area with their gates set far enough back to allow him to creep between homes without being seen from the street. He learned that if he wore dark clothes and stood perfectly still, nobody would notice him. He could look right in and watch a family get ready for dinner. He'd mainly watch the wives, but really, anybody could keep his attention. He'd only masturbate if he was given reason to, like the time he saw one mother watching TV wearing nothing but a towel. There was the time he saw a woman exercising, and there was the time he saw the same woman sweeping her floor.

On one occasion, while standing between houses looking in on an empty room, he was discovered by a neighbor. The gate to his left just popped open, there was no crunching of gravel, no warning, and George found himself face-to-face with a tired-looking man. He ran. There'd been a horse trailer in the driveway of the house, and he almost fell avoiding it on his way out. When he got home, his mother seemed to sense something was wrong. She asked him where he'd been. "I was at Cody's," he told her. Her face looked angry, though, hateful. He went to his room and quietly closed his door.

It was around that same period that he got involved in the online world. He'd never been comfortable with social media, but Reddit, after a while, started to feel like a place he could fit in. He started lurking on subreddits about weapons, about anime, and then he found one called r/incels, where guys talked in a way he hadn't heard before. They talked honestly about what losers they were, how ugly they were. How women hated them, and how they hated women. Women, they said, were evil. They needed to be raped. He couldn't believe people were talking like this. He loved it.

From there, he jumped over to 4chan, where the hatred was more explicit. He found /r9k/. This was harder stuff, real stuff. Funny stuff. Soon, he found another board, /pol/. This one wasn't just about women; it was the blacks, the Jews, the Mexicans, the Arabs, the faggots. They were all ruining America. George didn't post anything at first. He just lurked. But after a few months he started posting little memes he'd make. Pictures of women with black eyes. Pictures of black men in handcuffs, with little funny messages on top: *Talked back once. Put this gorilla back in his cage. Another customer for the cock carousel.* People started liking his posts. They were getting a response. People were replying. He had his own style.

Soon, he was on Discord, spending all night in chat rooms, talking to other trolls like him. He was making a name for himself. He'd play video games with them, but that wasn't why he was there. He was there for the community. People would spend all day in these groups. Guys would sleep with their cameras on themselves while they slept. George loved it.

Eventually, one of the boys, a kid called smallhands, told him he should meet this dude that lived near Denver. "Small," as George called him, said that the guy's name was General Dearing, and that General Dearing was looking for men like him. Smallhands invited George to a Telegram group and introduced him to the general.

George began chatting one-on-one with General Dearing, daily. The general, clearly, was a man of great importance. He wasn't, it turned out, in fact a general, but he'd been in the actual military. He knew all kinds of things about the world. He'd listen to George, and when George would talk about all the hatred he was feeling, all the hatred for the bitches, the whores, the Jews, the blacks, the fags, General Dearing would validate all of it. He'd hear him, and he'd tell him he was exactly right. And then one day, he said they should meet. George, feeling excitement in his belly, the kind of excitement he hadn't felt before, sat there in the dark, looking at his screen. "We should meet," the general wrote. The general kept typing, and after a moment, a new message popped up on George's screen: *I can come to you.*

"Y'all are saying, *Where's this? Where's that?*" said Bunny. "I'm saying they're shooting guns, man. ARs all day long, and you want me to sketch a map for you?"

The agents had picked Bunny up and brought him out to a trailhead at the Rocky Mountain Arsenal, a deserted old open space not far from Rayton's trailer. It was nighttime, and Bunny stood with the agents at the back of the car, so they could all look at pictures together. Agent

Howley had his flashlight turned on some maps on the trunk. It was a little chilly, and Bunny did not want to be there.

"Bunny," said Howley. "Relax."

"It's been over two weeks since the dude got shot, and y'all are sitting on your hands. Sitting in your offices, as far as I can tell."

"You heard shots. You didn't see anyone get shot. You didn't see a body. It sounds like nobody started acting different. We wrote it up, Bunny," said Howley. "Briefed it up the chain, the damn US attorney's gonna hear that one."

"And now these kids are out there, shooting all day long," said Bunny. "And you don't care about that."

"We're not diminishing that," said Howley. "This is what the case is about. We're here working it, man. We're gonna get into all of that."

"Bunny," said Gana, clearing his throat, "the case we're building and what we signed you up to help with . . . this is a paper case. This is about an *enterprise*. We need to show the inner workings of your uncle's group. I'm being real with you. I'm trying to help you out. That's what's gonna help us."

"And that's what's gonna help you," said Howley.

"Paperwork?" said Bunny.

"Documents," said Howley. "Have you made any progress on that? Have you found your uncle's office?"

Bunny felt himself deflate. He looked out toward the dark plains. His mouth went dry. These two cops clearly did not understand what was happening out there in Castle Rock. "What do you want me to say to the guy? *Where's your office? I want to root around in your paperwork?*"

Howley appeared to get a text message right then. He took out his phone and responded. Bunny looked at Gana. The man had closed his eyes and appeared to be doing some kind of breathing exercise, like he was trying to calm down.

"Do you like sports, Bunny?" asked Howley, looking up from his phone.

"I like basketball."

"Okay," said Howley. "It's the fourth quarter and time is running out. You got about four minutes left in the game and you're down by six points. It's time to start pressing. You know what a full-court press is?"

"Yeah."

"You gotta start looking on a full-court press, man. You gotta be pressuring the ball and you gotta get yourself into your uncle's office, find his safe. I'm trying to spell it out for—"

"Get in and do what?" asked Bunny.

They all stood there silently for a moment. On the road, about a hundred yards from them, a semitruck with no trailer drove by.

"I'm gonna read him in," said Howley.

Gana blew air through his lips.

"Your uncle has a ledger," said Howley.

"What the hell is a ledger?"

"A notebook. It's supposed to be a black notebook. Like a fancy black notebook—black leather. He keeps it in a safe. That's what we need you to get, Bunny. That's the name of the game."

"How the hell am I supposed to get that?"

"We can walk you to the finish line, but we can't run the race for you."

Bunny looked at the cop. "I think I need to talk to my lawyer about this."

Agent Gana turned hard on Bunny like he wanted to fight him.

"Hey, hey, hey!" yelled Howley, holding his partner back and standing between them. "Calm down!"

"Talk to your lawyer?" said Gana. "I will murk you." He started trying to get around to Bunny again. "Anything you say or do will be used against you in a court of law," he hissed over Agent Howley's shoulder. "And if we say you're going back, your bitch ass is going back on a one-way ticket to Cañon City." He took a step back and looked at his partner. "Okay," he said to him, like he was saying the storm had passed. He turned back to Bunny, pointed at him, and whispered, "I will fucking murk you, dude, I swear to God."

"Chill out," said Howley. "Calm down."

Bunny didn't say anything.

"So, that's where we are," said Howley, turning all the way back toward Bunny and pointing the light down at his feet. "Black book, or we gonna have to issue a failure-to-cooperate report. Let's go. That's it. We're done."

They drove Bunny back and dropped him off at the park. He watched them drive away and disappear around a corner. Then he took his phone out of his pocket and stopped the recording he'd been making. He scrolled through it and listened to a random part to check the audio quality. "Hey! Hey! Hey!" yelled Howley on the recording, clear as day. "Calm down!" Bunny put the phone back in his pocket. A backup plan for the backup plan.

Jerry spent the first couple of weeks out of jail in a kind of daze. He was anxious, but rather than dealing with anything, he hid out in his basement and played *Call of Duty*. When his mother was out, he'd sneak upstairs and eat food.

On day ten, he started making moves. First, he sold his steroids back to the guy he'd bought them from for twenty-five cents on the dollar. It wasn't good business, but Jerry had no intentions of going back to jail for anything. He sold his personal stash of acid and ketamine to Best Buy Johnny.

"You going clean?" asked Johnny.

"Trying to," said Jerry. "Trying to do the work."

The second thing he had to do was deal with Bunny. He'd been by Bunny's house a few times, knocking on the door. He thought he could hear Bunny's uncle in there watching TV, but the man never answered or called out or anything.

Finally, feeling like enough was enough, Jerry set up shop outside his friend's trailer, sitting on an oil drum in the shadows off to the side, waiting for Bunny to come home.

He'd only been there for about forty minutes when Bunny finally walked up. Jerry hopped off the oil drum.

"Fuck," said Bunny. "You scared the shit out of me."

"Why you so jumpy, man?"

"Look at you, though. Fresh and free." Bunny opened his arms for a hug.

Jerry stepped toward Bunny and gave him a half hug. "We gotta talk, dude," said Jerry.

"Hold on, I'm gonna grab us a couple beers, so we can toast for real." Bunny looked at him, shook his head. "Waiting out here like a damn creeper-peeper."

Bunny got the beers and led his friend back to the park, where they sat on a bench facing the street. They both snapped open a can, wiped their hands on their pants, and sipped from their beers. "Damn," said Bunny, shaking his head. "What a fucking mess we fell into."

They sat for a second. "I'm sorry to do this, but I gotta ask if you're cooperating," said Jerry.

Bunny, his face looking shocked, turned and faced him. "Cooperating?"

Jerry's plan was to go soft at first, get Bunny to confess, and once that was done, he could dissuade him. He whispered, "You can do what you need to do, Bunny, I understand. But I need to know if you're planning on testifying."

"Testifying?" said Bunny. He looked genuinely confused. "For what?"

"Against me, Bunny, if you're gonna testify against me."

"You thought I was snitching on you?"

"You got out fast, man."

Bunny sat there for a second, biting his thumbnail. Then he turned in his seat, making sure nobody was around. "They got me doing something else," he whispered.

"What?"

"They got me working on my uncle."

"Rayton?"

"A different uncle, a blood uncle of mine. They want me to do some shit on him. They got me going over there, like, every freaking day. It's bullshit, man. They got me pulled into a wasp's nest. I'm up about yea high in shit, man, holding a straw for air."

"Damn," said Jerry.

"Yeah," said Bunny. "They were gonna give me twelve years, and my lawyer was like, fucking do it, and truthfully, I kind of low-key hate this uncle anyway. So I was like, *yeah, shit, well, fuck* . . . you know?"

"Damn."

"They're paying me, though, a little bit, so it's all good."

"I wish I had that kind of deal," said Jerry. "You're lucky, man."

"That's what they said, too. I tried to get the same deal for you. They said they couldn't do it because it was me that was family with him."

"I guess that makes sense."

Bunny took a sip of beer, and then his face looked like an idea had occurred to him. "Matter of fact, though," he said, "they had me working this other job first, at a car lot, with this dude. He was paying fifteen an hour. All you gotta do over there is wash the cars and keep the lot clean and all that."

"I do need a job," said Jerry. "I don't like jails. I'm cool with all that. I'm done with the grimy life."

"I'll bring you over there. I don't see a problem with that. Shit, you could become a car salesman, too, if you stick with it. You already have the sales background."

"Shit."

"You do."

They drank from their beers.

"I'm glad to see you out and free," said Bunny. "For real, man, I was worried to hell about you."

Jerry leaned back on the bench. He felt suddenly uplifted. This was why he liked hanging out with Bunny in the first place. The guy always had a can-do attitude. He always had a plan of some kind. Jerry lifted his beer, and they bumped their cans together.

"Thank you, Bunny. I feel better seeing you, I always feel better seeing you, man. Shit, I'm sorry I even entertained those negative thoughts."

"Yeah, man, I'm not gonna snitch." Bunny took a big swig from his beer, licked his lips, stared off into the distance. "Not on you, at least."

⁂

The next day, Jerry cleaned himself up like he was headed on a date. He put on a nice T-shirt and his best jeans, and he slipped his gold chain on over his head and set it outside his shirt.

He went to a flower shop and bought a bouquet of white roses: a peace offering. He spent some good money on them, too. They were high-quality flowers, fresh, with tight buds. The girl selling them smiled when he paid, and Jerry took that as a good sign.

It was still a little early to drop by, so Jerry drove his Blazer around downtown, parked, and watched some TikToks. He smoked a cigarette and stared out at the street. He looked for friendly faces but didn't see anybody he knew.

Then he headed over to Helen's place. Her name was listed on the intercom. Feeling nervous, he buzzed her apartment. She wasn't home, though, so he had to wait in his car and watch her door.

A little over an hour later, he saw Helen walking to the front door of her building. She wore a black sweatsuit and carried two reusable shopping bags filled up with what looked like groceries. *Jesus, help me*, Jerry prayed, taking a deep breath. Then he got out of his car.

"Hey," he yelled, crossing the street.

He held the flowers behind his back, like a surprise. It was a stupid thing to do—she looked scared when she saw him. He showed the flowers and said, "I come in peace."

She still looked uncomfortable.

"I'm sorry," he said. "I'm gonna give you these and then I'm gonna be on my way. I just wanted to say thank you for getting me out. That's all." His heart was pounding in his chest, and he felt strangely defensive.

He stepped closer and held the flowers out to her. After setting her groceries down, she lifted the flowers to her face and smelled them. "Roses," she said, and her face softened a little. "You brought me roses. Look at you."

Her eyes filled up with tears; his did, too. He couldn't help himself. They both stared down at the ground for a second, blinking, and Jerry shifted his weight from foot to foot.

"You want to come up?" she asked. "We could drink a glass of wine."

Inside the apartment, Helen said she had to shower. Jerry looked around her place. It was even nicer than he'd imagined. All the furniture and appliances were new, and the ceilings were high. The floors were shiny. The walls were white, and there were framed pieces of art hanging here and there, candles in candle holders. It was clearly the home of an adult woman, and Jerry, waiting on the couch for her to come back out, felt self-conscious.

Finally, she came back in, wearing jeans and a button-up shirt. She'd put on a little makeup, too, and her hair was wet.

She went to the kitchen and came back with a bottle of white wine and handed Jerry a glass. They touched glasses, and Jerry thought about Bunny for a second, about the toasts they'd made last night.

"You gonna bring flowers to Sam, too?" asked Helen.

"Sam?"

"From the gym. He posted your bond, I just paid for it."

"Shit, I didn't know he did that." Jerry rubbed his forehead.

"We couldn't let you rot away in there," she said.

"I need to ask your advice about something," he said.

She looked at him.

"My case is still going," he said. "They're talking about sending me to prison." They sat there for a second. Jerry's ears began ringing. "I don't know how to ask this."

"What?"

He took a deep breath. "I'm wondering if there is any way to make this thing go away."

She stayed silent.

He continued, "Maybe you could . . ."

"What?"

"Talk to the guy, your ex, the dude? See if he might wanna drop the charges?"

Her face did the opposite of softening; it hardened. She turned her head toward the television, which was off, and sat there staring at it. "Is that why you brought me the roses?"

"I brought those to thank you."

She closed her eyes. "Jesus, Jerry. I don't think you understand what an uncomfortable position this puts me in."

"You know, the first day, when they brought me out to the jail, I came in the pod and one of the guys threw shit on my face. Like actual human shit, right onto my face."

Helen covered her mouth with her hand.

"He did that because my lawyer filed a complaint on one of the guards. The guard had been trying to molest me. There was a guy in there, this motorcycle dude with long hair, like an Aryan dude, that wanted to stomp me out because I made conversation with him. And this was all just at the jail, just normal people. Not prison. This was just the Denver County Jail."

Helen began to sob, and then she crumpled over onto her side and shook and cried into the couch. Jerry had never seen anyone cry like that. He scooted a little closer and put his hand on her back. He could feel her ribs expanding and tightening and he felt uncomfortable and removed his hand. It went on for some time, and then she just lay there breathing.

Finally, she sat up. Her face was covered in snot and tears. The little makeup she'd put on had run down from her eyes. "I'm sorry," she said. "It's my fault. My life is . . . I am a horrible person."

Jerry put his arm around her. She continued crying into his chest and he rubbed her back and looked around her apartment and his eyes settled on the window, and he stared out at the dark blue sky. He certainly hadn't expected any of this to happen.

"Oh God," she said. She got up and walked to the kitchen. He heard her blowing her nose.

When she came back, she went straight for the couch and lay down. She put her head on Jerry's lap. They didn't do anything sexual, though. She just lay there like that and eventually, after a long time, she fell asleep. Jerry got up, put a blanket on her. Then he left quietly and walked back out to his Blazer.

Bunny spent the next three days working at the ranch. He did a lot of digging, but that wasn't the only job that Nelson put him on. He helped clear a build site of rocks. He helped demolish one of the shacks near the main compound. He also spent a few afternoons painting the outside of one of the smaller buildings.

He wasn't, while he worked, overly concerned with the ATF agents, or what they wanted him to do. It felt, to Bunny, like the work *was* the sentence he was serving. Like he was just running down the clock. Like he'd just keep working until they told him to stop or sent him back to jail.

Still, he couldn't help noticing a few things. He saw cars coming and going. One of them was a dark SUV that carried four middle-aged white men. The men parked in front of one of the smaller buildings, and Nelson, who was waiting for them, escorted them in.

There were, Bunny had decided, three types of men who came to the ranch. The first type was a criminal class—these were the guys he worked with, the ex-cons and misfits. Second group was the younger guys, the kids, *the weirdos*, as he'd come to think of them. Bunny didn't know what the hell was going on with them. Finally, there was a third group, a more professional class.

Men like Nelson, older guys. They were more polished. They had military vibes. Truth of the matter was, some of them looked like cops. This group, the four men in the SUV, fit into that last category.

Bunny was painting outside when that group showed up. He stopped painting for a second and just stared at the car. There was a man working with him, a bigger guy, called Victor. Bunny looked at him and said, "What's up with those guys?"

Victor looked toward the SUV, frowned, and then shook his head. "Those are Nelson's friends," he said.

Bunny's eyes went from the SUV to the Big House. Willard's wife was standing there. She was looking right at Bunny, so Bunny gave a little wave. She returned his wave, and then Bunny went back to his painting.

They ended work early that day. Before they left, Nelson had all the men who had been working with Bunny—there were twelve of them—line up in two rows, six across. "In line," said Nelson, motioning them here and there. "In line. Scoot."

Bunny followed along as best he could. He stood behind Tall John and imitated his posture. "We're going to go back to work," said Nelson. "Get in line." He pointed. "There. Step up, straight. We're gonna end each day on a march. Teach y'all some discipline." He looked at Bunny, as if to say, *For you.* "Arm length apart," he said. Bunny followed what Tall John did in front of him and measured out an arm's length to his right.

They spent a long time working on just turning to their left. Nelson would say, "Your left," and the men would all make a quarter turn to their left.

Then they marched around the compound, trying their best to stay in step. Nelson marched with them and kept time by clapping his hands. "On line, march," he'd say. "And left, your left, left, left, left."

Bunny felt a little silly doing it. But there was something gratifying about getting into a rhythm like that.

When they finished, the men drank water, smoked cigarettes, and talked shit to each other. Bunny couldn't help noticing the SUV that the four men had come in was still sitting there, and he wondered if those men had something to do with all this marching.

Bunny, as he always did, caught a ride home with Spider. As soon as they were moving, Bunny took out his cellphone and texted Jerry: *Pick me up at 530.*

Bunny's phone buzzed: *OK.*

"Gotta get my buddy a job," said Bunny.

"Out here?" asked Spider. They were bumping along the dirt road, headed toward the gate.

"Nah," said Bunny. "At a car lot."

They got to the main road and drove in silence for a minute. Then Spider told him a long story about a friend of his who did some bank robberies in Colorado Springs. The man got away with the robberies, and then moved to Texas.

"He was doing it for fun," said Spider.

"You couldn't do that, though," said Bunny.

"Why?"

"All of them face tattoos would get you caught."

"I'd put a mask on."

"You better wear goggles, too," said Bunny, pointing at the cobweb near his eye.

"I got that one in prison."

"I bet you did," said Bunny.

When they got to Bunny's block, Spider stopped in front of the trailer park. He leaned to look and asked which one Bunny stayed at.

"I'm in there," Bunny said, pointing. "You can't see it from here. Just ask someone. Everyone knows where Bunny sleeps."

"Okay," said Spider.

"You want gas money?"

Spider, as he always did, said, "No need for that." And then he took off.

An hour later, showered and wearing fresh clothes, Bunny jumped into Jerry's Blazer. He was shocked to see Jerry sitting there in a T-shirt and jeans.

"You didn't want to put on nicer clothes?" asked Bunny. "A button-up shirt?"

"You didn't tell me to do that," said Jerry, lifting his hands off the steering wheel.

"It's a job interview, you gotta look fresh and tight."

Jerry winced.

"It's okay," said Bunny. "If it doesn't work out, we could always go to the cigarette store. She only pays twelve an hour, but it's under the table."

"Yeah, I don't think twelve's gonna do it for me, though."

"Okay, baller," said Bunny. "You got that two hundred forty dollars for me, then?"

"I'll get it for you," said Jerry.

"I need it," said Bunny. He looked around at the little brick bungalows they passed on Steele Street. "I wanna get out of this place."

"Me too," said Jerry. "San Diego. A whole new scene. I want the beach and the sun."

"Let's go," said Bunny.

"As soon as we get out of this little pinch."

"I'm serious," said Bunny.

"Me too," said Jerry.

When they got to Ventola's, Bunny pointed them through the gate and Jerry drove onto the lot. There was nobody outside, and for a second Bunny felt nervous, like he was making a mistake doing this, like Gana and Howley were going to get pissed off if they found out he was mixing these worlds up. But what could he do? They hadn't told him not to, and his friend needed a job.

He got out of the Blazer and Jerry, pulling at his T-shirt and touching the back of his pants, followed him toward the sales building. Bunny opened the door and the bell chimed. Ventola was standing over Blanche's desk, reading something on her computer screen with her. They both looked up when they heard the chime.

"Look what the cat dragged in," said Blanche.

"Hi, Blanche," said Bunny.

"You brought us a customer," said Ventola.

"Actually, I was thinking he could maybe fill in and take my old spot," said Bunny.

Ventola led them outside, pulled out his vape pen, and sucked from it. He blew out a big cloud of vape smoke and then scanned the lot and the street, like he was looking for surveillance. "Why do you want work here, instead of going out there with him?"

"He doesn't like to dig ditches," said Bunny.

"Let him answer."

"I wanna sell cars," said Jerry.

"You gonna pick up trash like he did?"

"Yes, sir," said Jerry.

"You gonna sweep and clean the bathrooms?"

"Yes, sir."

"Come in tomorrow, ten a.m., get set up with Jimmy Dean, he'll run your references and all that."

"Okay," said Jerry.

On the way out, Ventola pulled Bunny aside for a second. "That uncle of yours is causing a lot of tension within the community," whispered Ventola.

"What community is that?" asked Bunny.

"Our community, Bunny."

Bunny felt his forehead become hot. "I don't really know about that."

Ventola leaned in closer. "Well, tell him he needs to slow his roll. All this White Power shit gonna interfere with our business interests. If you understand my meaning."

Bunny took a deep breath. "I don't talk to them like that. They say dig, I dig. They say carry something, I carry it. They don't ask for my opinion about things."

"You're his family," said Ventola. He spit on the ground. "He'll listen to you."

That same night, Bunny got a call from Agent Gana. The cop sounded drunk, again. He asked if Bunny had located his uncle's office.

"I think it's in that big building," said Bunny. "He's always coming and going out of there."

The phone stayed silent for a long moment, then Gana said, "I'm not impressed, Bunny." He dropped his voice down to a whisper. "I can't keep covering for you, dog. You gotta give us something and you gotta do it soon."

⁂

Delivering Ventola's message was as good an excuse as anything else. That's what Bunny kept telling himself. Finally, right before lunch, he found one of Nelson's men, a bald-headed, long-bearded motorcycle type called Big Red. "I need to pass a message to my uncle," said Bunny.

"I'll tell him. What is it?" asked Big Red.

"It's a personal message."

"He'll be out soon."

"I don't think it should wait," said Bunny. He turned and looked over his shoulder. "Do you?"

Bunny was hoping he'd be brought straight to Willard's office. Instead, the man led him to South House. "Wait right here," he said, pointing at a metal stool.

Bunny had to wait in the hall for about twenty minutes, but finally his uncle came out of one of the rooms. When he saw Bunny sitting there, he shook his head like he knew bad news was coming. "What is it, Bunny?"

Bunny stood up. "Ventola wanted me to tell you something?"

"Monte? What the hell does he wanna tell me?"

"He said you should slow your roll."

Willard's face became stern. He took a deep breath through his nose. "Come in here with me for a sec, Bunny. I want you to tell my friends what you just told me."

Willard opened the door, and when Bunny stepped into the room, he saw the four men from the SUV seated around a table. Nelson, his face looking worried, sat there, too.

"These are our associates," said Willard. He introduced the four men by name, but the names slipped right out of Bunny's mind. "This is my nephew, my little sister's boy, Bunny Simpson."

The men, at least the three near ones, looked like they'd been around. They had a kind of hardened look to them. The fourth man, the one seated farthest away, had a friendly face; Bunny focused his attention on him.

"Pleased to meet you," Bunny said.

"Tell him what you said, Bunny."

"Well, I used to work with Monte Ventola, and I saw him yesterday, and he said that you"—he lifted his hand to indicate his uncle—"should slow your roll."

Some of the men shifted in their seats; one used his knuckles and knocked on the table. One of the near men sighed.

"You from Grand Junction?" asked the friendly-faced one. He looked like he was about forty years old. He wore a blue button-up shirt. His brown hair was neatly cut, and his face was shaved.

"Yes, sir," said Bunny.

"I grew up outside Durango."

"Beautiful place."

"Different now, though, right?"

"Yes, sir. Everything has changed up there. That is for certain."

"Okay," said the friendly-faced man. He nodded to Willard.

"Alright," said Willard, guiding Bunny toward the door.

"Nice to meet you all," said Bunny, on his way out.

"You as well," said the friendly-faced man. The other three men never said a word, but one of them nodded. Bunny's uncle stepped out into the hallway with him.

"Sorry," said Bunny, again.

"For what?"

"Interrupting you."

"Nah," said Willard. "These men need to hear that."

Right then, a door down the hall from them opened, and one of those weirdo kids stepped into the hallway.

"I was going to the bathroom," said the kid, looking down at the ground like he was scared he was about to receive a beating.

"That's okay," said Willard, leading Bunny toward the room he'd just come out of. "Bunny, this is Baby George."

"Hi," said Baby George. This was the kid Bunny had seen on the first day. "I want to show him your quarters."

Willard guided Bunny into the room that Baby George had just come out of.

The place smelled distinctly of bad breath. Bunny winced from the smell. There were four bunk beds set up, and some military-type clothing chests pushed against the wall.

Only three of the young men were there right then. They all wore khaki pants and blue polos. They were each seated on one of the lower bunks, and they all had cellphones in their hands. "Boys," said Willard. "This is my nephew, Bunny Simpson."

"Hi," said Bunny.

"Hi," said one of the young men.

"You boys okay?" asked Willard.

"Yes, sir, very good," said one of them, a brown-haired, heavyset one.

"Mason," said Uncle Willard. "Tell Bunny about yourself."

The boy stood. "My name is Mason Cawley," he said, speaking right to Bunny. "I'm from Vacaville, California. I went to junior college, and I was in the ROTC program during that time."

"Cool," said Bunny. "I'm Bunny. I'm from Grand Junction."

"You boys need anything?" asked Willard.

The three young men shook their heads. "We're all good, sir," said Mason.

Willard walked Bunny back out into the hallway, put his arm around him. Bunny could smell a hint of booze and cigarettes on his breath. They walked toward the front door. "So?" Willard said. "Anything else?"

"Where's your office?" Bunny asked.

"It's back there in the Big House," said Willard, pointing. "Why?"

"I was looking for you earlier," said Bunny. "Couldn't find you anywhere."

They got to the door that led outside and Willard opened it. "You don't have to be shy around here, Bunny. You're free to go wherever you want." He gestured out toward the property. "This place is for me and you. It's your house."

"Yes, sir," said Bunny. "I appreciate you, Uncle Willard."

"Well, Bunny, you're telling us the same thing you've been telling us," said Agent Howley, turning in his seat and speaking like he was yelling at a child. They were in Gana's SUV, traveling on East Forty-Sixth Avenue; on their right, I-70 cut into the ground like a valley. Gana guided the SUV into an abandoned construction yard. It was nighttime. Bunny sat up in his seat, looked around the lot.

"You're saying his office is in the main building," said Howley. "That's not worth anything. You've been saying that. That isn't new information. You gotta get in there. You gotta take pictures inside, take pictures of the whole building."

Gana stopped the car right next to a large dump truck, put it in park. "You're stalling, Bunny," he said. He turned the car off. "You're stalling, you're stalling, you're stalling. Get out of the car."

"You serious right now?" asked Bunny.

Gana pushed his own door open and stepped out. A second later, Bunny's door flew open, and he felt himself being yanked out by both ears.

Howley had already joined them, and Bunny was pushed against the SUV. The cops had him pinned there. "You fucking with me?" asked Gana.

"Easy," said Howley.

"What'd I do?" asked Bunny.

"You trying to fuck with me?" asked Gana. He punched Bunny hard in the gut. Bunny felt the air leave his body; he felt instantly starved for oxygen.

Howley crowded right on top of Bunny and wrapped his arms around Bunny's head, so he couldn't move. Bunny was stuck standing there. The fabric from Howley's coat was in his face and eyes. Gana hit him again in the same spot. And then again on his side, near his liver. Bunny couldn't breathe at all. He felt like he was drowning. His legs went numb, and he pissed his pants. Howley let him go, and Bunny fell to the ground.

"I could shoot you, and call it self-defense," said Gana, spitting the words out. He put his foot on Bunny's head and kept it pinned to the ground. Bunny felt himself trying to suck air in, like a fish on land.

"Chill out," said Howley.

Gana let up, and Bunny turned onto his side.

Next thing Bunny knew, Howley was squatting down near him. "We can't help you anymore, Bunny. That's what we're saying. We're out of options."

"He hit me," said Bunny.

"He's frustrated with you. You're pissing him off."

Gana bent to look at Bunny, too. For a second, the cop's face looked almost inquisitive, like he was worried if Bunny was okay. "You got exactly one week," he said. "I'm trying to help you, dude. I'm trying my hardest."

Bunny looked away from the cops and turned his gaze to the sky above them. There were no stars up there. He had once looked at the stars with a girl named Pepper, and he thought about her for a second. He'd lain in the grass with her and stared at the stars. He closed his eyes, but it wasn't Pepper he saw in his mind, it was Pastor Dan. Then Bunny heard car doors closing, and he turned his head that way. The SUV didn't move, and Bunny stayed where he was and watched it. Finally, after a minute or two, it started up and pulled out of the lot. Bunny was thankful, because he didn't want to get in with his wet pants. He lay there for a minute and had a good cry. Then he took his phone out and stopped the recording. He didn't feel good about it, though. He felt scared.

When Helen was twenty-six years old, in law school, and still living in California, she had a boyfriend who physically assaulted her. That guy's name was Ben Heiden. He went to Stanford and worked in finance. They'd been out at a bar. Back in Ben's apartment, they argued about Helen hanging out with a male friend of hers. They were both drunk. He called her a slut. Helen started frantically packing the few things she kept there: a sweater, a toothbrush, a few of her books. She was in his bedroom when he grabbed her from behind and swung her onto the ground. As soon as she landed, he was on top of her. She was belly down, and he pinned her like that. She couldn't move. He began slapping her with an open hand on the top of her head. He was a big guy, he'd been on the swim team, and it felt like he was slapping her as hard as he could.

He let her go, and she ran out of the apartment without any of her belongings. It was the only time she'd been hit by a man. She decided not to report the incident to the police, believing, at the time, that all the trouble wasn't worth it. The following morning, she broke up with him by text. She never spoke to him again. She was done with him. There'd been no visible injuries, but she had unquestionably been scarred.

Now Helen—in her car, in a parking garage, downtown, near the civic center—was thinking about that incident. It had been one of the most traumatic events of her life. She'd been degraded. Ultimately, it was the reason she'd left California and moved to Colorado. It was also the reason she'd started lifting weights in such a serious way. That was her old therapist's theory. She was obsessed with bodybuilding because she never wanted to feel weak again. *So therefore, you, Ben Heiden, you piece of shit, are responsible for this entire mess.*

She thought about Tad throwing that glass of whiskey. What else had he done? He liked to bang his fist on a table when he got mad. *Banging your fists. Slamming doors. Yeah, you're a regular piece of shit, too, asshole.* Her thoughts shifted to Sam, her friend from the gym. She saw him on top of her. *Fucking me like a gyrator? I'll put you in there, too. You piece of shit.*

Helen checked her lipstick in the rearview mirror; she checked her face, checked her hair, and then thought about Jerry for a moment. He'd never shown her any of these abusive strains. "Jerry." She said the word quietly. "Jerry." In her mind: *Jerry, this is my mother, this is my father. Yes, Mom, we're married now.*

She opened her car door and stepped out. Then, after putting the little parking stub into her purse, she looked around to remember where she was: section 3B.

The day before, Helen had called Jerry's lawyer and informed the woman that she had "relevant and helpful information for Jerry's case." Ms. Costa-Tenge had sounded skeptical, but she'd agreed to meet at a coffee shop in the Sixteenth Street Mall.

Helen stopped at the window and looked in. She recognized the lawyer from a Google Images search. She was sitting at a table with a man. Helen swung the door open, stepped inside, and—hand extended, smile on face—walked right up to the table. "Ms. Costa-Tenge, Helen McCalla, pleased to meet you."

Helen's appearance—she'd dressed up in a hot-pink suit, and she looked good, sharp, business-ready—seemed to surprise the public defender. It wasn't, apparently, what she'd expected. Perhaps she'd expected someone more like Jerry.

"Really nice to meet you," said the lawyer, standing up and shaking hands. Her gaze went up and down Helen's body. "This is my investigator, Jose." She nodded toward a man with a pockmarked face, who also stood and shook hands. "We've got coffee, would you care for one?" asked the lawyer.

"I'll get it," said Helen. She went to the barista and ordered a double cappuccino. While she waited for it, she checked her phone and pretended to respond to a text message.

When she sat down with her drink, Helen said, "I was hoping we could speak in private."

The lawyer made a face and shrugged. "Sorry," she said. "We'll keep everything you say discreet."

Helen looked around the coffee shop. "I want to give you information. I'm going to tell it to you, but it comes with a caveat. The caveat is that I'm not prepared to testify about this, and if you subpoena me and bring me to court, I'll deny that I said it."

"Okay," said April Costa-Tenge. She gave the investigator a look, and he capped his pen and set it on the table.

"First off, I'm not having an affair with Jerry. Okay? He's a friend." The lawyer stayed silent. "Tad Mangan was my husband." Helen's eyes filled up with tears and her voice dropped down to a whisper. "He's a violent man. An abusive man. He physically assaulted me." She stopped talking.

"I'm sorry," said April Costa-Tenge, with apparent compassion. "How many times did he do that?"

Helen's eyes went back to the table. Tad had never been physically abusive with her. But he had thrown the whiskey. He'd pounded multiple tables. He slammed countless doors. "He was physically abusive with me, probably, five times. He was mentally and emotionally abusive throughout our marriage."

"When he was physically abusive, how did this manifest?" asked April Costa-Tenge. "What would he do?"

"He would pin me down, on my belly, and he would slap my head. The top of my head. And he would scream at me and hold me there."

"Did you ever report any of this to the police?"

"No."

"Did you take pictures? Or tell a friend? A family member?"

"I was too ashamed."

The public defender leaned back in her seat. She rubbed her face with her hands. "Okay, so"—she thought about what she was going to say—"we appreciate you telling us this. It is very relevant. Whether the judge hearing the case agrees with that is another question. If we were able to question Judge Mangan on the stand about this stuff, we would need you ready to testify, in case he denies it."

"I told you, I can't. I'm sorry," said Helen.

"Well, it's information to have," said April Costa-Tenge. "At the very least."

"It's information to use," said Helen.

"The only way to use it," said the public defender, "is through your testimony."

"He is coming up for reelection next year," said Helen. "I think he would be rather averse to all this coming out in the press. I think you could call and ask him about it and tell him that a reporter has been calling you about it."

"I can't do that," said April Costa-Tenge. "That is illegal. You're a lawyer, you should know that. It's a crime. That's dissuading."

Helen pointed at the investigator. "Well, he could go, he could question him about it. Maybe ask some pointed questions. Get creative."

April Costa-Tenge's face looked pained. "He could do that," she said. "But your husband—sorry, your ex-husband—is a judge. I think it's probably safe to say that he will turn down any offers of being interviewed by our investigator."

The man shifted in his seat. He put his hand on the table. Helen stared at his wedding ring, a gold band around yet another hairy finger.

“I need to think about this,” said April Costa-Tenge. “Speak to my supervisor. But the only path forward that I see is you sit down for a more formal interview with Jose.” She gestured at Helen not to interrupt. “Jose writes up a report, and we give it to the prosecutor and tell them that we *intend* to call you.”

Helen couldn’t hide her disappointment.

“He’s a judge, Ms. McCalla. We need to be cautious with this.”

Helen closed her eyes for a moment and shut out the world around her. Then, after a deep breath, she opened them and looked at the ceiling. She would have to clean this up herself. She sipped from her cappuccino. “Well, okay then,” she said. “Let me know what your supervisor says.” She got up and left.

Within the first few days of working for Ventola, Jerry sensed that he’d landed right back in another criminal group. The endless stream of people that came visiting did not appear to be car shoppers. They were criminals, mostly white, some Latino, a few black. It was the same thing that Bunny saw, but Jerry saw it through different eyes. Bunny gave everyone the benefit of the doubt. Jerry was more skeptical of the world.

The second day Jerry was working there, a woman drove onto the lot and parked her old Crown Victoria near the garage. Jerry was using a steel wool pad to clean some hubcaps and spraying them down with water. The woman was a white lady, forties, gray pallor to her skin; she looked like she’d been around the block a few times. She popped her trunk open, pulled out a blue IKEA bag, and walked toward the office. Jerry’s hand kept moving over the hubcap, but his eyes stayed on her.

About fifteen seconds after she went into the office, Jimmy Dean and Blanche walked out. Jimmy, with a phone to his ear, went straight to his car, got into it, and drove away. Blanche walked toward the street, lit up one of her extra-long cigarettes, and gave Jerry a look.

Jerry turned so his back was to the office, and he scrubbed away at the hubcap, made it sparkle. He didn't even see the woman leave.

Later that same day, Ventola came out to the lot and looked at the stack of hubcaps Jerry had cleaned. "You know the old saying? Clean the hubcap, you get a price-jack."

"Yes, sir," said Jerry.

"Well, clean the engine, you get a pension."

Jerry liked working at the lot. He was happy to not be selling steroids or acid. Drug dealing never suited him; it always made him feel like he was going to get ripped off. He'd wake up in the middle of the night panicked, thinking his little stash was gone. Disposition-wise, Jerry needed a job like this. Something where he could put his head down and do the work. That's why he wanted to learn how to write code. Which isn't to say this job at the car lot was worry-free.

There was tension in the air. Ventola held a grudge against Bunny for leaving. He seemed to hold a grudge against Bunny's whole family.

"They get a little bit of money, and they start acting different," Ventola said one day. He was talking about Bunny's uncle. "You know the type?" Ventola asked.

"Yeah, I do," said Jerry. They were inside Ventola's office. Car prices were up, and Ventola was having Jerry call a whole list of numbers to see if anyone was interested in selling their car back to him.

"Driving his truck and walking like he's a son of a bitch," said Ventola. "I want to tell him, *You're not rich enough to be acting like you're the king of the jungle*."

Jerry didn't know what the man was talking about, but he nodded and made a face like it all made sense. He was between calls and his finger was holding down the hook switch on a desk phone. Ventola seemed to be done, so Jerry lifted his finger and dialed the next number.

There was another incident. It happened that same day, right as Jerry was leaving. "You gonna see your friend tonight?" asked Ventola, referring to Bunny.

"I don't think so," said Jerry, pulling on his coat.

"We got a nice little thing here," said Ventola. "We make good money." He wiped his nose with his palm. "Don't know why anybody would want to jeopardize that."

"What are they doing?" asked Jerry.

"It's what they want to do," said Ventola. But he didn't say more than that, and Jerry left the lot feeling confused and a little unsettled. He headed west on West Mississippi Avenue. The mountains sat in the far distance of his view. He thought about calling Helen but decided against it.

Later that night, tucked away in his mother's basement, he called Bunny. They spoke for a long time, comparing notes on the two spots where they were working. Jerry told Bunny he thought Ventola was selling drugs or something.

"Yeah, it does seem that way, doesn't it?" said Bunny.

"He's pissed at your uncle, though."

"Yeah, my uncle can make people feel that way. *He got skipped on the charm line* is what T-Ma would say."

"He said your uncle's planning something."

Bunny didn't say anything. Jerry listened to the sound of the television coming through the phone. Bunny must've been in his trailer, with Rayton. They were watching *American Ninja Warrior*. Jerry recognized the sound of that.

"You heard me?" asked Jerry.

"Yeah," said Bunny. He sounded sad.

"So, what the hell is he planning out there?"

"Don't know," said Bunny. "But they do a lot of shooting, and there's a lot of scary people coming and going."

The next day, Bunny was back at the ranch. They got pulled off the trench-digging and were helping another group of men raise some framing on a building a little farther into the compound. Bunny had never seen these guys. There were six of them. They were all white. Some of them looked a little grubby, one of them was missing some front teeth, one of them had a face that appeared to be scarred from fire, one had a swastika tattoo on his chest. To Bunny, these men seemed more professional than his group. More competent as builders, that is.

During lunch, Willard and Nelson came down and ate with the men. At one point, Willard went walking down a dirt road to go check on a fence line. They were out in the plains; it was just brown grass and a few scrubby trees, reddish-brown soil in the tracks of the dirt road. Bunny followed behind the old man and caught up to him.

"Who are those guys?" he asked, referring to the new men he was working with.

"Those are men who have been released from prison, Bunny. We're trying to get a program going out here." He looked up at the sky for a moment. "Gotta give back to the community."

"Is that what those younger kids are doing?" asked Bunny.

"You could say that."

The young men had been shooting their guns again, and running drills that Bunny couldn't see, but he heard them yelling on and off all day long. "What are they training for?" asked Bunny.

"Training?" Willard stopped walking. He turned and looked at Bunny with anger in his eyes. For a moment, Bunny was transported back to his youth, and he felt almost frozen in fear. Then Willard's face softened a little. "There's a war coming," he said. "You know that, right? If we're not prepared for it, we're gonna get run off this land. Lose our country. It's happening. It already started. All of them Black Lives Matter? They gonna put you in prison, Bunny. They gonna put you in a camp. Make it illegal for you to walk the streets of Denver. Do you wanna pledge allegiance to President George Soros?"

"I don't know," said Bunny. "I don't know about any of that stuff."

"You do know. You're white. You're Christian. Wake up." He clapped in Bunny's face, not hard, but it was still aggressive.

"So what are those kids gonna do?"

"They're not kids, Bunny. Those are young men." He turned, and they continued walking down the dirt road.

Bunny, while he walked, thought about an old fight he'd seen between his mother and Willard. It happened in the little apartment that they used to live in on Walnut Avenue. Bunny and his sister had been playing with their toy cars when he heard Willard and a few of his friends come into the apartment. The men were loud and drunk, but for a while nothing happened. Then there was a dustup. Bunny and his sister were in their mother's bedroom, and he stepped out and peered down the hallway toward the kitchen. Bunny's mother was arguing with Willard. Bunny watched her snatch the paper out of his uncle's hand, crumple it up, and throw it away. Willard marched right out of the apartment. The men he was with followed behind, doors slamming and heavy feet echoing down the stairway. It hadn't been a big drama; in fact, Bunny hadn't even thought of it since it happened. But he thought of it now. He'd gone and pulled the pamphlet from the trash. It was some kind of white supremacy paper. They used to pass them out in Grand Junction. Hand-drawn Jewish stars crossed out, pictures of the Ku Klux Klan, a bunch of words about having pride in the white race. Even at that young age, it made Bunny feel sick to know his uncle was carrying around that stuff.

"Home on the range," said Willard, interrupting Bunny's memory. Bunny looked over and found Willard staring at him. "We're peaceful people, Bunny, you know that. But that don't mean we're gonna take anything lying down. You get old, you get up to my age, you see patterns more clearly. It's not hard to see. God willing, you gonna understand it yourself someday."

"Yes, sir," said Bunny.

In the background, way down to the south of the property, gunshots cracked in the air. Willard turned, looked at Bunny, and nodded.

During the car ride home that night, Bunny breached the subject with Spider. "I like guns. I like shooting them. I like big guns. The bigger the better. But is something else going on out here?"

Spider—cobwebs tattooed on his face—kept his eyes on the road, both hands on the wheel. "It feels that way," said Spider, smiling a little, like he was entertained by it all. "Like enough play acting. Let's start doing. You know what I mean by that?"

"I do," said Bunny. He crossed his arms and nodded his head.

During dinner that night—frozen pizza and frozen French fries with ketchup—Bunny told Rayton everything that had happened.

"You need to tell those cops," said Rayton.

"I have been, they don't care. They just want the damn papers. That's all they care about. They keep saying it's a paper case. They're about to end up with blood on their hands."

"You should check in with that lawyer of yours," said Rayton.

"That's a good idea right there," said Bunny, pointing at Rayton. "That's a damn good idea right there."

After dinner, Bunny went to Rayton's room and searched through the area reserved for his paperwork. He found Rendelman's card and then went outside to the park and called him. The call went to voicemail, and Bunny left a message: "Hi, Mr. Rendelman, it's Bunny Simpson, your old client from that case out in the park. Hey, I wanted to check in with you, because there's been some weird shit going on with those ATF agents and all that. I wanted to just run it by you. All this stuff is new to me, and I don't really know how it's supposed to work. If I'm gonna be honest, I think there's some weird shit going on. Anyway, call me back." He gave Rendelman his number, repeated it, and ended the call.

On his way back to the trailer, on the street, he ran into a guy he used to smoke crank with. The guy was called Gator; he was a big white dude with a milky eye. He lived downtown, but his mother lived in the trailer park. He was wearing a white button-up shirt with a loose black tie. It looked like he was coming from church.

"What's good?" said Gator. "You alright?"

"Yeah man, I'm just stressing on life," said Bunny.

"I heard that," said Gator. "My mama got cancer, my sister got locked up on a warrant, my grandma died from the Covid, my homie

Lil Dee Wop— Remember Dee Wop? He got shot in Laramie. Shot in Laramie! Can you imagine that shit? Sounds like a country song. I rest my head in Denver, but I got shot in Laramie."

"You should write it as a song," said Bunny.

"I will," said Gator. "I got a little bit o' hee-haw if you wanna go smoke?"

"I'm good right now," said Bunny. "But I do appreciate you. Keep your head up and don't let life get you down."

Gator opened his arms and Bunny stepped toward him and accepted a hug. Gator was a bigger man, and he hugged Bunny tight for a long time. Bunny looked over the man's shoulder and stared at the dark sky, which still had just a little bit of sun left in it, setting down behind the mountains.

Helen was in her apartment with Ginger, the clerk from her office. She'd invited the woman there for a glass of wine. Ginger, punctual, had arrived ten minutes early. She wore a dress with a blazer over it, pearls, and makeup. Helen, seeing her like that, felt a stab of guilt. She had a plan for Ginger, something she wanted her to do, but she hadn't really considered the woman's feelings.

"This is my place," said Helen as they stepped into the living room. Ginger looked around with a wild expression on her face, like she was shocked at the magnificence of it all.

Helen pointed to a cheese plate and then gestured at the couch. She poured big glasses of white wine for her and her guest. After putting on a playlist, she sat down on the couch next to Ginger. They clinked glasses. "To friendship," said Helen. Ginger repeated the toast. They made small talk for a while. They talked about their families. Ginger spent a long time talking about her little brother and how smart he was, some kind of computer expert. The conversation moved to work. Helen talked about the changes she would implement if they made her a full partner.

As they drank, the conversation became more personal. Helen asked if Ginger was dating anyone and Ginger closed her eyes, shook her head, raised a hand, and said, "Oh, no, no, no." They sat in silence and then Ginger asked, "Are you?"

Helen shook her head no.

"My thing," said Ginger, "is that they always try and get me to do something that I don't want to."

Helen felt her eyes narrow; she nodded.

"They go on and on about *Oh Ginger this* and *Oh Ginger that*, but at the end of the day"—she turned, looked at Helen, whispered—"all they want to do is have sex."

"Yep," said Helen.

"I mean, you must go through it," said Ginger. "You're so beautiful and powerful and everything." They stayed silent for a second. "Donnie likes you," said Ginger, referring to Helen's boss.

"Oh God," said Helen.

Ginger's face lit up into a big smile. "I heard him talking to Peter. They were in the kitchen. Donnie said, *Helen's the cougar for me.*"

"No," said Helen, shaking her head vigorously.

"Yes," said Ginger. "*My cougar*. He likes you. I see him staring at you, too."

"Should I open another bottle?" asked Helen, trying to change the subject.

"I took the bus," said Ginger. "I can get as drunk as I want."

Helen went to the kitchen and grabbed a second bottle of wine from the fridge. She didn't want Ginger to be too drunk for this, just drunk enough. She went back to the living room and filled both of their glasses again.

"Actually," said Helen, pretending the idea was just occurring to her. "I wonder if you could do something for me?"

"Of course," said Ginger.

"I wonder if you could play a prank on him."

"Donnie?" said Ginger, aghast.

"Not Donnie, my ex-husband."

"Oh," said Ginger. She moved her head from side to side, stretched her neck, like she was looking for a lost hat on the ground. "I thought you meant Donnie. Yeah, not gonna prank our boss. Don't want to get fired."

"No, no," said Helen. "My ex-husband." She leaned back in her seat, crossed her arms in front of her breasts. "He had an affair."

"Oh my God," said Ginger. She became instantly focused.

"Yeah, he's with the woman still. They're married now."

"That's horrible," said Ginger, reaching out and touching Helen's arm. "Freaking men," she said, shaking her head. She finished her glass. Helen filled it up again.

"Yeah," said Helen. She got up and walked over to her desk, opened a drawer, and pulled out a sheet of paper. Typed up on the paper was a script. She handed it to Ginger. "I want you to call him and leave a message," said Helen.

Ginger fished her glasses out of her purse, put them on, and read from the script: "Hi, Mr. Mangan, this is April . . ."

"Costa-Tenge," said Helen.

"Costa-Tenge," said Ginger. "I'm a public defender in Denver. I'm representing Mr. Jerry LeClair, who is charged in your assault. I wanted to reach out to you because I've become aware of some alleged incidents of domestic violence involving you and your ex-wife." Ginger stopped reading aloud for a moment and read forward in silence. Then she continued, "I thought you might appreciate doing this quietly rather than in open court." She took a long pause for the last line. "Keeping it out of the press would probably be best for everyone."

When she finished, Ginger set the paper down on the coffee table. They were silent for a long time. Finally, Helen, trying to sound as light and humorous as possible, asked if she would do it.

Ginger's face suddenly looked miserable. "No. I'm sorry," she said. "I can't. It doesn't feel . . . I don't know."

Helen dropped her gaze to the floor. She sat there breathing through her mouth and tapping her forehead with her fingernail. A song lyric played in her head: *Sometimes I'm in love in the morning / Sometimes I'm alone at night.* She closed her eyes and began to cry. She took a deep breath to try and stop herself, but this only opened the floodgates more. She tried to get up so she could run to the bathroom, but Ginger clawed her arm and pulled her back down.

"No, no, shhh," said Ginger, wrapping her up in a hug and pulling her close.

The woman smelled like baby powder. Helen snapped out of her crying. "Oh my God," she said. "I'm so sorry." She looked up at Ginger, who was staring at her with a very worried expression. "I'm drunk."

"Don't beat yourself up," said Ginger. She grabbed Helen by the shoulders and gave her a little shake. "Don't do it."

Helen, in a daze, repeated, "I'm just drunk."

"Me too," said Ginger. "It's fine."

Helen reached out and took the piece of paper from her guest's hand. She crumpled it, set it on the table. "You're right. It's not a joke," she said. "It's serious. I don't know what to do. I just want to make him stop."

"Have you tried talking to him?" asked Ginger.

"I can't," said Helen.

"You'd be surprised what people are willing to do if you just ask from a sincere place," whispered Ginger. "That's what my mother says."

"Oh God," said Helen. She felt her face crumple like she was in pain; then it relaxed. "I knew I should call you. I knew there was a reason for it."

"We're friends," said Ginger. "We have to look out for each other."

Something happened around lunchtime that sent Ventola into a good mood. He was walking around the lot smiling, joking with Jimmy

Dean. He even tried to sell a car to a customer. Jerry had never seen the man move around like that. He looked twenty years younger.

It turned out he'd closed some kind of complicated real estate deal. Sold an apartment building on West Colfax and was about to double his money. "I thought this day would never come," he said.

At closing time, he was still happy. He and Jimmy Dean came out of the office, and Ventola looked over at Jerry, who was scrubbing his hands with Lava soap at the outdoor sink. "Come on in here, Jerry," he called out. "We gonna have a drink. Make a toast to our success."

Jerry dried his hands on a rag, set the rag down, and headed for the office. When he stepped inside, he saw Blanche pouring Scotch from a big bottle of J&B. She turned, looked at Jerry, and nodded, like *Yep, this is something you gotta do.*

Jerry, feeling shy, accepted a red plastic cup from her. He turned toward Ventola and Jimmy Dean. "To Monte Ventola," said Jimmy Dean, raising his cup. "Car king of Denver."

"Real estate king of Denver," said Ventola, dropping his chin.

"That too," said Jimmy Dean.

Everyone—including Jerry and Blanche—drank. "Fill 'em up again," said Ventola.

Blanche, muttering to herself and holding the bottle with two hands, filled the cups again. It occurred to Jerry that he was joining in on the tail end of things.

"Paid fees for over two years," said Ventola, looking at Jerry. "Paid the taxes on it, paid to heat it in the winter. They said I was an idiot."

"I didn't say that," said Jimmy Dean.

"No, you didn't. You, my friend, understand the power of patience."

"Amen," said Jimmy Dean.

"You understand that business *is* timing."

Jerry glanced at Blanche. She stood there, lifting her cup, waiting for the toast, but she seemed halfhearted.

"To timing being everything," said Ventola.

Everyone drank, so Jerry did too. Then he wiped his mouth with his hand. “Cheers,” he said. Blanche began putting her coat on.

“No,” said Ventola. “Come on.”

“Monte,” said Blanche. She had an angry look in her eyes, and she glanced toward Jerry like she was about to say something, but then she decided not to. “Don’t get in any trouble.”

“We won’t,” said Ventola. “Come here.” He made Blanche give him a hug, which she did with some reluctance. Then he watched her leave. “Pour us another one, Jimmy.”

Jimmy Dean poured shots, and Ventola disappeared into his office. Jerry leaned his butt on Blanche’s desk and looked down at his cup without drinking from it.

“Gonna celebrate,” said Ventola, coming into the room again. He held up a baggie of coke. It looked like an eight ball. “Jerry, you partake?”

“Sometimes,” said Jerry, pushing himself up off the desk.

Ventola tapped out a big pile. “Welcome to the big leagues,” he said.

Jimmy Dean had already rolled up a fifty-dollar bill, and he handed it to the boss.

“Not with that,” said Ventola. He reached into his pocket, pulled out a roll of money, and took off a hundred-dollar bill from the top. “Roll this up.” He handed the bill to Jerry, then he took out an ID card and cut a little out of the pile, chopped it up, and formed a few lines.

Jerry rolled the bill up and held it out to Ventola. “Nah, you go first,” said Ventola.

For a moment, Jerry felt apprehensive, like he was about to get in some trouble, and not the good kind. Still, he bent down and sniffed the line. He wiped his nose and held the rolled-up money to Ventola.

“Nah, you keep that. I’m not catching Covid from you,” said Ventola. He pulled out his own pre-rolled hundred-dollar bill from his shirt pocket, bent down, and loudly snorted a line. Jimmy Dean went next.

They spent about thirty minutes sniffing coke and drinking J&B, hollering, arguing, and talking tough. Jerry got a little less shy, and by the end of the half hour, he was carrying on like the other two, slapping backs, hooting and hollering.

"Should we take him to the spot?" asked Ventola.

A serious look came onto Jimmy Dean's face. He turned and studied Jerry. "Yeah, I guess he's ready."

"What spot?" asked Jerry.

"It's a surprise," said Ventola.

It was dusk when they stepped outside. The three of them piled into Ventola's truck, a black F-350 Super Duty. Jerry sat in the backseat of the cab, smacking his lips. Ventola handed him the bottle of J&B and he took a little sip. His reluctance had disappeared. He felt glad to be there, glad to be brought into Ventola's inner circle. If there was one thing in life that Jerry liked, it was being included in things.

They headed east on Mississippi Avenue, out toward Aurora. The radio was on low, and a nonstop string of commercials played. "Put some music on," said Jerry. "Play some hip hop." Ventola changed the station and different commercials played.

Ventola and Jimmy Dean were arguing about some kind of money issue. Jerry didn't know what they were talking about, and he pulled out his phone to check if he'd missed any calls. He took a quick trip through Instagram and Facebook, and when he came back out, Ventola had changed the subject and was talking about Bunny's uncle again.

"Well, someone convinced him," said Ventola.

"Wish they would've convinced me," said Jimmy Dean.

"Convinced you of what?" asked Jerry.

"To buy Bitcoin," said Ventola, glancing in the rearview.

"First time I heard of it," said Jimmy Dean, "the price was seven hundred dollars a coin. Can you imagine that? Buy a hundred coins! They were trading at sixty thousand!"

"Well, they're back down to twenty," said Ventola.

"Twenty K," said Jimmy Dean.

"You wouldn't know what to do with that kind of money," said Ventola.

"I wouldn't be pushing rust buckets for you."

"It's a pyramid scheme," said Ventola.

"Everything is," said Jimmy Dean.

"We're living in a simulation," said Jerry. "Mathematically speaking, it's more likely than not."

"Put me on the Matrix," said Jimmy Dean.

"You're already there," said Ventola.

"We all are," said Jerry.

They continued talking like that. Ventola pulled over at one point and they all did another bump of coke off his key. Then Ventola got on Highway 225 and took it north all the way out to Green Valley Ranch. Jerry had never been there before. It was one of those suburban neighborhoods where every house looked alike. He couldn't imagine what they were doing there. "Where we going?" he asked. "I gotta piss."

"Hold it," said Ventola. "We're almost there."

Ventola stopped in front of one of the houses. It was a normal place, big, two stories tall. An American flag hung on a pole by the door. There were a few trucks, like the one they were in, parked outside, two on the street, one in the driveway.

"What is this place?" asked Jerry.

"It's a club," said Ventola. "One more bump, come on." He killed the engine. They all sniffed some more coke. "There we go," whispered Ventola.

"There we go," repeated Jimmy Dean, popping his door open.

As they approached the place, Jerry noticed that all the windows had their curtains drawn. He looked at the truck in the driveway and saw it had a construction decal on the door that read, MASTRO, along with a phone number. "Mastro," whispered Jerry, tapping his pockets to make sure he had his phone and wallet.

Ventola pressed the doorbell, and all three of them sniffed hard through their noses. The door opened and a white lady in her fifties stood there. She wore a beige cashmere turtleneck sweater and some loose-fitting gray sweatpants. "Well, I declare," she said, giving them all the once-over with her eyes and then looking beyond them out at the street. She opened the door all the way and they stepped into the house.

Jerry, when he entered, smelled cigarette smoke in the air. He could hear a muffled television playing somewhere. He didn't want to be there, and he wondered whether this was some kind of drug house, and if it was, whether they'd be smoking meth or not.

"Come on," said the lady, walking them past the stairs into another room.

In the living room, Jerry saw four women, all Asian, all dressed in cheap-looking negligees and wearing shawls over their shoulders to ward off the cold. A television stood dark against one of the walls. There were no pictures hanging, no plants anywhere, and the mood in the room was dark and tired and not festive at all.

One of the women stood up and walked right to Jimmy Dean like they were already a couple. "Look at you," he said to her, patting her backside and putting an arm around her. They walked back out toward the stairs. "I been thinking about you," he said.

"He's with me," said Ventola, pointing at Jerry. "I'm paying for him."

"Well, which girl does he want?" asked the white lady.

Right then a man appeared in the doorway on the other side of the room. He was a big white guy with stubble on his face. He gave a tiny nod to Ventola and then withdrew back through the doorway.

Fuck, thought Jerry. He didn't want any of the women. He was disgusted by the whole thing. But he didn't know what to say; he was high, and he felt unable to act in a sensible way.

One of the ladies stood up and walked to him. She looked like she was about thirty-five. She had dark circles under her eyes and a bruise on her neck, and she was wearing Cookie Monster slippers. She grabbed Jerry by the hand and led him the same way Jimmy Dean had gone.

"Go on," said Ventola.

Jerry followed the woman up the carpeted stairs. His mouth had somehow become even drier. The woman led him down a hallway, and Jerry heard a man grunting like an animal and a bed squeaking from behind one of the doors. *I'm in hell*, he thought. *This is it. I'm here.*

The lady led him into a room. There was a bed, a dresser, a lamp, and a trash bin. Nothing else. Jerry's eyes went to two cigarette butts on the carpet. Right away the woman started trying to unbutton his pants, but Jerry grabbed her hands and pushed her back a little. She got an angry look on her face and tried again.

"I'm sorry," said Jerry. "I can't." He grabbed her and sat her down on the bed and then sat next to her. "Are they holding you here?" he whispered.

"Me?" she said.

"Yeah."

"No."

She moved toward his belt again, and again he stopped her. "I can't. Let's just sit here. I'll tell 'em you gave me a good time. They'll pay you."

The woman dropped her head down to her chest like she'd fallen asleep. She took a slow, deep breath and then lay down on her side with her back to Jerry.

His forehead was sweating, and he wiped it with his hand. He thought about rubbing her back to comfort her but decided against it. He pulled out his phone and looked at the time. It was 8:24 p.m. He figured he should stay in there for about twenty minutes.

He looked at a UFC blog for a minute, scrolled through the news there. Then he texted Helen: *Hey! You wanna hang out tomorrow?*

Helen's cellphone buzzed in her pocket. She was at a juice bar in Cherry Creek. She took the phone out, expecting to see Tad's name, and instead saw Jerry's. Her anxiety expressed itself by raising her internal temperature. She set the phone down, finished her protein shake, and blinked her eyelashes out toward Second Avenue, waiting for her ex-husband to show up.

When he did arrive, he walked in like he'd come straight from the gym—trendy sweatpants, sweatshirt, sneakers. She squinted at the outfit: *Mr. Fashion now?* The expression on his face hinted at aggrievement; Helen's blood pressure rose. They exchanged greetings and asked each other if they were okay. No, he didn't want any juice. He settled into his chair and looked at her with an expression like *Why did you ask me to come here?*

Helen wiped her mouth. She glanced outside and then looked back at him. "I have a weird thing," she said.

"What is it?"

"It's such a weird thing . . ." She shook her head like she regretted that she had to say this. "I found out about what happened in the park."

Tad sat there staring at her. His eyebrows turned in slightly. He didn't say anything. "The kid that you fought. I know him."

"What?" said Tad. His face showed equal parts confusion and rage.

"He's a friend," said Helen. "Calm down. I know him from the gym. It's such a stupid thing." Pantomiming extreme weariness, she rubbed her forehead and then her eyes. "I'm sorry. I can't believe this happened. Listen. I'm just going to say it. I told him about what you did. I told him about how you cheated on me."

"What?" said Tad.

"We were talking."

"What are you saying?"

"I'm saying, I think he got a weird idea that he was trying to help me."

They sat in silence for a moment. The buzzing of the lights and appliances was the only sound in the room. Helen prepared herself. She closed her eyes for a moment and saw Tad and his wife in their kitchen. The woman was pregnant. There was a Christmas tree somewhere.

"The kid's lawyer called me," said Helen. "That's how I found out. Her name is April something. She said she was going to subpoena me. She wants me to talk about some of your"—Helen put a hand on her head like she was trying to remember the phrasing—"your propensity for violence or something."

"What are you talking about?"

"I guess he told her about your throwing the whiskey bottle and all that."

"Whiskey bottle? I literally don't know what the fuck you're talking about."

"The glass." Helen looked at him. "A glass of whiskey." She looked him dead in the eyes. "The problem is"—she breathed into her diaphragm—"there's that reporter from the paper. What's her name? Marcella Bonafante?"

"Helen."

"She's always sniffing around for stories. A judge? Domestic violence? It doesn't sound good."

A cold smile passed over Tad's face and his eyes shined with tears. "Jesus, Helen. You are truly psychotic."

"Tad."

"You are a sick person." He was whispering. "You're hanging out with freaking homeless kids? Druggies? Having them attack me?" He shook his head. He looked at the woman behind the counter, then looked at the ceiling. He looked back at Helen. "I should have you locked up."

"I know," she said.

"You could be arrested for this."

"It's a mess. I'm sorry I opened my mouth. I'm sorry I brought Vanessa into this."

"Okay, stop. Freaking stop," said Tad. "Stop. It's sick. It's *gross*. Just tell me what you want. Tell me what the hell you think you want."

"I want you to call the DA and tell them to drop the charges."

Tad's eyes moved around while he thought this through. "I'll do it," he said.

"Good," she said.

"But we'll need to amend our divorce agreement. No more shared property. We take your name off the LLC. You just walk."

She suspected he might react this way. She sat there for a moment. "I give up my share of the building and you drop the case?"

"That's what I'm saying," said Tad.

"Okay," said Helen. She held her hand out.

Tad said he'd talk to his lawyer, have him draft something up, and then he got up and left. Helen sat there for a minute. She wanted to leave, but she wanted to give him a chance to clear out first. She tapped her fingernails on the countertop, *one, two, three*; then she pulled out her phone and responded to Jerry's text: *Yeah, sure!* Then she just sat there, looking out the window for a long time without doing anything. She had a strange feeling inside her. She felt good. A light feeling settled in her. She could do good things. She was capable of being a good person. That's all she wanted.

When Bunny and his sister were kids, they didn't just dig for water. They also used to dig holes in the dirt on the side of their house and bury knickknacks: bottle caps, thumbtacks, and spools of thread that they'd stolen from their mother's room. A cluster of little gray stones would mark the spot. Occasionally, they'd dig their booty up, see what they had, and then bury it all again.

Bunny was thinking about this as he unloaded lumber from a truck at the ranch. It was a clear, bright day—hot in the sun. He set down some planks and turned and looked at the building they'd been working on. It was going up much faster than he'd imagined it would.

"Some of those men gonna move in as soon as we're done," said Willard. "Imagine that." The older man walked right up next to Bunny and put a hand on his shoulder. "You could, too."

"I gotta take care of Rayton," said Bunny. He regretted mentioning him.

"Bring him."

"He complains too much. You don't want him out here."

Willard became distracted by some of the workers trying to place a ridge beam the wrong way. "Hey, no, no!" he said, walking that way to sort it out.

Bunny continued unloading the wood. If anybody looked at him, they would have thought he was carefree and lost in his work. In fact, he was suffering from anxiety. It felt toxic. He felt it buzzing in his chest and belly. He felt tense as hell.

Later in the day, toward the end of it, Willard gathered the men in a circle and led them in prayer. "Lord, Jesus," he said. "I wanna thank you for guiding these men here, where they can, with your blessing, fulfill the duty of their lives. Lord, we all done things in our past that we're not proud of. Let these men and their work be an example for all white men." Bunny opened his eyes and looked at the group of workers. They stood there frowning; most of them had their eyes cast down.

Willard continued, "Lord, I pray that you protect them and their families as we continue on our path to redemption. Lord Jesus, I want you to shine down on these men and protect them with your love. They are good Christian soldiers, and they are ready to bleed their blood just like you did."

"Amen," said one of the men.

"Amen," said a few of the others.

In the distance, across the ranch, Bunny heard three solitary shots. All the men, including Willard, looked that way. Willard raised his eyebrows as if to say, *Funny timing.* Then Willard shook hands with a few of the shirtless men before walking toward his truck. Bunny trailed after him.

"Uncle Willard," he said. "You got a fax machine up there?"

"Sure," said Willard. "Nelson does."

Bunny, feeling nervous as hell because he was being deceitful, pulled some folded papers from his back pocket. "I'm trying to get into the Clean Slate program up in Grand Junction. Gotta clear my record up there."

"That's a good idea," said Willard.

Willard started the truck and soon they were bumping along the road, headed back up to the main compound. It was a five-minute drive, and halfway there, they came across three of the young men out walking with a fourth man. Bunny had never seen the fourth one before.

Willard stopped the truck next to them. "Reverend Anderson," he called out. "Come meet my nephew."

The new man, Reverend Anderson, stepped up to the truck. To Bunny, he looked normal in a way that a lot of the other men out there did not. Bunny could imagine him as a dentist or something. He had light brown hair that was thin on the top. He wasn't a worker; that much was clear. He put his hands on the door and bent down.

"Reverend, this is Bunny," said Willard. "He's my little sister's boy."

"Pleased to meet you, son."

"Pleased to meet you, sir."

"The reverend's got a ministry over there in the Springs," said Willard.

"You should come," said the reverend, raising his eyebrows and smiling with an open mouth at Bunny.

"I will," said Bunny. He looked past the reverend at the three young men. All three of them were staring back at Bunny. One of them was moving his mouth around like his jaw hurt. They weren't wearing their uniforms. They were dressed just like normal teenagers—jeans, T-shirts, and sneakers.

"I was just telling Scotty there," said the reverend, pointing back at one of the boys, "that we have some beautiful young women in our church."

"You hear that?" said Willard.

"Yeah," said Bunny.

"I'm something of a matchmaker up there," said Reverend Anderson. He bent his head and examined Bunny. "A boy like you, that face, yes sir, we'll fix you up nice. Get you settled in. I got just the young girl in mind for you." He whispered, "Really nice." Then he looked at Willard. "God bless your family, Mr. Haggerty."

"And yours," said Willard, putting the truck back in drive. They started moving again. Bunny turned in his seat and looked back at the reverend. He was watching them go. The young men were staring, too.

"He's our spiritual advisor," said Willard.

When they got up to the compound, Willard pulled in right next to another parked truck. Nelson and two men that Bunny didn't know were gathered around the back of it. They were all looking down at something. Willard and Bunny got out and joined them.

"What do we got?" asked Willard.

"Take a look," said Nelson.

Willard and Bunny stepped closer. There was a large cooler in the back of the truck. It was filled up with vacuum-sealed steaks. Pink meat with white fat and bone.

"Ribeye, flank, skirt, and chuck," said one of the men, a potbellied guy in a white T-shirt and a MAGA hat.

"He gonna throw in fifty pounds of ground chuck, too," said Nelson.

"And you gonna eat it with us," said Willard.

"Yes, sir," said the man. He gave his partner a little friendly elbow in the gut. "We always like to break bread with our customers."

Willard told Nelson that Bunny needed to use his fax machine.

"Come on," said Nelson. He led Bunny toward the big house. Willard stayed behind with the two men and asked after some of their mutual acquaintances.

"Your hands are getting rough, I bet," said Nelson.

Bunny looked down at them. "All that digging," said Bunny. "Yep."

"It's good for you."

They got to the big house and Nelson pulled out a ring of keys and opened the door. As they walked down the hall, Bunny heard at least two female voices speaking from somewhere.

"Yep," said Nelson, unlocking the door to his office.

It was a little more cluttered than the last time they'd been in his office. Bunny noticed a map spread out on a big table. He went to it, looked down, and recognized Denver. A cluster of roads had been marked with highlighter pens and stood out in orange, green, and yellow.

"What do you want to send?" said Nelson.

Bunny pulled out the paperwork and handed it over. "It's going to the public defender," he said. "Up in Grand Junction. The number's on top there."

Nelson leafed through the paperwork and looked at every page. He took his time with it. Bunny breathed in and out and tried to calm his heart from its beating. This was the first step to getting into Willard's office.

Then, while Nelson typed in the number, Bunny turned back to the map and looked at it again. The streets that had been marked were all around downtown, near the Sixteenth Street Mall.

Bunny, while he looked at the map, thought about a girl he once met at the Conoco on Speer Boulevard, over there. She was one of those Rainbow Family girls. Bunny had used a fake ID and bought some beers. They poured them into soda cups and went to Fishback Park. The girl was Rainbow Family but all she wanted to talk about was the Bible. Then a dude in a wifebeater came and started trying to fight Bunny, and the girl left him there.

"There you go," said Nelson. He handed Bunny back his paperwork. "You want the receipt?"

"Nah."

Bunny followed Nelson out to the hallway and waited while the man locked the door. Fear in Bunny's stomach was making it hard to get the words out, but right when Nelson finished, Bunny said, "I need to put these on Willard's desk," holding the paperwork up. "He asked me to do that." His heart was pounding in his chest from the lie, but he tried to look as bored as he could. There was a moment, just a split second, when Nelson gave him a deep stare, like a cop looking at a suspect. Then he said, "Okay," and led Bunny farther down the hall.

They went up some stairs, then down a dark hallway, and stopped at the last door on the left. Nelson fussed with his keys again. Then he unlocked a deadbolt and pushed the door open. Bunny hadn't ever been in Willard's office, and when he stepped into it, he held his breath from nerves. He felt almost instantly disappointed because he didn't see a safe. There was just an old desk, made from fancy carved wood; a bookshelf with some books on it; and a table on the far side, pushed against the wall. Bunny stepped to the desk and put his paperwork on top. When he turned, he saw Nelson in the doorway, staring at him. Then, to Bunny's left, in the corner of the room, he saw it: a medium-sized black safe, sitting bolted on the ground. There it was. He wanted to snap a picture on his phone, but that, obviously, wasn't happening.

He stepped back out into the hallway and waited while Nelson locked up again. His heart raced in his chest, and he felt energized equally from fear and from success. He didn't like those agents at all, but he couldn't help feeling happy. He liked to succeed at things. *All you gotta do is try*, he told himself. *Try and try.*

When they got back outside, Nelson made a point of telling Willard that they'd gone into his office. "He left the papers on your desk," said Nelson, speaking loudly.

Willard turned and examined Bunny's face like he was trying to make sense of Nelson's words.

"Put 'em right on top," said Bunny. "Right where you could see 'em."

"Okay," said Willard. "Good boy."

Later, in the middle of the night, Bunny woke with a start. He was on the couch in Rayton's trailer. He'd had a bad dream about a snake, and his mouth was dry. First thing he thought about was the map on Nelson's table. He could see the little colored lines, and he knew they meant something awful. The problem was, everyone wanted to ignore him. His lawyer still hadn't called him back. Bunny got up and grabbed his phone from the charger. It was 3:24 a.m. As soon as it was a reasonable hour, he was gonna call Agent Howley and tell him again that something bad was being planned out there.

He closed his eyes, but he kept hearing gunshots on a loop in his mind. He saw images of his own father. He saw Pastor Dan. He saw

Frazier Haggerty. Willard. *No, sir*, thought Bunny, tossing and turning on the couch. *Nothing good is gonna happen out of any of this.*

He never did fall back asleep, and finally, at 6:02 a.m., he texted Agent Howley: *Hey. Please call.*

At 6:48 a.m., his phone buzzed. Bunny was already outside, on his way to the bus stop. "Bunny, tell us something we wanna hear," said Howley.

"I told you something you wanna hear," said Bunny. "I'll say it again: They are gonna do something real. I'm talking specific plans. This isn't theoretical, I'm talking real life."

"Yeah, no shit, Bunny. Why do you think you're out there?" asked Howley. "Why do you think we're spending all this time on this case?"

Bunny plugged one ear with his finger and looked around at the morning streets. "We just keep having the same argument, though."

"We're not arguing, Bunny."

"I'm saying you need to tell your lieutenant, or whoever the hell's in charge of y'all, that something is coming down the pipeline, and you're still only talking paperwork and this and that."

"Bunny, listen. Everything you say to us gets briefed up the chain. Come on, man. I'm gonna write up this call. It'll be written into a report. You are not being ignored. You matter, Bunny."

"But you gotta make arrests," said Bunny. "Not write reports."

"We are," said Howley. "We're making arrests. But it's not going to mean shit if we don't do it the right way. You want them to walk back out? What do you want to charge them with? Shooting guns on their own land?"

Bunny saw the bus coming. "I don't know," he said. "I'm saying, I'm throwing a flag. I'm saying something needs to be done."

"We know," said Howley. "Listen, we're gonna pick you up tonight. Be at your bench at nine p.m. I'm gonna brief the entire team on this call, and we're going to come up with a master plan."

"Okay," said Bunny. He didn't know what that meant, but he liked the sound of it.

The bus pulled up and he got on.

That same morning, Helen arrived at work carrying a small box of expensive chocolate. She walked right over to Ginger's desk and found the woman sitting on her chair, examining something on the sole of her shoe.

"I brought these for you," said Helen.

"For me?" said Ginger.

"I wanted to thank you. You really helped me." She pushed the box into Ginger's hands.

Ginger lifted it and gave it a little shake, as though wondering whether the box actually contained chocolate. "See?" she said. She licked her lips, then added, "I got in a fight with my mom last night because she said I didn't have any friends. Well? What do you call this?" She rubbed the top of the box with her fingers.

Helen tried to smile.

"I wanted to tell her about you," said Ginger. "I wanted to tell her about Nancy, too." She pointed in the direction of Nancy's desk. "I don't know, my mom's kind of weird."

"Mine too," said Helen.

"She's always on me about friends and boyfriends. She doesn't have any. I told her! She said, *I'm too old to have friends.*" Ginger gave the box another little shake. "I said, *You're never too old for friends.* I'll give these to her."

"Well, make sure you have some, too," said Helen, turning and walking away. "They weren't cheap."

Helen spent the rest of the morning doing actual work, which felt good. Then, right before lunch, she got a Slack from Donnie, her boss: *Can you poke your head into my office?* She squinted at that phrasing, and then responded, *Sure.*

When she got to his office, she was unpleasantly surprised to see Sandra Ung, from HR, and Dale Sigworth, one of the founding partners, already seated. For a moment, Helen thought this might be related to

Tad. The periphery of her vision blurred, her movements stiffened, and her breath became shallow. *Fuck,* she thought. *What have I done?*

"Take a seat," said Donnie.

Helen brushed the front of her pants, forced herself to smile, and sat.

"Helen, I'm gonna get right to the point," said Donnie. "The partners"—he raised a hand toward Dale—"have decided that we're not going to be offering you a partner position at this time."

"Excuse me?" said Helen. She felt blindsided. *Tad did this*, she thought. She looked at Sandra; the HR woman's face looked pained, like she understood exactly what Helen was feeling. "You assured me I was on track," said Helen, turning and speaking to Dale.

"I would take issue with the word *assured* in this context," said Dale. "I would say I was *encouraging*, but—"

"So what happened?" asked Helen. Happy voices floated in from outside the room. She didn't want to yell. She turned and looked at the door. Then she looked back at Donnie. "You're my supervisor. What happened?" she asked in a whisper.

"The firm wanted to go in a different direction," said Donnie.

"With who?" asked Helen, astonished. "If you may be so kind. With who?"

"We're going to announce, tomorrow, that Leanne Tenedou is going to be made partner," said Sandra. The woman then glanced at Dale, looked back at Helen, and continued, "We hope you'll stay on board, and we want to be very clear that the path to partnership is not closed. This was a strategic choice for the firm. It reflects the direction we're hoping to take things at this moment."

Helen looked down at the ground. She knew the truth was the exact opposite of what Sandra was saying. The firm was done with her. They weren't ever going to make her partner. This was a soft firing. She was done here. The last six years of her life had been a waste. Her time at Sigworth, McKenzie & Harper was finished. It all happened so fast.

At that same moment, Jerry—across town and in the garage at Ventola's—was sweeping the floor with the slow and deliberate movements of a man who was not watching the clock. He was thinking about a time he teased a childhood friend for being poor. He felt awful about it now and he cursed himself for being mean.

Right then, Ventola stepped into the garage. "Come on," said the older man. His voice sounded snappy, and Jerry, scared he was about to be yelled at for something, held his breath while he leaned the broom against the wall.

"Bring that thirty-sixer," said Ventola, pointing at a thirty-six-inch pipe wrench on the worktable. Jerry pictured a burst pipe somewhere. He picked up the wrench. It took two hands to carry it.

"Cocksucker wants to argue with Jimmy Dean," said Ventola. They were crossing the lot toward the front entrance. Jerry saw a few men gathered around a car. He had to hustle to keep up with his boss.

"What's the problem?" said Ventola when they reached the other men.

"I said we could do six, he wants eight-five," said Jimmy Dean.

The men with the car—it was a Subaru Forester, 2012, in fine condition—were rough-looking white dudes. The one who seemed to be doing the negotiating was a big guy; he was pushing 250 pounds. He had a tired expression on his face, like he'd been up all night, and scruff on his cheeks and neck, like he hadn't shaved in two days. He looked at Jerry and his eyes went down to the wrench, then they shot back to Jimmy Dean.

"So walk," said Ventola. "You don't like the deal, take it to another dealership."

The big guy doing the negotiating whispered to one of the smaller guys and then spoke to Ventola. "He said he'd do eight," said the man, pointing at Jimmy Dean. "I wouldn't have *bought* it from my guy if he hadn't said he could do eight."

The smaller guy who had been whispering—a dark-haired dude with a crooked nose—got Jerry's attention with a nod and then pointed at the wrench and motioned like he should put it down. Jerry looked at Ventola, who nodded, and then Jerry set the big wrench down on the ground.

"You said eight?" asked Ventola, turning his anger on Jimmy Dean.

"Hundred and fifty-seven thousand miles on it, though," said Jimmy Dean. "He didn't *say that*."

"So roll it back," said the smaller man. "Not like you don't roll all the other ones."

"Pop the hood," said Ventola.

Jimmy Dean popped the hood and Ventola pulled out his phone, turned the flashlight on, and looked at the engine, moving his head this way and that. "It's pretty dirty," he said. "I mean, we'll clean it, but it's still pretty dang dirty."

Ventola went to the driver's side door, opened it, and examined the interior handle, running his fingers over it like a high-end appraiser. He shined his light down on the brake pedal, bent down there, and touched the rubber padding. He looked at the driver's seat, tested the springs with his hand. "It's all worn down, Reggie—nobody's gonna believe this thing's under a hundred."

"They like Foresters, though," said Reggie.

"You want eight-five, we can give you six-eight," said Ventola. "That's it. That's the best we can do." He looked at Jimmy Dean. "I'm sorry he's making unrealistic offers outside these premises. Tell me this—did he make this offer after he'd been drinking?"

Jimmy Dean looked down at the ground and gritted his teeth. His face turned red.

Reggie whispered with the smaller man, and then said he'd take the six-eight. They closed the deal in the office. Jerry felt happy to have been included; it gave a little pep to his step.

Later that day, Jerry was in the office scrubbing the toilet when he got a text message. The text was from his friend Best Buy Johnny.

Johnny wanted to hang out that night. Jerry stopped his cleaning and sat down on the toilet to respond. He told Johnny he couldn't make it. Then he opened TikTok on his phone and spent almost a half hour watching videos. When he was done looking at TikTok, he finished cleaning the toilet and then sprayed down the sink and wiped it clean with a paper towel. Then he dropped the towel in the trash.

Jerry, when he stepped back out, walked right in on Ventola having a meeting with that same lady who had visited the other day, the one who looked like she'd been around the block. The one with the bad vibes. He startled them. The lady was sitting on a stool in front of Jimmy Dean's desk. Ventola was sitting behind the desk, and there was another canvas shopping bag right there between them. Blanche and Jimmy Dean were nowhere to be seen.

The look on their faces said everything Jerry needed to know. Even in that half second, Jerry could guess that she was selling and Ventola was buying. Jerry apologized, put his head down, and walked right out the door. He didn't see Ventola for the rest of the day and he never saw that woman again. Still, he felt uneasy all day long and into the night.

"This isn't the way we wanted it to go," said Agent Howley. "But there are bigger wheels turning than our own, and we have to recalibrate. That's all we can do."

They were sitting in a booth, in the back of an empty Mexican restaurant in Commerce City. The place was lit with fluorescent tube lights and the walls were painted yellow. Bunny had ordered chicken tacos. The two cops had both ordered carne asada burritos, but none of their food had been brought to the table. Bunny glanced toward the kitchen.

"Definitely not the way we planned," said Gana.

Gana took out his phone and held it up for Bunny to see. "I talked to the DA." He pointed at a number in his call log. "The lady you met. She said everything'll be cool. Just get that notebook. That's all she needs."

Bunny wiped his nose, nodded.

"Tomorrow, at eleven a.m., we're gonna come in with the warrant. It's gonna be a crowded field"—he counted on his fingers—"ATF, DEA, FBI, DPD, Douglas County. The way we see it, Bunny, we're gonna hit that gate, and you're gonna have about ten minutes of chaos before you get cuffed up."

"Cuffed up?"

"You're gonna get booked, and then we'll pull you."

"Trust me," said Gana, "you want to get booked. You want everyone to see your ass getting booked."

"So we're gonna hit the front gate," continued Howley. "From the time we hit the gate to the time we arrive at the compound, you gonna have a little less than ten minutes. It seems like a good chance that during those ten minutes, your uncle is gonna wanna move that notebook. That's gonna be your window. That's your chance."

"Jesus," said Bunny. "This is BS."

"Yeah," said Howley. "We're saying the same thing. BS across the board. We didn't want you to have to do it on raid day like this, but here we are."

"Why don't you guys just come and get it?" asked Bunny. "You got the warrant, just take the damn notebook. Take the whole safe. Why you gotta include me in this?"

"Because he will burn it, Bunny," said Howley.

"He will burn that notebook, guaranteed," said Gana.

"He burns it," said Howley, "that's it. Can't do nothing for you. Sayonara."

"When we first made this deal," said Bunny, "you guys said all I had to do was give you information. Just good info. You didn't say I had to strong-arm my uncle."

"The notebook *is* the information," said Gana. "That's the information you need to give us. That's all we need. That's it. It's black and white."

The waitress came to the table and delivered three Coca-Colas and some chips and salsa. "Thank you," said Howley.

"Thank you," said Bunny.

The woman left and they sat in silence until she went back into the kitchen. Bunny took a deep breath. "There's something else that's been bothering me," he said, sounding regretful. "You guys said I'd be paid every day I was in the field. I've been out there for eighteen days. That doesn't even count my time at the car lot. You gave me one hundred, so you still owe me seventeen hundred."

The agents didn't say anything.

"I'm sorry to be a hard-ass," said Bunny.

"We'll give it to you tomorrow," said Howley, looking grim.

"Before I go out there," said Bunny.

"After you give us the notebook," said Howley.

"Get the job done," said Gana, looking back toward the kitchen. He fussed with something on his lap, then set a brown paper bag down on the table between them. He slid it over to Bunny.

Bunny, hoping it was money, put his hand on it. He could tell right away it was a gun. He pulled the bag off the table and opened it on his lap: a black Glock 19.

"We took the firing pin. You're not going to be able to shoot that one," said Howley, whispering. "Don't need you accidentally killing anybody."

"So you're giving me a gun that doesn't work?"

"It's for show," said Gana. "That's only if you need it. Don't get your ass killed. You gonna wait for your uncle to open up the safe. Just get the fucking notebook. Secure it and wait for the cavalry. The two of us"—he pointed at his partner—"are gonna come straight for you, we take the notebook, you're gonna give it over, and that's it." He leaned forward. "Bunny, listen to me now. Don't give it to anybody else, only him or me. You understand what I'm saying?"

"This is sensitive," said Howley. "We don't trust everyone else on this task force, and you shouldn't either."

Bunny grabbed a chip, dipped it in salsa, and ate it. He realized he was starving, and he took another one, dipped it, and ate that too. "You guys got me all fucked up," whispered Bunny.

"We know," said Howley. "We understand this is hard, Bunny."

"We're here for you," said Gana.

The agents dropped Bunny back at the park at 11:49 p.m. They told him they'd send a text message ten minutes before the raid began. The text would be from a number he didn't know, and it would read: *All the cars R painted black.*

After they left, Bunny sat down on the bench in the park. He was too wound up to sleep. He pulled out his phone and opened Google Maps and punched in the ranch's address. Then he looked at the area for a bit and wondered how he was going to have ten minutes from when they breached the gate. It only took about five minutes to get from the gate to the ranch. He looked at the area surrounding the ranch. He thought about his uncle inviting him to live there.

Bunny thumbed his way over to his contacts, found Rendelman's number, and called him. He didn't care what time it was. The phone rang five times and went to voicemail. Bunny waited for the beep and left a message: "Hi, Mr. Rendelman, it's Bunny Simpson. I really need to talk to you. I mean, I really, really, *really* need to talk to you. If it's a money issue, I'm sure we could work that out. This thing's taken a turn, though. I need legal advice, sir. I need help. Please call me back as soon as you can."

When Bunny got home, he found Rayton awake and on the couch. The older man closed his laptop and set it down and asked Bunny where he'd been.

"Man," said Bunny. "This shit is getting too much."

"What is?"

"Hold on," said Bunny, walking to the back of the trailer. He found Rendelman's card and then sat down on his uncle's bed, and using his phone, he emailed the lawyer copies of the voice memos he'd recorded of the cops. He hadn't gotten every meeting—that night, for instance, he'd been too nervous to record them—but he'd gotten a few, including the one where Gana kicked his ass. "I hope I'm not doing something wrong by this," said Bunny.

"I didn't hear you," said Rayton.

"I'm talking to myself," said Bunny, walking back to the front door. He opened it and peeked outside. The place was dark, and nobody was there. The only sound came from a car stereo a block away that was blasting some Mexican music. Bunny took the gun from his jacket pocket. It was still in the paper bag. He set it down on Rayton's bookshelf and turned to the older man. "Those cops are going cuckoo for Cocoa Puffs, man."

"What'd they do?" asked Rayton. He took his glasses off and looked up at Bunny with a face like he might start crying. Bunny had never seen him look so concerned; that made Bunny even more nervous. He told him everything that happened that day.

"Shit," said Rayton. "You call your lawyer?"

"I did," said Bunny. "I've been calling him. I just emailed him too."

"Okay, Bunny, you gotta tell them no. Say you can't do it. Tell them you don't feel comfortable. The court's gotta work it out for you. They can't expect you to waylay your uncle. They can't ask you to commit a crime. That's too much. They're going too far."

"Yeah, you think?" said Bunny angrily. Then he changed his tone. "I'm sorry," he said. "I'm pissed at them and I'm taking it out on you."

"You gotta walk into the court tomorrow and ask to talk to the judge. The lawyer not calling you back. Federal agents asking you to do things. No, sir, that's a no-can-do. You gotta speak to the judge."

"The judge doesn't care about me."

"They're people, Bunny. A judge is a person. He'll hear you out."

Bunny leaned down and put his head between the sofa cushions and started to cry. He felt Rayton's hand rubbing his back. He had a good cry, cried for about a minute, then leaned back up and wiped his face with his shirt. "I'll just go out there," said Bunny. "I'll try and do what they want. I'll see if I can, and if I can't, I'll just get arrested. I'm not gonna rob Willard. I'll tell the judge I did my best."

They stayed up for a few more hours, talking and drinking beer. Finally, after it was three in the morning, Rayton insisted they go to bed. "You gotta have your wits about you tomorrow," he said.

Bunny lifted his uncle off the couch and carried him to his bed. "Listen," said Bunny. "If I don't see you—"

"Don't start with all that shit!"

"I might get arrested. I *will* get arrested. So, if I don't see you for some time, I want to thank you for putting me up." He looked at Rayton's face. The older man looked suddenly young somehow. "I think we had a good time here," said Bunny.

Rayton's eyes shined with tears. "We did, Bunny. We had a really good time here, the two of us."

Bunny wiped the tears from his own eyes. "I love you, Uncle Rayton."

"I love you too, Bunny."

Then Bunny lay down on the bed next to him, and they lay there without saying anything until eventually they both fell asleep.

Bunny woke at 5:21 a.m. He'd been dreaming about his sister, Reecey. They were in a kitchen in Grand Junction making pancakes and Bunny knocked over a big bowl of batter and it smashed down on the floor and made a mess everywhere. That's when he woke up.

He got out of the bed, gave Rayton a pat on the back, and then went and brushed his teeth at the kitchen sink. He poured himself a bowl of Frosted Flakes, then filled it up with milk and brought it to the couch and ate it. Then he changed his clothes, putting his best pair of blue boxer briefs on for good luck.

Before leaving, Bunny turned and looked around the trailer. He studied it, like he might not see it again. Then he rapped his knuckles on the wall for additional good luck. He put his coat on and slipped the gun, which was still in the paper bag, into his pocket.

⁂

During the bus ride to Five Points, Bunny sat there and watched the brick houses pass by like he was in a movie. His hand, while he watched, stayed in his pocket holding the gun in place. His thoughts, meanwhile, drifted from subject to subject, stopping for a moment on his fantasy of owning a motorcycle shop, and then moving on to picturing a string of different girls that he'd known. Random girls passed through his mind. One lived downtown. Her name was Lucy-Ann. She was sober. He could imagine going someplace with her. She was a good cook. He thought about his mother, who was not a good cook. She didn't have any natural skills in the kitchen. Burnt everything she touched. The kitchen was not a happy place for her.

Bunny looked at a man sitting on one of the sideways-facing seats in front of him. The man had dark hair and wore black sunglasses. He carried a leather-bound book that looked like a Bible in his hands, but Bunny couldn't be sure what it was. Somehow, that man brought Jerry to mind. Jerry had gotten him into this whole mess. Bunny took his phone out and texted him: *You up?* But he didn't get a response.

At his stop, Bunny got off the bus and began walking toward Champa Street. Spider, as usual, was already outside, sitting on the hood of his car, having a cigarette. A nervous feeling opened in Bunny. Everything seemed suddenly real. Today was gonna be the day that all things came to a head. *Had to be sometime*, thought Bunny.

"Wassup, big pimp?" said Spider.

"Cold ass day, man," said Bunny, looking up at the cloudy sky.

They got into the car and fastened their seatbelts. Spider took a moment adjusting the rearview mirror, and Bunny looked at him like *You don't have any idea that you're about to get arrested. You didn't stop and look around your room or anything like that. You got no clue, Spider.*

Bunny took out his phone and checked the time. It was 6:58 a.m.; they were seven minutes ahead of their schedule. "You guys own that house?" asked Bunny.

"My mother does," said Spider.

"She lives there with you?"

He told him she lived in Stockton with his sister.

"Where's Stockton?" asked Bunny.

"California."

"That's wassup," said Bunny. He rubbed his hands on his pants and nodded at a woman jogging by. "She's out jogging," he said.

"Makes you feel good."

"Not me," said Bunny.

They talked like that for a while, passing comments back and forth. Then Bunny closed his eyes and slept for a little more than half an hour, bumping along and feeling warm in the car.

They were outside Castle Rock when he woke up. Clouds had rolled in, and it looked like a spring storm was brewing. Bunny rubbed his face, then felt nervous and checked his pocket for the gun. He found it there, and he kept his hand outside his pocket, holding it in place.

A dude called Timmy Licks was manning the gate when they got there. That had been the routine lately. There had been so many workers coming and going that it made more sense to station someone up there than to drive up every time and unlock it.

Bunny looked at the man as he approached the car. *Who was gonna be on gate duty when the Feds came?* That's what Bunny wondered. Whoever it was would be the first man arrested.

Timmy Licks looked in on them like he was pretending he didn't know who they were, scrutinizing them. He checked the backseat, leaned his head close to the driver's window. "Bitch and bimbo," he said. "That's my name for you two."

"Nah, we're Spider and Bunny," said Bunny. "Check the web, we're gonna have a movie made about us."

"A romantic comedy?" asked Timmy Licks.

"Open the gate," said Spider.

Timmy Licks opened the gate, and as they rolled by, Bunny locked eyes with the man and held up a two-fingered peace sign. Bunny only noticed right then that there was an AR-15 resting butt down against the gate swing. A dreadful feeling rose in him; he felt panic pulling on his insides, and his lungs felt squeezed with fear. "Fuck," said Bunny.

"What?" asked Spider.

"I don't want to be here today," said Bunny.

Spider turned and looked at Bunny. "Work is work, man," he said, narrowing his eyes in a kind of warning. "Get a hold of yourself."

"I am," said Bunny.

Spider pulled the car in front of the Big House and killed the engine. They both sat there for a second without opening the door, then they got out. Bunny looked around and estimated a count of about sixteen men. Some of them were gathering tools onto a truck. They wore coats and some had hats on. Some were smoking, some were looking in the trunk of a car. Bunny recognized almost all of them, but there were a couple he hadn't seen before. None of the young weirdos were out this morning, and he didn't see Willard or Nelson. One of the workers, a guy called John Teacup, walked toward Bunny. "Greetings," said the man.

"Greetings to you," said Bunny, rolling his shoulders like he was loosening up for work. He turned to Spider. "Thanks for the ride," he said.

Right then, about thirty feet away, Nelson pulled up on his four-wheeler. He was wearing a green military-style sweater. Bunny walked toward him. "Morning," said Bunny.

"Morning," said Nelson. Bunny looked at the man. He had to be one of the main targets of the raid. Did he seem a little distracted? Maybe, but that wasn't unusual for him. He was the kind of man who always had his thoughts going in multiple directions.

"Is my uncle here?" asked Bunny.

"He's on a call."

Bunny stood there scratching his head. "What are we doing today?"

"They're gonna bring some hay," said Nelson, pointing at a group of the men. "And you boys are gonna insulate the house with it. Stack it up in the walls. Old-school style, the pioneer way." He looked at one of the trucks. "Hey, Cup!" he called out in his deep voice. "Make sure you got that handsaw!"

Bunny, trying to act casual, drifted away from Nelson and walked toward some of the men smoking cigarettes. One of them, a guy called J. J., turned to Bunny and said, "Don't be bumming, you said you weren't gonna do that anymore."

"I'm not bumming," said Bunny.

"Okay then," said J. J., tossing him his pack. Bunny pulled one out and leaned forward and held J. J.'s hand steady while he lit it for him. J. J. looked to be in his midfifties. He had short gray hair and a rough and beat-up face like he'd been a boxer as a young man. Bunny categorized him in the group of convicts, but he wasn't sure if that was an accurate categorization.

"You tell him," said J. J., nodding at a man next to him. "I'm saying you work harder if you don't eat breakfast, and he's saying the opposite."

"I always have to eat," said Bunny, smoking his cigarette. "All the meals. Sorry."

"Y'all don't get it," said J. J. He shook his head, then spit at the ground in front of Bunny's foot.

"Watch it," said Bunny.

"Sorry," said J. J.

"Where the hell is that hay?" said one of the other men, a guy who Bunny always thought of as the Rat. All the men in the group turned and looked up the road toward the main gate, like the truck full of hay was going to come rolling down right then. Nothing came, though. *Oh Jesus, just help me*, thought Bunny.

"Okay, ladies, let's head on down to the site," said one of the guys, a dude called McHenry, who served as the foreman. The group began moving toward a couple pickup trucks. Bunny felt his panic attack rise back up. He put his hand on the outside of his jacket and pressed his chest. Then he put the same hand down on the pocket and held the gun hard against his side. While he walked, he stared down at the ground like a man walking on wet rocks in the dark.

Bunny dropped his cigarette and stamped it out. His brain shuffled through a series of images: he saw his uncle's mean face—the younger version, which was even meaner than the current one. It was looking down on Bunny, all screwed up with anger. He saw his mother on her deathbed in a dirty hospital, even though she hadn't died. Then he saw Rayton in a bathtub. His skin had a blue shine to it, the water all drained out of the bath. Bunny saw all that in a series of flashes lasting not longer than one second.

"You alright?" asked Big Les, a man with a shaved head who clearly belonged to the convict group.

"Need to talk to my uncle," whispered Bunny.

"You gonna throw up?" asked Spider, who had stepped next to him.

The idea of throwing up brought on a whole new wave of images and bad feelings. He closed his eyes and saw a bloodbath—just blood everywhere. He opened them and looked toward the trucks and saw a few of the men watching him. One of the dogs, Darcy, stood next to the truck and barked twice at Bunny. "I'm okay," whispered Bunny. But he realized he was clenching his anus shut, and he became scared he was about to shit his pants in front of all these men.

Bunny turned and staggered toward the Big House. Before he'd gone even a few steps, he buckled over and threw up. White milk and wheat-colored cereal splashed down on the ground.

"Damn, Bunny," said Spider.

"Go on," said Bunny, turning and looking at him. "I'll come in a minute."

"What you do, turn up last night?" called one of the men at the truck. "You got faded without me?"

Bunny nodded and waved them on. "I'll come in a minute," he said.

Bunny tried to kick dirt on the vomit. It didn't do much, and he went to the Big House and sat down on the stairs that led to the door. He sat there breathing and squinting against the sunlight. It took a long time, but finally all the men climbed onto the two trucks and the trucks started moving.

❧

"Did you eat something bad?" asked Nelson. He was leaning over and looking down at Bunny's face.

"I don't think so," said Bunny. "If you give me the hose, I'll clean it up, though."

"Nah, don't worry about that. I'll have Rhonda take care of it." Nelson put his hand on Bunny's forehead. "You feel a little hot. Let's go get you some water."

Bunny felt another wave of panic rise in him. It made him moan out loud. He covered for the noise by pretending it came from the effort to stand.

Back on his feet, Bunny spit on the ground; he took his shirt and wiped his mouth with it and looked up the driveway toward the road. Then he turned to Nelson and found the man staring at him in a way that seemed to split the difference between suspicion and interest.

"I'm okay," said Bunny.

Nelson held the door open for him. Inside, Bunny stood blinking at the dark hallway as his eyes adjusted to the low light. "Come on," said the man, leading Bunny back to a little kitchenette. Nelson opened a cabinet, found a coffee mug, and filled it with water.

"Thank you," said Bunny, taking a sip. His feeling of panic kept growing; it was so severe that he was ready to confess everything to make it stop. "I need to talk to my uncle," he whispered. He was going to tell his uncle the cops had turned him into an informer. Just lay it all out on the table.

Before Bunny even made it out of the kitchen, he felt another overwhelming round of pressure on his anus. "I need the bathroom first," said Bunny. *Fuck,* he thought. *Fucking help me, God—with all this. I got too much on my plate.*

Nelson led him to the bathroom. *My plate is filled up*, thought Bunny. *I surrender.* He locked the door behind him and pulled his pants down, sat, and exploded with diarrhea. That went on for some time. Bunny's forehead became sweaty, and he sat there breathing through his lips.

Then, still seated, Bunny took the gun out of his pocket. He pulled it from the bag, held it in his hand like something fragile. He pointed it at the door. "Fuck," he whispered to himself. Then he lifted the gun to the side of his own head like he was going to shoot himself; he held it there for a second and then put it back in the paper bag and slipped the whole thing back into his pocket. *Next time, give me a gun that works*, he thought as he cleaned himself up. He washed his hands at the little sink, rinsed his face, and looked in the mirror: *Fucking dog, dude*, he said in his head, trying to pump himself up. *You are a fucking dog.*

When he finally came out of the bathroom, Nelson led him up the stairs and down the hallway to his uncle's office. Bunny could hear the old man's voice coming from inside. *I was in too deep*, thought Bunny, practicing what he was going to say to Willard. *They had me jammed up*. He wanted to slap himself in the face. *I fucked this one up good. I'll take whatever you wanna give me.*

Nelson knocked softly on the door, and a moment later, Willard, his cellphone to his ear, opened it. His eyes went from Nelson to Bunny, and for a second, Bunny thought he saw anger in there. "Chief, let me call you back," said Willard into the phone. "Okay, okay. Yes, sir, I will."

"Wants a word," said Nelson.

"Come on," said Willard, opening the door wider. Bunny stepped in alone, and Willard shut the door. The old man motioned to a chair in front of his desk, and Bunny sat down on it.

"I was sick," said Bunny. "Threw up."

"You know, your mother used to have a weak stomach, too," Willard said, sitting back down behind his desk. He picked at something on his scalp, pulled it off, looked at it, put it in his mouth, and chewed. "Teenager, she'd throw up every time her cycle came. Every month. Daddy used to call it her holy war. *Your holy war*, he'd say. She'd be throwing up, bitching and moaning. Lord have mercy upon our souls." He made a disgusted face. "You talked to her?"

Bunny shook his head. He crossed his arms in front of himself, stared down at the ground. "You haven't told her you working out here?" asked Willard.

"Nah," said Bunny.

"She's liable to start asking for money again." He paused for a second, shook his head. "Never understood us, did she?"

Bunny, in his mind, saw his mother working at their kitchen sink, cleaning up after his sister and him. Scrubbing dishes, not hurrying, but going at a steady pace. Bunny put his hand on the right side of his forehead and rubbed it, like that might help him. "She tried," said Bunny. "She's got issues, that's for sure, but she always tried as best she could."

"Is that what you think?" asked Willard.

"It's not what I think," he said. "It's what I know."

A clock hung on the wall behind Willard. It looked like it had been taken from a school. The clock read 8:48 a.m. The second hand moved slowly. Bunny watched it and scowled. He bent his head and looked at the safe on the ground. "She always tried," said Bunny again, whispering.

"Tried sucking dick for dope, that's for sure."

"What'd you say?" said Bunny. On the one hand, he wasn't sure he'd heard right. *Rick* and *rope*. On the other, he knew exactly what his uncle said. The old man sat there staring at him with his ugly face. A dog barked outside.

"Say it again," said Bunny.

"Boy, she loved sucking dick for dope. You can't deny that."

Bunny, in his mind, saw his mother with her head in a man's lap. He saw his grandmother staring at the stars above her. Pure anger opened up inside him, and he popped up and ripped the gun out of his pocket. The paper bag fell to the floor. "What the fuck did you say?" asked Bunny.

"Sit your ass down," said Willard.

Bunny stepped to the old man, pulled the gun back, and hit him on the side of the head. Willard stayed in his seat, but after a second, he turned his face up to Bunny. There was no blood, but the man had a crazed look in his eyes. He looked like a demon. His eyes went to the gun as if he were just noticing it. "What the fuck are you—"

Bunny leaned over hard and wrapped his left arm around Willard's head, like a hug, so the old man's face was forced into Bunny's chest. He straddled him and pressed the gun against the side of his head. He held him there for a long moment and looked around the room. Then he released Willard's head a little, but kept the gun pressed to his temple. He stepped back and put his finger to his lips. "Keep your mouth shut."

"Bunny," said Willard, speaking quietly. "I'm gonna bury you in the earth just like I did your daddy."

"What'd you say?"

"You heard me."

Like I did your daddy. A feeling of shame washed over Bunny. His uncle had killed his father. That's what the man went to prison for. Bunny had never understood that. He felt so stupid. How did he not put that together? Everybody must've known it. It was an unspoken truth. His mother knew it. His sister knew it. Everyone in town knew it. Bunny felt mean and stupid.

"Let me ask you a question," said Bunny.

"Go on."

"Why did you do it?" Bunny whispered.

"He kept putting his hands on your mother," said Willard. "What'd you want me to do?"

Bunny took a breath, held it in his lungs, and exhaled. His world had been flipped inside out.

"Stand up," said Bunny. "Get up."

Willard rose to his feet. Bunny turned him around and pressed the gun into the back of his head. "You're going to open that safe, or I'm gonna blow your brains out."

"There ain't nothing in there."

"Open it," said Bunny.

"It's my papers, you shitty, ungrateful half-breed," said Willard.

"You got three, two—"

"Fuck you," said Willard. But he got down on his knees and started working the dial. "It's my damn accounting!" He was panting, whistling somehow when he exhaled. "You're doing this for what? For my, for my . . ." He turned the dial back and forth. He had to do it a few times before he succeeded. Finally, he latched it open. "See!"

Bunny bent his head and looked in. He saw the black notebook. It was the only thing in there. "Hand that over," he said.

"That's my personal—".

"Don't talk," said Bunny, tapping the old man's skull with the gun. "Give it here."

Willard handed the notebook over, and Bunny took a step back and thumbed through the pages. It looked like a bunch of indecipherable accounting. Just handwritten numbers and lists. The agents were right. Willard was right. Here it was. A bunch of bullshit.

Bunny looked at the clock. The minute hand hadn't moved. He glanced out the window and didn't see anything that way except for the open plains, and above the plains a gray sky. He bent down and looked back in the safe. It was still empty.

"Put the gun away," said Willard. "You're right. I shouldn't have spoken about your mother that way." He raised a finger into the air and shook it for emphasis. "She's my sister—don't forget that, though. That's part of it. That's part of everything, Bunny. I served time for her."

"Stop!" said Bunny. "Stop fucking talking! I need to think!"

Bunny, holding the gun on him, went to the old man's desk and started opening drawers. In the second drawer, he found a roll of white duct tape.

It took him a bit to free the end of the tape, but when he finally did, he went back to his uncle, who was still on one knee. Bunny tried to wrap tape around the man's head to gag his mouth. It didn't work the first time—the tape got tangled up, and Bunny had to rip it off and start again. On the second attempt, he looped the tape around his uncle's big head four or five times, over the mouth and under the nose.

"Get the fuck down," said Bunny, forcing him onto his stomach. He bound his hands together behind his back, using the tape like cuffs. When he finished, he taped his legs together at the ankles. "There," Bunny said. "There you go." He was out of breath. "There it is."

Uncle Willard lay on his side, staring at Bunny with that same hateful expression on his face, looking like he wanted to kill him. Bunny grabbed the black notebook again. He tucked it into the front of his pants. Willard was moaning some kind of threat at him. Bunny went over, squatted down next to him.

"I can't hear you," said Bunny. "Stop talking. You're not gonna convince me to let you go, so just shut the fuck up."

Willard stopped. He lay there without moving, panting through his nose.

"I wanna tell you something, though," said Bunny. He put his fingertips on the man's shoulder and spoke right into his ear. "Whatever happened between you and my father, that's between you and him and God. You're gonna have to deal with that. Not me. For real, though. I wanna tell you, you're not better than us. My mom, you always thought you were better than her. You're not. She's a better person than you." Bunny looked at the door that led to the hall, then looked back at him. "You gotta understand that."

Bunny grabbed his uncle by the shirt collar and dragged him across the floor to the closet. He tried to force him into it, but Willard resisted. They scuffled around like that for about ten seconds until Bunny finally got him all the way in, legs included, and slammed the door shut.

"Dang it," said Bunny. "Fuck." He squatted there for a second, rubbing his chin, then he grabbed his uncle's chair and angled it against the knob to keep the closet door jammed shut. "Okay," he said when he finished. "All this mess and you got me doing all this and that," he whispered to himself.

Then he took a second and straightened his clothes out. He checked his pants and dusted himself off. He patted his hair down. After making sure he had the notebook, he put the gun back into his jacket pocket. He stood there, looking at the closet, shaking his head. "You wanna kill my father?" he said. "You wanna bury him in the ground? Then I'm gonna tie your ass up." Then he stepped out into the hallway and closed the door.

The hall itself was dark and quiet. The only sound in the air was a band saw cutting wood somewhere. Bunny's plan, insofar as he had one, was to walk right out the front door. Walk out to the road. Find some cops in the area getting ready for their raid. He'd just give himself up. Turn himself in, turn his wrists up, give them what they wanted.

He opened the door to the outside. Standing right there, with his back to him, was Nelson. The man appeared to be sending a text message. He looked over his shoulder at Bunny, then turned to him. "You okay?" he asked.

"I'm cool," said Bunny.

"You look like you seen a ghost."

Right then, a truck rumbled up to them. Big Les was driving. A man Bunny didn't know rode shotgun. Three men, all standing up and facing forward, rode in the back. Bunny couldn't tell if they'd been called by Willard somehow. He wanted to put his hand on the gun again, but he was too scared.

"What's up?" said Nelson, speaking to Big Les.

"Truck's still not here," said Les, stepping out. "Willard's gotta call him."

"Nah, it's okay," said Bunny, trying to speak with as much authority as he could muster. "He said he wants me to go meet them out there."

"Say what?" said Nelson.

"He told me to go meet them," said Bunny. "He said to take his truck."

"To Rampart?" asked Nelson.

"Yeah," said Bunny. "To Rampart."

"Nah, that doesn't make sense," said Nelson. "I'll go out there. You stay right here."

"I gotta talk to him about the roof line, anyway," said Les. The man started moving toward the door again.

"You know," said Bunny, holding his hands up like a bouncer, "it's not a good time." He looked up toward the road, licked his lips. "He's having a family talk. Kind of a tough talk with my mother. They're in there on the phone. It's a whole thing," said Bunny, shaking his head and standing tall.

Big Les cursed under his breath.

Right then, Nelson's phone rang in his pocket, and he took it out. Bunny felt certain it was Willard texting him somehow. He even stepped a little bit away from Nelson. He was ready to run.

Nelson looked at his phone, then put it away. Then he looked at Bunny. "I'll go to Rampart," he said. "I'll get the hay. You stay here."

"Can I borrow your quad to drive down to the site?" said Bunny.

"Bring it back at lunch," said Nelson.

"I will," said Bunny. Then he turned toward Les. "Talk to him after lunch," he said. "I think that'd be better. He's in a foul mood, man. I swear to God, he almost bit my head off."

The other men were jumping off the back of the truck now. Bunny had to walk past them to get to the four-wheeler. He lifted his eyebrows and nodded to them on his way past, but he felt too scared to turn and look back at Nelson or any of them. Somewhere, the saw continued buzzing; Bunny's ears were ringing, too.

He got on the four-wheeler. The keys hung from the ignition. He touched the notebook at his waistband and then turned the key and thumbed the ignition switch on. He only realized right then that he probably shouldn't drive it straight out in front of all these men. They would wonder where the hell he was going. That wouldn't work. Jesus, how much time did he have before they found Willard? Five minutes? Ten minutes?

He started moving and went the same way the truck had come from, down the dirt road deeper into the compound, toward the building site. That was the only way he could go. He didn't have any other option.

After a minute of driving, Bunny came to a little turn in the road. He stopped for a moment, stood on the foot pegs, and looked behind him. His hands were cold and he was feeling as scared as a chased jackrabbit. He sat back down on the bike and steered it off the road and onto the dirt and grass of the plains. He'd drive offroad for about half a mile and then cut back to the main road.

There was more brush and rocks than he'd imagined, and the going was rough. It took all his effort to keep the thing moving. At one point, the notebook fell from his waistband, and he had to jump down and grab it. While he was off, he took the gun out of his jacket and secured it in his pants pocket. It was swinging around too much.

There was a lot of stopping and starting and maneuvering around bushes and through gullies. Bunny had to stand on the pegs and rock the thing this way and that. It was exercise, and after a few minutes, even in the cold weather, he was drenched with sweat. Every now and then he stopped and looked behind to see if he was being chased. He thought about all those pit bulls and dreaded the idea of them being set free. But if Nelson and the others found out that he'd put Willard in a closet, he'd be lucky if the dogs came for him. At least he'd be killed fast.

After about fifteen minutes of rough riding, Bunny came to a barbwire fence. He looked at the thing. It was just the barbwire and studded T-posts; Bunny thought he could crash through it. Before he did, he stood on the seat of the four-wheeler so he could have a better view. He couldn't see any of the buildings behind him, and he didn't hear any kind of commotion coming from that way, either. On the other side of the fence, about a quarter mile to the west, he could see the road that he and Spider traveled on every day. Right then, he noticed a few snowflakes falling from the sky.

Bunny sat back down on the seat and then drove a wide circle back around so he could give himself a little runway. He pushed himself up, knees on the seat, and he slowly rolled up toward the fence. About ten feet from it, he gunned the gas and popped the front wheels up and sent the machine crashing through the wire. He jumped off before it hit, and he slammed down against the ground, knocking the wind from his chest. He lay there for a moment, looking at the dirt on the ground, the little pebbles and the dry grass. *Help me*, he prayed.

The four-wheeler had knocked through the wire, but the wire now appeared to be tangled up underneath the carriage. Bunny tried to fuss with it for a minute, but he couldn't get it loose. He got back on the quad, backed it up, and pulled forward. The wire was caught fast, though. He tried to force the issue and power through it; the wire popped free from a few posts but then jerked him almost all the way off and the wheels spun. "Dang it!" said Bunny. He hopped off.

In the near distance, a car drove past. Bunny decided to ditch the quad. He walked through the long yellow grass toward the road, checking himself for injuries as he went. His elbow hurt bad from the crash. His jeans looked dirty, and he was soaked with sweat. The snow was beginning to fall harder, and his lungs burned a little from all the exercise mixed with the cold air.

There were no cars on the road when he reached it. Bunny began walking north, away from the ranch. If the men were searching for him, they'd be searching this road.

His mind, while he walked, started looping around the issue of the money he was owed. By his accounting, those cops owed him seventeen hundred, eighteen if he counted today. He had no intention of letting that slip. That was a significant amount of money. *Don't try and fucking cut me out*, he practiced saying in his mind.

Bunny's phone vibrated in his pocket and damn near gave him a heart attack. He was certain it would be Willard, telling him to get his ass back there and accept his punishment like a man. He pulled it out and was relieved to see Jerry's name.

"Aw fuck, man," said Bunny, answering.

"Wassup, player? I got your text."

"Dude, I'm"—Bunny turned a circle and looked all around—"I'm out here near Castle Rock. I need help. I need help, bad."

"What?"

"I need you to come get me!"

"I'm at the car lot," said Jerry.

"Tell him you got a family emergency, man."

"Are you serious right now?"

"I'm dead serious," he said. "They're gonna kill me."

Bunny looked behind him and saw a car approaching. His first instinct was to run, but then he realized it was a compact car and not a truck. "Hold on," he said into the phone. "Hold on." Bunny stepped a little bit out into the road and held a hand up. The car looked like a Toyota Corolla, an older one. The driver was a girl. "Hey, stop. Stop, please," said Bunny. Waving his hand at her, he put a little pleading smile on his face.

The car slowed and then stopped. Bunny, trying to make himself seem as unthreatening as possible, walked to the window. "Sorry," he said, bending over. "I got an emergency. Can you give me a ride to a gas station?"

The girl appeared to be younger than Bunny, possibly even as young as sixteen or seventeen. She wore a striped T-shirt under her jacket, and she had light brown hair with bangs. The scent of bubblegum came wafting out of the car. "You okay?" she asked.

"Can you help me?" said Bunny.

"Jeez," she said. "I guess so."

She leaned to unlock the passenger door.

Bunny walked around the front and got in. "Thank you," he said. "God bless you." He looked at his elbow to see if any blood was coming through the jacket.

"Are you okay?" she asked.

"Crashed my quad back there," said Bunny, pointing to the plains. "Sorry, one second," he said to her. Then he lifted the phone back up. "Hey dude, just start driving toward Castle Rock, I'll tell you where. This young lady's gonna help me, she gonna drop me off at a gas station, I'll tell you where, but you gotta go right now, man."

Bunny ended the call. "Sorry," he said to the girl. "This dude's tripping." He motioned his hand toward wherever Jerry was.

"That's alright," she said. She used her hand and fixed her bangs. Her hazard lights ticked on and off. She put the car in drive and started to move.

"What's your name?" asked Bunny.

"Liza," said the girl.

"I'm Bunny."

"Bunny," she said, quietly.

"Thanks for stopping."

"My daddy says there are two types of people in this world." She sat up straighter. "Those that want to help strangers, and those who do not."

"That's wassup," said Bunny, nodding his head. "Helping strangers."

He took a deep breath and looked in the side view mirror. Nobody was behind them. When they finally passed through an intersection, Bunny leaned forward and looked all around for law enforcement but didn't see any sign of them, either.

"Do you live out here?" asked the girl.

"I live in Denver," said Bunny, settling back into his seat. "But I been working out here."

Bunny looked at his elbow again; he pulled the sleeve up. The flesh was a little raw, but not bleeding; still, he sucked air in through his teeth when he touched it. The snow came down harder now, in big, slow-moving flakes.

Right then, a truck came barreling toward them from the opposite direction. Bunny sank a little lower in his seat, but the driver didn't look like any of the men he didn't want to see. He glanced at the girl and gave her a little nod to try and put her at ease. He shrugged and sighed. "What about you?" he said. "Where do you live?"

"I live right back that way, about eight miles from where you were. It's a farm. I'm going to visit my sister, she lives in Foxfield. You ever been over there?"

Bunny told her he hadn't. While they chitchatted, Bunny's thoughts stayed fixed on the issue of the cops. He realized he could just call them and have them pick him up. That would've probably been the safe way to go. Two things stopped him from doing that. The first was the money they owed him. The second was him worrying that the cops were not going to honor their word, that they were going to send him back to prison no matter what he gave them. Bunny wanted assurances made, and he wanted those assurances made to a lawyer or a judge or something. He was tired of playing with these cops. He didn't trust them at all. And now, finally, he had a bargaining chip.

"My daddy went to the University of Nebraska," said the girl. "Out there in Lincoln, so that's where he wanted me to go."

"Never been there," said Bunny. "Never been to the state of Nebraska at all."

For a second, the girl's eyes drifted up toward the sky, and Bunny became scared she wasn't watching the road. He prepared himself to grab the wheel, but then she looked back down. "He passed away," said the girl. "Last spring."

"I'm sorry," said Bunny. "Mine did, too. A long time ago. It's not easy."

"No," said the girl, almost whispering. "It's not."

They rode in silence for a minute, then she spoke again. "We used to talk about this college thing, like where I should go and all that. He used to say, *The thing about life*"—she raised her chin in imitation of the man—"*is that there are all these little choices you make that will have a huge impact on your future.*" She lowered her chin, gripped the steering wheel. "Like for example, if I went to NU, I would meet different people and make different friends than if I went to CU. You understand what I mean?"

"Mm-hmm," said Bunny.

"Maybe I would meet a different boy, and we would have a family. So, those kids would be totally different depending on what university I chose to attend."

"Yep," said Bunny. "Life is an open road. Sometimes it can feel like too much."

The girl turned to him and smiled. "Yeah," she said. "You can get frozen from too many choices."

"I feel like that all the time," said Bunny. He wanted to reach out and hold her hand. He wanted to have her pull over to the side of the road so he could kiss her, but he didn't do anything. He just rode along, his face tense, and looked out the front and watched the snow fall and the road come at him.

Eventually, in Parker, in the suburbs again, the girl, Liza, pulled into a gas station. "You'll be alright here?" she asked.

"Yeah, I will," said Bunny.

"Are you sure?"

She was looking him in the eyes, and she seemed to be genuinely concerned about his well-being. Bunny felt half touched and half sad.

"I am," he said.

He held his hand out for a handshake, and they shook hands like they were closing a car deal. Their hands lingered like that for a second. "Thank you," he said.

Bunny stepped out of the car and watched it pull away. He was about to call Jerry when his phone buzzed. He pulled it out and saw a text from a number he didn't recognize: *All the cars R painted black.*

The cops were about to do their raid. *Goddamn, if it doesn't rain when it pours,* thought Bunny.

Jerry, still in Denver, was already on I-25 headed south toward Castle Rock when Bunny called him from the gas station and told him to come to Parker.

"Where the hell is Parker?"

"I'm at Circle K on South Parker Road. Just put it into your Maps, man. Shit, just type it in. You have no idea what I been going through today."

"Chill out, dude," said Jerry. "I'm coming. The cavalry is on the way."

"Hurry up."

"You said Circle K on where, though?"

Bunny gave him the cross streets again and Jerry ended the call. Eyes going up and down from his phone to the freeway—windshield wipers swiping the snow—Jerry punched the cross streets into his phone. Twenty-four minutes. He called Bunny back. "Twenty-four minutes," he said when his friend picked up.

"Okay, sweet, hurry up," said Bunny.

Jerry hung up again and put his music back on. He rapped along with it: "Got my swag, got my bag, got my ring, it's a diamond, got my boo, she's called Diamond."

Ahead of him, on the side of the highway, was a cop sitting in his car, holding his radar gun on him.

"Nope," said Jerry to the cop. "I got you." He glanced at the speedometer, sixty-three in a sixty-five. He checked the rearview and saw the cop's car standing still.

His eyes went back to the road. That morning, he'd had a disturbing interaction with Monte Ventola. He'd been cleaning one of the SUVs at the front and Ventola had approached him from behind. "Make it shine," he said. "Make it sparkle."

Jerry turned to him and said, "Yes, sir."

Thinking back on it, it looked like the man had been out partying all night, like he hadn't gone to sleep yet. His clothes and everything else were normal, but he had that kind of toxic vibe coming off him.

"We gonna party tonight?" Ventola asked.

"I got a date," said Jerry.

"If I say you got a date with us, then you got a date with us."

"Is that how it is?"

"You're damn right."

"Alright then," said Jerry.

A semitruck slowing down in front of Jerry interrupted his memory. He hit the brakes, changed lanes, and thought about Helen. He'd seen her two nights ago. They'd met at a bar near her house. Jerry, in his own humble estimation, thought he'd played the date perfectly. He hadn't acted thirsty at all. He'd just gone and hung out with the woman, asked her questions about herself, which she was more than willing to answer, and didn't put any romantic pressure on her. He gave himself a ten out of ten on that one. Yes, sir.

Toward the end of the night, she said she had to go get some sleep. Jerry paid for their drinks, he was happy to do it, and she said, "Aww," and rubbed his back. At the front of the bar, before they stepped outside, she turned to him and gave him a little hug. Her body was like the body of a damn Olympian. They didn't kiss or anything, he just held her like that for a second. She had her head right next to his, and he could feel her breathing. "I should go," she said into his ear.

"Alright," he said. Then he walked her to her car, and she drove away. He thought about that date all the way to Parker. When he saw the Circle K, he turned the stereo off and pulled in. He looked at his gas tank and saw that it was one-third full. *You're gonna fill me up*, he planned on telling Bunny. *You're gonna fill me up.*

The door of the Circle K popped open, and Bunny marched out. He looked tense as hell. Dirty, too. *What the hell is going on here?*

Jerry rolled his window down. "Fill her up," he said.

"You serious?"

"Yeah, we need gas."

"Damn it, man, I'm trying to bounce out of this damn town, and you're trying to get gas?"

"We need gas, man, come on. This thing doesn't run on fumes." Jerry popped the door and stepped out. "I'll do it," he said. He unscrewed the gas cap. "Least you could do is pay for it."

"You still owe me two forty!" said Bunny.

"Shit, that's right."

"Yeah, it is right," said Bunny, opening the passenger door and getting in.

Jerry filled up the tank, topped it off, and looked around. It was a small town. An old, white-haired woman was filling up nearby; she used both hands to hold the nozzle. She looked at Jerry, and Jerry smiled politely at her. The snow continued falling, and it was sticking to the ground now.

When he got into the car, Bunny was in the middle of pulling his phone out of his pocket. "Shit," said Bunny. "That's the cops calling."

"Pick it up," said Jerry.

Bunny sent it to voicemail, then sat there staring out the window, making a little clicking noise with his tongue.

Then he wiped his face. "So what the hell is going on?" asked Jerry.

"Well, my uncle just told me he killed my father, so—"

"What?"

Bunny started telling him but was interrupted by his phone buzzing again. "They're calling again." He sent the call back to voicemail and then turned his phone off.

They sat there for a second.

"Yep, I was a little kid, so I wasn't exactly told everything. But yeah, he told me that, and then I had to lock him in a closet, tie him up, and steal a four-wheeler."

"Shit, you're gonna get me caught up in all this," said Jerry.

"Caught up?" said Bunny. "This is your thing! You pulled me into this! I'd be in Commerce City selling cigarettes if it wasn't for you! And I'd be plenty happy there, too."

"Shit," said Jerry. "You're right. My bad, man."

"You're damn right I'm right."

"Calm down," said Jerry.

"No, I'm not gonna calm down. You pissed me off."

Bunny took a deep breath. "Okay," he said. He finished telling Jerry what happened that morning. Told him about the notebook, and the men, and the raid.

"Let me see the notebook," said Jerry.

Bunny pulled it out and shook his head at the thing like it was a gift certificate to a clown supply store. He handed it to Jerry. While Jerry thumbed through it, Bunny, out of habit, looked at his powered-down phone.

"Fucking numbers," said Jerry.

"Yep," said Bunny.

"Bunch of gibberish."

"That's what they wanted."

Jerry looked through rows of shaky handwritten notes. Some of it was smudged pencil marks. There were lists of things to buy: grain bagger, seed tender. There were prices. Jerry read through some of them. Agricultural bullshit. Things for running a farm. There were ledgers that looked like money owed, or debts, or something. But they didn't seem very big: $731.02, $41.06, $618.00; the biggest one Jerry saw was for $2,602.88.

Jerry skipped ahead then, and about twenty pages in, he came to a new section. He squinted and read the words out loud: "And straightaway the father of the child cried out, and said with tears, Lord, I believe; help thou mine unbelief." He skipped forward through the pages. "Bible shit," he said.

"Yeah, he's always saying Christian stuff," said Bunny. "Quoting from it."

Jerry continued turning pages. He came to a new section and read silently to himself: *Wedding liar February play claim begin level protect fee multiply cost finger purchase lizard arrange hybrid pilot smart fence step indicate gate mechanic chef.*

"What the hell is all this?" he asked.

"Don't ask me," said Bunny.

"Slam poetry or some shit," said Jerry. "You need a cryptologist to understand this." Jerry sat there for a second, just looking at the words. Then he felt an electric shock run through his body. "Hold on!" he said. He used his finger and counted the words. "Holy shit!" he whispered when he finished.

"What?" said Bunny.

"You know what this is?"

"What?" asked Bunny, looking concerned, scared even.

"This is a fucking crypto key."

"What?"

"Remember Johnny?"

"Best Buy Johnny?"

"He said people stamp them on copper and screw the copper plate into the attic, in case the house burns down."

"But that's not copper," said Bunny.

"It's not the copper that's important, it's the words, dude. Twenty-four random words. He talked about that shit all night: twenty-four fucking words."

He counted the words again, out loud, one at a time. "That's a twenty-four-word phrase right there! I mean, come on. There's only one thing that's gonna be."

"What?" asked Bunny, still confused.

"Crypto, man! Are you not listening? The fuck you think I'm talking about?"

"How much?" asked Bunny.

"Don't know," said Jerry. They sat there for a second, looking around, making sure they weren't going to get ambushed. "You said those cops were trying to get it, though."

"Damn!" said Bunny. "You're right. They were trying to get it for themselves. Fucking dirty-birdies, man. They told me not to talk to any other cops about it. What the hell is going on here? They're trying to use me to rip my uncle off."

"Ventola talked about your uncle and crypto. I didn't even pay attention to it."

"Lord have mercy upon our souls," said Bunny.

"Alright, stop the bullshit," said Jerry. He closed his eyes for a second, waved his hand in the air. "This is where things sometimes go wrong. You understand what I'm saying?"

"No," said Bunny.

"Like in a movie, this is where people could start fucking each other up."

"Who?"

"You and me, man," said Jerry.

Bunny sat there looking at the notebook.

"Do you want to do this?" asked Jerry.

"Do what?"

"Take this shit, man. Take their money."

"Yeah," said Bunny. "I do."

"Then we gotta split it fifty-fifty. There's no getting around that. We gotta vow that we're gonna split it. That's the only way we can make this work."

"Yeah," said Bunny. "I agree to that."

"Whatever it is," said Jerry. "We gotta swear right now."

"Yeah, okay."

"'Cause Bunny, it could be ten thousand dollars, it could be ten million, man; I don't know."

"Okay."

"Say, *I swear.*"

"I swear," said Bunny. "You say it, too."

"I swear, too," said Jerry. They shook hands, but that didn't feel sufficient, so they leaned across the center console and hugged each other.

"Okay," said Bunny, leaning back. "California?" he asked.

"Yeah, man," said Jerry. "San Diego. It's time to start living our lives."

They sat there, both looking in their respective side view mirrors, both of their faces slack. "We just need some gas money to get out there," said Bunny.

Jerry pulled the Blazer into Ventola's lot and parked right in front of the office. "You sure we should be doing this?" said Jerry.

"He's the only person I know," said Bunny.

"Alright," said Jerry.

"Tell me how you're gonna say it," said Bunny.

"I'm gonna say, *We wanna trade this Blazer and you could pay us the difference in cash.*"

"For a cheaper car," said Bunny. "We need a thousand in cash, walking-around money."

They entered the office and found Ventola, Blanche, and Jimmy Dean sitting there with the television on.

"What the hell is this?" asked Ventola when he saw Bunny.

"How are you?" said Bunny, holding his hand out for a shake.

Ventola pushed himself up and walked to Bunny, looking at him suspiciously. "You don't write, you don't call." He shook hands with Bunny, clapped him on the back.

"I been busy," said Bunny.

"Shit," said Ventola. "Busy jerking off about twenty times a day."

"Monte," said Blanche. "Don't bully the boy."

"I'm not," said Ventola.

"Can we talk to you?" asked Jerry.

"You are talking to me."

"Outside?" said Jerry.

"Jesus," said Ventola. "What the hell is going on with you boys? You're acting like a bunch of doula dolls."

They stepped back outside into the cold day; the ground was wet from the snow, but it hadn't stuck here in the city. Jerry took a deep breath and looked at Ventola. “Monte,” he said. “I want to thank you for taking me under your wing.”

“What is this?” asked Ventola.

“I have to resign my position from the dealership,” said Jerry. He nodded toward Bunny. “We’re gonna hit the road. We’re going to Kansas City. We got jobs waiting there. High-paying construction work.”

“What about your uncle?” said Ventola.

“Yeah, I told him about it,” said Bunny. “He’s cool. He understands.”

“I wanted to see if I could trade my Blazer for one of those Hondas, or that Toyota,” said Jerry, pointing at a couple of the cars. “And you could maybe give us a little cash back, like a thousand or so.”

“What the hell have you boys done?” asked Ventola.

“Nothing,” said Bunny.

“That Blazer’s only worth about forty-five hundred,” said Ventola.

“Come on,” said Jerry. “That’s worth at least ten large. That’s my baby. It’s in damn near-fine condition. The stereo in there is worth damn near two thousand.”

“I’ll give you the Honda and six hundred,” said Ventola.

Jerry looked at Bunny. Bunny shook his head.

“Could you do that Avalon?” asked Jerry, pointing at a 2007 Toyota Avalon. “Plus a thousand cash?”

“You give me a thousand cash?” asked Ventola.

“Stop playing,” said Jerry.

Right then, Ventola’s phone rang. He had it to his ear before the boys even knew what was happening. “Hello?” he said. Then, in a serious tone, “You said what?” An alarmed look came over his face. His eyes went from Bunny to Jerry, and then they dropped to the ground. “Mm-hmm,” he said into the phone. “Okay, let me call you back.”

He ended the call. His lips, as he pulled air into his lungs, formed a little circle like he was gonna whistle a tune, then that circle turned into a little smile. “I’ll go get the paperwork started,” he said. He turned toward the office and started walking that way.

Before he'd taken a step, though, Bunny was already on him with the gun out. "Hold up," said Bunny.

"What the hell are you doing?" whispered Jerry.

"He knows," said Bunny.

Ventola stopped walking.

"Shit," said Jerry.

"Into the office," said Bunny.

"You boys are making a mistake," said Ventola. "Get back in your car and just get the hell out of here."

Jerry turned and looked around the lot. Nobody was there to see what was happening. Down the block someone honked their car horn.

Bunny pointed at the office. "Go on," he said. Then he stepped to Ventola and pressed the gun into his back. "Let's go."

They pushed into the door of the office and the bell chimed again.

"Get them down on the ground," said Bunny.

Jerry walked toward Blanche and Jimmy Dean, who were seated at their respective desks. Jimmy Dean looked alarmed, but Blanche didn't appear to understand what was happening. "Down on the ground," said Jerry. "I'm sorry, Blanche. I really am."

"What?"

"Blanche, do what they say. Get down on the ground," said Ventola.

"What is this?" asked Blanche.

"They're robbing us," said Ventola.

"We're not robbing you," said Bunny. "We wanted to trade our car."

"Do you want me to call the police?" asked Blanche.

Jerry went right up to her, grabbed her by the shoulders. "You have to get down on the ground, now, Blanche," he said. "I'm sorry about this."

"Stay right where you are!" said Bunny, speaking to Jimmy Dean.

"Face down, right here. I'm sorry," said Jerry. He guided her down to her knees, and then down onto her stomach. Then he had Jimmy Dean do the same, right next to her. He frisked Jimmy Dean, made sure he didn't have a gun on him.

Bunny, meanwhile, had moved Ventola back to his office and was making him open the safe. It was the second safe he'd broken into that day; Bunny marveled at that. He'd never been inside a safe in his life.

"Bunny, this is not the path you want to take," said Ventola.

"Yeah, no shit," said Bunny. "Open it up. Come on, Monte, I don't want to kill you, I really don't." His voice sounded sad, and this seemed to frighten Ventola. The safe was on the ground, and the car salesman worked the dial silently, getting down on both knees as he worked.

"Open it slowly," said Bunny.

"You dummies," said Ventola. He opened the door slowly, but then his hand darted to the inside of the safe.

Bunny was ready for this; his pistol was already swinging down and catching Ventola in the back of his bald head. The man fell forward, away from the safe, but caught himself like he was preparing to do a push-up from his knees. Bunny was right on top of him, legs on either side like a horseback rider. "Down on the ground!" said Bunny, pointing the gun against his head. "Flat on the ground."

"I didn't do nothing," said Ventola. "What the hell did you hit me for?"

"Stay flat, man. I'm not playing anymore!" said Bunny.

"You okay?" called Jerry from the other room.

"Yeah, just hold them."

Bunny leaned down to whisper, "You stupid son of a bitch, you had to be a tough guy."

He went to the safe, looked in it. There was a black .357 Magnum lying there. Bunny shook his head. "You were gonna try and buck up on me?" He looked at Ventola, then bent down and looked deeper into the safe. There was some cash, one small stack, rubber-banded. Bunny pulled it out and leafed through it. It looked like a couple thousand; he winced at the fives and tens. "This all you got?"

"That's it," said Ventola.

Behind the cash, there was a big Ziploc freezer bag. Bunny pulled it out and looked at it. It was meth, must've been about a pound. "You got a bag I can put all this shit in?"

"Blanche does."

"Alright, get up."

Bunny moved Ventola into the other room, had him get down on the ground. He showed Jerry the .357, handed him the Glock, and made a face. "Where's the duct tape?" he asked.

The three hostages stayed silent.

"There's packing tape in Blanche's desk," said Jerry. Blanche shot him a look.

"Lay on your stomach," said Bunny, getting the tape from the desk. "We're just gonna tape your hands. First give us your phones. We're gonna leave them in here."

"Boys," said Ventola. "Come on."

"No, no," said Bunny. "It's gotta be done."

Bunny taped their hands behind their backs, then marched them one at a time out to the lot and helped them into the trunks of three separate cars. He put Ventola in first—stuck him in the back of a Cadillac so he'd have room. He had to work to get the big man in there, lying down with his hands bound behind his back.

"Where's Juan Carlos?" Bunny asked, referring to Ventola's mechanic.

"He's in Colorado Springs," said Ventola, hatefully.

"Tell me his number."

"It's on the wall in my office," said Ventola. "On a Post-it note."

"Okay," said Bunny, "he'll let you out." He closed the trunk on Ventola.

Bunny hurried to the office, found Juan Carlos's number and stuffed it into his pocket. Then he walked Jimmy Dean out to the lot and put him into the trunk of a white Buick LaCrosse. "I'm diabetic," said Jimmy Dean, when he was lying flat. "I'm gonna die in here."

"Nah," said Bunny. "The mechanic will let you out. We just need to get a little road between us."

Jimmy Dean looked petrified; he licked his lips compulsively, and his eyes bugged out. Bunny shut the trunk on him, too.

Both Bunny and Jerry took Blanche out. They led her to a red Kia Forte. The trunk was already open, waiting for her. When she saw it, Blanche became rigid and refused to move. They lifted her up together and set her into it. She looked absolutely pissed off, ready to kill.

"You are gonna rot in hell for this," she said. Bunny glanced at Jerry. His friend was looking down on the woman regretfully, his brow knitted up like he was in pain. "You stupid fucking cunt-boys, we're gonna hunt you down and feed you to the pigs for this. Fucking flea-rats. *In hell!* I'm gonna find you in hell if I have to!"

Bunny closed the trunk on her. They could hear her inside, issuing a steady stream of muffled curses.

They had a quick chat and then they went and opened Ventola's trunk and spoke to him again. "Alright, Monte," said Bunny. "We're gonna call your boy and let him know you're in here, so you won't die or anything like that."

"We're not ripping you off," said Jerry. "I'm gonna leave you the Blazer. This is a deal, fair and square."

"You can write up the papers and sign for him," said Bunny.

"But you're not gonna tell the cops about this," said Jerry. "If you do, we're gonna have to tell them about your little meth operation with that white lady that comes by."

"Your best option," said Bunny, "is to let this go. Just let this one go."

They stood there for a second, looking down on him. A semitruck blared a horn out on the street. Ventola lay there, shaking his head.

"Thank you," said Jerry.

"Yeah, thanks," said Bunny.

Then they closed the trunk on Monte Ventola.

"There he is," said Jerry, guiding their new Avalon toward the curb. The car was silver and clean, and felt strange, like they were riding around in a grown-up's car. The sky was still overcast.

Angel stood there with his arms crossed, looking suspicious as hell. Underneath a big down jacket, he wore a white Juicy Couture sweatsuit, a girl's style. Thick eyeliner around his eyes, stubble on his cheeks. Jerry hadn't seen him since he'd gotten the ride home from him after he got out of jail.

Bunny rolled down the window so Jerry could speak to him.

"Who's this?" said Angel.

"This is Bunny, he's my guy, don't worry about him. Jump in, come on." Angel looked at Bunny, looked at the back of the car, looked at Jerry, then looked all around the street before finally getting in.

"Alright, look man, show it to him," said Jerry. He put the car in drive and pulled back out onto Humboldt Street.

Bunny turned and handed the Ziploc bag to Angel in the backseat.

"Shit," said Angel. "Damn, you're not playing. Okay, Mr. Big Dick. How much you trying to get for it?"

"We were thinking two thousand," said Jerry.

"Nah," said Angel. "That's not quite a half pound. I can feel that in my hands. Anyway, that'll trade in Denver for eight hundred."

Bunny turned in his seat and looked at Jerry's friend. "How much can you do?"

"I only have seven hundred and twenty-one dollars in the bank. I can give you more later, or you can sell me just half of it for four."

"Shit," said Jerry. "That's two grand worth."

"I can give you seven," said Angel, speaking with his eyes closed like he was addressing a child.

"You have it on you?" asked Jerry.

"Come on, girl, I don't have that kind of cash on me. You gotta take me to the bank. Go over there near Whole Foods."

Jerry looked at Bunny, who nodded.

They let Angel off at the bank near Whole Foods and then circled around and parked in the lot.

"Check your phone, see if there's any news stories on that raid," said Bunny.

Jerry pulled out his phone and muttered to himself while he checked. "Raid . . . Umm, police . . . Castle Rock . . . Yeah man, right here!"

"What?" said Bunny.

"Yeah, right here. Press release. US Attorney's Office, District of Colorado. Listen." Jerry read from his phone: "Twenty-six individuals with alleged ties to white supremacist group arrested on weapons, drugs, and racketeering charges in Douglas County. Wednesday, April 2, 2022. That's today, dude."

"Let me see," said Bunny.

Jerry handed him the phone. Bunny read the names and ages of the people arrested. "There's my uncle, right there, Willard Haggerty, sixty-eight, of Castle Rock," said Bunny. "Peter Vinson, twenty-eight, Denver. That's Spider. They got Lester. Bessie. Rhonda. They got Arnold D. Man," said Bunny. "They got everyone. Wrapped up the whole gang." He looked like he could hardly believe it. He kept reading. "They didn't get Nelson, though. I don't see him here. He's the real one. They didn't get any of those kids, either. They had these younger guys there. I don't see any of them on the list. Youngest person on the list is John Foote, twenty-seven. I don't even know who that is."

"That's a government operation right there," said Jerry. "Big time."

Bunny handed him his phone back. "Damn," he said. "That is an operation." He had a hair in his mouth, and he tried to grab it with his finger.

"Hey, you gotta ditch your phone, man," said Jerry. "They're gonna be on that."

"Shit, you're right," said Bunny. "Throw it away?"

"Yeah, toss it," said Jerry. "We'll get you a new one."

Bunny got out of the car. He dusted his clothes, rubbed his elbow, and then walked toward the entrance of the Whole Foods. On his way, he took his phone out. He thought about turning it on for a second, checking his messages, but then realized he better not even do that; he didn't want to ping anything. He saw a trash can and he slipped the phone into it.

Shoppers were coming out of Whole Foods. A woman, pushing a cart, walked right by him. She had large breasts and wore a pink sweater. She appeared to be totally oblivious to his existence. He was a ghost, a man on the run now. The woman was followed by a guy, speaking loudly into his AirPods. He was saying something about things not being "satisfactorily addressed." Bunny patted his pocket where his phone should be, found it missing, and then remembered he'd just gotten rid of it.

When he got back in the car, Jerry looked at him and asked, "Yeah?"

Bunny said, "Put it in the garbage."

"We should've sold it."

"Come on, man."

A few minutes later, Angel opened the door and sat in the backseat. "Okay, let's go," he said. "Take me home."

When they arrived at Angel's apartment, Angel invited them up. "You don't want to party?" he said.

"We can't," said Jerry. "Got too much to do."

"Next time," said Angel. Then he handed forward a bank envelope. The car became quiet while Jerry counted the seven hundred-dollar bills.

"Alright," said Jerry. "Thank you."

Angel, meanwhile, sat up straight and leaned back a little, so he could fit the freezer bag into the front of his pants. Then he looked at Bunny, like he wanted to stamp a romantic memory into his brain. "Okay, you two, be careful," he said.

"We will," said Jerry.

When Angel was out, they added their money together. "Two thousand eight hundred and fourteen plus seven hundred . . . is . . . twenty-nine, thirty, thirty-one, thirty-two, thirty-three, thirty-four . . . Three thousand five hundred and fourteen," said Bunny. "Hey, that's not bad."

"No, it isn't."

"I wish those cops would've paid me," said Bunny.

"That would've been cool, too," said Jerry.

"Hey, we gotta call that dude," said Bunny. "Call that dude, Juan Carlos, let him know about those three in the trunks."

"Shit," said Jerry. "I almost forgot all about that."

The young men, riding in their new Avalon, left Denver behind. They took Highway 6 and headed straight into the Rocky Mountains. On their left was the white water of Clear Creek. On their right, the mountain face: the ground a little snowy, except where the rocks pointed out—some aspen, a few pines, and some bushes here and there. Jerry drove and Bunny rode shotgun. The only thing they carried with them was their money, the black notebook, and the two guns, which they'd hidden between the seat cushions in the backseat. The car still smelled faintly of Angel's perfume. They called Juan Carlos from a blocked number on Jerry's phone, told him the situation. He didn't seem overly concerned.

"We should've kept a little bit of that crank for the drive," said Bunny.

"Nah," said Jerry. "It's time to clean up."

"You're right again," said Bunny, slapping his own leg. "It's time to clean up."

"We gotta live like mercenaries now."

"I'd like to go vegan," said Bunny.

"Shit, me too," said Jerry. "Let's do that. I wanna get in shape, too. I don't need to lift weights, but I'd at least like to be able to run a mile in under seven point five minutes."

"Yeah, we gotta get our beach bodies."

"It takes discipline, though."

"That's true," said Bunny. "It does."

Bunny sat there thinking for a second, tapping his head with his fingers. He could only imagine how angry those cops felt. His thoughts moved to Rayton, and his body felt a little influx of guilty feelings for not having said a proper goodbye. *I guess we did, though*, he told himself. He tapped his pocket again, where his phone should've been. "Shit, I just thought of something," he said out loud.

"What?"

"Those cops might not be able to see where I am."

"Yeah?"

"But they're gonna see who I called, who called me."

"Shit," said Jerry, sitting up in his seat. He looked in the rearview, then checked his side view like he was searching for an active tail.

Bunny looked that way, too. The road was empty behind them. "It's okay, chill out," said Bunny.

Jerry said he was going to pull over and pointed ahead of them, across the highway, at a little scenic overlook by the creek.

"You can't cross the highway," said Bunny, putting his hand on the dashboard.

Jerry slowed down and did it anyway. They crossed against the double yellow lines and cut in front of a trucker, who flashed his brights in anger. Then they bumped against the side of the road and hit the dirt pull-out spot and skidded to a stop.

"Jesus," said Bunny.

"Sorry," said Jerry. "That was a little more chaotic than I wanted it to be."

"We get pulled over for something like that, they're gonna find a warrant on me," said Bunny.

"Damn, now it's your turn being right."

"Like you said. Come on, now. We can't be doing that kind of stuff," said Bunny.

"Okay, let me think for a second," said Jerry. He sat there with his eyes closed, thinking. Bunny wondered whether his friend might be having second thoughts about this whole venture. Finally, Jerry opened his eyes and looked at Bunny. "I'm gonna call my mom real quick. Tell her I'm going off the radar for a bit."

"Yeah, that's a good idea," said Bunny. "But tell her we're headed to Kansas City."

"Yeah, okay," said Jerry. He pulled out his phone, looked at it, and then opened his contacts and looked at Helen's number. He had a sudden desire to call her. "Shit," he said.

"What?"

"Nothing," said Jerry. He took a moment and repeated her number to himself. In his stomach, he felt something like a tension that wanted to break. He stepped out of the car, and Bunny felt the cool mountain air come in. He watched his friend walk away, and then he spent a moment looking around. The sky had cleared, and the sun had already dipped behind the mountains, and they were fully in the shade. The creek was rushing by. It was pretty out there, mountain vibes, snow on the ground. He wanted to get out, too, but he wanted to give his friend a moment to talk to his mother first.

While Bunny waited, he thought about his own mother. They were going to head right past her. He knew he should stop, give her a kiss, and tell her he was going to be fine. *We're gonna make a whole lot of money*, he imagined telling her. For a second, his dad crossed his mind; he saw the man begging for his life. He forced that thought from his mind, watched Jerry finish his call, and then got out and joined him.

"Left a message," said Jerry. "Said I'm headed to KC for a job, and I'd be in touch soon." He shook his head, like he was feeling sad. "Yep."

"Gotta let the moms know you're safe and sound, though."

"Yeah," said Jerry. He kicked a rock and then asked, "Should I get rid of it?"

He seemed to be experiencing the same feelings that Bunny had when he ditched his phone. Like pushing off to sea. No turning back from here.

"Yeah," said Bunny.

Jerry tossed the phone far, all the way to the creek, like a baseball player throwing a runner out at home plate. It disappeared into the water, didn't even make a splash, just plunked right in.

"Nice throw," said Bunny.

"Thanks," said Jerry.

They both stepped forward and peed down the hill toward the creek. Then they got back into the Avalon. "Need to buy some paper maps," said Bunny.

"Keep going west," said Jerry, pointing uphill. "Get to the Pacific Ocean and you swing a left."

"That's true," said Bunny. "We don't need a map, for that. The sun always sets in the west."

"Mercenary style."

"G-style. Let's go," said Bunny.

"Should I cut against the traffic?" asked Jerry.

Bunny looked all around, up the hill, down the hill, back up again. "Yeah, I guess so."

The wheels spun and kicked up dirt; they crossed back over the double yellow lines and started heading uphill again, west, following the sun. Bunny crossed his arms in front of him and stared out at the road. "We don't have music anymore," he said.

"Yeah," said Jerry. "Like we're lost at sea."

Bunny nodded, sighed. He started thinking about things and his worries moved in on him like a big storm front and then they spread through his body like wind through a canyon. "Shit," he whispered.

"What?"

"Just shit."

"What?"

"This is gonna be kind of complicated," said Bunny. "Like I don't know anything about crypto. Do you?"

"No." Jerry shook his head. "Not really."

"Like, how—assuming there is some money—how are we supposed to get it out? Like, what the hell? You go to a bank or what? How you gonna get this money out?" His hands were sweating now, and he wiped them on his pants. The mountains that had just looked nice suddenly looked cold and inhospitable.

"You think we're making a mistake?" asked Jerry.

"Nah, look. Truth is, I don't know about you, but I have to go. By now— Shit, I already got a contract on my ass. Real talk, man, I'm not even playing, I got a kill sight on my head." He tapped his head. "The cops looking for me, too? I'm not trying to serve twelve years."

"Mm-mm," said Jerry. "No, sir."

"You don't have to come with me, though," said Bunny.

"I'm tired of living at my mom's house," said Jerry. "I gotta live my life at some point, you know what I'm saying?"

"Yeah, I do." Bunny nodded. "But we need some help for this. We should've folded Best Buy Johnny in on this one. We need some tech support."

"We could try and find someone in San Diego," said Jerry.

"My uncle's gonna lock that money up," said Bunny.

"Time is not on our side," said Jerry.

A man on a Harley rode past them in the opposite direction. "Too cold to be riding a bike up here," whispered Bunny. They both watched him go.

"You know what?" said Jerry.

"What?"

"You know who could help us on this?"

"Who?"

"Same lady that got us into this mess."

"Her?" asked Bunny, shocked.

"She's a lawyer, man. She'll know what to do."

"You think so?"

"Yeah."

"Damn," said Bunny.

"She's cool," said Jerry. "We been hanging out a little bit."

"What?"

"Not like that, man, just on the friend side. But she's cool." Jerry reached for his pocket to get his phone and remembered it was gone. "Shit," he said.

"I keep doing that, too."

They rode for a moment, feeling a little more perked up. "How we gonna get her to help, though?" asked Bunny.

"Cut her in," said Jerry. "We'll have to give her a percent. Say ten percent. Or a flat fee. We'll say ten K, just to kind of advise us. That kind of thing."

"'Cause in a way, we got money now," said Bunny. "We can pay for advisors. Pay for lawyers, all that. That's what rich people do."

"Yep."

"You gotta act rich to get rich," said Bunny. "Acting rich attracts money that way."

Jerry pointed at a sign on their right. "Idaho Springs, fourteen miles."

⁂

They found a motel on the far side of Idaho Springs. The place accepted cash. It was $72.06 with tax included, plus a two-hundred-dollar cash security deposit. The clerk, a big-bellied cowboy with wrinkles around his eyes, looked at them suspiciously. He pointed at a handwritten sign above the check-in desk: CHECK OUT AT 11 AM.

Their room was on the ground floor, two twin beds. The place was dark and smelled like Pine-Sol and other cleaning chemicals. "I never stayed in a motel before," said Bunny, testing the mattress by pushing down on it.

"Never?"

"You have?"

"A few times," said Jerry. He found a little pad of paper and a pen, and he wrote down Helen's number. "I memorized it," he said, showing the number to Bunny.

"Are you in love with this girl?" asked Bunny. "Are y'all about to turn me into a third wheel on this?"

"It's not like that," said Jerry. "Trust me, she's cool. She's gang, you'll see." He picked up the desk phone, dialed her number, and after a few rings, he left a message: "Hey Helen, it's Jerry." He paused. "Hold on, let me call you right back." He hung up.

"What was that?" asked Bunny.

"I don't know what number she's supposed to call me back at. Go ask the front desk man."

Bunny stepped back outside. A few doors down, a woman stood in front of one of the rooms scrubbing something off her jacket. She looked up when Bunny closed his door. Her hair was dyed black with gray roots and her face was gaunt from meth. To put her at ease, Bunny nodded, smiled, and then crossed the parking lot.

Except for an airplane flying in the distance, and an occasional truck passing, the place was quiet. When Bunny entered the office, the clerk, startled, turned off his television with a remote like he'd been caught watching something naughty. Then he turned to Bunny with his chin and eyebrows raised, like *Yeah?*

Bunny asked about the phone number and the man showed him a card with the motel's name and number on it. "You're in room eighteen," he said. "Tell them to call *this* number"—he tapped the number on the card—"ask for room eighteen. I'll transfer 'em through." He handed Bunny the card and then folded over into a coughing fit.

"Yes, sir," said Bunny. "Thank you."

With the man still coughing, Bunny stepped outside again. He crossed the lot, looking around for danger. There was no sign of anything out of the ordinary. When he stepped back into the room, he found Jerry sitting on the bed, hunched over and not looking at all like a mercenary. He looked more like a scared kid.

"You got it?" asked Jerry.

"Yeah," said Bunny, handing him the card. "Tell her room eighteen."

Jerry called back and left a second message. He gave Helen the phone and room numbers and asked her to call him back as soon as she could. When he finished, he looked at Bunny. "You want to watch some TV?"

Bunny grabbed the remote and turned it on. He flipped through the channels for a minute until he found some motocross. "You cool with this?"

"Yeah." They sat there watching the motorcycles for a while.

"I'd like to jump those," said Bunny.

"You ride motocross?" asked Jerry.

"No, but I'd like to," said Bunny.

The motel phone rang. They both looked at each other, a little shocked, like they couldn't believe she called back.

Jerry picked up the phone and Bunny listened to him have a conversation. He basically told her that they were in trouble, that they needed help, and that they all might be able to make some *real* money off it. He gave her the motel's name and told her they were in Idaho Springs. He repeated the town again: Idaho Springs. Then he hung up and looked at Bunny. "She's coming," he said. "She is definitely coming."

"Damn," said Bunny. "That's cool as hell."

A little less than two hours later, Jerry hopped up when he heard three quiet knocks on the door. He turned the TV off, opened the door, and found Helen standing there in all her glory. She wore a black ski jacket and tight black leggings. She had red lipstick on, too. Jerry couldn't believe his eyes. She looked like a movie star. She didn't belong in Colorado—she needed to be in Hollywood. Jerry's confidence, upon seeing her, shot straight up. He felt certain that they'd done the right thing by calling her. "Come in," he said.

She stepped into the room, and Jerry turned his attention to Bunny. Bunny didn't get up or say anything; he just stared at her. It occurred to Jerry that Bunny was a damn good-looking man himself, and he felt a pang of jealousy.

Jerry introduced them to each other.

"Pleased to meet you," Bunny said, finally speaking and standing up with his hand held out.

"You too," said Helen, leaning forward and shaking hands with him. She turned to Jerry. "He's the one who helped you with my thing?"

"Yep," said Jerry. "He went to jail, too."

"I'm sorry," whispered Helen. She took a deep breath and studied Bunny for a second. "That turned into a mess, didn't it?"

"That's okay," said Bunny, sitting back down.

Jerry went to the window, pulled the blinds back, and checked the lot. There was no movement outside. Feeling suddenly cold, he rubbed his hands together, made fists, and blew into them, one at a time. "We want to tell you what's going on," he said.

"Please," said Helen, pulling a chair out from under a desk. She unzipped her jacket, opened it, and sat.

Jerry and Bunny took turns and told her the story as best as they could. They told her about the cops recruiting Bunny. They told her about Ventola. Told her about Bunny's uncle, the ranch, and the men out there, the guns, the shooting, the white power stuff. And then they told her about the notebook and how it was all the cops could think about.

"So we got it," said Bunny.

"And I'm looking at it," said Jerry. "And you know what I find?"

"What?" asked Helen.

"Twenty-four words," said Jerry. "You know what that is?"

"No," said Helen, glancing at the door behind her.

The boys continued their story. They told her how Ventola had mentioned Willard making his money in crypto. "Drugs and crypto," said Jerry. "Need money to buy drugs," said Bunny. They described the ranch to her and told her that Willard regularly paid some twenty men to work out there. They showed her the notebook, which Bunny had been holding, tucked into the front of his pants. They showed her the page, pointed at the twenty-four-word phrase. She squinted, and her lips moved a little while she read it.

"So, how can I help?" Helen asked.

Jerry thought she looked sad. Like somehow this whole thing had disappointed her; this made him sad, too. He took a second to think about what he wanted from her. Then he realized he just wanted her to join them. He wanted her to trust that he was onto something. He looked down at the floor, which was a maroon linoleum tile. "I guess we wanted . . ." His voice came out sounding like a whisper. "I guess we just wanted a little help. Because we don't know how to get from point A to point B."

"We need guidance," said Bunny.

"How much do you think it is?" asked Helen.

"Could be a thousand," said Jerry. "Could be a million."

"Could be nothing," said Bunny. "We don't know. We just don't want to screw anything up. Set off the wrong alarm bell, anything like that."

Helen, still seated, put her head in her hands and her elbows on her knees and sat there. It looked like she was crying. Jerry glanced at Bunny, who shook his head at him.

After a long time, she finally looked back up. "Could be nothing," she said, sighing. "If there's nothing there, then there's no risk for me. If it's something, then you're asking me to join you in a criminal conspiracy. You're talking about ripping off a white supremacist gang. You're talking about stealing from police officers."

Jerry felt nervous hearing it spelled out like that. It sounded more serious coming from her mouth. He tried to form a verbal response, but it was Bunny who spoke first, and all he said was "Yep," and then "Mm-hmm."

"I'm a lawyer," said Helen. "My fee is fifty percent."

"I think that might be a little too much," whispered Jerry. He looked at Bunny. They all sat there for a moment, holding their breath.

"There's three of us," said Bunny. "We should split it in three: one, two, and three."

Helen looked up at the ceiling and made a face. "Okay," she said, looking back down. "But I make all the decisions and my word is final. I'm sorry, but that's the only way I can do it."

"Okay," said Jerry.

"Yeah, okay," said Bunny. He walked to her and held his hand out. Jerry watched them shake, and he noticed their hands linger together for a moment afterward, like they were already in love, like this was the consummation of their love. Then he stood and shook hands with her, too.

"I'll call in sick to work," said Helen. "I'll tell them I have Covid. I'll have to do research. I'll have to find a computer here in town. I'm not going to do anything from my phone. I'll figure it out. That's what it's all about, right? Anonymity?"

"Yeah," said Bunny.

They all three stood there for a second, nodding their heads. Then Helen clapped her hands together. "I'm hungry," she said.

The only open place in town was a Chinese restaurant on the main strip. It was decorated with colored Christmas lights, which cast a nice glow and made everything seem romantic. Except for one other family, the place was empty of customers. The boys ordered fried rice, sesame chicken, string beans, Mongolian beef, and egg rolls. Helen ordered steamed chicken with steamed vegetables. They didn't have liquor, but they served beer, and all three of them ordered one and then kept ordering more throughout their meal.

Helen, while they ate, asked Bunny questions. She asked him where he was from, how long he'd lived in Denver, how old he was, all kinds of things. Bunny seemed to like the attention, and as the meal went on, he became more and more gregarious. Apparently, Helen was having troubles at work. And at one point, Bunny asked her if she'd like to accompany them to California.

Helen glanced toward the kitchen, glanced back, and whispered, "If it's more than a million, I'll come to California with you." She looked at Jerry, then looked at Bunny and smiled. "We can be a happy family, all of us living together."

"That would be cool," said Bunny. He held out his beer bottle and she lifted hers and they clinked their bottles together. "Right?" he said, turning to Jerry.

"Yeah," said Jerry.

"Cheers, then," said Bunny.

The three of them clinked their bottles together and they all drank to seal the deal. Then Bunny and Helen started talking about lifting weights. Helen said she'd be perfectly happy not having a job. She could devote herself entirely to her bodybuilding. Bunny said, "Yeah, I could do that, too. Just go all full-in on something. Like yoga, or jiujitsu."

Jerry sat on the sidelines of this conversation. As the night wore on, he became more and more resentful of Bunny. He wasn't mad at him; he was just jealous of the way the guy could carry on without giving a damn about anything else. Bunny had a lightness to him. Jerry, sitting there, tried to summon that lightness. *Okay, here we go*, he thought—and he dug down into himself, but there was no lightness there. He drank from his beer again, burped quietly, looked around the room. "I gotta go to the bathroom," he said, and he pushed himself up from the table. Neither of them looked at him; they just continued talking.

In the bathroom, he told himself he was being stupid. He spit into the urinal and then peed into it. Before leaving, he washed his hands and looked at himself in the mirror, raised his chin a little, turned it side to side. Then he tossed his towel in the trash, and on his way out, he noticed that someone had written the word *arrow* on the door. *Change my name to Arrow*, thought Jerry. *Hey, I'm Arrow LeClair.*

When he came back, he found Helen in the middle of a story. Jerry sat down and pushed his plate to the side. He was stuffed. Bunny sat there listening with his arms crossed in front of his chest.

"I'm telling him," said Helen, turning to Jerry and speaking in a kind of spaced-out way, "that when I was in junior high, I was camping, and we had an accident, and my face got burnt pretty bad. I was disfigured. I looked like a monster." She lifted a hand toward Bunny. "He was asking why I started bodybuilding." She shrugged. Her eyes filled with tears, and she sat there staring down at the table and blinking. "That's why."

"I'm sorry," said Bunny.

"Me too," said Jerry.

"It's not supposed to be a sob story," said Helen. Her affect changed and she sat straight up. "The point is, life is short. You have to live it as well as you can."

"Yeah," said Jerry, hitting the table with his fist. He felt himself become more energized. "That's what I been saying. That's what I've been trying to say."

"Yeah," said Bunny. "Me too."

"Hell yeah," said Jerry. He looked up at the ceiling, looked around the room, and felt suddenly alive. Helen was looking at him with a little smile on her face, like *I've been trying to tell you*. Bunny smiled, too, and Jerry leaned over and bumped fists with his friend. "Damn, I feel better now," said Jerry. "You said exactly what I needed to hear."

Helen insisted on paying for dinner. Before they left, she went to the bathroom, and Jerry and Bunny had a moment alone. "She's cool," said Bunny.

"I told you."

On their way back to the motel, they stopped at a liquor store to buy some whiskey. They were already a little tipsy from the beers, and Helen took hold of Jerry's arm while they walked down the aisle of the store. They got a big bottle of Diet Coke to go with the whiskey. The clerk who checked them out, an older woman with thick glasses and dry lips, treated the whole transaction with a seriousness that made all three of them become quiet.

The motel had an ice machine, and they found two glasses and a paper cup, and they made a round of drinks. At first, they drank sitting down, but as the night wore on and they became more and more drunk, Helen started playing music on her phone and the three of them, each in their own way, began dancing to hip hop.

Helen said the lights were too bright, and she put a towel over both lamps. Bunny, perhaps because he was feeling like a third wheel, kept mainly to himself, and danced in his own space. Jerry and Helen, meanwhile, sometimes would touch each other, but mainly they danced apart, too.

At some point, they moved the end tables and pushed the two beds together in the middle of the room. Helen looked at their work and said, "Now we've got a king-sized bed." She flopped herself down and the boys lay down on either side of her. They turned the lights off, and Helen changed the music on her phone to Johnny Cash. She put her arm around Jerry, and he lay there with his head toward her neck, and he could tell that she was holding hands with Bunny, but it didn't even bother him because her hair smelled like melons. He breathed that smell in and eventually he fell asleep, and everything went black.

Then, quite suddenly, Jerry emerged from the blackness and found himself shoveling snow with his mother. In the dream, he must've been younger, because his mother was showing him how to shovel, and the snow was heavy and hard to lift. His shoes and gloves were wet, but he didn't feel cold. The air smelled like snow and pine trees. Somewhere down the street a car was stuck, and its wheels kept spinning and whining for a grip on the road. Jerry turned that way and stared down the street and his breath came out in little puffs of clouds.

The next morning, when Jerry woke up, the room, except for right around the curtains, was still dark. His head hurt and his mouth was dry. He reached with his hand and tried to touch where Helen's hip should've been, but there was nothing there. He pictured Bunny and her wrapped up in a romantic embrace. Instead, when he turned, he found Bunny lying there on his belly with both arms tucked under him and a pillow over his head.

Jerry used the bathroom and then drank water straight from the faucet. He went to the window, pulled the curtain back, and squinted at the parking lot. He didn't see Helen's car. His gaze, when he turned back to the room, fell onto the notepad where he'd written her number. The pen was sitting right there next to it. A bad feeling started in his stomach. His palms began to sweat. He pulled the curtains open, and the sun lit up the room.

"Hey," he said, shaking Bunny's shoulder.

Bunny pulled the pillow off his head and turned onto his side. He looked confused. "What?"

"Do you know where she went?" asked Jerry.

"No," said Bunny.

Jerry felt like crying. "You have the notebook, though, right?"

Bunny, blinking, stared at him for a moment. "I think it was . . ." He reached behind the bed. "I think it was under my pillow."

Jerry lowered himself down to his knees and peered under the bed. It was dusty down there—he saw a lot of hair, a hairpin, and a candy wrapper. "Check the bed," he said.

Bunny got up and pulled the blankets off. He shook them out. They both pushed the beds apart, checked all around them, near the frames, and then set them back near their original places. "I don't see it," whispered Bunny.

"Me neither," said Jerry.

"You think she's just getting a start? Maybe doing some research?"

"I don't think so," said Jerry. "I got a bad feeling about this."

Bunny sat down on a chair, stared at the dark television, and with one hand, he rubbed his face like he was trying to wake up. "Are you saying that you think she took it?"

"Yeah," said Jerry. "That's what I'm saying."

"But you think she'll come back?" asked Bunny. "Just say what you think."

"I don't think so," said Jerry. "I feel like she would've woken us up, written a note."

"Damn," said Bunny. "We got fucking jacked, didn't we?"

"Yeah," said Jerry. "Damn it. I think we did."

"And we can't just go get it from her."

"Not in Denver."

"First thing she'd do is call the cops on us."

"That's what I'm thinking," said Jerry.

"Drinking and dancing. Asking all those fancy questions. She had us in checkmate the whole time. Hook, line, and sinker."

"It's my fault for bringing her into this."

"Nah," said Bunny, waving his hand. "It's not you. We flew too close to the damn sun is all. We got cocky. Thought we were gonna be rich." He shook his head.

"Mmm-mm," said Jerry.

"Shit, some people are born rich, even if they're not," said Bunny. "They got that quality. Some people are born poor. We were born poor. That's just how it is."

They sat there in silence for a minute, both shaking their heads. Finally, Jerry spoke, "How much do you think it was?"

"I think it was one point five million," said Bunny. "That's pure speculation, mind you, that's the number that popped into my head."

"We could've gone to Mexico on that. Retired down there," said Jerry.

"Open up a club or something. Bunny's Place."

"You gotta keep your name off it, though," said Jerry. "Don't want someone to just google you." He pretended to be typing. "What's Bunny up to?"

"Shit," said Bunny.

They sat there for a second, then Jerry said, "I'll call her." He went to the phone, picked it up, and dialed her number. "Straight to voicemail," he said looking at Bunny. Then he spoke into the phone. "Hey Helen, it's us. We're wondering where you went. I gotta be honest, we're kind of surprised you just dipped out on us like that. I'm gonna call you back in an hour. Can you please pick up your phone? Thank you. I hope everything's okay with you. Hope you're alright for real. Bye." He hung up. "Damn," he said to Bunny. "I feel like if we keep on losing . . ."

"What?"

"I don't know."

After a while, they decided they should check out of the motel just in case she called the cops.

They went and got some Sausage McMuffins and coffee and parked across the street from the motel so they could keep an eye on the place in case she came back. But after a few hours of cursing their bad luck, and another unanswered phone call placed from the motel office, they decided it was unlikely she was going to return.

"There's nothing that suggests she is," said Bunny. "Like all she had to do was tell us."

"I really didn't think she was that kind of person," said Jerry.

"Me neither," said Bunny. "But you know what? God's got a plan for us. He does. I always believe that. And if God didn't want us to have that money, then God didn't want us to have it."

Helen had woken up in bed with the boys at 3:48 a.m. She was hungover, and panic began churning inside her belly and chest as soon as her eyes opened. She pushed herself up and staggered into the bathroom, shut the door, turned the lights on, stripped her clothes off, and took a shower. At that point, she wasn't even trying to be quiet or keep the boys from waking up. She was cursing them.

It was while she showered that things began to come into focus. She was in the middle of a criminal conspiracy. She'd already provided aid and comfort to the boys. She'd helped them steal and move evidence. She was part of it. There was no denying it.

And that wasn't even getting into the matter of the Nazis, or whoever the hell they were. They were going to want their notebook back. How did she end up involved in this? And, on top of everything else, no partnership at the firm. She shut the shower off, dried herself as fast as she could, and pulled on the same clothes she'd been wearing the night before, which was something she hated to do.

Her plan was to leave. She was going to jump in her car and drive back down the mountain and resume her life. She stepped out of the bathroom, and when she bent down to look for her purse, she saw the black notebook sitting right there under the bed. She picked it up and sat down on the chair and looked at it. These boys were going to get into a lot of trouble if they held on to this thing. If she took it right then, she'd be doing them a favor. They'd already made the deal with her. She was in charge; she didn't have to ask permission. Anyway, she certainly didn't want them knowing what she was doing. No, it would be much cleaner if she just took the notebook with her. If she looked into it on her own. That's what she told herself. That was the story.

Before she left, she took one last look at the boys. They lay there in bed, their backs to each other, breathing quietly like little children. She decided it was best not to leave a note. "Bye, boys," she whispered. She didn't know it right then, but she would never see them again.

In the car, driving back down out of the mountains, headed toward Denver, her mind started wandering a little. She couldn't help herself. What if there was some money in that notebook? What if there was enough to start over? Her mental state while she drove fluctuated between optimism and fear. There was part of her, too, that felt thrilled to be involved in something as extraordinary as this. She was living her life. Fuck you, Judge Mangan!

A semitruck passed on her left, and as she watched it hug a curve, she fantasized about appearing on one of those *Dateline*-type documentaries. She imagined an interviewer asking her pointed questions. She saw herself seated on a black set, wearing a suit. *What you have to understand*, Helen would say, *is that I was an attorney. I'd been hired to help my clients. And that's what I was doing.*

As soon as she got home, Helen started researching crypto currency. She scrolled through Reddit forums, watched some YouTube videos, read some news stories, read some random blogs. It all felt a little overwhelming, though. Just like the boys, she didn't want to make any mistakes. Helen closed her eyes for a second and her friend Ginger appeared in her head. *Ginger.* Ginger had once mentioned that her younger brother was something of a crypto expert.

Yes, she thought. *Roll forward with momentum.* She picked up her phone and called Ginger.

Bunny and Jerry went in the opposite direction of Helen. They continued west, toward California. The highway eventually led them down the same winding path as the Colorado River, and as they approached Grand Junction the cliffs above them became dramatic and looked like they'd been taken from postcards and movies. Jerry had never been this way before, and he bent and looked and took it all in.

Bunny guided them through Grand Junction, and they finally left the highway near Fruita. He pointed Jerry toward Loma, where his mother was staying, and told him to keep going. It was farmland—big open skies and snow-covered fields that stretched out toward the hills in the far distance. Thin clouds hung in the sky here and there.

"You lived out here?" asked Jerry.

"Sometimes," said Bunny. "Sometimes we did."

"I didn't know you were a farmer."

"Not like that," said Bunny. "Slow down up here."

Bunny leaned his head and squinted at a long row of mailboxes on the side of the road. "Go that way," he said, pointing to their left. "M Road," Bunny whispered to himself, reading from a street sign. "Yep, I think this is it." His mother was caretaking for a woman named Ruth Ortiz, an old family friend. Bunny hadn't been out this way in years.

They drove slowly and looked at the houses, which were mostly simple ranch and mobile homes. "Yep," said Bunny, nodding. "Keep going straight."

He always felt emotional coming back here, and right then was no different. He felt sad; he could sense time passing. It had been so long since he'd been a kid. He looked at the fields and thought about his sister, his mom, his father, his uncle: they all swirled around in his head. He thought about his uncle's kid, Frazier, and how Frazier used to put live insects into a jar and keep them alive like little pets. He thought about Frazier dying in the back of a car somewhere, a needle plunged in his arm. He thought about his uncle burying his father in some homemade grave, probably somewhere not too far from where they were. He thought about Willard sitting in jail right then, plotting to kill him. Old Willard probably wanted nothing more in the world than to kill poor Bunny dead. That kind of knowledge did not sit well with him.

They rode on in silence.

"Slow down," said Bunny. "Yeah," he said, pointing up ahead. "There we go."

"Go in?" asked Jerry, looking at a dirt driveway that led up to an aluminum-sided ranch home. A split-rail fence surrounded the property, and a little past the northern border of the fence was a cluster of other small homes, trailers, and tractors. Everything was quiet, and the place—with trash scattered here and there, with patches of dirty snow—had a depressed feel to it.

"Yep," said Bunny.

It was 5:35 p.m.; the sun hadn't set, but it had dipped behind a cloud. In front of the house were two trucks, and off to the side was an SUV. Bunny had his eyes on the SUV. It was black, and a newer model than you would expect to see out at Ruth Ortiz's place. He knew it didn't belong to her, his mother, or any guest who'd come visiting. But he didn't say anything. He was scared that if he put the thought into words, that would make it real, so he kept his mouth shut.

Jerry parked the car back from the house. He seemed to be thinking about the SUV, too. There was a worried vibe in the air, and they both just sat there for a second, biting their tongues.

"Maybe we should drive on? Call her later?" Jerry finally whispered.

"I can't do that," said Bunny.

"You want me to come with you?"

"You should wait here."

"I'll come," said Jerry.

"Probably better if you wait," said Bunny.

"You wanna take the gun with you?"

"Nah, I'm just gonna see what's up."

Bunny got out and closed the car door as quietly as he could. He ran his hands through his hair, then brushed some crumbs from his shirt and pants. Then he bent and looked in at Jerry and gave a little nod, which he hoped expressed gratitude toward his friend.

The only sound was a dog barking in the next lot and a little wind pushing by his ears. Bunny pulled his pants up and walked toward the front of the house. Ruth Ortiz used to be one of his mother's best friends. The woman used to be something of a marksman, too; she could shoot a can right off a fencepost. Now she needed caretaking, and soon enough, Bunny's own mother would, too.

Bunny looked all around, but nothing else stood out as unusual, so he stepped onto the plank stairs, pulled the storm door open, and knocked on the front door.

Right away, he heard his mother call out, "Yeah?" She stretched the word out so it sounded like *Yeeeaahh*, and in the sound of that word,

Bunny heard a warning that said: *Run away, boy, run as fast as you can*, but he ignored it, and he turned the knob and pushed the door open.

Inside, the place smelled like soup; underneath that, it smelled like damp wood, and a little moldy, too. Bunny thought there must be a leak in the roof. His eyes adjusted to the low light, and he saw framed pictures of little kids on the wall: Ruth Ortiz's grandchildren, some of whom he'd known. To the left of the entryway was the living room. A television played quietly in there. He stepped that way now, conscious of the creaking sound his feet made on the floorboards underneath the carpet.

The first thing Bunny saw, when he got to the room, was Ruth Ortiz, sitting on one of those medical recliner chairs, with oxygen running to her nose. "Hi, Ruth," said Bunny. He stepped further into the room and saw his mother sitting there on the couch, scowling. Agent Howley sat next to her. Near the window, back from everyone else, stood Agent Gana. He had his arms crossed in front of his chest. Howley picked up the remote and turned the TV off and the room became awfully quiet.

"Well," said Bunny. "I'm here."

"Better late than never," said Howley.

"They said you're in trouble," said Bunny's mother.

"Ma'am," said Howley. "If you could take Ms. Ortiz back to her room. We need to talk business with these boys."

"I'll bring LeClair in," said Gana, looking out the window and then moving toward the front door. Bunny braced himself to be hit, but the man walked right on by without incident.

Bunny's mother looked at him. "It's okay, Mom," said Bunny. "Take her back. We're gonna straighten everything out. Don't worry." He shifted his gaze to Agent Howley. "We'll get it all sorted."

"That's right," said Howley. The cop stood, too, and helped Bunny's mother get Ruth onto her feet. It took a little bit of work, and when she was finally standing, Bunny went to her and gave her a one-armed hug. "I'm sorry," he said.

She whispered in his ear, "Hi, Bunny."

Bunny turned to his mother. "It's okay, Mom," he told her, again. The woman looked like she'd aged twenty years in the five years since he'd seen her. She wore a rough-looking, moth-eaten sweater. She'd lost weight, her hair had thinned, and she had a deep crease in between her eyes. He gave her a hug, too, and patted her bony back and repeated, "It's okay."

Bunny glanced at Howley, and the man shook his head at him again, like he had all kinds of ill will stored inside him. Bunny's mother, meanwhile, began helping the older woman out of the room. Howley then stepped to Bunny and turned him against the wall, gave him a quick pat down, his hand rubbing up and down his legs and around his waist. Bunny heard Jerry and Agent Gana coming back into the house.

"Take a seat," said Howley, pointing at the couch.

Bunny sat, and a second later, Jerry—who, considering the circumstances, seemed to have a casual air about him—joined Bunny on the couch.

"What the hell?" whispered Jerry.

"I don't know," said Bunny.

Gana stepped back to the window and peered out of it like a hostage taker. Then he turned back toward the room. A gust of wind blew against the house.

"Do you have the notebook?" asked Howley.

"Nope," said Bunny. "Sorry, we don't."

Howley stepped toward the hallway that Bunny's mother had disappeared into. He looked that way, then came back into the room. He grabbed a chair and set it down between himself and the boys. "Come sit over here, Bunny," he said. "Come on."

Dreading the fact that he was probably about to be beaten, Bunny stood back up and walked to the middle of the room. He sat down where he'd been told, and before he knew what was happening, Howley zip-tied his right arm to the arm of the chair. The cop was breathing heavily while he did this, and Bunny tried to lean his head away from the man's breath. When he grabbed Bunny's left arm, Bunny resisted for a second, but didn't follow through with it, and his arm was fastened tight.

"Am I under arrest?" asked Bunny.

"Yep," said Howley. He turned to Gana and told him to cuff Jerry.

Bunny watched as Gana cuffed Jerry's hands behind his back. Jerry, while this was happening, kept his eyes on the ground. It looked, to Bunny, like his friend was contemplating all their missteps, adding them up, and filing them away. When he was done, Gana sat Jerry back down on the couch, helping him by holding his arm.

"Okay," said Howley. Bunny looked at him and saw that the man had garden shears in his hand. For a second, Bunny thought he was going to cut the restraints off his arms. But then he watched Howley step over and hand the shears to his partner, and a cold and desperate feeling ran through Bunny's body. Gana stepped right up next to him. Absurdly, Bunny smelled cologne on the man.

Bunny decided right then and there that it was better to have never had the notebook than to have had it and lost it. "I don't have it," he said, with all the passion he could muster. "We don't have it. It wasn't there. I opened the safe, and it wasn't fucking there. I did everything you wanted me to. It was not there."

"Okay," said Gana.

The cop bent down and grabbed hold of Bunny's left hand, which was bound to the chair at the wrist. Bunny and the cop struggled for a moment, leaning into each other and pushing, until the cop freed Bunny's thumb and held it isolated from his hand. Bunny felt the shears press against the base of his thumb. He was stuck. The chair he sat on rocked back and forth like it might snap and break itself.

"Stop, or I'm gonna cut it," hissed Gana. "Stop moving, I'm gonna cut it off."

Bunny felt the blades dig into the base of his thumb. He stopped moving, pulled his head away and closed his eyes. "I don't have it," he said. "I don't have it. On my mother's name. I do not fucking have it. Please."

"I'm gonna take your thumb. I'm gonna cut it off," said Gana, panting. "Then, I'm gonna take the other one and you're gonna be walking around with no thumbs for the rest of your life."

The blades pinched down on his thumb and Bunny imagined firetrucks and dirt and light. All his muscles tensed up. The wind seemed to be rocking the house.

"Where is it?" asked Howley from his side of the room.

Bunny turned and looked at him. "Please," he whispered. The man was framed by the light in the window. He stood there with his arms crossed in front of his chest. *Come on, you're the good one*, thought Bunny. They'd gotten on okay. Bunny stared at him and tried to direct his prayers that way: *Help me. I'm just a kid.* "Help me," he said. "Please. I didn't do—"

Without any warning whatsoever, Howley's head popped like a pulverized melon. At the same time, his legs crumpled, and his body fell forward, and black blood and pink brain matter spilled out. Next thing Bunny knew, he was on the ground himself, on his side, the chair still connected to him at his wrists. From down there, he watched Gana take cover against the wall. It only occurred to Bunny right then that the shot had come from outside the house.

Agent Gana had his gun out, and he held it against his chest with both hands. Bunny watched the man take a breath, watched his chest fill up and expand with air. It was the last breath he would ever take. Automatic gunfire ripped through the wall, and Gana's body twitched with it and then fell, and a gaping hole stood where the wall had once been. Dust from the drywall floated in the air. A buzzing noise filled Bunny's ears.

"Mommy!" called Bunny from the floor, yelling as loudly as he could. He pulled against the restraints, but they held fast. He tried to look for Jerry, but a coffee table between them blocked his view. "Mommy!" he cried, again. He couldn't help himself.

"Bunny!" said Jerry.

Bunny tried to speak, but a sob got stuck in his throat and he couldn't form any words. He moved his left thumb to check if it was still there. At the same time, his eyes went down to the rug, and he looked for his own blood but there was none. He took a deep breath and pulled against the restraints on his arms, but they wouldn't break, and he was still trapped.

Bunny turned his head toward the ceiling. There was a water stain up there; he heard the word *mold* in his head, and at the same time, he caught some movement in his peripheral vision, and he looked that way and saw the blur of a head descending from one of the windows.

"Fuck," Bunny said.

"What?" said Jerry.

Bunny didn't answer. He was too busy listening to a voice outside. He couldn't make out the words, but it wasn't hard to understand that a man was reporting on what he'd seen inside. Bunny had time to take a deep breath, and he tried to pull his arms free again, but his hands were tied tight.

The sound of the storm door opening stopped his efforts. Bunny looked that way. He saw a blond-headed boy walk into the room. The boy had a rifle in his hands. He was skinny and his eyes were bugged out. Because he was dressed in desert camouflage, Bunny, for a second, thought he was being rescued by some kind of army operation. Then he recognized the kid as Baby George, one of the youngsters from Willard's camp.

The fear of death can express itself in wild ways; right then it came on as pure pain in one of Bunny's back molars. The pain was paralyzing. Baby George walked right up to him. He held the gun pointed at Bunny's head, close enough for Bunny to see the blackness inside the barrel. *I'm gonna die.* He could feel the shot coming and he braced himself to take it like a punch.

Right then, behind Baby George, Nelson stepped into the room. He wore gloves and carried a sawed-off shotgun. It looked like he wanted to cry. He looked scared as hell, like they were on the front lines of a war. Bunny felt an immediate urge to apologize, but instead, all he could do was whisper, "Help me." Nelson stared down at Bunny. Bunny wanted to tell him that everything was a mistake, it had all been a giant mistake. Things had just gotten mixed up. He couldn't find the words, though. He couldn't make his mouth work.

Instead, it was Nelson who spoke. "You have ten seconds to tell us where your uncle's notebook is," he said, holding his gun on Bunny. He started counting backward. "Ten, nine"—Bunny's mind went *Gramma, Mama, Daddy*—"eight, seven, six—"

A blast from the hallway interrupted Nelson's counting and sent him crashing sideways into the near wall; and the whole room shook. The kid next to Bunny lifted his gun toward the hallway, like he was going to shoot that way, and Bunny used all his force and swung his foot and kicked the gun toward the wall. The kid, right then, went flying back, too—like he'd been yanked by a rope—and the sound of a second blast filled the room. Bunny looked to the hallway, and he saw his mother standing there in her sweater, a twelve-gauge in her hands. She looked like an animal, she looked wild, like she wanted to fight the whole world. She looked, Bunny thought, staring up at her, just like Willard.

Bunny watched his mother going from man to man, checking them, turning their faces, touching their necks. Nelson was still moaning a little. Ruth appeared from somewhere, walking on her own. "He's not gonna make it," she said. "They're all dead."

Bunny's mom then went outside for what seemed like forever and checked if there were any more men. "If there were any," she said when she finally returned, "they ran."

"Tiffany's gonna be mad," said Ruth Ortiz. Bunny had no idea who Tiffany was.

"Get her oxygen back on," said Bunny's mom, like she was giving herself instructions. "She's gonna start coughing soon." She leaned the shotgun against the wall and marched to the back bedroom.

"Bunny?" said Jerry.

"Yeah?"

"Are you okay?"

"Yeah, are you?"

"I think so," said Jerry.

Bunny's mother came back in and, using Howley's shears, cut Bunny loose. "What the hell did you do?" she hissed at him. She looked as upset as Bunny had ever seen her. She looked ruined with anger, like this anger might not lift.

"I don't know," said Bunny. He pulled his hand up and looked at his thumb, moved it this way and that. A little cut at the base, but nothing serious.

When he looked back at his mother, he found her crying. "This is Ruth's house," she said through her tears. "You brought trouble to her home."

"I know," said Bunny. "I'm sorry."

His mother sat there, shaking her head and breathing through her nose. "Look at this place," she said.

Bunny, meanwhile, stared back at her. He thought about his murdered father and felt a mix of anger and sadness. He felt mad at her for any part she had in it, and he felt ashamed and disgusted for feeling that. He wanted to ask her about it, but he couldn't. Maybe another day. He felt too clamped right then. The words wouldn't come.

Instead, Ruth spoke up. "It's okay," she said, waving a hand at her mangled house. She had the oxygen tube back in her nose. Bunny, his mother, Jerry—they all turned their attention to the older woman. "The way I see it is this. Those officers came in," said Ruth, taking a breath and pointing at Agent Howley's lifeless body. "Then those men shot the cops. Then your mama shot those men." She shrugged. "That's what happened, anyway. A bunch of damn nonsense. All of it." She looked down, coughed into her fist. "Go get them bolt cutters for your friend. You boys need to get the hell out of here before the sheriff shows up."

❧

Helen, upon meeting Ginger's brother, felt intense trepidation. He looked like he couldn't have been more than fourteen years old. He wore the same kind of round eyeglasses as his sister. His face was a little chubby like hers, too. His hair was medium length, and he wore a loose navy-blue cotton sweater. He came right into Helen's hotel room, set his backpack on the ground, and then lay down on her bed. He put his hands behind his head, crossed one foot over the other, looked at the ceiling, and—as though he were performing some kind of comedy act—said, "The hotel is nice, but the location is not ideal."

It turned out, Harold was sixteen. "My mom was eighteen when she had me and thirty-eight when she had him," said Ginger.

"But we do have the same mother and father," said Harold.

Helen got right to the point. "Ginger says you have a little experience with crypto?"

"A little?" said Harold, craning his neck to look at Ginger.

"I said you had a lot," said Ginger.

"Did you tell her I'm kinglord.eth?"

"No," said Ginger.

"Well," said Harold, pushing his glasses up, "I am."

Helen turned to Ginger. "Can I talk to you in the bathroom for a moment?"

They stepped into the little bathroom and closed the door. "Ginger," Helen said. "What if I told you I was about to steal crypto from some Nazis?"

"Real Nazis?"

"American Nazis," said Helen.

Ginger looked at the door, wet her lips with her tongue, then looked back at Helen. "I don't know."

"Is that something you might be interested in?" asked Helen.

Ginger looked crestfallen. "I mean, for me—no. I don't like getting involved in those kinds of things. That sounds dangerous and scary."

"Is it something that your brother could help me with?"

"I think so."

"Okay," said Helen, whispering. "Let me ask you one more thing." She put both of her hands on Ginger's shoulders and stared into her friend's eyes. "Can I trust him?"

"My brother?" said Ginger, matching Helen's whisper. "Of course."

They stepped back into the main room, and Helen jumped right into it: "Okay, this is the deal, Harold," she said. "I have a twenty-four-word passcode for what is presumably a crypto wallet."

"Seed phrase," said Harold. "It's called a seed phrase."

"Alright," said Helen. "A seed phrase. Listen, the wallet belongs to a despicable person. He's really a piece of shit. I'm going to be honest with you. He's a Nazi. He's a racist. I want to take all his, you know, whatever he has, and move it to a safe account. Is that something you could help me with?"

Harold took off his glasses, wiped his eyes, and put the glasses back on. "I think so."

"Wow," said Helen. She could hardly believe this was happening. She felt dizzy. "I mean, do we need to make a deal or anything? Are there some terms you need met or anything like that? Do we need some kind of contract?" She glanced at Ginger, who frowned and shook her head.

"No," said Harold. "I don't think so."

Helen went to the desk and grabbed her laptop. She brought it to Harold, who looked at her like she was offering him a dead cat. "I don't use Apple computers," he said.

He got his own backpack, opened it, and pulled out a rather large, sticker-covered laptop. "I have my own computer," he said.

"So, what do we have to do?" asked Helen.

"Well," said Harold, "we'll have to see what it is. Poke around." His fingers started working the keys. He waited for a second. "Can you show me the seed phrase?"

Helen, her heart racing, showed him the page.

"Hold it open for me," said Harold. "I'm going to import it into a wallet app—we like Electron."

She held it open, and the kid, his face looking serious and not betraying any kind of nervousness, typed in the twenty-four words. When he was done, he sniffed in through his nose and leaned his head back. Helen could see the screen change in the reflection of his glasses. "Yeah." He smiled. "It's Bitcoin."

Helen joined him on the bed so she could see the actual screen. It showed what looked like a regular bank's website. Harold scrolled through a bunch of transactions. "So, it looks like your friend bought a hundred thirty-two coins on November 20, 2015." He pointed at the screen, then turned and looked at her. "They were priced at three hundred twenty-two dollars and three cents." He waited for a second, then added, "USD."

Helen thought she sensed amusement in his eyes. "Is that— What is that? Is that a lot?" she asked.

Harold pointed at other transactions. "He took some out here, added some there. Little bit out, little bit out, added some. See all these? He has a hundred and twelve point eighty-two now. It's trading at thirty-nine thousand four hundred and ninety-seven dollars and seventy-seven cents. He has a balance of— Sorry, *you* have a balance of four million four hundred fifty-six thousand one hundred and thirty-eight dollars and forty-one cents."

"*I* have a balance?" asked Helen.

"We have the wallet. It's yours now," said Harold. "This is it. It's your account now."

"What do we do?" asked Helen. "Should we move it? I'm freaking out."

"Yeah, you're probably gonna want to tumble it. Mix it up. Hide it from that guy."

"Okay," said Helen. "Yeah, yeah, yeah. Can we do that?"

While his fingers tapped, Harold said, "We'll need to set up a new wallet." He waited a second, tapped some more keys. Waited, typed some more. "There," he said. "You have a new wallet. Now"—he cleared his throat—"to blend it, my associates seem to like *Coinomize*. I don't have anything to hide, so I don't really *blend* coins. Also, I'm never cashing out, but that is neither here nor there." He opened a new window, typed, waited, typed. Then he copied some text from one of his screens, pasted it into another, and repeated that. Then he pulled out his phone and responded to a text message he received. Helen saw a series of emoji on his phone. She noticed her own mouth hanging open, and she forced it shut.

"Okay," said Harold. "We'll set the delay to three hours. The fee from the tumbler is three point seven percent." He winced at that. "Is that okay?"

Helen told him it was.

"Okay," said Harold. He smacked the key, made the transaction, and put his hands behind his head. "In about three hours, you should have the *new* clean coins in your *new* wallet."

"That's it?" asked Helen.

"That's it," said Harold.

Helen sat there for a long moment. Her forehead was sweating; she could feel that. *I want to be a good person*, she thought. *I want to be good. I want to do good.* She closed her eyes, opened them, looked at Ginger and her brother. "I want to give you guys fifteen percent for helping me."

Ginger shook her head no.

But her brother said, "If you want to, we'll take it."

Bunny and Jerry continued west. They passed through Green River. They did not stop and visit Bunny's sister. Instead, Bunny looked out the passenger window and said, "I'll see you next time, Reecey." They never made it to San Diego. They got sidetracked on Highway 50, and a little over twelve hours after leaving Grand Junction, they ended up in Reno, Nevada.

The truth is, they were too traumatized to make a big journey. They didn't talk much on the drive; they mainly just rode in silence. Bunny, on a constant loop, kept seeing Agent Howley's head snapping forward. Jerry's thoughts were more fragmented: Ventola's angry face, Blanche in the trunk. He'd see Helen dancing one second, then the next he'd see the cop against the wall. His mother at her home. The kid with the gun. Blood on the wall.

All that ruminating didn't stop them from being hungry, though. They were starving when they got to Reno. They went to an old casino and had all-you-can-eat eggs, bacon, hash browns, sausage, and pancakes. They felt better after that, and when they were done, they decided to try their hand at roulette. They put a twenty-dollar chip down on Red and the ball landed on Black. That was the last they gambled during that stop.

Later that afternoon, they went to a dark bar on East Fourth Street. While they were drinking beer, they met a punk girl named Chastity. Her hair was dyed bright green, and she had GAME OVER tattooed on her knuckles. She invited them to stay with her for the night.

The first day they were at her house, they saw a news report about the shoot-out in Grand Junction. Ruth Ortiz was treated as a kind of local hero, and the news spun it as a random incident. None of the stories mentioned Bunny or Jerry, but that didn't stop them from checking over their shoulders every time they stepped outside. They didn't talk about the incident around Chastity. And she didn't even seem to notice any of this.

On the third day, Chastity hooked them up with a dude called Jaden. He had horrible teeth and he sold used cars. They traded their Avalon for a beat-up Honda Odyssey. They gave Jaden the guns, too, a broken one from the cops and an operable one from Ventola. In exchange, Jaden gave them some California plates, and he swore they were clean and registered and would not raise any alarms with law enforcement. "Trust me," he said.

Chastity lived in Northwest Reno, right on the edge of the desert. She lived in a suburban area where all the houses were painted off-white and looked like they had Spanish roofs. It was a nice neighborhood. But she lived with an older female roommate who did not seem to appreciate the boys crashing in her living room. After a few days, they decided they should continue west.

Before they left, Chastity told them she had an uncle in Eureka, California, who could hook them up with a job in a sawmill. Their funds were already starting to run thin. Gas and food were expensive. They didn't know anything about Eureka, but when she said it was on the coast, they were sold.

"Yeah, man," said Bunny. "Surftown, USA."

After they loaded the car with their few possessions, Chastity leaned forward and kissed Bunny on the mouth. They hadn't fooled around or anything the whole time, so it caught him by surprise. She had a wet mouth, and the kiss left him wondering if he should have stayed with her in Reno. He thought about her all the way until they crossed the state line and entered California. Then, for a few moments, on the dry, scrubby straightaway of Highway 395, his thoughts leaned toward the future, and he didn't worry about the past.

Eureka, when they got there, didn't look anything like they'd imagined it would. The place was gray and foggy. There wasn't a bikini or palm tree in sight. The air smelled strange, too: briny, sulfuric. People on the streets looked like they had serious drug problems. It was worse than Denver in that way. Still, a job was a job, and the boys called up Chastity's uncle and introduced themselves to him.

"We could bring you in on the cleanup crew," said the man when they met. "It pays twenty-one dollars and twenty-two cents an hour. Work your way up to millwright, you'll be making forty."

"That's not bad," said Bunny.

"No, it's not," said Chastity's uncle, Anthony.

"We wanna stay off the books, if possible," said Jerry.

Anthony took a moment thinking, then he said, "In that case, you'll have to work the night shift."

"We can do that," said Bunny.

He hooked them up with a place to stay, too. They shared a room with some Mexican mill workers, out on the edge of town, at a place called the Pine Motel. Those Mexicans liked to drink, and Bunny and Jerry drank with them every chance they got. Depending on the vibe, they either toasted and carried on with them or matched their moods and became quiet and thoughtful.

The work was hard; they had to be sweeping and cleaning and lifting boards and scraps all shift long. They worked the second shift, too, which meant they got off at two a.m. and wouldn't fall asleep before daylight. When they did lie down, they'd hear the buzzing and whining of the saws in their ears, and they'd feel the dust in their lungs and splinters in their fingers and palms.

Still, they got into something of a rhythm. Living like workers, coming home tired, drinking their beers. It felt mature and American to be working a job like that. "Look at you," Jerry would say to Bunny. "Look at you," Bunny would say back.

When they got their first paychecks, the boys moved into their own room at the Pine Motel. On weekends, when they weren't working, they drove over to Arcata and tried to pick up girls from the college. Occasionally, they'd go out to the beach, look at it, and shake their heads. Neither of them had ever seen the ocean before. Once, they even tried to go swimming, but the water was freezing, and they didn't make it in past their waists.

About seven weeks after they arrived in Eureka, Jerry, lying in bed, scrolling on his new phone, checked in on his email and found a message from somebody named Yaxeni O. The message read: *Dear Jerry, sorry it took so long. Call me at this number: 720 291 4219.*

Jerry stared at the message for a long moment. Then he googled the name "Yaxeni O." A female bodybuilder popped up, and he knew it was Helen emailing. He shook Bunny by the shoulder, woke him up, and showed him the message.

The phone rang six times before making a strange sound like a fax machine. Jerry couldn't leave a message. He tried back again, and the same thing happened. "I don't know," he said to Bunny.

Six hours later, right before they had to head back to work, Jerry's phone rang. The number was blocked. When he answered it, he heard Helen on the other end. "Hey," she said.

"Hi," said Jerry. He looked at Bunny and mouthed: *It's her!*

"How are you?" asked Helen.

"We're good. We're in California. Where are you?"

"Denver," she said, after a pause.

"Denver," he repeated back to her. His mouth had gone dry. He didn't know why, but he felt sad. He looked out the window and saw some clouds drifting in the sky.

"Listen," she said. "My plan was to wait a couple years before I got in touch. I wanted to keep you out of trouble. But the market has been dipping. Do you have a pen?"

"Hold on," said Jerry. He looked at Bunny. "Give me that pen right there." Bunny handed him a pen and an envelope to write on.

"Okay," said Jerry.

"Right now, you two are looking at about eight ninety-five each," she said.

"Eight hundred and ninety-five dollars?"

"Thousand," said Helen. "Eight hundred ninety-five thousand dollars."

He put his hand over the phone and whispered to Bunny, "It's eight hundred ninety-five thousand dollars."

"What?" said Bunny.

"You have a pen?" asked Helen.

"Yeah," said Jerry.

"I'm going to give you a new seed phrase, just like you gave me. Are you with Bunny?"

"Yeah," said Jerry.

"Okay. Hi, Bunny."

"Hey," said Bunny.

"I got you on speaker," said Jerry.

"Okay, write down these words." She read him a list of words and then spelled out each one. "Say them back to me," she said.

Jerry looked down at the list of words and read them back to her: "Topic adapt tennis employ current tank doll secret spawn—"

"S-P-A-W-N?" said Helen.

"Yeah," said Jerry. "Okay, so, spawn original timber—"

"T-I-M-B-E-R?"

"Yeah, yeah," said Jerry. "Timber young merit junk general moment visit trick mad waste—"

"Spell *waste*."

"W-A-S-T-E."

"Okay," said Helen. "Go on."

"So, waste school skirt ahead race."

"Okay, that's it. Listen to me, you guys. If you lose those words, you lose the money. If someone takes that list, you lose the money. If you store it in a computer, and someone hacks your computer, you lose the money."

"Okay," said Jerry. "We understand."

"I would suggest going to a bank and getting a bank vault," said Helen. "Put it in there. Keep it safe. Okay? If you cash out the money, you're going to have to pay taxes on it. If you want to avoid all that, I have a guy in Vegas that I've been using. I'll give you his number. He'll buy your Bitcoins and give you cash. He takes a seven percent fee." She gave them the guy's name and phone number. "He's good," she said. "You can trust him."

Jerry looked at Bunny. His friend was biting his thumbnail and nodding his head. "Can you give me a number to reach you?" asked Jerry.

"I'm sorry," she said. The phone went silent for a second. "I don't think we should talk again. I want to. But we can't."

"Alright," said Jerry. He looked down at the floor. His face felt hot.

"Don't lose that phrase," said Helen.

"I won't," said Jerry.

"I want you boys to know something," said Helen. "You are *good* people. Don't ever let anyone tell you otherwise."

"Thanks," said Jerry. "We won't."

"You are, too," said Bunny.

There was a long pause, then she said, "If things were different . . ."

"Yeah," said Jerry.

She ended the call.

Jerry sat there for a second, then he looked up at Bunny. "Eight ninety-five, dude," he said. "We're fucking rich, man. Like beyond dreams kind of rich." Then he bent over and started crying into the crook of his arm. He didn't even know why he was crying. The tears kept coming. Bunny scooted over to his friend and rubbed his back.

Things happened fast after that. Some of them good, some of them horrible.

First, Jerry got in touch with his old public defender, April Costa-Tenge. He didn't want to show up in Vegas and get arrested. She told Jerry that she'd been contacted by Bunny's lawyer, Adam Rendelman. Rendelman had shared the recordings of the cops that Bunny made. The public defender and Rendelman then brought the recordings to the district attorney. Those recordings—in combination with the question of why those two ATF agents had ever even gone to Grand Junction in the first place—had the potential of turning into a huge scandal. Jerry knew why they'd been there, they'd wanted to steal the crypto, but he didn't say anything, he kept silent about that. The case against Willard Haggerty and the other twenty-two men and four women who were arrested out there was going to move forward. It just wouldn't have anything to do with Bunny Simpson or Jerry LeClair. Their cases were going to be dismissed.

"Can we at least sue the cops?" asked Jerry.

"It would probably be best to leave this one alone," said April Costa-Tenge. She seemed to be hinting at something, and Jerry knew enough by now to accept that kind of hint and move on.

They were still working at that point, and about a week after the call with the public defender, someone at the sawmill showed Jerry their phone. There had been a mass shooting at a Juneteenth festival in Denver. Two white men had taken rifles to the Sixteenth Street Mall and gone on a killing spree. They killed twelve people. Later, Bunny looked for pictures of the shooters. He was not surprised to recognize them from the ranch. It was two of the younger men who had been doing all that rifle training. "Yep, they were there," said Bunny. "I told those cops this was going to happen. I spelled it all out for them, location included."

"Yes, you did," said Jerry.

"I warned them."

"They didn't want to listen to you."

"Twelve people," said Bunny. "Those were sons and daughters, man. Mothers. They had families. I'm getting sick of all this shit. Stupid, hateful shit. Ignorant fucking racists."

"I know," said Jerry. "It's a sick world."

Six days later, there was a shooting at a synagogue in Boston, and the public's attention shifted over there. Three weeks after that, there was a shooting at a gay bar in Phoenix. A little over two weeks after the shooting in Phoenix, eighteen people were killed at a Dollar Store in Gainesville.

The following spring, Bunny and Jerry finally made it out to Las Vegas. The broker Helen hooked them up with was named Parviz Farahani.

He was about the same age as them, but he seemed much older. He knew all kinds of things. He told Bunny and Jerry to meet him in the parking lot of a laser tag place in Summerlin. He said, "Meet me on the far west side, right in front of the Marie Callender's. That's my cousin's place. I'll be in a white van, parked facing the lot. We can sit in there. Smoke a hookah, relax a little, have a nice chat."

When they got there and parked across from him, he flashed his brights. They had told him that they only wanted to cash out forty K. He charged twenty-eight hundred dollars for that, which seemed perfectly fine. When they got to the van, a Sprinter, the passenger door slid open and Parviz leaned out and said, "Yeah, yeah, come on, wassup." He wore a black Armani shirt, and his hair was slicked back. There were two other guys in the van with him. Bunny got in first, and Jerry followed. "Don't be nervous, boys, come on," said Parviz. He closed the door.

"Let me just see your ID real quick," he said.

He looked at Bunny's driver's license. "Bunny Simpson, I like that, dawg. That's the shit right there." He said something in Farsi to his two partners, and they smiled and nodded. He checked Jerry's ID and said, "Alright, wassup with you, cousin?" He gave them each a cold bottle of Coca-Cola and said, "So, what are we doing? Are we ready? Don't be nervous, this is a small transaction. Come on, you're in Vegas now, it's all good."

Parviz had already explained how the transaction would work. Now he helped Jerry open his phone and transfer $42,800 worth of Bitcoin. "Give me the box," he said to his partner. His partner handed him a shopping bag. Inside it, Jerry found a small Nike shoe box, like a box for baby shoes. He opened it up and saw four banded stacks of hundred-dollar bills, ten thousand each, forty K.

"You wanna count it?" asked Parviz.

The boys counted the money, then they both shook hands with each of the three men and told them they'd probably be seeing them again soon.

Back in their own car, Bunny said he was hungry.

"Let's go to one of them all-you-can-eat places," said Jerry. "We'll get the big trays and load them up with as much as we can."

"Okay, but not one of your fancy places," said Bunny. "I wanna go to just a normal place."

"That's what I'm saying," said Jerry.

They found the kind of place they were looking for on Fremont Street, an old casino with an empty dining room. They loaded up with breakfast food—pancakes, eggs, sausage, bacon, sweet rolls, French toast, regular toast, pineapple, home fries, coffee, orange juice—all of it.

"I feel crazy," said Bunny, setting his tray down. "I feel amped up."

"Me too," said Jerry. "Should we get some champagne?"

"I don't think so," said Bunny.

Jerry squinted at him like he was trying to see if he was joking, but Bunny didn't say anything, so Jerry didn't either. A waitress walked by, humming to herself, and they both watched her go. Outside, a big rig rolled past, shaking the restaurant's windows as it went.

"I want to tell you something," said Bunny, looking serious.

"Yeah?"

"I want to thank you for riding with me. I feel like I couldn't have had a better partner to share this time with."

"Come on," said Jerry. "Stop all that nonsense."

"Nah, it's true. You saved me back there in Castle Rock. Probably saved me in Grand Junction, too." He looked deep into Jerry's eyes. "I want to apologize to you. I feel like I got you into all this trouble."

"Nah, we're cool," said Jerry. "You know that."

"You don't always get friends you can trust, but we found each other. That's wassup. That's worth more than all that money. You know what I'm saying?"

"I feel the same way," said Jerry. "I agree with you."

"I'm gonna raise this glass of orange juice up to you, 'cause here's the deal." He raised his glass of orange juice, and Jerry raised his. "The way these things go— Shit, you're probably gonna find a girl, get married, have kids. You gonna be like my sister and end up strung out on life."

"You're gonna do all that, too," said Jerry.

"I'm saying, though, while we're sitting here at this table, while we're still young, while we have our lives ahead of us, I want to say cheers to you, I want to raise my glass, you're my best friend."

They touched glasses, sipped from their orange juice. Both of their eyes had become shiny.

"I love you, Bunny," said Jerry. "Shit, you know that. Come on, man."

The two of them sat shaking their heads for a moment, looking down at the table. Then they picked up their silverware and began eating their food.

Acknowledgments

Thank you, Charlotte Sheedy, for being my wonderful agent. You've taught me so many things. I'm so happy to be your friend.

Thank you, Morgan Entrekin, and everyone at Grove Atlantic. I'm honored to publish these books with you.

Thank you, Jesseca Salky and Kate Garrick for for helping shape and sell this book.

Thank you, Walter Green for another beautiful cover.

Thank you, Eli Horowitz, Ally Sheedy, Jason Schwartz, Basho Mosko, and David Hoffman for your generous notes on early drafts.

Thank you, Aaron Lammer, PJ Vogt, Evan Ratliff, and Frank Coffer, for patiently answering my questions about cryptocurrency. Thank you, Elle Reeve, for answering my questions about white nationalism and incel culture (for more on these subjects, I highly recommend her book, *Black Pill*).

Thank you, Kent Simpson, for answering my daily questions about Denver. Thank you, Haeya Yim, for your advice on law firms and lawyers. Thank you, Taffy Brodesser-Akner, for all the advice and help you've given.

Finally, most importantly, with love, thank you, Reyhan Harmanci. I don't know where I'd be without you!